Even to my uneducated eye, it was obvious that something was about to happen. The creature had suddenly raised its head higher than ever, and it swayed slowly from side to side on an impossibly elongated neck, towering over us, higher even than the bridgehouse. Its jaws opened and it roared at us, a wet, gravelly sound that hurt the ears, and I thought I caught the faintest hit of its corrupt breath, although that may have been my imagination. The deck lurched under our feet as the captain tried to steer us away from the beast, but riverboats are designed for comfort, not speed or maneuverability. One of the young women behind us screamed, but whether from fear or excitement, I could not say. As terrifying as the dragon might be, it seemed somehow unreal.

MANAGANSETT PRESS

Don D'Ammassa is the author of:

Horror
Blood Beast
Servant of Chaos*
Caverns of Chaos*
Wings over Manhattan
The Gargoyle
That Way Madness Lies*
Little Evils*
Passing Death*
Date with the Dark*
The Devil Is in the Details*
Living Things*

Science Fiction
Scarab*
Haven*
Narcissus*
Translation Station
The Sinking Island*
Alien & Otherwise*

Mysteries
Murder in Silverplate
Dead of Winter*
Death at the Art Gallery*
Death on the Mountain*
Death on Black Island*

Fantasy
The Kaleidoscope*
Elaborate Lies*
Perilous Pursuits*

Nonfiction
The Encyclopedia of Science Fiction
The Encyclopedia of Fantasy and Horror
The Encyclopedia of Adventure Fiction
Masters of Detection Vol I & II*
*Published by Managansett Press

PERILOUS PURSUITS

Don D'Ammassa

Managansett Press First Edition 2015

PERILOUS
PURSUITS

CHAPTER ONE

One irate dragon can ruin your entire day.

The first few days of my trip down the Mississippi had been blissfully uneventful and I had spent most of the daylight hours on deck, watching the scenery slip gracefully past to the tune of water rushing off the paddlewheels at either side of our vessel. I exchanged pleasantries with my fellow passengers, dozed in a deck chair, and occasionally read one of the half dozen light adventure novels I had purchased before coming aboard the *River Warlock,* unaware of the fact that my own life would shortly be far more exciting than that of any fictional hero.

At night I frequented the saloon, trading drinks with some of the commercial travelers or playing cards for small change, although I was careful to avoid sharing a table with the two or three men and one woman whom I suspected were professional card players disguising their talents. Sometimes I stepped out onto the observation deck and smoked a cigar, lighting it with the ornate pocket lighter my father had given me on my last birthday. My life had afforded me few opportunities for relaxation and I intended to savor this rare break to its utmost. Some of my fellow passengers were openly bored and paced the deck restlessly but I've always had an antipathy toward unnecessary excitement and I'd chosen a riverboat rather than a faster steam launch or some form of overland travel expressly to avoid any unwelcome stimulation. The last time I'd been aboard a launch it had foundered, and bandits, broken axles, and bumpy roads might sound wonderful in a four penny thriller, but they were grossly over rated in the real world.

So I wasn't particularly pleased when we sighted a river dragon just north of Memphis. It wasn't one of those relatively tame European varieties, the ones that were brought over by the first wave of aristocratic settlers and subsequently set loose in the wild during the Revolution. Europeans dragons are usually quite timid and can generally be driven off by a few pistol shots or even a lot of shouting and arm waving. Because of their inclination to raid farmland, tearing up crops and occasionally carrying off the odd cow or horse, farmers had hunted them nearly to extinction on both sides of the Atlantic. It was now considered bad form to kill a dragon unnecessarily, particularly since in their absence the numbers of rabbits, squirrels, wood pixies, and other lesser pests grew dramatically. Unfortunately, they bred very infrequently and it would require the better part of a century before their numbers would increase significantly by natural means. In parts of Europe biogenetic spellcasters were laboring to speed up the process and restore the balance of nature, but in the new world other problems were more pressing.

This was an oriental dragon, and very close to its full growth as best I could judge, a creature equally comfortable on land or in the water. The 1860 Accord with the Emperor of China had theoretically prohibited their presence in all but the coastal cantons far to our west, but every provincial administrator kept at least one of the beasts as a symbol of his sacred authority and it was inevitable that some of the beasts would escape and go rogue. They were much more intelligent than their European cousins, as well as larger, fiercer, and more frightening in appearance. The specimen we encountered was at least a couple of centuries old. Its throat scales bore the rusty red hue of maturity and its jaw flaps were fully formed and iridescent. The sinuous body moved through the water like an eel, and the impact when it struck our hull was violent enough that several people were thrown to the deck and we nearly lost one passenger over the side.

"Looks like a big one." Jeb Walker, with whom I'd been engaged in a casual railside conversation, leaned further out over the water to appraise the situation. My own inclination was to retreat to the roundhouse. There were stories of dragons plucking passengers off the decks of vessels, all supposedly apocryphal, but frightening nonetheless. Jeb took the pipe out of his mouth and regarded it solemnly. "You wouldn't have a light, would you?"

I loaned him my lighter although I felt reluctant to have it even momentarily out of my possession. "You don't think there's any real danger, do you?" I intended that my voice remain calm, perhaps even casual, but I suppose the tremor in my throat was as obvious to Jeb as it was to me.

"Probably not. Keep your head up, though. Never can tell what these beasts will do." I couldn't read his expression through his bushy beard and perpetually guarded eyes, but I thought I heard a trace of amusement in his voice. I didn't know whether to be annoyed at his presumption or relieved that he considered matters light enough to be joked about. Certainly there was considerable turmoil elsewhere. Passengers were darting back and forth – the brave or foolhardy seeking a better view, the timid or just cautious moving back toward shelter. I could see at least three crewmembers, one up on the wheelhouse, waving his arms slowly and pointing, two others moving along the deck carrying the heavy poles that they used to fend off floating tree trunks and other waterborne debris. None of them appeared to be unduly alarmed and I felt my heart slowly sinking back into place.

There was another bump, not as powerful this time, and one of the pole wielders came back our way, moving a bit more quickly.

"Looks like she's curious," said Jeb. His eyes twinkled. "Or unusually hungry."

I watched the crewman climb up toward the bridge and saw the captain emerge from his sanctuary, holding two long barreled muskets. "They're bringing out the guns," I said.

Jeb didn't answer, just kept a watch on the roiling surface of the river, his rawhide jacket flapping loosely in the breeze created by our passage. Drops of sprays glistened in his beard and his unruly hair. Past his head, I caught a glimpse of an immense, scaled body as it surged toward the surface briefly, then went back under, apparently swimming parallel to our course and matching our speed. The river ran quite deep here, and the water was a murky, opaque brown.

"What do you think it wants?"

Jeb answered without turning in my direction. "Can't rightly say. It might just be curious, in which case it'll go its own way. On the other hand, it has a fresh scar on its flank. If someone's been hunting it, the creature might have a bone or two to chew with us." He turned and a wry grin was visible even through his beard. "Metaphorically speaking, of course."

I cautiously joined him at the rail and seconds later we saw the head break water, the jaws gaping wide enough to have swallowed a bullock, the eyes like dinner plates. Its stare raked the deck for a few seconds, and a good number of the remaining onlookers retreated cautiously. Jeb, on the other hand, leaned further over the side, and nodded his head. The rhythm of our paddle changed and I realized we had slowed and were changing our heading, apparently in an attempt to turn away from the dragon.

"We're in luck. It's not the fire breathing sort. I didn't see the crest well enough last time she broached, but there's no doubt of it. And there's no trace of firebalm sacs along its throat either. The fire breathing ones, they're the worst. Some of 'em can spit that flame farther than a man can shoot, and they're smart enough to sit out of range and wait till the firing's died down before charging. I saw one attack a settlement once. Lucky to get out with my skin that time."

I'd already noticed that Jeb had a tendency to spin tall tales, but this was too much to swallow. "That's a little hard to believe, old timer. There hasn't been a firebreather in this part of the world for more than a century. They were banned from the continent by treaty and the ones already here were shipped back to China."

He stepped back from the rail, no longer interested in the dragon, which had submerged once again. "That's the way it's supposed to be, all right. But the Kurosakans brought some over before the Tang Dynasty gobbled them up, and at least a few escaped and went wild during the consolidation. I talked to a man said he saw one down toward Mex country a few years back, and there's been rumors of them in the Saskatch as well. Remember when they had all those forest fires up there a couple of years back? They blamed it on the dry weather at the time, but I heard stories there was a rogue firemaker heating the place up, trying to attract a mate most likely. The females only come into season every twenty years or so, but when they do, they can cause a lot of damage trying to find Mr. Right."

Our conversation was interrupted at that point by a cadaverously thin steward who hopped nervously back and forth until we acknowledged his presence.

"Excuse me, sirs, but the captain has asked us to poll the passengers to see if there's anyone aboard who might be able to lend us a hand."

I had no idea what he was talking about but Jeb didn't even look surprised. "He wants to know if you or me's got any useful magical talents, lad. A powerful avoidance spell or something that could scramble our visitor's eyesight for a little while would come in mighty handy about now."

"Who? Me?" The very idea was absurd. The Parkhurst family hadn't produced even a minor arcane talent for as far back in our lineage as we could trace, not even one of the useless ones like beer dowsing or milk curdling. But now I understood why the steward seemed so uneasy. It was considered very poor manners to inquire about paranormal powers, a legacy of the horrible pogroms of the previous century when innocent people were driven from their homes and sometimes attacked and killed simply because they had inherited a talent for magic. Some of the rarer abilities had been all but eradicated during the two decades of repression, particularly in Europe, and since the arcane genes were always recessive, no one knew how many talents had disappeared completely. In our supposedly more enlightened country, magical heritage was still considered something of an embarrassment, and most people never made the effort to find out whether or not they had the gift. Even among those who practiced openly, it was considered gauche to do so publicly.

"No, I'm afraid not," I said quietly but firmly. "You'll have to try elsewhere."

The steward nodded politely and turned to my companion.

"Sorry, nothing that would help. I'm a pretty fair water dowser, actually," he gestured with one arm toward the rushing water beyond the rail. "But I don't suppose that's a talent you get much call for on a riverboat."

After a mumbled acknowledgement that might have been a thank you, the steward moved on to the next group, a cluster of young women who had emerged from the dining room during our conversation and were now hovering halfway between the doors and the rail, trying to decide whether curiosity or discretion was the more powerful motivator. The original panic had subsided and more and more of the passengers were venturing out to watch the beast, a situation which would not be viewed favorably by the crew.

Until now, the voyage had been utterly bland other than a brief delay when we broke a paddle in the portside drive chamber, necessitating a short visit to a riverbank town named Mantonville where the local forge quickly put the situation right. The captain had suggested that anyone who wished to go ashore do so, but only if we were certain that we could return before dusk. Mantonville was a small farming community with little to attract tourists, and I'd spent less than an hour wandering its streets, discovered that its tiny dancehall wasn't even open until evening and that the even smaller Illusion Chamber featured conjured stories so old that most of them were already in the public domain. There was an empath with a small office not far from the dock, however, and I considered using her services to send a message back to my family, but unfortunately there were several people in her waiting room, including one unfriendly looking fellow I'd seen aboard the *River Warlock*, and I had not been patient enough to wait. To be entirely honest, I wasn't unhappy to have abandoned the attempt; mindlinks always made me uneasy and I rarely resorted to them unless it was unavoidable.

I joined Jeb at the rail now that it appeared an attack was not imminent. Indeed, the dragon was giving us quite a wide berth, and the perturbations of the river's surface were growing less violent with each passing moment. "It seems to have lost interest in us," I ventured.

"Maybe," Jeb answered noncommittally

As if it had heard me speak and wanted to prove me wrong, the dragon suddenly altered course. The swell of water was capped with white foam as it headed diagonally toward our bow. It was moving faster than we were and I heard bells clanging as the captain and crew tried to avoid a collision. The deck tilted slightly and I clutched at the guardrail and spread my feet while shouts and cries sounded on every side.

"She's coming up on us." Jeb seemed as calm as ever but I could see that his knuckles were white where his hands gripped the rail alongside my own. Just ahead, on the port side of our bow, the water exploded into churning froth and the dragon's head rose up on its ridiculously long and narrow neck, high enough that it peered directly down onto our foredeck.

If you've never actually seen a mature Oriental dragon in the flesh, any description I might offer will necessarily be inadequate. They have much heavier muscles than their European cousins, and their bodies are longer, more serpentine, better adapted for an aquatic environment. They are fresh water animals, thankfully, which is why there are no native varieties in either America or in New Hindustan. The head is disproportionately small, although that's obviously a relative term. The triangular ears are actually quite broad when extended, but while swimming they were folded into recessed cavities. The snout is much longer and narrower than seems proper, and the teeth are strong and sharply pointed. European dragons hunt by tearing the flesh of their prey so that they bleed to death; Oriental dragons crush the bones and tissues to pulp, and while the former are often content to subsist on vegetarian fare, the latter are by preference carnivores.

They also differ radically in temperament. Centuries ago, French and Prussian farmers domesticated dragons and used them to till their fields, and others became performers in traveling circuses. Efforts to harness them for use in warfare had been largely unsuccessful due to the animals' nervousness around loud noises and the difficulty of feeding them in the field. The Oriental breed could not be broken to harness, not even with magical assistance. They were more likely to till the farmer than his land, they wouldn't distinguish between friend and enemy in a battle, and the fire breathing variety were so difficult to handle that even in interior China, where they were still revered as demi-gods, their eggs were often destroyed in order to keep their numbers down.

A captive dragon was the sign of great personal power among the Chinese, however, and when their warlords and noble class expanded to the continents of America and Cantonia, they brought dragons with them. The kangaroo, a once common mammal in Cantonia, was hunted nearly to extinction by wild dragons two centuries ago. Fortunately, in most places the wild dragons have nearly exhausted their food supply and natural pressure reduced their numbers, although pessimists predicted that they'll be driven to predation against humans eventually.

This particular dragon was now swimming parallel to our course once more, but she held her head high and watched the deck with undisguised avarice. I say "she" because Jeb so identified the creature, claiming that he could determine gender by the shape of the two twisted tusks that curled up from the end of the snout, and the curvature of the horns that arched back behind the now rampant ears. "Males have thicker tusks and the horns are heavier and curve slightly forward. This one's a lady, all right."

I tried to examine those features dispassionately but it was the creature's eyes that held my attention. They were large, deep set, and dark, and would have been beautiful if they hadn't seemed so full of malevolence.

"Step back lively, Jimmy lad. She's making to lunge at us." Jeb grabbed my arm and pulled me back from the rail.

Even to my uneducated eye, it was obvious that something was about to happen. The creature had suddenly raised its head higher than ever, and it swayed slowly from side to side on an impossibly elongated neck, towering over us, higher even than the bridgehouse. Its jaws opened and it roared at us, a wet, gravelly sound that hurt the ears, and I thought I caught the faintest hit of its corrupt breath, although that may have been my imagination. The deck lurched under our feet as the captain tried to steer us away from the beast, but riverboats are designed for comfort, not speed or maneuverability. One of the young women behind us screamed, but whether from fear or excitement, I could not say. As terrifying as the dragon might be, it seemed somehow unreal.

A series of sharp, popping sounds came from somewhere above and behind us, the crew apparently opening fire in a vain attempt to drive off our unwelcome companion. Jeb pulled me back from the rail and we half ran, half staggered across the deck, finally reaching the wall of the forward deck house, where I braced myself with both hands on the window frame. Jeb stood next to me, feet splayed apart, the fingers of one hand wrapped around a bit of piping that ran up the wall and across the roof.

"They're just going to piss it off even more," he told me, his voice as calm as ever. "We're in its territory and it's not going to back off until we leave."

"I imagine the captain is attempting to do just that!"

I glanced around and saw that most of the other passengers had elected to quit the deck, a decision I hoped to emulate at the first opportunity. The door to the deckhouse was on the opposite side from where we stood, but access to the canteen was only a few steps away. Unfortunately, it would be necessary to cross directly in front of the dragon's looming head to reach it. Several wooden crates and barrels had been piled on the deck nearby, secured with a cargo net, and I would have to bypass that obstruction to reach safety. I was considering making a dash for it when I felt Jeb's hand rest on my shoulder.

"Don't do it, lad. It'll most likely pluck you right off the deck if you attract its attention. Dragons don't see all that well, but they're attracted to movement."

The roaring cut off abruptly and I glanced upward. The nearer eye seemed to be staring directly at me and I felt a sudden weakness in my legs. Then the head darted forward, directly toward me, and I confess that I opened my mouth to scream, and would have as well, if it hadn't bent its neck and disappeared under the waves in a burst of spray that exploded over the deck, soaking me thoroughly.

Jeb grabbed my arm. "Grab onto that netting, lad, and hold on tight. She's going to ram us."

We barely had time to wrap our arms through the rough mesh before the entire world seemed to jump beneath us. My left hand slipped free as the deck rose at an unexpected angle and I flailed around for what seemed like an eternity before I caught another hempen strand. The *River Warlock* righted itself abruptly, and I slammed back down hard enough to leave me momentarily stunned. A spray of water splattered my face and I blinked and slowly turned my head, trying to assess my situation. I was lying on my back, both hands raised above my head and tangled in the netting. The deck wasn't completely level and my feet were actually elevated slightly. I must have been suffering from mild shock because I felt suddenly calm, disconnected really, with no sense of alarm or distress. I might have remained there quite contentedly if Jeb hadn't grabbed my arm.

"We can't stay here. No telling what it'll do now."

I had to replay his words a couple of times before they made any sense. "What happened?"

"The stupid animal's got herself fouled in the drive chains. Hit the port paddle chamber direct, looks like. Can't tell how much damage she's done already but as soon as she realizes she's caught herself, she's going to raise hell trying to get free. If she rakes the hull with her claws, she'll tear right through and sink us."

It took a real effort to uncurl my fingers from the netting and shift my body around so that I could sit up. I hadn't felt any pain till then, but I'd bruised my back pretty badly and had come near to dislocating my right shoulder. The *River Warlock* shuddered every few seconds as the dragon shifted its body, trying to extricate itself. "She's not completely stupid," Jeb told me. "Knows enough to try to ease herself away. If we're lucky, she'll do just that."

There were shouts on every side and I saw people running back and forth, apparently without purpose, crew and passengers alike. I learned later that half a dozen people had fallen overboard and some of the confusion was caused by efforts to rescue them.

"Can you stand, do you think?"

I glanced up at Jeb and nodded. "I'm all right. Just had the wind knocked out of me." And I did get to my feet, although my legs felt as though the bones had all turned to jelly and I had to pause a second while my head stopped spinning.

We made our way slowly toward the stern. A musketman had fallen from the aft deckhouse and one of his mates was using a belaying pin as a temporary splint on his right leg, but that was the only serious injury we saw. Later I heard that one of the assistant cooks had broken three ribs when a barrel of molasses hit him in the side, and one of the passengers struck her head and was mildly concussed. Part of the port side railing had broken loose and fallen into the river but we saw no other serious damage until we reached the wheel chamber. The housing was a total loss, reduced to shattered panels and jaggedly broken framework. We couldn't see the dragon, but we could hear her heavy breathing, and the *River Warlock* lurched every few seconds as she tried to pull free.

Jeb must have realized that I was still suffering from mild shock because he steered me over to the dining salon and pushed me down into a chair before disappearing to see if he could be of assistance elsewhere. For such an innocuous looking, rough edged man, he seemed unusually cool and competent in an emergency. I didn't know much about him; we'd met because there were no private cabins available and we'd been cabin mates for the trip. He was not inclined to say much, particularly about his past, but that's not uncommon among frontiersmen, many of whom have unsavory pasts.

"I'm mostly retired now. Spent all my life on one frontier or another, trapping, hunting, trading with the Iroquois, even did some survey work for the Department of Cartography." He lived on the border between the American Federation and the Iroquois Free State and was on his way to New Orleans for a vacation. "A long overdue vacation, I might add."

I estimated his age at about fifty, although it was hard to tell what might be concealed behind that long, unruly beard and those curly locks that covered his forehead and ears and brushed his shoulders. There was the faintest hint of gray in his hair, but if he'd spent most of his life outdoors the way he claimed, then the sun might have bleached it prematurely. So he could have been younger than he appeared. On the other hand, a graying retardation spell didn't cost much more than a haircut and he might actually have been closer to sixty. A gentleman never admitted to using magic to improve his appearance, of course, but you saw the service being offered in more and more places lately so there were obviously plenty of customers.

My wits returned fairly quickly. The heavy thumping below the deck level had grown less frequent and I wondered if the dragon was tiring. I hadn't heard any screaming for a while, although there was still considerable shouting in the distance. A few passengers had ventured back out into the open, trying to find out what was going on, and I saw a flustered looking steward trying to urge a small group away from what remained of the port rail. The deck remained slightly canted, but not enough to make walking particularly difficult. I rose and took a very tentative step and was pleased to discover that my legs were willing to support me once more.

I could hear the steam engine pumping away and realized that both paddles were stopped, the one on the port side at least partially destroyed, the starboard one disengaged. There was still movement as the river current urged us gently forward and occasional shudders and jerks, as though the *River Warlock* was trying to free itself from some unseen hindrance, or vice versa. At least a score of men, mostly crew, were clustered near the ruined paddle chamber, several of them using poles to prod at something I couldn't see. Some of the wreckage had fallen onto the deck and other crew members were attempting to clear this away, aided by a handful of passengers. Thinking I might be of some use there, I headed in that direction.

From near at hand the damage seemed even worse. The housing was quite obviously a complete loss and most of the shattered remains had fallen onto the deck. Two men and one of the female passengers were throwing some of the lighter debris over the side and I joined them, nodding silently to the young woman.

I had barely had time to clear away a half dozen pieces before there was a particularly violent shudder and the ominous sound of wood splitting and nails tearing loose somewhere below.

"Cut through the goddamned chain before she rips the side out of us!" I recognized the captain's voice although I couldn't see him. Captain Martin was a difficult man to overlook – tall, broad shouldered, with a full head of snow white hair and a moustache that would have made a Prussian noble proud. He was built like a wrestler and when he'd greeted me during the boarding process, my hand had disappeared in his palm like that of a child with a parent. His carriage and demeanor were self assured and calm, and if there was ever a living archetype for ship's captain, it would have looked very much like Captain Martin. His only flaw was his voice, which was pitched just slightly too high, making him an easy target for caricature among the passengers. Probably among the crew as well, although much more circumspectly. I wondered why he hadn't chosen to have it altered, but perhaps he was one of those rare immunes for whom magical cures were at best temporary.

There was a shower of sparks from somewhere out of my line of sight, presumably a torch trying to sever the chain in which the dragon was currently entangled. I pitched a few more pieces of wreckage over the side, then retreated quickly when a section of sinewy body suddenly reared up just beyond the rail, then crashed back down into the water.

"She's getting tired!" shouted someone.

"Just getting her second wind!" came the answer, and I thought the voice was Jeb's, although I couldn't see him anywhere.

A moment later someone shouted an inarticulate warning and I saw several people move quickly away from the port rail. A broken bit of drive chain came shooting up from below and slammed into the only remaining support stanchion for the paddle housing. I was close enough to see that the oversized spindle had split into two parts and the bulk of what remained of the wheel lay pressed against the hull, supported by the drive chains and anchor supports and pinned in place by the dragon, around whose body the rest of the chain was now loosely wrapped. The housing and wheel would both have to be replaced entirely; the missing portions which had not landed on the deck were already drifting away downriver.

The deck moved violently beneath me and I staggered forward as the list to starboard suddenly became a sharper list to port. Fortunately the rail was undamaged ahead of me and I was able to stop myself before I was thrown over the side. I glanced down in time to see the enormously powerful scaled body of the dragon twist itself free of the last section of chain and disappear under the water.

Freed at last, the dragon appeared to have had enough of us because I could tell by the swell of the water that she was moving rapidly and powerfully toward the far shore. Her gigantic tail broke the surface and slapped down like a thunderclap, sending spray in every direction. I'm a fair judge of distance and based on the forward surge of water where her head ploughed forward, the beast must have been fully forty meters long. They said that the Royal Dragon of Teiping measured more than sixty meters fully extended, making this one seem pretty ordinary in comparison, but she was still quite extraordinary by my standards.

The deck had returned to a more or less horizontal position and the crewmen were already examining the wreckage to determine the extent of the damage, although it was obvious even to my untrained eye that the port side paddle was a complete loss. More of the passengers appeared from below deck and from the dining salon and elsewhere despite efforts by the stewards to restrain them. I saw Jeb emerge from a cluster of people. He nodded in my direction, then raised a hand to shield his eyes as he peered toward the dragon's wake.

I started toward him but had only taken a step or two before the dragon's head erupted from the swiftly moving river once again. She had turned beneath the water to face us, and she did not look happy. Even at this distance, she looked menacing.

People began scurrying about and I heard the crackle of renewed musket fire. I looked for Jeb but he had disappeared as if by magic. My eyes went back to the dragon, which appeared motionless but somehow larger, and I realized that she was moving toward the *River Warlock* steadily but cautiously, having learned from her previous mistake. The jaws were open and she roared, a deep rumbling that rolled across the river like distant thunder. I'm sure it was just my imagination but the two unblinking eyes seemed to have fastened onto me specifically. The musket fire continued, sporadic and ineffective, the shots bouncing uselessly off armored hide. Everything was dreamlike, unreal, and at that moment I don't think I even felt any fear. But I was numb rather than courageous.

I might have remained standing there until those jaws had closed around my body if I hadn't been startled back to reality by a rush of sound to my right and a plume of thick black smoke that seemed to have burst from the deck itself. I thought the ship must have caught fire and exploded, but then I saw Jeb backing out of the sooty cloud, waving his arms to clear the air. A sudden breeze swept across the deck and I had one second to glimpse a peculiar mechanical device before a muffled thud drew my attention back to our attacker.

The dragon screeched in outrage and jerked her head away from a boiling mass of pitch black smoke that had appeared directly in front of her snout. The water roiled around her as she came to an abrupt stop.

"Goddamned dud!" Jeb glanced in my direction. "Give me a hand here, lad."

His voice was different, commanding, and I found myself kneeling at his side before I realized that I had responded to his orders. "What should I do?"

"Brace the two forelegs against the deck. Press down as hard as you can so I can line things up properly."

Once more I found myself obeying without consciously deciding to do so. I wrapped my fingers around the two forward legs of the tripodal device, which appeared to be some kind of wide breached musket, and leaned forward to hold it steady. There was a cylindrical chute or channel mounted on a pivot, which Jeb adjusted carefully while he placed a tapered object nearly as long as my forearm within its cradle. The dragon roared again, sounding angrier than ever, and closer as well.

"Hold it steady now, just a bit longer. We won't have time to take another shot."

I didn't dare turn and look out across the water. Instead I focused my eyes on the patch of deck visible between my thighs. The *River Warlock* could use a fresh coat of paint, I told myself. Then there was a flash and a roar, not the dragon this time, and the tapered shell rushed up the chute trailing black smoke. I recoiled instinctively, lost my balance, and fell onto my back. There was a loud explosion and a flash of light and I closed my eyes, half expecting to feel dagger sharp teeth biting into my body.

The roaring turned into a shrill scream and I chanced opening my eyes, twisted my body in time to see that enormous head, towering high in the air and distressingly close, streaming flame and smoke. The dragon whipped her neck back and forth, still screaming, then withdrew under the water so quickly that I blinked my eyes, not understanding what had just happened. Although Jeb told me later that he doubted we'd done the beast any permanent harm, we'd obviously discouraged it and that was the last we saw of her other than a trail of bubbles and disturbed water as she turned and vanished upriver.

I was sitting on the deck, still rather stunned, when Captain Martin appeared. He grasped Jeb's hand and began pumping it enthusiastically. "Well done, sir. Well done indeed."

"I had to break into the locker to commandeer your flare launcher, Captain. There wasn't time to ask for the key." Jeb sounded more like a discovered truant than a hero.

"That's the least of our problems right now." Martin gestured toward the ruined wheel housing. He turned in my direction. "And thanks to you as well." He shook my hand, his grip firm and warm, an action I found totally incomprehensible. After all, I hadn't done anything worth of congratulations. Had I?

"I would be pleased if the two of you would dine at my table this evening." He sighed with unusual theatricality. "Although I suspect that dinner will be served a bit later than usual today."

"We'd be honored." Jeb answered for both of us, which was just as well, since I'm not certain that at that particular moment I still retained the power of speech.

"Good. I look forward to it. If you'll excuse me then, gentlemen." And with a tap to the brim of his cap, Captain Martin turned and strode away.

I got up onto my hands and knees, made my way to the railing, and vomited over the side. Jeb seemed to find this quite amusing.

CHAPTER TWO

It didn't require any expertise about riverboats to realize that we had a serious problem. The *River Warlock* wasn't really a luxury vessel; her appointments were adequate but plain compared to the elaborate facilities provided on the Twain Line ships like the *Admiral Washington, Ambassador Clay*, and *President Cholmondesley*. Originally a cargo ship, the *Warlock* had been converted to take advantage of the lucrative passenger trade, catering to business travelers and tourists who couldn't afford the more expensive vessels, an enterprise even more profitable at present because of a chronic shortage of berths. As I have already noted, a new coat of paint would not have been unwelcome. Meals were well prepared and wholesome but there were few choices, the cabins were smaller and less well equipped than on the major lines, and there were not nearly as many personal services aboard. We had neither a barber nor a tailor, for example, and made do with an old fashioned laundry service rather than a cleaning spellster. But I had made inquiries before taking passage and heard nothing but praise for Captain Martin and his crew. They ran a clean, efficient ship and had an enviable safety record.

Once the worst of the wreckage was cleared away and a closer examination made, Captain Martin immediately informed his passengers of the details of our situation. With a single operable paddle, we could still make some progress, but we would necessarily be slower and less maneuverable. The hull showed some signs of strain but nothing alarming. Sealing balm had been spread over the affected area and the associated lower compartment had been closed off in case of a breach. Barring further misfortune, there was no reason to be concerned about the safety of the ship.

That was the good news.

Portions of the wheel structure had been salvaged and were now lashed against the side or tied down on the aft deck, but for the most part, the entire works were beyond repair. An unscheduled stop at a small riverside town called Sanders Ferry would be necessary so that equipment and assistance could be found to lift the rest of the surviving structure onto the deck and secure it in preparation for a full refit which could not be accomplished until we reached

Memphis. Under the best of circumstances, the *River Warlock* would be dockbound there for at least four days while repairs were being completed. There was a possibility that those of us with deadlines to meet might be able to arrange alternate transportation, either overland or aboard another ship, but the choices for the rest would be either to remain aboard while repairs were being completed or find temporary accommodations in the city. Captain Martin hinted that his superiors might be willing to pay for any reasonable expenses, but he was unwilling to commit himself to anything specific until he'd had time to communicate with the company and receive authorization to make promises.

If this had been simply a vacation, I wouldn't have minded waiting. Memphis is a very cosmopolitan city, one I had visited briefly on several previous occasions, always on business, always just long enough to stimulate my curiosity, never long enough for me to satisfy it. Unfortunately, although I intended to mix pleasure with business this time, and despite the fact that there were several days remaining before my meeting with the exporting consortium, I wanted to reach New Orleans as close to my original schedule as possible. There was other business to be conducted there. My competitors would be in New Orleans as well, and if much more time passed before I arrived, it would be less likely that I'd find sufficient unallocated cargo space for this season's goods, forcing me to rely on less reliable and more expensive alternatives. Realistically, if I was delayed more than ten days, I might just as well have stayed at home and dealt with the gypsy freighters and New Hindustani cargo runners.

So I was not in the best of moods that evening as we prepared to dine with the captain. Jeb surprised me by having a set of reasonably formal garments tucked away in his luggage, a high necked silk shirt with tastefully minimal shoulder braid and a stylishly narrow waist sash. "Always be prepared to blend in with the scenery, lad. That's the mark of a good hunter."

"We're having dinner, not hunting for it," I responded irritably.

"You might be surprised how much a dinner at the Captain's table can resemble a hunt," he said quietly.

The formal dining room provided less elaborate fare than could be found on the fancier ships, but the staff on board were more than competent and I'd had no reason to complain about the food. Meals were served at specific times, however, much more inflexible than what I was used to. Those who couldn't accustom themselves to this schedule could usually find something to eat in the crew kitchen below deck, or they could purchase sandwiches and other small items in the lounge. I couldn't remember ever seeing Jeb in the dining room before, so I assumed he made do with whatever the crew was having. We attracted some curious looks when we arrived, and I suspect that at least a few of our fellow passengers didn't recognize Jeb without his rawhide jacket and buckskin leggings. He had even combed out his beard and dragged his curly locks back from his face. If I hadn't known better, I might have mistaken him for a gentleman.

The Captain's table was at the far end of the main dining room, raised slightly above the others so that everyone seated there would be readily visible from each of the other tables. Perhaps three quarters of the seats were filled when we arrived, but conversations were more subdued than usual. A handful of stewards hustled back and forth, dispensing wine, coffee, ambrosia, and other beverages.

Captain Martin greeted us warmly and introduced the other five people at his table. Two were crew members, Chief Engineer Luttrell and the ship's doctor, Edna Snow, a gaunt woman who rarely spoke spontaneously and who had never smiled in my presence. There were three other passengers, including an Adjudicator from Madison named Beck, whom I'd spoken to earlier in the voyage. She was taking her first vacation from her duties since her appointment and planned to sail from New Orleans on a tour of the Prussian colonies in Cuba and Dominica, possibly even pay a visit to the Ishthmian canal.

The other two passengers were both military men, a colonel of musketry named Sykes, on leave from his posting in the border town of St. Paul, and a naval engineer, Lieutenant Commander Davis, recently transferred to New Orleans from the Great Lakes Command. I had played cards with Davis on two occasions and knew that he was quite reticent about his recent duties, which I assumed had something to do with improving the fortifications along the border. The Duke of Toronto was still refusing to rescind his secession from the New British Empire, as our northern neighbors were styling themselves ever since the arrival of the exiled Royal

Family, and it was feared that a border incident might be manufactured to draw either the American Federation or the Iroquois Free State into the quarrel. The Iroquois were notoriously unwilling to involve themselves in foreign disputes, but they were clearly concerned about the military buildup. The Federation Congress was currently in session in Boston and a number of anti-monarchal speeches had been quoted in the newspapers, stirring up barely dormant animosities left over from the Revolution. Most people believed this to be no more than political posturing; the Congress was decidedly isolationist and certainly had no intention of interjecting itself into the conflict. But there was always the possibility that circumstances would cause things to slip beyond their control, and there was serious concern that trading patterns in that part of the world might be disrupted unpredictably.

"And are you gentlemen traveling with us on business or for pleasure?" It took me a second to realize that the captain had addressed his remarks to Jeb and I.

Jeb hesitated, so I spoke up. "Both actually. My father and I run a wholesaling business out of Lansing. We front for a large number of small manufacturers, farmers, artists, and so forth. We deal in everything from luxury items and art objects to grains, pelts, potions, firecharms, and fabrics." We had also briefly represented a munitions firm and had traded muskets and powder quite profitably, but when one of our shipments ended up in the hands of one of the New Hindustani pirate states, the authorities had asked some rather pointed questions and we'd elected to sever our ties to that particular industry. It was not an episode I preferred to advertise.

"I just completed a trip to the Tuang Sheng province up north and I have a warehouse filled with jade, screen paintings, silk, and jewelry, which I'm hoping to sell through our connections in New Orleans. But I'm also overdue for a vacation, so I had planned for a slow, unexciting trip." I smiled to indicate that I didn't hold Captain Martin responsible for the day's aberration.

"I wouldn't have thought there was much opportunity for trade with the Empire lately." Davis was frowning slightly and I immediately pegged him as an Expansionist.

He was right, though. Relations between the Federation and the Empire had been deteriorating for some time. Although the border was still officially open, and for all practical purposes could

not be closed since it ran through large tracts of unexplored
wilderness, several Federation merchant vessels had recently been
refused use of the Isthmian canal despite treaty obligations
specifically assigning us Most Favored Nation status. Excuses had
been offered – suspect cargoes, problems maintaining the spells
which regulated the continuity of the sea level, improper
documentation, human error, and so forth, but most of these had
been flimsy excuses and, more importantly, had clearly been
designed as deliberate affronts.

It was all because of that damned play, of course. Albee's
Who's Afraid of Empress Su? It was an acerbic and obvious satire
directed at the current Chinese ruling family, particularly Empress
Lu, who was not known for either her sense of humor or her
tolerance of criticism. Ling Hwa, the Governor General of the
Changsha Territories, the Empire's holdings in this part of the world,
was known to be less than enamored with the Empress himself, but
that didn't stop him from reacting predictably and negatively when
foreign nationals made light of the throne to which he was sworn.
The full trade embargo that the Emperor had decreed would never
have worked; the Changsha were too dependent on providing
American markets the bulk of their excess goods and the border was
so long and unsettled that it was more a funnel than a sieve. For that
matter, Ling Hwa was almost certainly avoiding taking steps that
would cause serious harm to the economy on his side of the border.
The Emperor was far away and usually preoccupied with his western
provinces and the border war with the Tsar's vassal states while the
prominent merchants of Changsha were close at hand and very
vocal. He was also preoccupied with the depredations of the savages
in the southwest and hoped to convince Congress to tighten
restrictions on trade along the Texican border.

It has always been my experience that the pursuit of profit
generally triumphs over transient political differences. Anti-Chinese
sentiment had stimulated some backlash in our domestic markets and
the troubles to our north were causing people to become more
circumspect about their purchases, but it was a temporary aberration.
Even so, we were exerting ourselves to open up new markets in New
Hindustan, the Prussian Carib states, and elsewhere. Although we
were not obligated to help our business associates in Tuang Sheng
by taking their excessive inventories off their hands, it would be to

our advantage to do so. The Changsha would feel dishonored if they did not return the favor at some future time. Even if we disposed of the merchandise at cost through subsidiary dealers and shipped them to the Zulu Republic, we'd lose nothing of importance and gain an immeasurable amount of good will.

"There is some resistance to Chinese goods at the moment, Commander Davis. You're right about that. But there's still a healthy market overseas, and the present strained relationship provides us with considerable leverage in our dealings with our oriental friends."

"Still, doesn't seem very patriotic. No offense meant."

"Not at all, Commander." Adjudicator Beck came unbidden to my defense without even looking up from the fruit cup which she was examining as critically as she would a legal brief. "Even the most isolationist members of our Congress won't suggest a counter embargo. The balance of trade is enormously in our favor. We export fully one third of our wheat and corn to Changsha, and significant quantities of other crops. The present situation will end as soon as Empress Lu finds something else to outrage her sensibilities."

Davis subsided with an inarticulate sound that managed to convey his dissatisfaction with the situation, even if he couldn't express it more eloquently.

Captain Martin tactfully changed the subject. "I'm afraid that we may be delayed longer than I'd initially expected. The last time I passed through Memphis, the refitting yards had their hands full, and my cargo master tells me that the situation is reportedly much worse now. Even if the company is willing to offer a premium, it's not likely that we'll be going anywhere any time soon. We could probably find small contractors willing to reset the paddles and run the chain, and the housing can be refitted with unskilled labor, but we need an entirely new spindle, a portion of the hull will have to be removed and replaced, and there's been some strain on the engines as well."

The Chief Engineer nodded sullenly in agreement.

"I thought as much," I replied. "I don't suppose there's a telegraph in Sanders Ferry?"

"Not that I know of. Never actually stopped there before except to drop off mail. It's a backwater, used mostly by cargo steamers and fishermen and probably a few river pirates. Pretty good sized community though. There might be an empath there who could establish a mindlink for you."

I nodded, but my reservations about that form of communication remained. No matter how focused the connection, unintentional thoughts and memories often slipped through, depending on the skill of the empaths at either end of the linkage. There was little chance that a small, out of the way place liked Sanders Ferry would have attracted one of the more talented of their kind, if indeed they had an empath there at all. On one occasion, while attempting to expedite a shipment through customs, I had picked up some particularly revolting memories of a sexual perversion I will not describe, and I was always troubled about the possibility that some of my childhood peccadilloes would slip past my guard and become public knowledge.

"I imagine I can wait until Memphis. You don't expect to layover in Sanders Ferry for the night, do you, Captain?"

"No, a few hours should suffice to bring what's left of the wheel aboard and secure it. We won't be able to make our usual speed downriver, of course, but the Chief tells me he can manage some temporary adjustments to make the ship more responsive than it is at present. Another night's travel should see us there safely. With luck, you'll be able to have your breakfast ashore."

The stewards began removing our empty fruit cups at that point and brought on the main course, which slowed the conversation somewhat. We were offered the choice of chicken cooked with chestnuts and brown rice or unicorn steaks. I'm rather fond of the latter; the taste is a trifle gamey and unless cooked well the meat can be rather tough, but when prepared properly it is far superior to pork, mutton, or even to my mind the overpriced centaur. Beef was still the prince of meats, of course, but its rarity had priced it far beyond my means, and it would certainly never have shown up on the menu aboard the *River Warlock* or any of its sister ships.

"And you, Mr. Walker, business or pleasure?"

It was a second or so before I realized to whom the captain was speaking. Jeb had told me his full name when we'd first introduced ourselves, but I'd never had occasion to use it or hear it again.

"A little of both, same as Mr. Parkhurst here. I've been calling myself retired for the last few years, but I still keep my hand in. I put aside some savings through the years, but not nearly enough to make me a gentleman of leisure. Courier work suits me; I get to travel on someone else's dollar. I carry messages too complicated, too big, or too confidential for mindlink or telegraph." He glanced at me and smiled. "Done some bargaining a time or two myself, negotiated a few deals. Nothing on the scale of Mr. Parkhurst here, but enough to put a few bills in my wallet."

"Well, I hope this delay isn't going to cost you your delivery bonus."

"Nope. There's no deadline hanging over my head this time, or at least not one so close that it casts much of a shadow. I might still jump ship in Memphis though. Can't say that I'm particular partial to that city, or interested in spending much time there. Too organized, if you know what I mean. Last time I was there they was trying to pass some silly law against carrying guns inside the city limits."

"It passed." Adjudicator Beck didn't look up from her chicken this time. "No firearms to be worn or carried openly or concealed within municipal limits without a permit." She forked a chunk of white meat into her mouth and chewed it. "Legal challenge pending at the district court in Nashville. It's my understanding that few people pay much attention to the law, though; Memphis still has the third highest murder rate of any city in the Federation. Parts of the city are virtually lawless."

"Damned politicians just make things worse. As soon as Mayor Strait and his cronies got into office, they started looking for ways to tighten their grip on the city. You mark my words, there's trouble coming there." Surprisingly, this uncharacteristic outburst came from Doctor Snow.

"A certain degree of discipline is a requirement for any rational society." The previously silent Colonel Sykes weighed in. "Even within the military we've discovered that it is generally advisable to relieve our troops of their muskets when they're off duty and post a guard on the armory. There have been unpleasant incidents, particularly in some of the more remote outposts." He let his voice trail away but we all knew to what he was alluding. Dueling had been illegal for nearly a century, but old traditions die hard and it wasn't uncommon to see parties of young men trooping off into the woods of a morning on some mission of honor.

"What can you tell us about the situation up north, Commander? Can Toronto make a go of it alone? If the Brits let them go, that is."

Davis made a show of eating a bite of chicken, obviously trying to decide how much he could say without encroaching on military intelligence. "I'd have to say first of all that the Duke's timing is excellent. There's still considerable tension between the colonial administration and the new Parliament the King has been trying to organize ever since his exile." The northern colonies had refused to join the Revolution against the Crown back in the 1790s, but they had never expected to have to surrender their autonomy to direct rule by the royal family. But then no one had ever expected the British themselves to overthrow the monarchy in favor of the new Council of Governors in what now called itself the Peoples Union of Britain. "The Duke has made overtures to the Iroquois."

"I can't see that they have anything to gain by allying themselves with Toronto," interposed Sykes. "Their common border has been troublesome in the past and they can hardly be in sympathy with the Duke."

"No, but they would certainly rather be surrounded by many weaker rivals than a few stronger ones. They've formally recognized his government, but I doubt that we'll see any more substantial support from that quarter. They certainly don't want to be drawn into a war."

"The IFS has traditionally refused to involve itself in conflicts outside its borders," offered Beck. "They're more isolationist than even our own government. It's a simple question of survival. The Iroquois don't have a standing army, just an irregular militia. A determined attack by a modern, organized army would overwhelm them in a matter of days."

"Don't be so certain of that," objected Sykes. "They're undisciplined but determined and they know full well how to take advantage of the local geography. I won't say they could prevail, but I doubt that it would be a quick or bloodless conquest. I remind you that the Apache and their allies have successfully held off the Changsha for several generations."

Davis dismissed the objection with a gesture. "I defer to your expertise, Colonel, but the fact remains that they exist because none of the three continental powers can move against them without risking a military response from either or both of the remaining two. Three, if we assume Toronto gets what he wants."

"I hardly think Changsha would interfere." Beck sat back in her chair. "They have no common border, trade through the Great Lakes is limited, and Governor Ling is hardly an altruist who would withdraw troops from the southwest to help defend a people with whom he has no shared interests."

Colonel Sykes responded quickly, gesturing grandiloquently with both hands, one of which still held his fork. I noticed a large, crescent shaped scar on the back of his left hand, a white slash across otherwise deeply tanned flesh. "Don't underestimate Ling. It's true he wouldn't feel any moral compulsion to defend the Iroquois, but he's a pragmatist and an opportunist. If war broke out and he sided with the Federation against the Brits and the IFS, he could probably win trade concessions as well as our reciprocal assistance against the Apache. On the other hand, if he chose to associate himself with the Crown, it would give him an excuse to move against Wichita, St. Paul, and our other western outposts. He might well seize the Mississippi, lay siege to New Orleans, and capture a significant part of our farmland. The Apache are a thorn in his side, but he could withdraw into his line of forts and hunker down there while the bulk of his forces crossed the river and invaded the Federation. We're probably strong enough to drive him back, but not if we were simultaneously defending the northern states from attack."

The chief engineer shook his head wearily. "This is all too complex for me. Politicians always seem to make things so much more confusing than they need to be." He laughed. "I even got lost reading that spy story that everyone was raving about a few months ago."

It was the first opportunity I'd had to contribute to the conversation, as well as a welcome change of subject. "Are you talking about *The Maladjusted Mandarin Affair*? The latest Malachi Marks adventure?" I had just finished reading it the day before.

"That's the one. Read it cover to cover and still don't understand who was working for who, or why the Prussians were trying to murder their own agent."

It was the fifth adventure of Marks, a series whose author claimed they were based on the actual exploits of a mysterious Federation secret agent, although no one really believed that. The author was the pseudonymous "Richard Grenadier", supposedly a close friend of the real character who served as the basis for the novels.

"The Prussian had sold out to the Tsar's spies," I explained. "He was funneling information to the Persians to help them resist the Turkish occupation."

"Never had much liking for that sort of book," mumbled Jeb. "Not much more than fairy tales. You know right from the start that the hero is going to win the day." Jeb had efficiently cleaned his plate while the rest of us jabbered away and he was already spooning out seconds from the common platter. "Every time he gets into trouble, you know something's going to happen to save him at the last minute. Too many coincidences to my way of thinking. Life isn't like that."

"You've read them then?" I was frankly surprised. Jeb didn't seem the type to curl up with a book. I imagined him whittling on the porch, or cleaning his musket and pistols, or swapping tall tales over a pint at some local inn, not reading spy thrillers.

He glanced at me with a baleful eye. "Not all of us out in the wilds are illiterate, lad. It's only in your big cities where everyone's coming and going so fast that no one's got time to relax. Considering our relative ages, I reckon I've probably read a few more books than you. There's not much else to do when you're waiting out a storm in a cave someplace, or sitting in a blind waiting for game to put in an appearance."

Dad always said I had a habit of judging people too quickly and that I needed to look for more than the superficial, and I realized I had misjudged Jeb. "That wouldn't surprise me at all," I admitted readily. "I used to read quite a lot when I was younger, but not since I became a partner in the business. There's just never enough time."

"Bad for your body." Doctor Snow didn't look up from her food, every bite of which she examined carefully before placing it in her mouth. "Even a good healing spell can't reverse the effects of stress on the heart or other internal organs. Infections, wounds, chemical imbalances, those we can correct with the proper ceremony and herbal treatments, but once the muscle tone starts to go, particularly in the heart or lungs, well..." She let her voice trail off ominously.

"Can't keep your bow strung all the time, that's for sure," answered Jeb. "Loses its spring."

The rest of the party seemed more interested in food than conversation now. We finished the main course and few words were spoken until the steward had cleared the table and brought fresh coffee.

Adjudicator Beck asked if anyone objected to her smoking and when no one spoke up produced a small but quite elaborate pipe from some inner pocket. When she had lighted it and drawn the first few puffs, she turned to Davis. "Did you visit New Britain at all during your stay up north, Commander?"

He looked distinctly uncomfortable. "The details of my assignment are quite confidential, I'm afraid. I have visited the Crown colonies in the past, of course, but purely in an unofficial capacity."

I suspected that he might have been clandestinely evaluating the defenses along the border. There had been much talk recently of the need to reinforce our redoubts in the Great Lakes region, and the uncertainty caused by Toronto's rebellion could only have raised the level of concern.

If Beck noticed his reluctance to discuss the subject, she ignored it. "I was just curious whether you'd heard anything further about the political situation back in Britain itself. When I left Madison, there were persistent rumors that the Crown was preparing to finance a guerilla movement against the PUB." The Peoples Union of Britain was dominated by three young socialists from Liverpool, who were inspired by the political writings of an obscure philosopher named Lennon.

Davis shrugged. "There are always rumors. I've also heard that the Prussians were preparing to intervene because they feared that their own collectivist sympathizers might be encouraged to attempt a similar rebellion. Personally I consider that very unlikely. The Prussians are too thoroughly engaged in their hostilities with the Tsar's army to involve themselves in another foreign adventure. They'll posture a bit and growl a lot but they're too smart to act with a tactical disadvantage."

"We've also heard rumors that there is considerable resentment in the eastern provinces," I ventured. "They prefer the decentralized colonial government that's being supplanted."

Davis nodded. "King Winston ruffled more than a few feathers when he replaced most of the colonial administrators with his personal staff. Bad politics and bad management as well. His cronies are used to dealing with the relatively passive populace back in Britain; they're ill prepared to manage a society that still has much of the frontier about it. If you want my opinion, Winston will be preoccupied consolidating his new venue for the foreseeable future, perhaps the remainder of his reign. He's not a young man after all. And if Toronto can't be talked around, there will either be a costly war or a significant loss of taxes and resources. Either outcome will reduce his ability, and perhaps his willingness, to meddle outside his remaining borders."

"And remember, Toronto is the loudest dissenter, but not the only one. And he seems to be quite popular in his home province. I'm surprised though that he hasn't been assassinated before now." Sykes' voice had intensified; this was clearly a topic that interested him.

Davis nodded. "The British Secret Service has been quite effective silencing dissenters in the past, but the Duke has so far avoided their attention, or perhaps quietly disposed of them."

"Then there have been attempts?" I asked.

"As to that, I couldn't say." His face twisted uncomfortably.

"Is the Duke a popular figure then? Would his constituents defend him if attacked?"

Davis sighed. "Toronto has always been the best run of the provinces, ever since colonial days. If the rebellion had failed, the Duke might well have been tapped for Prime Minister. He's a handsome man, speaks well in public, is an able administrator, and commands the loyalty of his followers. But no man is universally loved, and some pledge allegiance only to further their own best interests. If war comes, I think the Crown will not be completely without friends within the Duke's forces. Whether the Duke can succeed despite that is an open question."

We adjourned a short time later. Supper had been delayed more than an hour and it was quite dark when we rose from the table to allow the stewards to clear away the last of the cups, glasses, and napkins. Jeb had fallen into conversation with Beck and the two invited me to accompany them to the lounge for a nightcap, but I'd developed a blinding headache during the last few minutes and declined with thanks. The rest of the party was also dispersing but I was quite alone when I reached the door of the cabin Jeb and I shared.

If I had been more alert, I might have heard movement or breathing when I entered, but all I could think of was to shed my clothing and crawl beneath my blankets. If the pain didn't subside quickly, I would have to look up Doctor Snow, but I've always been wary of healing spells and prefer to let my body adjust itself by more natural means. In any case, I heard nothing except the closing of the door behind me, and had taken two steps toward my bunk when I noticed the figure of a man at the far end of the room, crouched over my steamer trunk.

CHAPTER THREE

"Oh, excuse me, sir. I thought you'd still be dining."

Momentary alarm turned into mild annoyance as I recognized the intruder as Dana, the steward responsible for the second class cabins on this deck. He straightened up and I saw that he was holding my spare boots in one hand. "I was just going to have these polished, sir, since it appears that we'll be staying in Memphis for a few days."

"So it appears." I turned up the lantern in order to see him better. My head was hurting abominably and apparently the strain was showing in my face.

"Are you all right, sir?"

"A bit of a headache is all. Nothing to be concerned about."

"Should I summon Doctor Snow?"

"Not necessary, thanks. I just need a good night's sleep to put me right." I took a tentative step toward my bunk, hoping he'd interpret the move as an invitation to leave.

"I've just changed your bed clothing, sir, if you'd care to retire." He moved toward the door. "Sorry to be so late today, but we've all been put to work clearing debris and making minor repairs."

"That's perfectly all right, Dana." He seemed a likeable enough young man, barely out his teens, not too much younger than myself. I doubted that he'd remain in his present position for long because he was remarkably well spoken and self assured, and I'd seen indications that he was much more alert and intelligent than his fellows. Dana had a well developed sense of curiosity as well, and occasionally asked questions that some might consider impertinent.

"I could bring you a sedative potion from the dispensary. They're quite effective."

"I don't think so, Dana, but thank you for offering. I'll just lie down for a while and see if that helps, and if it doesn't, perhaps I'll look up the doctor later."

"Very good, sir. I sleep lightly so don't hesitate to ring the bell if you need assistance." He stepped past me, opened the door, and left with a polite nod.

I climbed into the top bunk without undressing other than to shed my boots and drifted off to sleep almost immediately.

When I next opened my eyes, the cabin was in total darkness. The lantern must have run out of fuel, or Jeb had returned and doused it. All around me was silence except for the lapping of water against the hull. I leaned over the side of the bunk but couldn't hear any breathing from below, which meant that Jeb had not returned or, if he had been back, had declined to remain. I lay back, relieved that the worst of my headache had subsided. I meant to go immediately back to sleep, but decided to undress properly first, so I moved my legs over the side of the bunk and sat up, then lowered myself gingerly to the floor.

The lantern was indeed empty, but I had a charmlight in my jacket pocket. I flashed it around the room and confirmed that Jeb was still absent, which wasn't surprising or out of character. He seemed to survive on a surprisingly small amount of sleep, and most of that came in odd catnaps at irregular hours. The weather was warm enough that he might well have elected to sleep in one of the deck chairs and take advantage of the night breeze, an option that had tempted me as well. The air got quite close in the cabins at times, and felt even closer in the darkness.

My headache had subsided but I was feeling unusually weary. I knew that I'd regret it in the morning if I slept in my day clothing, so I forced myself to pull off my shirt and pants, fold them and place them inside my trunk. It was warm enough to sleep comfortably in just my underwear, but I took the time to locate a cotton night robe which I had purchased specifically for this trip.

I was preparing to climb back up and retire once again when I heard voices from outside the cabin door.

I couldn't recognize either of them, nor could I make out most of the words, but both were almost certainly male and I did hear fragments. Although I wasn't curious enough to pay strict attention, a few words penetrated my waning consciousness as I lay back against the pillow, which I would recall quite distinctly the following morning.

One sequence in particular. The first voice rose above a whisper. "That's impossible! We've looked everywhere." An indistinct murmured followed, from which I could discern only the phrases "false trail" and "knows we're onto him".

The first voice resumed but faintly and I realized the speakers were moving away from me, or I was sinking away from them. Then one last word, spoken so clearly that I had no doubt of my memory when I recalled it the following morning. The second voice had used the word "archmage".

Even in these enlightened days, our society retains an ambivalent attitude toward magic. Although the pogroms of the past have been repudiated time and time again, they continue in less civilized parts of the world, particularly New Hindustan and eastern Russia. We know now that magic is a perfectly natural part of the world, that fey talents are genetically determined and bear no relationship to the character of the practitioner, and as a consequence magic and science have become integrated elements in society rather than opposing poles in a philosophical debate.

Despite the modern reconciliation, there remains a pervasive uneasiness about the arcane arts, a prejudice that defies easy explanation. I consider myself an educated, intelligent man, but even I generally resort to magic only when there is no other viable alternative. Every day, thousands of people use charms or spells routinely to retard hair loss, shed unwanted pounds, find lost objects, cure minor illnesses, suppress allergies, safeguard their possessions, preserve food, and perform many other useful services, but few will admit to it publicly, particularly if they have the talent to perform such charms, spells, and incantations on their own initiative rather than through a licensed spellcaster, demimage, or conjurer.

Most communities of any size have one or more Illusion Chambers, which are clearly arcane even if no one talks about that aspect of their art, and there's not a professional healer, physician, or herbalist who doesn't practice at least some magic, or call upon specialists to do so if they lack the ability. Mindlinks are essential in remote areas where no telegraph lines exist, and popular among those who consider their communications too private to trust to the employees of the various telegraphy or messenger services. Clairvoyants are popular as well, though many of these are fraudulent, and most are more or less hidden in less desirable neighborhoods.

Archmages are a different matter entirely. Although as many as one fourth of the human race possesses some magical talent, usually trivial, often useless, there are a very few who are capable of mastering a wide range of arcane skills, even develop new ones. Most archmages are conscripted immediately by their respective governments everywhere in the civilized world, and put to work detecting and countering any magical assault from foreign or domestic opponents, or perhaps to initiate a covert assault. Because of this balance of power, there had not been a successful arcane attack on an international level in living memory, or at least none that has been publicly acknowledged.

There was almost certainly a second purpose to the conscription, however. Archmages were too powerful, too potentially dangerous, to be allowed to operate without oversight. Although they were rewarded with princely sums of money and elegant lifestyles, they were encumbered by a team of personal bodyguards who were there to watch over the archmage's activities as much as to protect him or her. Their travel and communications were restricted and monitored and they had virtually no private lives.

Not every archmage was forced into government service, however. There were rogues who carefully masked their powers. Technically they were fugitives by definition, but if you knew where to ask the right questions in almost any medium to large city, someone would refer you to a friend of an acquaintance who knew somebody else, and the chain might eventually lead to an archmage.

I couldn't imagine that anyone aboard the *River Warlock* could be such a powerful figure, but then again, how would I know for sure? I'm not a sensitive, after all. While dressing, I tried to remember the rest of the conversation upon which I'd involuntarily eavesdropped, but could dredge up nothing but the few fragments I've already mentioned. Ultimately I dismissed it as of no consequence. Whatever the issue might be, it didn't concern me and I had other matters of much higher importance to deal with before the day was through.

We docked at Sanders Ferry at mid-morning, a bit later than expected. Word of our situation had preceded our arrival; the damage to the paddle chamber was visible from shore and we had passed several smaller settlements since daybreak. A larger steamboat had overtaken us during the night and inquired as to our condition, offering to carry word in advance so that we would be expected. A small delegation was therefore waiting on the dock as we moored, contractors anxious to bid for part or all of the temporary repair work, shills from local businesses hoping to lure passengers or crew into parting with their money, and the inevitable complement of curiosity seekers who were largely disappointed, since the damaged side of our vessel faced away from shore. Captain Martin announced that we'd be docked for a minimum of three hours if any of the passengers cared to visit the town, and that he'd sound the steam whistle three times half an hour prior to departure, just in case anyone lost track of the time.

Sanders Ferry was a quite small farming community with only a few marginal salvage services and other river oriented businesses. It looked to be fairly reputable if not prosperous, even a mildly attractive community, and since I was feeling considerably better after a night's rest and the hearty breakfast provided in the lounge, I decided that a brisk walk on solid land would be a welcome diversion. When I inquired about Jeb, who had not to my knowledge returned to our cabin at all the previous night, I was told that he had already gone ashore, leaping to the dock without even waiting for the ramp to be lowered.

I waited on the gangway, following hard on the heels of two married couples with whom I'd exchanged a few words earlier in our voyage, followed in turn by an elderly woman with her three less than well behaved grandchildren, the oldest of whom could not have been more than twelve. When my turn came to disembark, I was accosted by the shills, singing praises of the local eateries, taverns, hostelries, and even what purported to be an antique and gift shop.

Once I had passed through this gauntlet, I found myself facing a brace of warehouses that obscured my view of the rest of Sanders Ferry. There was a well worn path that wound up and between them, and I followed this, emerging onto an old fashioned but well maintained cobblestone street, and from that vantage point I could see that the town was considerably larger than I had originally thought. Since land was inexpensive here, plots were quite large and there were spacious gaps between the buildings. The only structures greater than two stories were three grain silos towering in the distance. The area to my left appeared to be largely residential, small cottages scattered through a fairly thickly wooded area, but to my right was a thoroughfare that led to what were quite obviously shops and professional offices. My fellow passengers were all headed in that direction, and I looked for Jeb as I walked, but he'd had enough of a head start that he was well out of sight.

I strolled about the town without any real purpose. The local Illusion Chamber was showing the revival of the classic Groucho Marx production, *Bullets and Bandits*, which I had seen during a trip to Detroit a year previously. I bought a cold drink from a street vendor, read the public notices posted outside the town hall, then visited the "antique" shop, where most of the merchandise had quite obviously been magically aged, and a tourist oriented craft shop that mixed mass produced items from the East Coast with some genuinely interesting examples of local work. There was a small restaurant adjacent which claimed to offer "authentic French cuisine", but when I examined the menu posted outside, I noticed that most of their offerings were American dishes with French names.

I spent a considerable amount of time in the craft shop, as I am always looking for potential new trade items. It was quite crowded, narrow aisles between makeshift racks filled with merchandise that varied quite dramatically in quality. Some of it was painfully crude – kitchen witches, straw brooms, wood carvings that showed no affinity for the wood. There were paintings on the walls, some fairly well done, at least to my uneducated eye. The graphic arts were still my father's province. I quite admired a large and intricately detailed model of a paddlewheeler, but it was much too large and delicate to transport readily. Some of the dolls were remarkably well made, and I found interesting items among the placemats, straw hats, aprons, and some of the woven fabrics and quilts. There was dust everywhere, unfortunately. It was evident that the stock did not turn over very quickly and that little effort was made to keep the place clean and tidy.

An elderly man sat in a cane backed rocking chair at the rear of the shop, working on an embroidery. He seemed to take no notice of my presence even though I was the only potential customer in his shop. I decided to make a mental note of the place, but it was unlikely that anything would come of it. Some of the merchandise was quite good, but not remarkable enough to justify a return visit.

I was turning to leave when I caught sight of the owls. There were six of them, each about the size of my clenched fist. They were carved from a richly grained wood, with ruby red eyes made of inset colored glass. The carvings were not meant to mimic nature; they were clearly caricatures. But they were quite strikingly original, cleanly cut, highly detailed, exaggerating certain features to emphasize their owlishness. They might almost have been fetishes. Used as a pattern for mass production, they could command a respectable sales volume. There were woodturning companies in Lansing and Peoria that could turn out a hundred or more a day with no difficulty once a good patternist composed a spell program for the lathes. I reached up to take one of them down and examine it more closely.

"Clever, aren't they?"

I hadn't noticed that another customer had entered. She was one of my fellow passengers, a young woman I'd seen once or twice before although we hadn't spoken and I didn't know her name. She was the one whom I'd seen pitching broken shards of wood over the side during our encounter with the river dragon. I hadn't had time to properly notice her on that occasion. Although I'm rather a tall man, nearly two meters, she was nearly my match in height. She was not as slender as current fashion recommended, but solid rather than fat, almost athletic. Her face would not have been called pretty either, although I found it personable enough, even a bit exotic. A halo of strikingly blonde hair framed her face, and I wondered idly if she'd had it magically augmented.

"They're certainly unusual. I thought one of them might make a good souvenir."

"I think you're right. Hand me down one of them, would you, sir? They're a bit high for me. The second from the left, if you would be so kind."

I did as she asked and took a second for myself, quite similar but with wider eyes and an expression that bordered on the sarcastic.

"Thank you. You're James Parkhurst, aren't you?"

She offered her hand and I took it. "You have me at a disadvantage."

"Kelly Masters. I apologize if I seem a bit forward, but Jeb Walker pointed you out one day and I remembered your name."

"I'm pleased to meet you, Miss Masters. Jeb seems to have quite a wide circle of acquaintances."

"Yes, he does get around." Her voice hinted at more intimacy with Jeb's activities than I had expected.

"Have you known him long? Before this trip, I mean."

She nodded. "We've met a time or two in the past. Do you suppose we pay that gentleman over there?"

We traded a quite reasonable amount of cash for our owls. I asked for a business card and the man stared at me as if he'd never heard of such a thing, but consented to write his name and address on a scrap of paper so that I could write to him. "My nephew does the owls," he admitted when I asked. "Never sold one of them before now." I wasn't prepared to suggest a business arrangement until I'd shown the owl to my father, but it sounded like we could acquire reproduction rights readily enough. Kelly disappeared while I was speaking to him, but I found her outside, and it thrilled me to realize she'd been waiting for me.

It seemed quite natural for us to walk together, and Kelly and I eventually ate a quite decent pot roast lunch at the local branch of the Bret Harte restaurant chain. I found her very easy to speak to and explained my reasons for traveling to New Orleans in much more detail than she probably wished to hear. She had the same destination in mind, as she was planning to visit an aunt, as well as investigating the possibility of relocating. She was currently engaged as a private tutor in a small lake front town named Chicago and was looking for steadier employment. I found her surprisingly easy to talk to. I confess that I had made little time in my own life for the opposite sex. Having grown up with four sisters, I had long labored under the admittedly unfair opinion that young women were frivolous, nasty minded, and altogether more trouble than they were worth, a predisposition I had not entirely relinquished.

My companion also displayed a surprising depth of knowledge about life along the Mississippi. "You sound as though you've traveled the river quite a few times."

She shook her head and laughed, but I thought for a second that a wary look had come into her eyes. "Not really. But I read constantly, and I'm particularly fond of travel books. There isn't much of anything else to do back home, unless you want to go down to the docks and watch them unload the fish or scrape the hulls."

"Have you traveled elsewhere then? The East perhaps?"

"On what I earn? Not likely. Why would you think such a thing?"

"Oh, it's just that you seem quite sophisticated for a lady from such a small town. I've been to Boston twice, as well as New Dublin, Managansett, Providence, and Chesapeake, but I fear I know less about these places than I should. There never is enough time to actually look around, you see. Our business is fiercely competitive."

"Then you should read more, James. There's nothing wrong with learning from the experiences of others. There's not nearly time enough to do everything for ourselves."

"There's quite a nice art museum in New Orleans," I mentioned sometime later. I knew of it by reputation only.

"Yes, I spent some time there during an earlier visit. The British were picketing it at the time, claiming that many of the paintings and sculptures belonged to them. That was before the present troubles, of course."

"It was a dubious claim at best." The state of Georgiana, which included New Orleans, had been purchased from George IX shortly after the Revolution. The English were short on cash, and it was easier to consolidate their New World holdings in the north than to hold onto the last of their colonies in the south. Prussia had already seized most of the islands, the Hindus dominated the southern continent, and the Chinese were consolidating their hold over Texicana. The area had largely been settled by the French, who were at that time still subjects of the British Crown, and when the Prussians were poised to take Paris, most of the contents of the Louvre were evacuated to New Orleans, where they were unaccountably forgotten for several years. After the transfer of sovereignty, several attempts were made to reclaim them through legal and diplomatic channels, none of which had been successful. It was my opinion that the Prussians had a stronger claim than the British, since France was now their vassal.

"How long do you plan to visit your aunt?" I remembered that my father had instructed me to take the time for some relaxation during this trip and that once my business was done I would be at loose ends in New Orleans. It would make my stay much more pleasant if I spent part of it squiring this intelligent young lady around to some of the more interesting attractions. "Perhaps we could have dinner some evening."

"I don't know." She seemed uncertain, even wistful. "I mean, we may be traveling on from there for a while. My aunt is quite well off and she's a bit of a wanderer. I've pretty much put myself in her hands for the first few days.

"Doesn't sound very exciting." My disappointment had overrun my judgment and I apologized hastily. "That was very rude of me."

Kelly laughed at me. "Don't feel badly. I promise you, I'm not offended. I imagine it all sounds pretty boring, but you might be surprised at how wrong you are. My family is rather unconventional, and if you ever have the opportunity to meet my aunt, I doubt very much that you'll find her boring."

We found a small open air market and Kelly bought so much fresh fruit than I offered to carry her owl with mine in my shoulderbag until we returned to the *Warlock*. When Captain Martin sounded the recall whistle a short time later, I felt a moment's regret. I feared that our new friendship was a matter of the moment and that it would not survive once we were back on the *River Warlock*. We might nod to each other pleasantly or exchange a few words when we passed, but it was unlikely that I'd again enjoy her exclusive attention for any length of time. But after we parted I realized that I was still carrying her owl as well as my own. Either she had forgotten to reclaim it or had deliberately left it in my charge to ensure another meeting. I chose to believe the latter explanation.

The change was immediately visible when we returned. The salvageable portion of the paddle had been tied down on the afterdeck, but to my untrained eye, it seemed we might just as well have cast it adrift. I couldn't imagine any repairs that would set it right without being much more complicated and expensive than fabricating an entirely new one. A tarpaulin and two cargo nets had been stretched across it, all secured by oversized metal clasps to turnbuckles in the hull. The local workmen had by then been paid off and sent ashore, and the only trace of their presence was a portable crane which a handful of men were winching slowly back into its place. We walked up the ramp together but once aboard Kelly immediately made her excuses and hurried off. I stood at the rail, feeling rather dispirited as the *River Warlock* was brought underway once more, her bow pointed toward Memphis, but that is when I remembered the owl and I felt somewhat better.

When I grew tired of pretending to watch the scenery pass, I wandered over to the forward lounge, where I found Adjudicator Beck and Commander Davis arguing about the admissibility of magically obtained evidence in criminal cases. It was an old argument, one I'd heard many times before, and I listened with only half an ear. Davis, unsurprisingly, was opposed to the introduction of evidence obtained through clairvoyance, scrying, divination, psychoscopy, or clairaudience. "If the evidence cannot be directly perceived by each and every member of the jury, then it shouldn't be allowed. How can a juror make an informed judgment based on the unsubstantiated statement of a psychic? How are we to know that it wasn't contrived by artifice rather than merely revealed?"

Beck countered in a considerably calmer tone by comparing clairvoyants to more conventional experts. "How many jurists are capable of matching fingerprint records? We rely on expert testimony in many non-magical situations. The alternative would be to eliminate several major sources of evidence, and the result would be to allow a great number of crimes to go unpunished simply because they were committed in secrecy and without observation. Even with non-conventional testimony, we're often unable to successfully prosecute cases where we know beyond any reasonable shadow of doubt that the defendant is guilty."

"But surely the authorities are smarter than the common criminal."

"It's the uncommon criminal that I'm concerned about. When there's premeditation, which is invariably the case with professionals, there is plenty of time to take countermeasures. If a thief can make use of a spell to mask his identity or use an orb of penetration to disable an alarm system, then the courts should be empowered to employ a clairvoyant recorder or a psychoscopologist to draw the truth from the past or from the mind of the perpetrator. Our legal system has always been a delicate balancing act between the rights of the accused and the rights of society to protect itself. If you deny magically acquired evidence to the courts, you put them at a serious disadvantage that will only encourage criminals to use magical artifices to protect themselves from discovery."

They went on in that vein for some time and although I sat near them and pretended to be listening, I was actually reliving my encounter with Kelly, wondering if I had missed an opportunity for greater intimacy. I made no effort to follow their arguments until my attention was caught by the mention of recording crystals, and only then because they were among the items we were hoping to export this year.

"I've no quarrel with crystals," insisted Davis, who seemed considerably less animated than when I'd arrived. Beck's calm, relentless arguments seemed to be carrying the day. "The jury can see and hear what happened and make their own judgment."

"You can see and hear in an Illusion Chamber, Commander. The better ones are indistinguishable from reality. That doesn't mean that they reflect the truth."

"Even low level seers can tell whether a crystal recording is genuine. A false record would be exposed immediately."

Beck pounced. "So you would allow magical testimony as to the nature of a recording, but not otherwise. Isn't that rather inconsistent?"

Davis was spared the necessity of responding by the arrival of another passenger, a government bureaucrat of some sort named Burgess, who entered the lounge in a very excited state. He began complaining loudly and offensively about the security aboard ship, insisting that his cabin had been ransacked while he was ashore. I had shared a table with Burgess my first day aboard, and I have rarely spent a more tedious and boring evening. He was a Clerk of Records from someplace in the east, not even Chief Clerk, but you would have thought that an entire municipality continued to function solely due to his administrative efforts. He was chronically loud, insufferably opinionated, and went on at great length on subjects about which his knowledge was clearly no more than superficial. I suspected that his complaint was as imaginary or exaggerated as was his characterization of himself.

When it was obvious that he had no intention of subsiding, I sighed and rose, intending to return to my cabin.

I arrived to find my dirty laundry had been cleared away, presumably by Dana, the steward, whom I intended to tip handsomely when I finally went ashore. He had been more than usually attentive and efficient. I had traveled aboard more expensive ships than this in the past without receiving such excellent service, and I wondered if Dana had perhaps worked for Cunard or one of the other major lines at some time in the past. Shortly after we came on board, he had partially unpacked Jeb's trunk and my own without being asked, somewhat to Jeb's annoyance I fear although I found it very helpful to have my clothing and personal effects properly disposed. The cabin was well maintained; he cleaned and aired it daily, as well as stopping by frequently to see if there was anything we required. If I had any complaint at all, it was that he was a bit too attentive. I know Jeb thought so. He once remarked that he half expected to meet Dana in the privy, inquiring about the status of his bowels.

I was still carrying the carved owls around with me, and I took the time now to wrap both with a spare hand towel and stash them in one of the side compartments of my trunk. There would be ample opportunity to return Kelly's, perhaps over drinks in the lounge that evening. Jeb still wasn't about, and I hadn't seen him since coming back aboard, but I thought it unlikely that he'd somehow been stranded back in Sanders Ferry. The afternoon had grown chilly so I changed into a heavier shirt before returning to the main deck.

Although I prowled the decks for some time and looked into the lounges and every other public place, I was unable to find Kelly Masters anywhere. I did run into Jeb finally; he was sitting with one of the crewmen in the stern, helping him replace some frayed rope. He was reminiscing about his days as a scout in the northwestern territories and although I meant to listen for only a moment, I was quickly caught up in the story, which was so clever and dramatic that I was quite sure he was making the entire thing up. The decks were nearly empty and the barman was closing the lounge when I finally made my way back to the cabin and my bunk. Kelly would have to wait until the morrow to reclaim her property.

Although we would normally have steamed through the night, there was storm debris in the water above Memphis and the captain anchored there, further delaying our projected arrival. I woke shortly before dawn and found myself in need of the privy, and when I left the cabin I could see the faint glow of the city's lights in the distance. I noticed another figure moving away from the privy just before I arrived, a trifle furtively I thought, which reminded me of the odd fragments of conversation I'd heard the previous night. My business there accomplished, I returned to the cabin and had no difficulty falling immediately back to sleep.

The morning was neither more nor less eventful than I had expected, but for some reason it seemed to drag by interminably. Perhaps the knowledge that I would need to find some other form of transportation made me impatient to arrive and eliminate the uncertainty. There was a perceptible rise in the irritability of my fellow passengers as well, although Jeb remained as imperturbable as ever.

"Decided yet what you're going to do once we reach the city?" We were seated in lounge chairs on the raised deck just forward of the bridge, which afforded us an excellent view of the lower deck and the river. I was still watching for Kelly, but with less intensity than before. Our conversation had faded to a pleasant memory.

"What do you suppose my chances are of finding quick passage out of Memphis?" I had started this trip with a comfortable margin of several days, but three of them had already been lost, and progress from Memphis onward was at this point unpredictable. There were trains running north, east, and west, but none directly to the south. The territory between Memphis and New Orleans was sparsely settled and poorly policed. Anarchist bandits from the Green movement were drawn to the region and preyed on travelers who ventured outside the larger settlements. The government had sent in an entirely inadequate military force that spent most of its time garrisoned. More active measures were subject to "budgetary constraints" which meant that since the territory was not yet formally represented in Boston, its constituents were more or less on their own.

"Depends on how desperate you are, lad. There's plenty of small boats that run up and down the river. If you don't mind a hammock and a diet that's mostly fish and biscuits, you could probably buy yourself a place on one of them. Have to watch out for the river pirates though. They won't tackle anything as big as us, but they're brave enough to roust fishers and couriers."

"Made any plans of your own?"

He frowned, scratching idly at his bearded chin. "Don't much like sitting in one spot too long. When there's a storm on its way, I'd rather be moving than hunkered down."

I automatically glanced up at the sky, which had been relentlessly blue throughout our trip. There were some faint white clouds threading the upper atmosphere, but no hint of rain.

"Wasn't talking about the weather, Jimmy." Jeb's voice had hardened a bit. "There's something on the move out there. I can taste it in the wind, hear it in people's voices, see it in the way they hold themselves. If you want to survive in the wilderness, you have to develop a sixth sense, learn to pay attention to everything around you. It's almost like magic if you can do it, but it's pure observation. I'd watch my step if I were you."

I started to laugh, but choked it off. Jeb might be seeing things that weren't there, but he wasn't joking. "From what I hear, Memphis is about as tame as a city can be."

"Don't fool yourself, lad. It's best to be careful wherever you are. I intend to find myself a safe place to wait things out, and I'd surely recommend that you do the same."

At the time, I dismissed Jeb's warning without a second thought. There was no reason to believe I was in any personal danger. I was a businessman on a routine trip to New Orleans and I couldn't possibly be of interest to anyone other than the people with whom I was supposed to be meeting. I had nothing to worry about except finding timely transportation and getting myself to where I was supposed to be at the time I was supposed to be there.

Unfortunately, someone else thought otherwise.

CHAPTER FOUR

During the approach to Memphis, I carefully packed my luggage, tactfully declining Dana's offer of assistance. A powered skiff met us shortly after first light, bearing an unsmiling representative from the company that owned the *River Warlock*. She met with Captain Martin in his cabin for a short time, after which he conveyed to the passengers the welcome if somewhat grudging news that we would all be offered complimentary accommodations at the Riverrunner Hostelry, not the most elegant establishment in the city but certainly acceptable. Appended to this was the pessimistic assessment that we would be unable to leave Memphis for a minimum of ten days, as the demand for refitting was at an unusually high level and even offers of premium payment had proven ineffective in jumping the queue. I would not, therefore, have any choice but to seek alternate transportation, and several of my fellow passengers indicated that they also were constrained by time. The Captain suggested in his remarks that this might prove more difficult than usual due to high traffic levels, but he was understandably interested in discouraging us from leaving his charge and I suspected he was casting the situation in the most unfavorable possible light.

Since it was unlikely that, once ashore, I would have any reason to return, I gave Dana a rather handsome tip when I next encountered him, for which he thanked me profusely. I assured him that I would have no further call for his services and expressed my appreciation for his courteous and conscientious service, then set off to find my breakfast. I did, however, hand him the second owl with instructions to return it to its rightful owner, although I confess that I no longer remembered which was hers and which my own.

Breakfast, I learned, was to be delayed at least half an hour due to a mechanical problem in the galley, so I decided to take a quick nap in my bunk. When I reached my cabin, however, the door was unlocked and inside I had a particularly unpleasant surprise. Both my trunks had been thrown open despite the locks, which had been bypassed rather than broken, and various of my possessions were strewn haphazardly about. The sight stunned me so completely that it was a few seconds longer before I realized that Dana was standing there, his expression equally startled.

"What in the world is going on?" I felt a simmering outrage at this invasion of my privacy.

Dana raised his hands defensively. "I'm terribly sorry, sir, but this is none of my doing. I heard a door close down this corridor, even though I believed that everyone was above, so I decided to investigate. Your door was ajar so I stepped inside. I wasn't certain whether I should tidy things up or report the situation. Sometimes passengers prefer that unusual events be handled discretely, if you understand me, sir. You can ask Benson if you doubt me; he was with me when I heard the noise and he can confirm my story."

I wasn't even close to being mollified. "Did you catch sight of the intruder?"

"No, sir. I'm afraid not. He must have been very quick. I came along this passage just a few minutes earlier and I checked all the cabin doors at the time."

I thought it must have been an opportunistic thief. "He may be in another of the cabins by now. It might be best to raise the alarm. We might still catch him in the act."

"I don't think so, sir. I checked the other cabin doors on my way, since I didn't know where the sound originated. This was the only one not secured."

I was too experienced a traveler to leave valuables in my cabin; all of my cash was on my person. The papers I needed during negotiations in New Orleans were crucial, but they had no intrinsic value, and a quick check reassured me that they were undisturbed. My clothing and personal effects were in considerable disarray, but it didn't appear that there was anything missing. Jeb's canvas suitcase and disreputable duffel bag appeared to be untouched. It seemed likely that whoever was responsible had bolted before finishing the job, perhaps having heard Dana's approach down the stairway. The side pockets on my trunk were still zipped shut, and the last third of my clothing was still in place. I checked to be certain, but my toiletries were in one pocket, and the carved owl in the other, exactly as I had left them.

"It doesn't look like anything is missing but I still think you should inform the Captain at once, Dana," I said pointedly.

"Yes, sir! Right away!" He started for the door in a rush and I caught his arm. "Circumspectly, please. The Captain may not wish for a general alarm just yet."

"Of course! Thank you, sir." And his expression became slightly more composed as he slipped out the door.

It was a surprisingly short time before I found myself ensconced with Captain Martin, Jeb, and one of the ship's officers named Humboldt. The Captain seemed to be personally insulted by the incident and apologized so tediously than I almost wished I hadn't told Dana to report it. Jeb and I both assured him that nothing was missing and that we believed the culprit to be one of our fellow passengers rather than a crewmember, although I frankly thought both possibilities equally likely. He suggested that we notify the authorities in Memphis, but I strongly requested otherwise, fearing that an investigation would force me to remain in the city longer than I wished. Jeb agreed with my decision, and made some disparaging remarks about not allowing a "dirty little sneak thief" to disrupt his vacation. Ultimately I think the Captain's decision was based on our willingness to keep what had happened to ourselves, which would obviously spare his employers additional bad publicity. River dragons were not something one could reasonably blame on the company or its employees; stolen property was an entirely different matter..

"If that solution is satisfactory to both of you gentlemen, I certainly won't object. Since it appears that nothing was taken, it is more in the nature of a nuisance than a crime, after all. I assure you that we will be tightening security aboard ship." He glanced at Humboldt, who looked uncomfortable but remained silent. "I won't tolerate such outrageous conduct on a vessel under my command. You will have nothing to fear for the remainder of your voyage."

I shifted uncomfortably. "I have no doubt of that, Captain Martin, but I'm afraid I will be leaving you in Memphis. My travel schedule isn't flexible enough to accommodate such a lengthy delay. Please rest assured that I have no complaints whatsoever and that I would have no reservations about traveling in your charge in the future."

Jeb had contributed little to the conversation thus far, which was far from typical of him, but he spoke up now. "Captain, would it be possible to get a message to Memphis in advance of our arrival?"

Martin frowned. "I suppose it might be possible to hail someone along the shoreline and convince them to send a telegraph, if there is a station anywhere nearby, but it's not likely, I'm afraid. If you had said something earlier, I could have asked the company representative to carry a message back with her. The skiff will likely have returned there by now."

The Captain was looking distressed again and Jeb reassured him. "It's not that important. I was just curious. I don't suppose anyone else had the same idea?"

"Possibly, but I doubt that anyone acted upon it. I saw Miss Fonda's skiff off myself and there was no mention made of any messages other than my own. I suppose it's possible someone might have approached one of her crew, but it seems unlikely. Was there some urgent reason to do so?"

I thought Jeb's voice had been unusually firm, but if so he reverted now to his usual light tone. "No, none that I'm aware of. I was just thinking I might be able to make arrangements for another bunk in advance of the rush. I'm not that fond of Memphis, or any big city for that matter, and I'd sooner be on my way than later, even if it means putting up with uncomfortable surroundings."

I don't think Captain Martin was convinced by this explanation, and I know I wasn't. Jeb had a strong reason for not wanting to stay in Memphis, and I wondered if perhaps he was in trouble with the local authorities. None of the stories of his past that he'd told me had involved anything more serious than a misdemeanor or two, but that didn't mean he had a spotless history.

The Captain pushed back from the table. "Well, if neither of you gentlemen is inclined to pursue the matter, I will abide by your decision. Dana will watch over your stateroom until we have docked to ensure there is no recurrence. We'll be keeping an eye on all of the cabins in fact. Let me apologize one last time for the inconvenience and wish you both the best whether or not you choose to continue your trip with us."

We rose and shook hands all around, except for Humboldt who nodded but remained in the background.

Docking was a considerably more elaborate affair in Memphis than it had been in Sanders Ferry. For one thing, the gangway was lowered onto the deck from shore rather than vice versa. It had a padded floor, wrought iron side rails, and was long enough that the angle of descent was comfortably gradual. For another, there was motor transport waiting for us, hired carriages waiting to bring passengers and luggage to the Riverrunner. There were shills here just as there had been in Sanders Ferry, and their numbers were greater, but they were dressed more finely and handed out discount coupons, sample menus, catalogues, and other come-ons rather than shouting the praises of their respective employers. It was a quieter if more litter prone arrival in that sense, although the rush of waterborne and ground traffic near at hand was loud enough to make casual conversation impossible until we had finally moved away from the dock area.

The two biggest vehicles were brand new steambuses, much more modern than anything we had back in Lansing. These were fitted with comfortable seats and accommodated only we passengers ourselves, with our luggage following in a louder, slower motor carriage or one of several horse drawn carts. I thought to watch for Kelly Masters, but the press of the crowd was too great and I was unable to recognize anyone not in my immediate vicinity. I thought once that I did catch a glimpse of her in the distance, but if so, we were boarding two different vehicles.

Based on what little I saw of the city during our trip to the Riverrunner, Memphis had not changed much since my last visit, at least in appearance. The trees outside the Changsha Cultural Mission were fuller and greener than I remembered, traffic along the main thoroughfares seemed a bit heavier, but the skyline was much the same, still dominated by the First United States Bank tower and the Benedict Arnold Memorial. The supposed trade embargo by Changsha had depressed the local economy but thanks to General Ling's lackadaisical enforcement, it was only a mild recession. Memphis derived most of its commercial life from river traffic, light manufacturing, and as a major processing center for the tobacco and marijuana farms to the south and east. Many of these were now enjoying subsidies from the federal government because of their importance to the balance of trade with Europe. Unfortunately the rest of the agricultural industry in the southeast was depressed and had been for many years. The heartland areas raised enough grain and corn to satisfy the Changsha as well as the domestic population, and the southeasterners from Florida almost to New Orleans had become increasingly marginalized and most had been forced to resort to marginal niche crops. Their economy had lagged sharply behind that of the rest of the Federation even in good times, and disaffection was one of the main reasons that the anarchist Greenies flourished in that part of the country.

We turned off the most direct route because of a traffic tie-up and used a bypass road that wasn't nearly as smooth. Smaller hotels, hostelries, restaurants, and occasional shops were interspersed with corporate housing complexes, apartment buildings, and small specialty manufacturers. I saw many familiar names, the restaurant and hotel chains that were spreading rapidly from the Atlantic to the Mississippi – the Guy Fawkes Inn, McDonald's Fine Dining, Delmonico's Tomato Pies, Howard Lovecraft's Seafood, and others. The Riverrunner was known to me only by reputation, noted for comparatively low pricing and fewer amenities, but clean rooms and good service. I looked out through the window while waiting for my turn to disembark, and it appeared well maintained, although in my experience the real test of any such facility was in the intangibles.

I looked for Kelly again as we milled around waiting for our luggage to arrive, but once more she eluded me.

The lobby was surprisingly large and elaborate, large considering the size of the building overall, elaborate because even though the hotel was clearly newly constructed it was decorated with carved woodwork, heavy drapes and tapestry, ornate lamp fixtures, and other signs of ostentation. The current trend favored simulations of natural spaces, gentle curves, earthy colors, landscapes on the walls, and plants both artificial and real scattered about. I found the Riverrunner a bit gaudy, actually, but they were certainly making an attempt to distinguish themselves from their competition. There were still significant numbers of people who would be drawn by these excesses of decoration.

We were quickly ushered into a half dozen lines of equal length so that we could be checked in as expeditiously as possible. Considering the fact that so many rooms were available on such short notice, the Riverrunner must have looked upon our arrival as a godsend. A sign posted above the counter informed us that a prescient was on duty so that our luggage would be delivered to the proper rooms even before we were officially registered. The state of Kennessee had passed the controversial Specificity Laws two years previously, which prohibited hotels from selling food or drink, but selected independent vendors were allowed to hawk their wares in the lobby and I was able to satisfy a rumbling in my belly with a paper of finger thin catfish sausages and a corn muffin, followed by a malt beverage that would have been better had it not been served at room temperature.

Adjudicator Beck was in my line, two places forward, and the two military men, Davis and Sykes, were together three rows to my right. I saw others of my casual shipboard acquaintances scattered through the crowd, but there was no sign of Jeb and when I finally did catch sight of Kelly Masters, she had already registered and was carrying a hefty shoulder bag toward the bank of levitators at the far end of the lobby.

In due course I held the passkey to room 403, and when I arrived there, my luggage was smartly arranged on a table just beside the bed. In contrast to the lobby, the room was almost Spartan, although still luxurious compared to my cabin on the *River Warlock*. A map on the door informed me that bathing and toilet facilities were located at the far end of each corridor, which was particularly convenient for me.

I unpacked just enough to see me through to the following day, as I hoped to spend only one night in Memphis. To do so I would have to find alternate passage quickly, and since there was likely to be considerable competition from the rest of those temporarily stranded here, I decided to move as quickly as possible.

The levitators delivered me safely to the lobby, although the descent was so slow that I suspected the spells needed refreshening. The lines had disappeared and lobby traffic had returned to normal, so I had no difficulty finding a desk clerk who was willing to help.

"The hotel can inquire about commercial bookings for you, sir, but berths downriver are in great demand at the moment. The *General Presley* developed engine trouble in St. Louis and is delayed indefinitely, and the Memphis to Jackson passenger shuttle was rammed by a fishing boat and foundered. Travel overland has been…uncertain of late, so the demand for berths has expanded far beyond normal. It all caught us rather by surprise, so there hasn't been time to put new ships into service."

"What about private charters?" It would be expensive and I didn't relish the idea of spending that much money, but it might be my only alternative. If I found something suitable, I might be able to split expenses with some of the rest of the *River Warlock*'s foundlings. "Surely there must be a local trader or hobbyist interested in earning some quick money."

The clerk merely shrugged and I felt a bit miffed at his lack of sympathy for my situation. "I wouldn't know about that, sir. Charters have to be handled through the city booking office. So they can collect the tax, you understand. There might be some willing to bypass the formalities, but it would be improper of me to mention them. I can give you the address of the booking office."

I nodded, and he took a blank envelope from a cubbyhole in his desk and scribbled on it. When he handed it to me, I noticed that there were two addresses.

"What's the second one?"

"I have no idea what you are talking about, sir. I only wrote the one." He kept a poker face and it took me a few seconds to understand.

"Oh, of course. My mistake." I slipped a bill out of my wallet and handed it to him. "For your trouble."

He made it vanish as quickly as a stage magician. "May I be of any further assistance?"

"Not at the moment, thanks. Wait, yes you can." I tucked the slip into my sash. "Could you give me the room number of one of your other guests? Kelly Masters. She checked in about the same time as I did. We got separated in the press."

"Certainly, sir. One moment please." He turned to consult the registration crystal, staring intently into the faceted depths. "Sir, we have no one named Masters registered at the moment. Are you certain that she's staying here? I understand that some of your companions went to the Roosevelt Regency."

"I saw her in the lobby, from a distance. Could her name have been recorded incorrectly?"

"That's unlikely, sir." His tone said it was impossible. "I could search again on her first name if you'd like."

I waited while he repeated the search. "We have three Kelly's at the moment. Abraham Kelly, Kelly Winslow, and Kelly Scott. I've met the gentleman, sir; he's one of our regular clients. The two young ladies both checked in today. Perhaps one of them is your friend." His voice was silky but I sensed sarcasm. The clerk plainly thought I was playing some obscure game to get information about a young woman whom I didn't really know.

"I don't understand." I was unhappy to hear a note of petulance in my voice. "Perhaps you're right and she decided not to stay here after all. Sorry to have inconvenienced you and thanks again for the help." I didn't tip him this time.

It was rather a puzzle. I was quite certain that Kelly Masters had checked in a few minutes before me. Something peculiar was going on here. Either she had lied to me about her name, or she was lying to the hotel for some reason. I was tempted to pursue the matter further, but recollected that my primary obligation was to reach New Orleans in a timely manner. Reluctantly, I told myself to forget about it, and forget about Kelly Masters as well.

The balance of the day was a succession of frustrations. The charter boat office on the city pier was crowded, dingy, and stiflingly hot. I had decided to attempt booking lawful passage first, and I had registered with the Memphis Charter Authority, paying a nominal fee for a thirty day license to negotiate passage. Virtually every legitimate vessel had a representative on duty, sitting at tables with their scheduling books. The desk clerk had been right; there was a sizable crowd of would be travelers, most of them in a decidedly unfriendly mood. It was possible to make a reservation with no difficulty, so long as one was willing to wait a fortnight or more before leaving. I spoke to three agents before realizing that I was wasting my time.

I was reaching into my pocket for the envelope on which the clerk had written a second address when a familiar voice rang out.

"Mr. Parkhurst? Is that you?"

I turned to find Edna Snow, the *River Warlock*'s doctor, bearing down on me.

"Good afternoon, Doctor Snow. How are things going with the *Warlock*?"

She shrugged good naturedly as we shook hands. "Captain Martin's in high dudgeon. Not that it will do him any good or speed things along. One week minimum before the engineers will even give us an estimate and allow the company to reserve a space in drydock. I gather you're arranging for alternate passage. Probably best, under the circumstances."

"Well, that's what I'm trying to do, but I'm not having a great deal of success."

She glanced around at the crowd. "I can't recall ever seeing it as busy as it is at present."

"It's a minimum two week wait and they're charging as much for hammock space as I was paying for half a cabin on the *Warlock*. It looks like I'm going to have to travel overland."

Snow pursed her lips. "I'm not sure how prudent that would be. The Greenies have been very active between here and Jackson for the past few months. Government troops and the state militia go out looking for them and they've managed to keep them away from the river for the most part, but they don't have enough men to cover the entire countryside. I know that the official line is still that they're just outlaws who will be tracked down in due course, but personally I think the Federals have written off everything twenty kilometers inland from the east bank except for the major cities and fortified outposts."

The Greenies, named rather derisively after their charismatic leader, August Greener, had originally been just another political movement, in this case organized to oppose the Treaty of Havana ceding the southern tip of the Florida Peninsula to the Union of Prussian Carib States. A century later their motives were less clear and their hydra headed leadership had fluctuated from advocating anarchy to calling for an independent nation composed of most of the southeastern portion of the Federation. They had attracted a variety of malcontents, poor tobacco and marijuana farmers displaced from their land by the bigger combines, the remnants of the outlawed American Revolutionary Peoples Party, anarchists, bandits, murderers, escaped convicts, and the usual assortment of miscellaneous crazies. Somehow they were held together despite their collective leadership's constant internal squabbles and in some cases they'd held off Federal forces in pitched battles.

"I might have to take the risk. It's crucial that I reach New Orleans in time to conduct my business."

"Well, you could always do the same as Mr. Walker. I can't say I'd want to travel that way, but as long as you don't mind the smell…"

I must have looked as puzzled as I felt. It took a second or two to before I remembered that Mr. Walker was Jeb, and then another to realize that he'd found a way to leave Memphis. Snow hastily explained. "He paid for deck space on one of the local barges. Most of the time they truck the city's more noxious waste products down river and dump it in the Gulf. At least that's where they're supposed to be dumping it. Some of their round trips are suspiciously quick, and there have been complaints from some of the smaller communities to the south about the fish dying off in parts of the river."

"But they take passengers?"

"Not exactly. They do some commercial hauling from time to time, livestock, machinery, bulky stuff that can be stored on deck and that doesn't mind bad weather. Legally, they're not allowed to carry passengers, but what some of them do is sign people on as extra deckhands. Supposedly you even get paid for making the trip, although in practice the money moves in the opposite direction. It's not strictly legal, but the Mayor and his people haven't figured out a way to pass a law against it just yet."

I can't say that the prospect of traveling in company with a herd of cows or pigs appealed to me, but unless some better alternative offered itself very quickly, I might have to reconsider my squeamishness. "I didn't see Mr. Walker at the hotel. Do you know if he's left the city already?"

Snow removed a pipe from her sash pocket and idly began tamping the bowl. "As to that, I couldn't say. I only know as much as I do because I ran into him in Magruder's Tavern and he kindly bought me a drink. A real gentleman, Mr. Walker is, despite his rough appearance. He told me about his arrangements in passing, but if he ever mentioned when he was leaving, it didn't make an impression on me."

We talked a bit longer and then I made polite noises and escaped, hailing a carriage to take me back into the city.

Memphis will never be one of my favorite cities, but it is certainly one of the more interesting places I've visited. It has always been one of the busiest ports on the Mississippi, and grew even more quickly when it was chosen as junction point for the trirails from Nashville, New Atlanta, and Tupelo. Then, just a generation or so back, the governor of New Orleans – which was still an independent city at the time – signed a mutual development treaty with the King of Texicana . The kingdom supplied the money to build a modern port facility in return for a substantial percentage of the city's profits for the next century. New Orleans shrewdly developed strong trade ties with the Carib states and Hindustan, and was able to do well by itself during the negotiations that preceded her entry into the Federation. When the king abdicated, New Orleans claimed to have no obligation to repay the successor government, which was so divided among its various interest groups that they had little time to pursue the matter.

The people of Memphis should have seen the writing on the wall, but they didn't. They continued to appropriate funds to expand the port facilities, counting on a steady increase in trade down river, underwrote the construction of several large warehouses, and mortgaged their assets to a future that had already been taken from them. At the same time, they neglected to support other areas of economic growth until it was too late. Now they had the highest tax rate in the Federation, city services were steadily declining, and most of the big commercial traders had shifted most or all of their operations to New Orleans. Only the tourist trade remained reasonably healthy.

The result was that portions of the city had been largely abandoned. The southern half of the waterfront was well maintained and prosperous, but to the north stood empty warehouses, rotting piers, the noxious Memphis Sanitation Depot, and many of the city's brothels and bars. Prostitution was legal in the city and there were licensed establishments scattered through the downtown, including one directly across from the Riverrunner. But the licensed places were forced to charge according to the municipal code, which included a healthy sin tax, and certain services were prohibited as well. On the waterfront, few paid taxes and if your pocket was deep enough, you could indulge almost any quirky desire.

I knew better than to wander into the northern waterfront alone. I'm fairly tall but narrow in the shoulders and certainly don't have a commanding presence. Even if I carried a pistol, I was inexperienced and could be disarmed easily, either by physical attack or a disabling spell. But between north and south was the Band, a narrow strip of land where the criminal element played straight, relatively, and the Civic Order Patrols, the COPs, turned a blind eye to certain low key illegalities.

The Band hosts a large farmer's market where you can buy fresh fruit and vegetables without paying the victualing tax, a bazaar where stolen goods were mixed indiscriminately with other wares, a few inexpensive rooming houses and eating places, more than a few bordellos, and various small businesses which had counterparts in the city proper, but which weren't quite as strict about adhering to the ever growing list of ordinances and regulations governing trade.

The second address on the envelope in my pocket was within the Band.

I investigated overland travel first, but it proved to be even more frustrating than my futile attempts to find a berth. There were no longer any steam carriages carrying passengers further than Loquacia, a military town on the northern edge of Greenie territory. Trirail passage was possible, but it was so roundabout that I would barely arrive on time even if all went well, and there had been so many stories about Greenies tearing up the tracks through Alabama and Terranglia that even the booking agent cautioned me against relying on their schedule.

I found a carriage that would take me as far as the Band but not into it. The carrier dropped me off near the bazaar with directions and a word of caution. I had no difficulty locating the address I sought, which turned out to be Bub's Bar and Billet, which claimed to be an inn rather than a tavern, but whose rooms were probably let by the hour rather than by the night.

I took a seat at a table in the rear, ordered a Bloody Jane from the bored waitress who materialized when my head was turned away, and tried to figure out how best to proceed. About three quarters of the tables in the room were currently in use, men flirting with women and vice versa, at least one card game, several parties who spoke in low voices and held their heads close together.

"Is there anything else I can get for you?" The waitress, an almost pretty redhead, set my drink down on the table.

I paid for the drink and gave her a reasonable tip, but I ostentatiously refrained from putting my money away. "You wouldn't happen to know where I might be able to book passage down river to New Orleans, would you?"

She frowned but didn't move away. "There's not much traffic headed that way right now, and what there is is filled up."

"I'd be willing to sacrifice comfort for speed." I placed a gold coin on the table, but kept my thumb on it.

She turned her head and glanced around the room for a second. "I'll be right back, Mr...?"

"Smythe," I told her. "Nathaniel Smythe."

She disappeared, returning in a surprisingly short time accompanied by a youngish, dark haired man whose acne pitted face was really quite hideous. He had a purple birthmark on his forehead, and his complexion suggested he hadn't been out in the sunlight since childhood.

"This is Mr. Hertz. He might be able to help you."

I nodded and slid the coin across the table so that she could take it. Once she was gone, Hertz sat down across from me. "I understand you need to get to New Orleans in a hurry." His voice had a pronounced rasp, as though his throat or vocal cords had been damaged at some time.

"I would like to leave Memphis as soon as possible, preferably by water. I'm prepared to pay a premium if that's what it takes."

Hertz licked his lips and I repressed a shudder of revulsion. "If discretion is what you're after, perhaps we should retire to some place more private."

Where I'd no doubt be relieved of my money if not my life. "I'm not in any difficulty with the authorities, Mr. Hertz; I'm simply in a hurry."

"There are regular booking services..."

"None of whom can help me." Hertz already knew this; he just wanted the point made to support what would probably be an outrageous price.

"I could ask around. There might be something available. But it would cost you a lot more than an ordinary ticket, and the facilities might be less than what a gentleman like yourself is used to."

"I understand the situation."

"How can I get in touch with you? If I find something, I mean."

"You could leave a message at the desk of the Riverrunner in the name of Nathaniel Smythe." There was no way that I was going to give Hertz my real name. "I look forward to hearing from you, Mr. Hertz." I started to rise and reached for my wallet, which was still on the table.

"I might have better luck if I could place a deposit in advance."

With deliberate casualness, I returned my money to my sash. "If you feel that's best, then do so with your own funds. You can repay yourself the advance when we do our final accounting."

Hertz seemed prepared to argue the point, but I had no intention of paying for a service yet to be provided. "Good day to you, Mr. Hertz." And I walked briskly toward the door.

I breathed deeply once I was outside even though the air was only marginally less stale and sour. I felt like an actor who was badly miscast; clandestine meetings and encounters with criminals were not normally part of my life. I'm not the adventurous type and am perfectly content to sit in an office, balancing inventories, arranging delivery schedules, and posting transactions into ledgers. I believe that I'm a fairly astute negotiator, and certainly my father has had little to complain of me since I became his partner, but I've never felt the thrill of it the way he does. I sometimes suspect that he would rather take a loss that he'd negotiated shrewdly than enjoy an inept profit.

The sun was just dropping behind the tops of the warehouses to my west and shadows were creeping stealthily across the bazaar. Many of the vendors were clearly closing up shop for the night, while others were simply changing the variety of merchandise they were offering. There was a slight surge in the number of customers, probably bargain hunters looking for last minute price cuts, but the general noise level had declined. This was obviously a different class of clientele.

I decided to be prudent rather than satisfy my curiosity and started walking briskly back toward the causeway that led into the more reputable part of the city. All might have gone well if I hadn't chanced to glance to one side just as I was about to pass through the last row of carts and stalls. A familiar figure stood about twenty meters away, apparently locked in an argument with a red faced woman who gestured quite dramatically with both hands while she talked. The light was failing and the angle was difficult, but I was quite certain that the young woman facing her was Kelly Masters.

Curious, I started toward her, but a team of horses passed between us and halted, and I was forced to detour around them. Human traffic and several carts blocked my way almost as though by plan from that point onward, and when I reached the area where I had seen the two women, there was no sign of either of them. A tinsmith who was in the process of packing up his wares eyed me suspiciously and I decided against asking him if he'd seen my quarry.

Darkness was falling fast and I decided prudence was preferable to curiosity. I turned back to my original course.

I dined alone that evening in a moderately priced restaurant whose name I cannot recall, then walked over to the Memphis Zoo, which is one of the finest in the world, although even there I saw signs of neglect. In addition to the usual exhibits of buffalo, unicorn, antelope, African apes, an aging hippogriff, and various feral cats, they also have a small family of the nearly extinct gargoyle, rarely found outside of Europe. Their gothic habitat had recently been expanded and refurbished and I spent quite a lot of time there, leaving only when the closing charm urged me toward an exit.

It was quite dark and the streets were emptying out as I made my way back to the Riverrunner. I checked for messages at the desk, but I hadn't really expected to hear from Hertz this quickly and was therefore not disappointed. I took the levitator up to my floor, suddenly realizing that I was very tired and that my feet were beginning to ache. Normally I spend most of my day sitting at a desk, not walking through marketplaces or museums.

The door lock recognized me as I approached and the door swung open, but it didn't issue the customary greeting, which should have warned me that the security spell had been tampered with. But I was tired and not expecting trouble, so I walked right into it.

As the door closed behind me, the room lights came on, revealing three masked figures who apparently had been awaiting my return.

CHAPTER FIVE

They wore masking spells to conceal their appearance, which meant that their voices would be distorted as well. Their clothing was nondescript and the light was dim, but I was reasonably sure that all three were male. The one in the center pointed toward a chair. "Sit down, Mr. Parkhurst." Since his two companions both held pistols, I decided to do as I was bidden. A gunshot might or might not raise an alarm inside the hotel, but I would not be surprised if they had silencing spells on their weapons. These did not appear to be casual burglars.

"Who are you? What are you doing in my room? I don't have anything worth stealing."

One of the armed men moved out of my line of sight, probably to guard the door. The second stayed where he was, but his arm moved slightly so that his weapon was still pointed at my chest. The third man settled back into the only other chair in the room. Although I could not see his face through the swirl of distortion that hovered around his head, I sensed that he was alert and tense.

"You know what we've come for, Mr. Parkhurst, or whatever your real name is. Suppose you just hand it over now so that we can leave you to enjoy a good night's rest."

My first impulse was to respond furiously, but I tempered it. They did not, after all, appear to be run of the mill brigands. "I have no idea what you're talking about. You must have me confused with another party. Are you sure you broke into the right room?" But they had called me by my name, so that couldn't have been the explanation.

My inquisitor sighed. "Let's not push professional courtesy too far, Mr. Parkhurst. Or should I call you Mr. Marks? You've led us a good chase, I have to admit, but it ends here and now. That gentleman over there," he gestured toward the armed man facing me," is a gandalf. You'd be quite foolish to lie to us at this point. I'm not noted for my tolerance of those who waste my time."

I glanced at the gandalf with considerable anxiety. Gandalfs are renegade archmages, fugitives from government service, who use their abilities to profit themselves and others. Government archmages are popularly known as merlins, both nicknames originating in the classic series of adventures of King Oswald of Camelot, *The Fellowship of the King* by J.R.R. Tolkien, and its more recent sequels by Paul Alan Sheffield.

"If that's true," I said slowly, "then he should be able to tell you that I'm exactly who I claim to be and no one else. And also that I haven't the faintest idea in the world what you're talking about or what you want."

The gandalf raised his head and his altered voice was low and gravelly. "He appears to be telling the truth."

The first man's agitation was audible even through the distortion. "That's impossible. You told me you'd scryed that it was in his possession."

I think the gandalf nodded then, although it was hard to interpret subtle movements through the masking spell. "It resonated in his presence. But I cannot feel its influence now. Perhaps it has been magically concealed." He moved across the room to my trunk so effortlessly that he seemed almost to be floating. Although I had not unlocked it, the lid opened at his touch and his hands were inside, rummaging through my possessions. I was about to protest but I thought better of it. Once they realized their mistake, presumably they'd trouble me no more.

He was thorough and efficient and the entire search couldn't have taken more than five minutes. When it was done, my clothing was stacked – neatly, I must admit – on the bed, with my toiletries, conference notes, the carved owl I had purchased, and other odds and ends.

"Well?" The leader's disguise didn't conceal his impatience.

"Truth is not immutable. He has passed it on, or someone has taken it from him. It is possible that he did not know it was in his possession. That would explain his truthfulness."

"Either that or a merlin prepared him in advance."

The absurdity of the situation overwhelmed my patience. "What are you talking about? What is it that I'm supposed to have that you want so badly?"

"The crystal, Mr. Marks! Don't pretend stupidity with me!" The masking spell shimmered as it struggled to contain what was clearly a sharp emotional jolt.

"My name is Parkhurst, I tell you. Not Marks."

There was a brief pause, broken by the gandalf. "He's not old enough to be Malachi Marks, is he?"

I shook my head in frustration. "Malachi Marks? He's a character in a book, for God's sake! He's not real!"

The seated man answered me, and he seemed to have regained his original calm. "There most certainly is a Malachi Marks, although he uses many names and only he knows which one he was born with. But I admit you're an unlikely candidate to be Marks himself, although I have little doubt that you are allied to his cause."

I was half convinced that I was dealing with a pack of madmen by now. "All right, you've made a mistake, that's all." Thinking furiously, I decided to play up to their delusion. "Someone has cast some kind of displacement spell to make you think I'm the person you're looking for. But I'm really just a businessman on a routine trip and I have very little interest in politics or anything of interest to you. I don't know what this is all about and frankly I don't much care. If you gentlemen are finished here, I believe I could manage to forget the entire incident. I just want to go to bed."

"It's not quite that easy Mr. Parkhurst, or whoever you are. You can't put us off by protesting your innocence. The crystal may not be here now, but we know that it was in your possession until quite recently. If you can't give it to us, then tell us where it is and we'll deal with the matter. It would be in your own best interest to cooperate."

Exasperated, I started to rise, but a hand grasped my shoulder from behind and forced me back down into the chair. It was a strong hand, but the fingers were icy cold, a supernatural cold that I could fee through my shirt. Too cold to be completely human.

"Look, I don't know what you're talking about. What does this thing, this crystal, look like? Maybe I've seen it and can help."

"Please don't try to be clever with us. I can't emphasize strongly enough how important it is that we recover the object. There is little that we would not risk in order to accomplish that."

"But I don't know anything that can help you!" I protested.

The gandalf moved back to his original position. "He is telling the truth as he knows it."

"That's impossible! If he's not Marks, he has to be one of his associates. Marks must have found a merlin more powerful than you to put a protective spell on him." The seated man raised a hand to run his fingers through his hair and that disturbed the masking spell, not badly enough to see him clearly, but sufficient to provide a glimpse of the hidden face. What little I could see looked vaguely familiar, but I couldn't place it, and it was gone so quickly that I couldn't even recall it from memory. I was about to look away when I noticed a distinctive scar on the man's hand, running from the little finger to the base of the thumb. It was a scar I'd seen before, and it took little effort to remember where. The leader of this little group of madmen was Colonel Sykes, former passenger on the *River Warlock*. I struggled to contain my amazement and prevent it from showing in my face, because I knew it would only worsen my situation if Sykes knew that I'd recognized him.

Fortunately, the gandalf had bridled at the implication that he'd been outclassed. "The truth could possibly be concealed, even from me, for a short time. But there is no one powerful enough to conceal the tampering itself. Given time, I can determine whether or not his memory has been altered although I may be unable to recall the lost knowledge. I'm no sideshow fortune teller or clairvoyant and I'm not easily fooled. When I scryed for the crystal earlier, it was in his possession. There is no way that I could have been mistaken. But it's gone now."

"I wish I could share your confidence in your abilities."

The other man stiffened and I realized that there was no love lost between the two of them. I wondered if there was some way I could exploit the tension to my benefit.

"Your employers have never had cause for complaint."

"Well, I'm certainly not getting my money's worth today. There must be something you can do!"

There was an awkward pause and I could almost feel the tension in the room. "The terms of our agreement were that I should ascertain for you the holder of the crystal. The information I provided was accurate at the time of the divination."

"But you claim that he's telling the truth when he says he doesn't know where it is!" I still couldn't recognize Sykes voice, but I recognized the way he gestured as he spoke.

"Obviously someone has taken very clever countermeasures. Either his memory has been altered or he is merely a dupe. I can enter his mind and find out which is the case, but to do so I need time and equipment. There will, of course, be an additional charge involved."

"And if his memories haven't been interfered with?"

The gandalf shrugged and turned in my direction. "Then he may be of no help to you. If the crystal was secreted among his possessions without his knowledge and subsequently removed, then nothing I can do will help you recover it.. If Malachi Marks is indeed your opponent in this, then he may have outsmarted you again. It's possible that he has been moving it from one innocent to another for some time. Scrying can only succeed when there is a prolonged association."

Sykes was silent for a long time and beads of sweat began to dot my forehead despite the coolness of the evening. Whether they were madmen or not, my usefulness to them appeared to be at an end. There seemed to be no compelling reason for them to harm me, and the fact that they had disguised themselves argued that they intended to leave me alive. Or so I hoped. I looked around as casually as possible, gauging the distance to the door, wondering if I could evade the third man long enough to reach it and escape. Apparently I wasn't as subtle as I thought, because he touched my shoulder again, as though warning me of the futility of trying to break free.

"All right," Sykes said at last. "We'll take him northside with us. Can you put a compulsion on him or something to keep him from raising an alarm or trying to escape?"

"A compulsion spell requires two hours of preparation and treatment. I could render his vocal chords immobile or place him in a coma for a short period, but the first wouldn't prevent him from struggling and the second would require that we carry him."

Sykes made a disgusted sound. "All right, Parkhurst, we'll do this the hard way. I'm warning you right now that there will be two pistols aimed at you until we're safely northside and if you think we'd have any second thoughts about killing you, you're sadly mistaken. You're of questionable value to us and I'm only taking you along so that we can be absolutely certain we haven't overlooked anything."

"Why should I cooperate if you're going to kill me in any case?" My voice shook a little and I felt like a character in an illusion play.

"Because in all likelihood, you'll get out of this alive if you cooperate. If you are what you say you are and you come along quietly, the gandalf here will finish with you and then erase your memories of the evening. We'll drop you off somewhere afterwards and you can go about your business. You'll have headaches and nightmares for a while, but you'll survive."

I wasn't sure if I could believe him, and even if I could, I wasn't happy about the idea of having the gandalf sorting through my brain at his leisure. Even commercial mindlink bothered me; the kind of intrusive activity he had mentioned made my skin crawl.

Since my captors couldn't unmask without revealing themselves to me, we could not leave by conventional means, the levitators or even the emergency stairwell. At their urging, I followed Sykes and the gandalf through the window of my room onto the fire escape, closely followed by the third man. We descended to ground level without incident.

A Cheviot steamcar was parked not far from the fire escape. The doors opened when Sykes mumbled some codeword I didn't hear. I hesitated and the silent man bumped into me. I knew that if I was going to escape, it would have to be now. Once I was inside their vehicle, I would be even more completely under their power than I was already. A hand gripped my arm and the moment was past, which was probably just as well. I doubt that I could have managed more than three or four steps before one of them killed me. It appeared that I had no choice but to go along with them.

Or that would have been the case if outside events hadn't changed things.

The Cheviot was parked in a narrow paved way that ran along the rear wall of the Riverrunner, not a public thoroughfare properly speaking but rather an alley to facilitate delivery of linens, maintenance supplies, and other goods to the hotel's laundry and service offices. On the side opposite the hotel's rear wall stood a wide expanse of undeveloped land, covered with a thick coat of low grass, dotted with small evergreen trees and scattered picnic tables. Beyond that stood another hotel whose name I couldn't discern from this angle, but which I thought must be the Sundowner. I heard the faint hiss of a steambus somewhere in the distance and the clatter of some hoofed animal drawing a carriage, but there was no traffic, either pedestrian or wheeled, anywhere in sight.

Despite the evidence of my eyes, I felt that we were no longer alone, and when the gandalf stopped in mid-step and started to turn his head, I realized he had sensed the same thing. Suddenly there was an inarticulate cry of warning, from Sykes I believe, followed by three small crackling sounds that I recognized as the discharge of a pistol or pistols. One of the balls came so close to my face that I felt the hot breath of its passage across my right cheek.

The silent man stepped away from me and was bringing up his own weapon when he was struck by at least two rounds; I heard the impact as they slammed into his body. Sykes fired his own weapon at a target invisible to me and I heard a cry of pain from somewhere in the darkness. Panicking, I started to run toward the nearest of the picnic tables, hoping to take cover behind it, but I tripped over the silent man's legs and fell sprawling on the pavement.

I untangled myself and rolled away, toward the steamcar this time. There was a very faint humming in the air and I felt my skin prickle. More shots were fired and I froze, then cautiously looked around. The gandalf was standing almost within reach, both arms raised above his head, and the darkness around us began writhing as if it were a living thing. I'd seen enough Illusion Chamber adventures to realize that he was summoning a shield of protection, although I'd never seen it done in real life. He had to be an unusually talented sorcerer to invoke the power this quickly.

I doubted that he was much concerned with shielding me from harm, but I wasn't ready to entrust my safety to whoever had attacked us either. The ambush was not the work of the COPs; even in Memphis they would not open fire without first shouting a demand that we surrender.

Having decided that I was probably in jeopardy no matter who won the current battle, I started rolling again, slipping under the steamcar and then wriggling my way across to the far side where I hoped I would be comparatively safe. I rose into a crouch, peering across the luggage compartment. A sphere of darkness marked the spot where the gandalf had been standing. I couldn't see Sykes anywhere but the brief bursts of pistol fire continued so I assumed he was still in the game. When the next pause came, I bolted toward the back of the Sundowner, expecting to feel the sting of a pistol ball at any moment, but I made it there safely. The service door was locked so, cursing heatedly, I ran around the side and toward the hotel front. When I stumbled in through the main entrance, I was so short of breath that the doorman thought I had suffered a stroke.

Once I was recovered enough to make myself understood, I explained the situation. When the COPs had been called, I felt considerably better, but my disheveled appearance apparently distressed the hotel manager because he insisted rather forcefully that I avail myself of his private office until the authorities arrived. I thanked him for his hospitality, even though it was quite obvious that he was more concerned with shielding his guests from me than in protecting me from my assailants.

As I sat waiting, I vowed that this would be my last ever visit to Memphis.

CHAPTER SIX

The Memphis COPs who responded to the call were visibly unimpressed by my story. They were willing to believe that something had happened, but implied that I was exaggerating an ordinary mugging into some exotic clandestine mystery. I was interviewed by a Lieutenant Turner, a narrow faced man with dark, unruly hair and a perpetual air of bored skepticism, while several of his subordinates conducted a desultory and unproductive search of the park between the two hotels.

"Let's see if I understand this, Mr. Parkhurst. You say these people had you confused with someone else?"

"That's right." I was trying to keep my voice under control, firm, businesslike, but my nerves were still on edge and there was a shrill note there that I could not eliminate. We had returned to the Riverrunner and were sitting in a small function room which the night manager had ungraciously offered. "They thought I was Malachi Marks. You know, the spy."

Turner made chewing motions with his lower jaw and looked away briefly, as though he'd found something indigestible and was looking for someplace to spit it out. "Aren't you a little young to be a master spy, sir?"

"Of course I am! I told you it was all a mistake!"

"Yes, you did. And you say they also had a sorcerer with them?"

I'd already told the entire story twice before, and it was hours past my normal bedtime. I was beginning to wonder if I would have been better off slinking back to my room without reporting the incident at all. "Yes, they had a gandalf. He was tall and thin and seemed to be quite powerful."

"But you wouldn't be able to recognize any of these men again, except for this..." he consulted his notes, "this Colonel Sykes. The man you met on the river boat."

"That's right. I told you they were all masked. I wouldn't have known Sykes if I hadn't seen the scar on his hand. I think Sykes is staying in this hotel. Why don't you question him?"

"We do know how to do our job, Mr. Parkhurst. Now, about these people who attacked Colonel Sykes and the others. Would you be able to recognize any of them, or were they masked as well?"

I shook my head. "I don't know. I never saw any of them. They were hiding in the shadows and once the shooting started, things happened too fast for me to take notes. All I was concerned with was escaping without being shot myself."

"Perfectly understandable, sir." Turner's tone did not match his words. "Let's talk about this object your assailants were looking for."

"A crystal of some sort."

"Yes, the crystal. Could you tell me more about it? Was it a precious gem, some sort of magical charm, a captured soul, or did it have any other significance?"

I shook my head wearily. "I have no idea, Lieutenant. As I've already told you, I don't know what they were talking about. To the best of my knowledge, I haven't had any kind of crystal in my possession during this entire trip. Either the gandalf made a mistake of some sort, or something was planted in my luggage earlier and then removed before I could discover it." I suddenly remembered that my luggage had been searched aboard the *River Warlock* and was about to mention it when I thought better of it. Turner would just assume that I was making up more evidence to bolster my story. "That's quite possible, now that I think of it. We never locked our cabins aboard the *Warlock*, and I've been away from my room here for most of the day."

Turner looked momentarily thoughtful. "The security system on your door was in fact tampered with, but the safeguards here are so rudimentary that my ten year old son could have gotten around them." For the first time, I thought Turner might actually believe my story. "You said that one of the men was shot. Can you describe the location again?"

I did so, to the best of my ability. "I think he was hit at least twice. He fell to the ground without making a sound."

He had been pacing back and forth, but now he came to a stop, facing me. "You have to understand our problem, Mr. Parkhurst. Other than your word, we have no evidence that any of this happened. There were no other witnesses, there's no sign of a struggle in the park, no traces of blood, and no Cheviot parked in the alley. I'm prepared to believe that you surprised an intruder in your room, perhaps an armed intruder, and that the two of you left by means of the fire escape, but beyond that..." He spread his arms dramatically.

"Are you implying that I made all of this up?"

"No, sir, I am not. What I am saying is that the only basis for my filing a criminal report is your uncorroborated testimony. If you insist, I will do exactly that, and an investigation will be conducted in due course. You will not, of course, be allowed to leave Memphis until the investigation is completed. On the other hand, you have suffered no harm or loss, the chances of our tracing the guilty party or parties is negligible, and it would expedite matters for both of us if this was handled less formally."

I shouldn't have been surprised. The Memphis COPs were notoriously understaffed and overworked. They would be more than happy to pretend that the entire incident never happened, and in return, I'd be allowed to leave as expeditiously as possible. But I made a feeble, last ditch attempt to salvage my dignity. "Couldn't you use a clairvoyant or even a merlin to find out the truth?"

Turner sighed again. "Mr. Turner, Memphis is experiencing some serious fiscal problems at the moment, and even in the best of times, law enforcement has never been well funded. Do you know what a clairvoyant charges for a consulting fee? We don't even have a merlin on the city payroll any longer, haven't had once since Lady Tipper was indicted for producing pornographic illusions. And if we did, this still wouldn't be an important enough issue to merit their attention."

"So what you're telling me is that you aren't going to do anything."

"I didn't say that. As a matter of fact, we did check on Colonel Sykes. Unfortunately, he checked out of the hotel earlier today, told the desk clerk he'd run into some old friends with a private boat and that he was leaving the city."

"That should be easy enough to check."

He shook his head. "I'm afraid not. City traffic control requires all commercial vessels to log in and out, even the fishing boats. But private traffic is just that, and there are so many little piers in the inlets that we could never monitor them all. It's entirely possible that he booked illegal passage in order to avoid the tax.

There are dozens of small boats that get around the laws one way or another. But it's unlikely that we could track him down even if I had the manpower to check into it. Besides, if he really does have a gandalf with him, he could cover his tracks so well we'd never ferret him out."

"You make it sound pretty hopeless." I was already resigning myself to the inevitable. As a child, I'd loved reading adventure stories. I had never realized that adventure could be so unpleasant.

""We will contact the military authorities and request an interview. Even if he's on leave, he will have reported his travel plans to his superiors. He'll be questioned in due course, at which point he will doubtless deny any knowledge of your troubles, and without probable cause, we have no basis to request a truthtelling. Unless something else happens that escalates the matter, your complaint will be listed as an open but inactive case. That certainly won't satisfy you, but it's the best I can offer."

Turner sounded almost sympathetic toward the last and, frankly, I was so weary that I just wanted an end to the interview. "All right, Lieutenant. I apologize if I was rude just now. This evening has been very upsetting and I'm not quite myself."

"Perfectly understandable, Mr. Parkhurst." He closed his notepad and made it disappear into his clothing.

"Will you be needing me any further?" I stood up and felt a wave of disorienting weariness.

"No, sir. As a precaution, I have requested that the hotel move your belongings to another room and strengthen the security spell, but I think it very unlikely that you'll be bothered any further. We do request that you stop at the local precinct office some time tomorrow to have your statement notarized."

"And I'm free to leave the city?"

"Once we have your completed statement, we'll have no reason to detain you further. The desk clerk can give you directions to our office."

"All right, Lieutenant. Thank you again."

I already knew where the COP building was located, just past the Memphis Municipal Prison. I had passed that way during the day, and the anti-contraband spell was so powerful that I had felt its effects while still two blocks distant. The prison was a sprawling complex of blocky buildings and towers, at one end of which a smaller building sat on an artificial island, surrounded by a turbulent moat, presumably the local vampire containment facility. Criminal vampirism carried a mandatory perpetual sentence under Federation law. The Supreme Court had ruled that statutes of Assumed Culpability were unconstitutional, so the law abiding undead could no longer be incarcerated without just cause, but they were still shunned and feared, and most lived in isolated colonies out of the public eye.

The desk clerk gave me my new room number but I could tell by the set of his mouth that he found the entire situation distasteful and blamed me for causing so much difficulty. He didn't acknowledge my mumbled "Thanks" and turned away without waiting to see if I had any further need of his services. Under ordinary circumstances, I might have been offended, but at that moment, my only thought was to fall onto my bed and go to sleep.

Unfortunately, fate had other plans for me.

The levitator disgorged me onto the fifth floor where I read the room numbers until I found 534. The door had, fortunately, been properly compelled to admit me. Once inside, I glanced around nervously, but there were no shadowy figures lying in wait, and my trunk was standing in one corner of the room. I turned and had just started to secure the manual lock on the door when someone knocked three times.

I leaned forward, let my forehead rest against the painted wood. "Who is it?" I asked wearily.

"There was a brief pause, and then a woman's voice spoke quite clearly. "It's Marlinn Beck, Mr. Parkhurst. Could I speak to you for a moment?" The name meant nothing to me at first, but she continued after a moment. "We met on the *River Warlock*."

It was Adjudicator Beck, the judge from Wisconsin. I couldn't imagine what she wanted with me, particularly at this ungodly hour of the morning, but it would be bad manners to turn her away. I opened the door, somewhat cautiously, and for a second I didn't recognize her. She was wearing uncharacteristically casual clothing. I had never seen her before without her formal adjudical sash.

"Good evening, Judge Beck. Is there something I can do for you?"

Her head turned from side to side, scanning the corridor in either direction. "We can't talk here, Mr. Parkhurst, but my room is just down the hall. Please hurry, before we're seen together."

I must have looked like quite the idiot standing there with my mouth gaping open. "I don't..."

She cut me off instantly. "Not a word, please! I'm taking a terrible chance as it is. There could be a recording spell or a clairvoyant eavesdropper nearby." Without further hesitation, she reached forward and grabbed me by the arm. Her grip was surprisingly strong and I pulled back instinctively, then froze as her free hand rose into view.

Judge Beck held a cocked pistol aimed at my forehead and her hand was absolutely steady.

Her room was identical to mine, and when we were safely inside with the door locked, she gestured for me to take a chair. The pistol disappeared so quickly that I never saw exactly where it went, and I was quite sure she could make it reappear just as efficiently if the need arose.

"Judge Beck..." I started, but she shook her head at me.

"Please, my name is Marlinn. My mother was an adjudicator so I use that as a cover, but I'm not really a judge."

I was beginning to get a headache. This ever increasing web of plots, secret identities, mysterious comings and goings, drawn pistols, and the like was too rich a broth for my palate.

"Would you mind telling me what's going on here? So far this evening I've been threatened, kidnapped, shot at, interrogated and now kidnapped again. I don't mean to complain, but this is a little bit outside my area of expertise."

She nodded sympathetically but remained silent for so long that I feared I was to be kept in the dark forever. But finally she relented, or more likely finished deciding just how much she should tell me.

"I know about your adventure earlier this evening. While I don't know the identities of the people involved, I can pretty much guess their loyalties."

So Beck didn't know that Sykes was involved, or at least she wasn't willing to admit that she knew. "Perhaps you can enlighten me then."

"I can't tell you everything; it would only make your situation more dangerous. Let's just say that there are two parties equally determined to acquire an object of considerable political and financial value, an object which they believe to be or at least to have been in your possession."

Which told me nothing I hadn't already learned. "And to which of these groups do you belong, Marlinn?"

She smiled. "Neither one, as a matter of fact. I would prefer that the object reach its intended destination without hindrance, and as quickly as possible. I hadn't planned to be anything more than an observer, but when I heard about your encounter, I realized I would have to take a more active role."

"And just what is this object? And why have I been drawn into it?" Questions spilled out of me before I could stop them. "Who are these people? Are they likely to attack me again?" I had more questions, but I ran out of breath.

"The object is a recording crystal, Mr. Parkhurst. Its contents could change the balance of power throughout the world. I can't stress how important it is that the crystal be delivered successfully."

"Are you trying to tell me I'm mixed up with a bunch of spies rather than common thieves?" I remembered the reference to Malachi Marks. But Marks wasn't real, was he?

"I prefer the term 'intelligence agent'."

"And you're one of them?" I felt an irrational urge to laugh. "Which government do you work for, ours or theirs? Whoever they are."

"I'm actually a freelancer, although I have certain standards about whom I will work for and what sort of assignment I'm willing to undertake."

"So who are you working for right now?" I asked bluntly.

"It would be imprudent of me to answer that, as I'm sure you must realize. I assure you that my current employer's interests in this case closely parallel those of the Federation. The crystal is, or at least was until recently, in the possession of an agent whose loyalty has never been in question. You may have heard his name before now. Malachi Marks."

This time I did laugh, though nervously. It was still hard to accept that grown people thought that Marks was a real person, but

Sykes had seemed to believe it, and now Beck was saying the same thing. Could it possibly be true?

"I'm finding all of this rather difficult to believe. If Malachi Marks is involved, why am I the one being rousted from my room at gunpoint every time I turn around?"

"I'm not in his confidence, I'm afraid, but I'm quite certain that he's involved. His personal style is very distinctive."

"Then you don't know him by sight?"

She shook her head. "No, we've never met. And he is almost certainly traveling in disguise. I'm strictly a small time operative, Mr. Parkhurst. I've provided commercial information to the Prussian Empire, served as a courier for the Duke of Toronto, visited London at the behest of the Federation, even worked as unofficial envoy for the Iroquois once or twice. But I've never fired my pistol except in practice and this is as close to genuine danger as I've ever been. My intrigues have all been rather petty, boring ones. I have neither the ambition nor the nerve to play for bigger stakes. When I accepted my current assignment, I had no idea of the degree of danger involved and, honestly, I'm not certain I'd have accepted the commission if I had known."

Despite my fatigue and frustration, I was growing curious. If a major shift of alliances was in the works, it might prove advantageous for my business to know what was coming. "Can't you at least give me some idea what this is all about?"

She closed her eyes and massaged her forehead for a few seconds. "I don't know the details myself, but you must realize that the displacement of the British crown to this continent has had and is still having a ripple effect through the international power structure. One of the parties interested in the crystal has strong links to the Royal Intelligence Service."

That couldn't be Sykes, I reasoned, because he was an officer in the US Army. But then I remembered that he'd spent a lot of time in British territory. "So what's in the recording?"

Beck shrugged. "As I already told you, I don't really know. Plans to suppress the Toronto secession, perhaps. The Federation and the Iroquois have both recognized their independence at least tacitly, and with Changsha remaining neutral, it would be difficult for the Crown to reassert its authority unless it acts pre-emptively. When I was first briefed, Marks was supposed to be on his way to

Philadelphia, but either that was a cover story from the start or he changed his plans. In either case, my sources tell me that he's en route to New Orleans now. I'm supposed to observe and report but not get involved unless it appears that Marks is experiencing some difficulty. So I took passage on the *Warlock* and I imagine other agents were sent aboard other riverboats with similar instructions."

"It looks to me as if I'm the only one experiencing any difficulty."

Beck did not appear sympathetic. "Sometimes the imperatives of a situation outweigh personal concerns," she said calmly. "I'm sure this inconvenience is a significant tragedy from your viewpoint, but I'm more concerned about the possibility of a major international conflict."

Kidnapping and pistol fire struck me as being slightly more than inconveniences, but I didn't argue the point. "All right, if Marks is working for the Federation and you're with some undisclosed friendly neutral and the people who kidnapped me are working for the British, then who was doing all the shooting?"

"There is any number of possibilities. Marks may have alerted a clandestine Federation unit to prevent your capture. The people in your room might not have been British agents at all, but some other party interested in the outcome, and the ambushers might have been from British intelligence. For that matter, there are enough factions among the royals that both could have been working for our friends to the north. The Prussian Empire may have taken a hand; they're determined that nothing should divert the Chinese from the war with the Russians. A major conflict on this side of the Atlantic could compel the Emperor to send additional troops to Changsha as a precaution. The Duke of Toronto may have agents working on his behalf as well."

"In other words, you don't know any more than I do. It could even be the Iroquois, I suppose."

"That's right. They have a definite interest in encouraging the fragmentation of British influence."

"So what has all this to do with me? If I had the crystal, it's gone now. I don't know anything that could help anyone. Why contact me? Why haven't you gotten a message to Marks?"

"I would love to do just that, if only because I'd like to know who he really is. His identity is a complete mystery to me. For that matter, he might well be a woman."

"The books describe him in great detail."

"The books are fiction. Even the identity of their supposed author, Richard Grenadier, is a closely held secret."

I was too tired to continue. "Look, I'll accept whatever you say. What do I need to do before you'll let me go back to my room and get some sleep?"

Beck stared at me for a few seconds, as though trying to decide how much to tell me, which was probably the case. "When I was told to book passage on the *Warlock*, I expected to find myself among strangers. Much to my surprise, an old acquaintance was aboard, someone with whom I've worked in the past. He told me that this was a routine trip rather than business, but he wouldn't necessarily tell me the truth. Ordinarily, I wouldn't have involved another agent without authorization, but I had no other resources available to tell me whether or not Marks was aboard, and my friend has a very rare and useful talent. He's an aura reader and a precog."

That perked my interest despite my fatigue. Precogs are extremely rare, and usually unreliable. Their predictions were often misleading and occasionally completely false.

"Unfortunately, his talent remained dormant through most of the trip and it wasn't until that night we shared a meal at the captain's table that he got a glimpse of something. It was very tenuous and he couldn't tell me any details, but it seems that you and I have intertwined futures. He had a very strong feeling that my mission would only succeed if I made you aware of the situation."

"But what kind of help can I give you? I don't know anything about this business!"

Beck opened her mouth to answer, but she never got the chance. A shadow moved at the edge of my vision and I turned my head just in time to see a figure emerge from the bathroom doorway. Its body was completely covered by a heavy cloak and a masking spell turned the head into a ball of shifting smoke. I intended to shout a warning and I think I'd even begun to raise one arm to point, but my reactions were too slow. A pale purple globe flew from the figure's hand, growing impossibly large, and I had a split second to realize that I was slipping out of my chair before darkness overwhelmed me.

CHAPTER SEVEN

I've had headaches in the past, sometimes very intense ones that robbed me of the will to do anything except sit quietly and wait for the pain to subside. None of those in my previous experience even approached the severity of the one I felt when I regained consciousness. The pain seemed to originate above and between my eyes, burning back along two diverging paths to the rear of my skull. My teeth ached and it felt as though my skin had been stretched to the tearing point. When I first opened my eyes, they refused to focus, and everything around me seemed distorted. I was lying prone on a hard surface, and my arms and legs were cramped. As soon as my head stopped spinning, or at least slowed to a tolerable speed, I rose cautiously to my hands and knees, then stopped as a wave of dizziness swept over me, leaving me breathless and nauseated.

All things pass, the bad as well as the good, and eventually I felt well enough to straighten up and look around, still on my knees, moving my head slowly to avoid rousing any slumbering pain demons. I was still in Beck's room, which was quiet now. There was no sign of the intruder, but that didn't mean he wasn't there. I made as little noise as possible as I stood up and surveyed my surroundings.

At first, everything seemed perfectly normal. Then I spotted a dark shape on the opposite side of the bed. It was Marlinn Beck and she was quite dead. If she and I had any future together, it was going to be quite brief. She was lying on her back with a dagger hilt projecting from her chest like an exclamation point above the dark stain, still wet, that covered the front of her body. I felt a moment of regret, but it passed quickly as I realized I might still be in danger.

My first inclination was to bolt from the room and call for help, my second to rush to my own room, barricade the door with every bit of furniture I could move, and then collapse onto the bed. Caught between conflicting impulses, I did nothing for several minutes, during which time my mind worked furiously.

What good would it do to report the attack? The Memphis COPs were already skeptical of my testimony and I could tell them even less useful information this time than in the case of my own abduction. For that matter, I was alone with a dead body in a room whose door, I noticed, was still locked from the inside. What conclusions were they likely to draw from that? I was half willing to suspect myself. At the very least, it would be impossible for me to leave Memphis in time to make my conference. I was frightened, uncomfortable, mystified, and starting to get angry. What right did Marlinn Beck have to get murdered in my presence?

The anger dampened my fear but not my caution. I systematically searched the room and adjoining bath. There was no sign of the intruder, and I had no idea how he had escaped unless he'd levitated himself through the single window, although if he was the same gandalf who had been assisting Sykes earlier in the evening, that might well be exactly what had happened. Why had I been left alive? Was I so insignificant that it didn't matter whether I lived or died, or was I meant to be implicated in the murder? I didn't have enough information to even begin to guess. It was entirely possible that if I returned to my room now and left Memphis in the morning, that would be the end of the matter as far as I was concerned. I would never know what was really happening, but on the other hand, I'd be alive and out of the line of fire.

On the other hand, it was equally possible that I'd been spared for a reason, and if that was the case, I needed to know more about what was going on, for my own protection. So I searched Marlinn Beck's belongings.

I suppose I expected to find something dramatic, a spy identification card, perhaps, or a copy of the instructions from her employers. There was nothing like that, of course, unless it was so well disguised that I couldn't recognize its true nature. There were some surprising items though, including a great deal of cash, which I left exactly where I found it. I am not a thief. There were half a dozen charms concealed in her carefully folded clothing, but the only ones I felt confident about identifying were a night vision charm, a moth deterrent, and a minor healing potion.

I almost missed Beck's pistol until I looked under the bed. It hadn't been fired and must have been kicked there during the struggle with our assailant. Although I considered taking it with me, I put it back instead. Somehow the idea of having a pistol in my possession made the danger seem greater, not lesser. I considered searching her pockets, but in the end I was too squeamish to do so.

Now that the time had come to leave, I was suddenly terrified that I might be discovered at the last moment and unjustly accused of the crime. I crossed to the door and slipped the lock free, then paused with my ear pressed against the wood, trying to determine if there was any traffic on the opposite side. Silence. I drew a deep breath and eased the door open, intending to slip out, return to my room, and pretend nothing had ever happened.

The moment I opened the door, it was forced back and out of my grip and a figure slightly shorter than me pushed into the room.

My heart hammered like a steamboat's engines. The newcomer was hooded and for a second I thought it was the mysterious assailant back to finish the job. The door was torn from my fingers and pressed closed, firmly but without making any unnecessary sound, and my companion turned, throwing back his hood.

It was Dana, the steward from the *River Warlock*.

His expression was neutral as he scanned the room, but I heard a sharply indrawn breath when he saw Beck's motionless body.

"I didn't do it," I protested weakly as he withdrew a pistol from somewhere inside his cloak. Was everyone I knew carrying a weapon? His hand was steady, his eyes level and unblinking and displaying none of the subservience I'd seen earlier. This was a new person I was seeing now, forceful and uncompromising.

He nodded but said nothing, and the pistol remained pointed in my general direction. I backed away as he moved forward to examine the corpse, kneeling beside it and studying the murder weapon closely.

"I didn't do it," I repeated. "Someone was hiding in the bath when we came in. He used some kind of magic to knock me out and when I came to, Beck was lying there just like that. I think he went out the window. It's closed, but not locked. I'll show you." I started toward the window, but his gun hand came up quickly.

"Please don't move just yet, Mr. Parkhurst." He stood up and glanced around.

"I told you, he's gone now. I searched the room as soon as I recovered."

"So you said. You don't mind if I reassure myself on that point, do you?" Even his voice seemed different, fuller, deeper, more confident. It was hard to continue thinking of him as Dana, the steward. "Sit down on the bed, please. And keep your hands on your knees."

I did as I was bidden and sat while he checked the bath, glanced through Beck's clothing, and peered into the corners of the room in search of I knew not what, magical wards perhaps. Once he was satisfied, he sat down in a chair facing me and seemed to relax slightly, although the pistol remained pointed at my chest. "Could you identify the assassin?"

I shook my head. "No. Whoever it was wore a cloak and a masking spell." My suspicion that it was the gandalf who had accompanied Sykes was growing, but I didn't say anything. If I described my earlier encounter, it would just lead to more questions to which I had no answers.

"You seem to have gotten yourself into a good deal of trouble, Mr. Parkhurst. What were you doing in Beck's room in the first place?"

Now that I knew I was not going to be shot out of hand, some of my anger returned. "I might ask you the same thing. Why were you waiting outside her door at this hour?"

A hint of a derisive smile lifted the corner of his mouth. "I think that for the time being I'll ask all the questions, Mr. Parkhurst, but I will tell you that Beck and I had a professional relationship of long standing and that I was invited here this evening. She sent a message indicating that she'd made some progress on a matter of mutual interest, but she made no mention of a third party."

I closed my eyes and thought furiously. Dana must be the precog. I knew that he was too smooth to be working on a tourist class vessel like the *Warlock*. "I'm out of my depth, Dana, if that's really your name." I waited but he didn't rise to the bait. "Somehow I've been dropped into the middle of some ridiculous game of spies and assassins and all I want to do is get some sleep and then leave this godforsaken city. At this point I'd be willing to walk or even swim to New Orleans if that's what it will take."

Dana nodded as if he understood, but I noticed that his pistol hand never wavered. "I heard something of your earlier adventure this evening. The hotel staff seems to think you've got quite a flare for invention."

"I told the COPs the absolute truth," I said huffily.

"Perhaps you'll find me a more sympathetic listener."

And so it was that I told the entire story again, the abduction, inadvertent rescue, and the less than satisfactory response from the authorities. Dana made me describe each character in excruciating detail, asking questions about their mannerisms, their way of speaking, anything that might identify them. He didn't even blink when I mentioned Sykes' name and, in fact, showed no reaction to anything I said. Earlier I'd thought him little more than a boy, with his smooth chin, delicate features, and deferential manner. Now he seemed to me at least ten years older, an altogether different person. It wasn't just the pistol that made him dominate the room; his composure commanded respect.

The moment I had finished he rose to his feet, walked over to Beck's trunk, and took from it a small cloth bag whose purpose I had been unable to determine. It was filled with a light gray powder, a pinch of which he sprinkled over the hilt of the knife embedded in Beck's chest. Then he tossed the bag to me.

"Rub a pinch of that over your fingertips, both hands."

I had no idea what he intended, but I complied. The powder had an oily texture and a very faint, bitter odor.

"Now come over here, next to the body."

I hesitated a second and the pistol focus rose from my chest to my face so I did as I was told.

"Be careful not to touch the knife, but move your hands as close to it as you can, and hold them there until I tell you it's all right to move away."

Again I followed instructions, crouching uncomfortably with my fingers curled around but not quite touching the ornate hilt while absolutely nothing happened. Beads of perspiration began to run down my forehead as I realized I might not leave this room alive, and might not even know the reason why I was being killed. The moment seemed to stretch endlessly, but eventually Dana relented. "All right, there's no affinity so you didn't kill her. Go sit down on the bed while I think about this." The pistol disappeared into the folds of his cloak, but I was quite certain it would reappear instantly if needed.

We waited in mutual silence, but only for a few minutes. Dana seemed to have made his decision because he gestured for me to stand up. "We need to get out of here. If what I suspect is true,

Beck was murdered for one of two reasons. Either she was very close to discovering who has the crystal and someone wanted to protect that knowledge, or someone wanted you out of the way for some reason and figured the best way to do it would be to frame you for her murder."

"But I don't have any idea what's going on, and I don't care either!"

"I'll take your word for that, Mr. Parkhurst, but even if you aren't concerned about the situation, the situation is concerned about you. Your future is tied up with Beck's mission in some fashion. I know that much, but I don't know whether for good or ill. It's possible you're just a distraction, a loose piece lying on the game board that someone is trying to push out of play. I don't know nearly enough to understand why they want you in custody or on the run, but for the moment at least it's to our mutual advantage to see that you retain your freedom of movement."

I shook my head wearily. "Where are we going?"

"Your room, at least for the moment. I don't know what's going to happen next, but it doesn't take precognition to guess that an anonymous report has already been sent to the COPs. It's fortunate for both of us that they're notoriously slow responding at this time of night. But they will show up eventually and we need to leave now, before they find us here."

I felt as though I was falling deeper and deeper into a morass of deceit and danger, but I had lost the will to resist. When Dana opened the door, I followed obediently. He closed the door behind us and the security spell bade us a whispered good evening as we walked away, moving quietly along the corridor until we reached my room. My own security spell had been reinforced and would not open for me until Dana had moved out of range, but once appeased, it made no objection when I invited Dana in, although I would have preferred that he just go away.

He had barely stepped inside the room when the door swung back into place with a bang and a dark figure emerged from the shadows, swinging a truncheon down across the back of Dana's head.

He dropped silently to the carpeted floor.

"Not you too!" I stepped back, raising my hands protectively.

Kelly Masters moved out into the light. Her arm dropped to her side but she didn't relinquish her grip on the weapon with which she'd struck down Dana.

"Not me too what?" Even in the dim light I could see that she was smiling cheerfully, as though she hadn't just committed a gross physical assault.

"You're another spy, aren't you? I'm beginning to think everyone on the *Warlock* except me was secretly working for one foreign power or another."

She nodded. "Not everyone but probably more than usual. And I'm not working for a foreign power. I'm employed by the Department of Internal Security of the Federation Congress." She glanced down at Dana's still motionless form. "Who is this?"

"You mean you don't know? Then why did you knock him out?"

She answered with an expressive shrug. "I figured anyone carrying a pistol and entering your room at this hour had to be up to no good. If I'm wrong, I'll apologize later, if I have the time. He'll recover."

"It's Dana. He was my steward on the *Warlock*. Or at least I think that's his name. Lately I'm not certain about anyone's real identity. Look, Miss Masters…"

"Scott. I'm Kelly Scott. Sorry about the false name but it was really necessary at the time."

"You see what I mean!" But I was beyond being surprised. "All right, Miss Scott, then. I've just about had it with this whole thing. I've been threatened, shot at, kidnapped, framed for murder, and held at gunpoint by half the population of Memphis this evening, and now when I finally run into someone who appears to be trying to help, you hit him over the head."

Her smile had disappeared during my outburst. "You said framed for murder. Who was murdered?"

I tried to start at the beginning, but she already knew about my encounter with Sykes and the gunfight that followed. So I went directly to my abduction by Beck, our truncated conversation, and Dana's subsequent arrival. I suppose I was less than circumspect in doing so. I had no idea if Kelly was whom she claimed to be. She had already lied to me at least once and for all I knew she was actually in the pay of the Emperor of China or the Zulu King. For that matter, how could I know for certain that she hadn't been the figure hiding in Beck's bath less than an hour earlier? I thought it was a man, but a really good morphing spell could have made her look like anyone or anything she desired.

"And this man, the steward, you say he was working for Beck?"

I nodded. "Beck said she had a contact on the *Warlock*, and Dana seems to match her description, although she never mentioned his name. I suppose either or both of them could have lied about that as well. She said they'd worked together in the past, that their encounter this time had been a fortunate coincidence."

"I very much doubt that. One of the first things my father taught me was not to trust coincidences. He was probably already working for someone else and either decided to profit from a little sideline, or was playing both ends of the game. Or just possibly his job was to insinuate himself into her good graces. I recognized Beck when she first came aboard. She's a freelancer specializing in commercial espionage and she's always avoided political entanglements. Apparently she should have stayed to that course. This Dana, or whatever his real name is, remains a cipher. Maybe he is what he claims to be and maybe he isn't, but we'll likely be safer without him."

"What do you mean 'we'?"

She smiled again, but this time I thought it was rather more artificial than not. "Mr. Parkhurst, Jim, I understand that all of this must be bewildering and frightening. I'm afraid that your involvement in all of this is largely my fault, for which I'm truly sorry, but there were a limited number of options available to me at the time and I only acted in the interests of our country."

"Your fault. You said it was your fault. Who are you anyway? Malachi Marks?"

I meant it facetiously. She couldn't be master spy Marks, assuming he really did exist. She was far too young for one thing. But Kelly's face was completely serious when she answered. "No, I'm not Malachi Marks, but I'm working with him at the moment."

While I was digesting that, she stooped to examine Dana, who had moaned softly but still hadn't moved.

"Are you trying to tell me that Malachi Marks is real and that he's actually involved in all of this...whatever this is? That he was on board the *River Warlock* with us?"

She stood up. "That's right. As a matter of fact, I've seen you speaking to him." Her smile was impish, teasing. "There's a story for you to tell your grandchildren, if you live that long." The amusement vanished from her face between heartbeats. "He's going to be coming around soon; I didn't hit him that hard. We need to leave before then. Why don't we continue this conversation in my room. I don't think anyone suspects me yet."

I crossed my arms and spread my feet stubbornly. "No way. I've been pushed and shoved all night and this is where I draw the line. No more adventures."

She sighed. "We can't risk talking here. I really can't take the chance of letting our sleeping friend eavesdrop on us. I'm afraid I'm going to have to insist." And she drew from her pocket yet another pistol.

I raised my chin and kept my voice level. "If you are who you say you are, then I can't believe you'd actually shoot me. I'm an innocent bystander and you know it."

"If circumstances warranted it, I would. The stakes in this are too big to be concerned about a single life, no matter how innocent. But it wasn't you I had in mind." She pointed the pistol at the back of Dana's head.

"Wait!"

She looked up at me, but the barrel of her pistol never wavered. "Yes?"

My shoulders slumped. I was pretty sure that she was bluffing, but I wasn't positive, and I wasn't about to gamble Dana's life on my ability to judge character, particularly considering my recent track record. "All right, I'll come with you." I looked longingly at my bed and followed Kelly out into the corridor.

Kelly Scott's room was two floors down from mine, but otherwise appeared to be identical, even to the landscape mounted on the wall. While she was securing the physical door locks, I walked to the bed and fell face forward onto it. "Now I know why spies are all so desperate and dangerous," I muttered loudly. "They never get enough sleep. What do you do? Live on anti-fatigue potions?"

"I never touch them. Anti-sleep potions slow your reflexes. But I make a point of taking long vacations between assignments." I couldn't tell whether she was serious or joking. She moved quickly around the room, checking the windows, touching each of several feathered charms scattered here and there. "All right," she said at last. "Not even a clairvoyant can listen in on us now. I guess I'll have to tell you the whole story."

I rolled over onto my back and stared up at the ceiling. "That would certainly be a change." I didn't believe for a second that she was going to tell me everything. Among other things, it was quite evident that she didn't even know the entire truth herself.

"I have an ulterior motive," she confessed. "I want your help and it won't do me any good if it's under duress."

I was off the bed and working at the door lock so quickly that I caught her completely by surprise.

"What in the world are you doing?"

I answered without turning my head. The locks seemed unusually complex and I couldn't quite figure out how to work them. "Leaving. I'm going to walk out of this hotel, go immediately to the waterfront, and hire on as a deckhand, if I have to. If no one will have me, I'll walk to New Orleans. Or more likely sleepwalk." The lock seemed to be quite simple, but I still couldn't get it to open.

"Sit down, Jim."

I tugged angrily at the main bolt, but it remained fixed in place. "It's been really nice talking to you, Miss Scott, but I don't think I'm even going to enjoy reading spy stories in the future. I certainly have no intention of getting involved in a real life version."

"The bolt won't work until I release it.. I always carry a few extra security spells with me when I travel. And you're already involved, whether you like it or not."

"Oh." I released the lock and turned to face her. "Will you release it, then, or shall I go out the window?"

She shook her head. "Neither. The windows are frozen as well. You can't leave until I'm ready to let you go."

"Wonderful. What am I supposed to do now?"

I meant the question to be rhetorical, but she answered it anyway. "Right now you should go sit and calm down." She moved toward the bath. "Do you want some coffee? I have a pot on."

"No thanks," I responded without thinking. "It keeps me awake." I started to laugh then, but it sounded funny and I forced myself to stop.

"How about some brandy then?"

"No. No brandy." I sighed. "I guess I'll have the coffee. Somehow I don't think I'm going to get much sleeping done tonight.. There's enough time left before dawn for me to be abducted at least six more times. Wouldn't want to miss that because I was too sleepy to enjoy the fun."

A minute later I was sipping a cup of surprisingly good coffee. The warm fluid felt wonderful when it reached my stomach and my badly jangled nerves actually felt somewhat soothed. "This is excellent," I observed grudgingly.

"Imported. And I added some calming herbs."

"So what's next on the agenda? I haven't been shot at for a while. We could try that."

Kelly ignored my sarcasm. "We're safe enough here, at least for the moment." She sat down and crossed her legs, looking thoughtful and, I must admit, rather attractive. "I'll tell you as much as I can now, and more later if necessary. As you've probably guessed, I don't know everything either. There are too many interested parties after that crystal and it's not clear to me where everyone's loyalties lie."

"It's not clear to me where anyone's loyalties lie."

She ignored the thrust. "How familiar are you with the political situation? Internationally, I mean."

"I try to keep abreast of things. Importing and exporting is almost half our business, so we have to keep an eye on the politicians. We deal with Changsha and New Hindustan, the Prussian Carib states, the Zulus, and others. Our primary international trading partners are still the British and the Iroquois, although we're trying to hedge our bets there."

"Then you're aware that Toronto has announced its secession?"

"Of course. It's common knowledge. And I know that the Federation Congress was fiercely divided about whether or not to recognize it as a sovereign state and the de facto resolution may yet be reversed."

"Much of that is pretense. They've already decided for recognition but they're posturing so that the British will think we're reluctant to commit. We've fought six wars with the British Empire over the last two centuries, and the animosities are as deep rooted as ever despite the supposed reconciliation. Some of our senators believe that the Duke will eventually sue to join the Federation, but that's very unlikely. He's an egomaniac and I wouldn't be surprised if he started calling himself the King of Toronto before the year is out."

"Is this what that crystal is about? Something to do with Toronto?"

"No, or at least only peripherally. The crystal is a recording of a meeting between Governor Ling of Changsha and a high ranking envoy from King Winston. The crystal was planted and later recovered by Malachi Marks, who smuggled it across the border into the Federation several days ago."

"I thought there were ways to safeguard against clandestine recording devices."

"There are," she admitted. "Ling employed a merlin to monitor the conference chamber and a second to keep watch over the first. It should have been nearly full proof. Nearly wasn't enough, though. Somehow Marks managed to subvert the process and get what he was after. I don't know how he did it yet; we've been unable to talk for more than a few seconds at a time."

"Is Marks a gandalf?" If that were true, it might explain some of the feats ascribed to him.

"No, and he'd be a merlin anyway. He works for the government, remember? But he's just a man, an extraordinary one, but with no noteworthy magic talents. Sometimes he seems almost precognitive, but as far as I know he doesn't have the talent."

I blinked. Dana was a precog. Was Dana actually Malachi Marks? But no, that was impossible. Kelly knew Marks and would certainly have recognized him after, if not before, she'd knocked him unconscious. So Dana couldn't be Marks. Or could he? After all, I only had Kelly's word that she actually knew the master spy. It was entirely possible that she was lying to me and actually worked for a foreign power. My head began to spin and I forced myself to stop thinking about the possibilities and concentrate on what she was actually saying.

"Eventually I reached Milwaukee, where we'd arranged to meet." I realized I had missed part of her story, but I said nothing. "By then word had leaked out and we had to stay on the run. Ordinarily he would have gone straight to Fort Romney and asked for a military escort, but we believe that they have suborned some of our military officers. We were also pretty sure that the British were prepared to violate the Treaty of Sardinia if they were able to definitely locate the crystal, and they'd be watching the fort."

I was shocked by this last comment. There had not been a major sorcerous attack by any nation against another for more than a century, ever since the destruction of Constantinople and the signing of the Treaty.

"Wouldn't that have the same result as releasing the information in the crystal, whatever it is? The Federation would have to declare war and they'd automatically recognize Toronto's independence at the same time."

She shook her head. "Not if the attack was disguised so that we couldn't prove where it originated. We'd know, of course, but the Federation would pretend not to in order to avoid being drawn into a war we really don't want to fight."

"Politicians," I muttered.

"Anyway, Marks and I laid a number of false trails, but there were so many agents beating the bushes that it was inevitable that some of them would stumble onto the right one. Since it's obvious that I'm not Marks, he gave me the crystal while we were aboard the *Warlock*; I wore it on a chain around my neck but under my clothing. He thought we'd be safe once we reached New Orleans, but he didn't confide in me so I don't know his plans once we'd arrived. Someone focused a scrying spell on us the day before we ran into that dragon and I was able to counter it well enough to conceal the exact location, or at least I thought I had."

"So how did I end up with the crystal?"

"That was my decision. I'm sorry, but I recognized one of our fellow passengers, a very efficient and dangerous foreign agent. You know him as Colonel Sykes, but I have no doubt that the real Sykes is dead, his body probably weighted down and thrown in the river. I don't think he knows who I am but I couldn't be certain."

I hadn't told her that I'd recognized the man I still thought of as Sykes so I feigned surprise when I heard his name. "So you decided to hide the crystal somewhere no one would think to look."

"That's right. It wouldn't deceive a scrying spell, but I didn't think we had any gandalfs traveling with us. I realized that it could pass as one of the faceted eyes of those carved owls we bought so I used it to replace one of the eyes in my owl. When you offered to carry it, I thought it might be best if it stayed out of my possession for a while. Then when I went to your cabin to get it back, I almost got caught redhanded; someone started checking the cabins before I found it and I had to sneak away."

"That was Dana," I told her. "We reported it to Captain Martin, but it seemed best to keep the whole thing quiet."

"Just as well. I thought everything was okay when you sent my owl back, but you kept the wrong one. After we checked in here, I waited for you to leave your room, then neutralized the security spell and switched the owls." She reached under her pillow and pulled out a small figurine that looked very much like my own. "I was afraid you'd notice the change. They're not as similar as I'd hoped."

I leaned forward, squinting, then began to laugh.

Kelly didn't seem to know whether to join me or be alarmed. "What's so funny?" There was a slight edge in her voice.

"You've screwed up. That's what's funny. That's my owl you have in your hands, not yours. I didn't remember at the time, but yours has straight ears, mine have them folded down. I noticed it the day we bought them."

It was almost comical the way her face cycled through a variety of expressions. She pressed one forefinger to each of the faceted eyes, then angrily threw the carving across the room. The plaster cracked where it struck the far wall.

"I know I took the right one! Come on." She was on her feet and headed toward the door. "Someone switched them again."

"Did they? Or did you just get confused about which is which?"

"I don't make mistakes." She sounded absolutely confident, and more than a little angry. "Someone has bypassed my wards. I don't know how they managed that; they've never failed me before. We need to check your room. It's just possible the real owl is there for some reason, although I doubt it. They might believe they could use you as a dupe the same way I did, but they can't believe I wouldn't spot the fake pretty quickly. And it's not Sykes' style. He would have left an explosive device or a magical trap of some kind."

Not to mention that the gandalf had been quite certain the crystal was not in my room. I was too tired to protest. Staggering a bit, I lumbered after her, reaching the door just as she finished unlocking it.

The door opened, but not to an empty hallway.

"Well, Mr. Parkhurst. We meet again." We were staring into the muzzle of Colonel Sykes' pistol.

CHAPTER EIGHT

By this time, I'd apparently gotten used to being held at pistol point because my stomach failed to leap into my throat, and I had to throttle back the urge to laugh. Or perhaps I was just too tired to react more appropriately. Sykes wasn't smiling though, or the man I still thought of as Sykes, nor was he masked. Kelly and I backed up slowly while he and three other men entered the room. One of them was Lieutenant Commander Davis, also lately a passenger on the *River Warlock*. The other two were strangers, to me anyway.

"No disguise this time, Colonel?" I couldn't see any advantage to concealing the fact that I'd identified him during our earlier encounter, and quite frankly I wanted to provoke a reaction from someone else for a change. I was tired of being cast as the ignorant innocent who had to be walked through every step of this charade.

His face twitched but he didn't miss a beat. "Impractical, I'm afraid. And unnecessarily expensive. The cost of clandestine magic has become quite outrageous lately." The intruders were inside and the door closed, isolating us from the rest of the hotel. "Your weapons, if you please."

Kelly handed over her pistol and then, after meeting Sykes' eyes steadily for several seconds, she relinquished a smaller one that had been concealed in her voluminous cuff.

"The boot gun as well, if you don't mind."

I watched her surrender the third weapon with a renewed sense that I was completely out of my league here. No one had even bothered to ask if I was carrying a concealed weapon, but that was unnecessary, of course, because I didn't have one.

"I apologize for inconveniencing you for a second time in the same evening, Mr. Parkhurst, but I'm afraid I really must insist that you accompany us. I promise you that this trip will be somewhat less eventful than the last. And you'll be coming along with us as well, Miss Masters. Or should I say, Mr. Richard Grenadier." His face displayed a brief smirk.

My own expression must have been considerably more picturesque because Davis laughed briefly before turning away. Sykes even deigned to smile slightly. "I gather she hasn't told you.

This young lady is the author of the Malachi Marks novels, among her many other accomplishments. I'm quite a fan of hers, as a matter of fact. She manages to create an air of authenticity without revealing any of the real secrets of his extraordinary string of successes. But then, I would expect no less from the daughter of the great man himself."

I had exceeded my capacity to be surprised. If Sykes had announced that he was actually the Duke of Toronto traveling incognito, I probably would have taken that in stride. I looked in Kelly's direction with a question in my eyes and she nodded slightly, admitting to the charge.

My brain must have become overloaded with new and incomprehensible information at that point because the next thing I knew, we were all riding down in the levitator.

As we reached the lobby, I couldn't resist pushing back a little. "Aren't you worried that we'll be ambushed again?"

"Not at all. That was all a misunderstanding. Commander Davis was regrettably left out of the planning and acted based on erroneous intelligence. We've come to an accommodation since then, as it appears that our interests run in the same direction, at least for the time being."

"Those men worked for you?" I turned toward Davis as the door slid open.

He nodded, but I could tell that he wasn't entirely pleased with what Sykes had told us. They might be allies for the moment, but they were uneasy ones. "I'm sorry to have involved you in all this, lad, but there are issues of the utmost importance involved. Sometimes the good of the many must supersede the good of the few."

Sykes laughed. "Don't pull our legs, Davis. You're in this for the money, just like me. You sold out the Federation to the Brits years ago."

"The Federation should never have abandoned the Crown in the first place," Davis responded angrily. "I consider myself a British subject and a proper patriot. My ancestors fought and died when Arnold's army took Quebec and my mother traces her family back directly to Governor Carleton."

Sykes didn't respond and our small party made its way across the lobby to the front entrance. I scanned the room, looking for anything that would offer a chance of escape, or delay, or some faint hope that I might get out of this in one piece. But other than one elderly gentleman reading a newspaper in a padded chair, and a pencil thin night clerk dozing at the front desk, there wasn't another living person in sight.

There were two steamcars waiting in the street in front of the hotel, both late model Drakes painted black. Davis and one of the nameless men took Kelly into the first while the rest of us piled into the second. The turbines were already thrumming and both vehicles moved away from the curb as though they'd been directed by a single hand.

Frightened or not, I found it impossible to remain awake any longer. I remember turning onto the main thoroughfare heading east from the hotel district, but I closed my eyes about then and didn't open them again until Sykes shook my shoulder roughly and told me to get out of the now motionless vehicle.

The sky was still as dark as velvet, but the moon had emerged from the clouds and provided enough light for us to examine our surroundings. I stepped out of the Drake and found myself facing a plot of unkempt, parched grass that ran in a broad band across the front of a dilapidated farm house. Just beyond was a barn, but even in the darkness I could see that part of the roof had collapsed and that the entire structure was leaning decidedly to one side. Judging from the general air of neglect, I guessed that the farm had been abandoned when the local agricultural business had plummeted about ten years back, providing a fresh crop of recruits for the Greenies to the south.

Kelly and I were escorted into the main house, which was much better maintained on the inside that I expected, almost clean in fact. I suspect that the building was used regularly for clandestine meetings by either Sykes' people or those working with Davis, or perhaps both. In one corner of the room stood a tall, silent figure with an ugly raw wound in his forehead, draped in clothing that hadn't been washed since this farm had been prosperous. The figure was entirely motionless except for the fingers, which twitched constantly. I recoiled involuntarily, recognizing it as one of the most illegal abominations of the modern world, a zombie. Reanimation of the dead had been outlawed in every civilized nation for over three centuries, although the practice had never completely died off and was supposedly still condoned unofficially in parts of demon haunted New England's northernmost regions.

"Sit down, both of you. We might as well be comfortable while we talk. There are still a few hours before the gandalf will be here."

"What else can you possibly want from us? You have the crystal. Just let us go."

Sykes ignored my remark and addressed Kelly instead. "Is he really this naïve, Miss Marks?"

She ignored him, turned in my direction. "He doesn't have it either. Sykes – or whoever he really is -works for Changsha. We've known it for some time but since the Federation and Governor Ling have often had unacknowledged common interests in the past, there has never been sufficient reason to move against him. That's a situation which will doubtless change now." There was no disguising the threat in her voice..

Sykes seemed to be amused. "If I can place that crystal in Ling's sweaty hands, Miss Marks, I'll be able to retire from this business permanently. I already have a safe haven waiting for me, far enough away that it won't be worth anyone's while to come looking for me."

"Don't count your griffins before they're hatched," she replied caustically. "Malachi has already taken the crystal and left Memphis. You've been following a false trail ever since we arrived there."

I figured this was a bluff, then wondered if it was true. She had seemed genuinely shocked to find the crystal gone, but could she have been pretending? There were so many layers of deception and conspiracy that I no longer trusted my own judgment. If it was a bluff, then who had the crystal now? Beck was dead, Dana unconscious and clueless, Davis and Sykes still searching for it. Or did one of them have it already? The alliance could have been a bluff to mislead one or the other. Or perhaps Marks had recovered the crystal from his daughter – if she really was his daughter – without telling her, either deliberately or under the press of events.

"I don't suppose I could convince either of you to cooperate and tell us what we want to know right now. The gandalf will get the truth from you eventually. Even your considerable charms, no pun intended, won't protect you, Miss Marks. He's one of the most powerful sorcerers I've ever met. His methods are always effective but occasionally unpleasant. I would hate to see either of you come out of this mentally or physically damaged."

If I had known anything worth telling, I might have given in then. I'll never really know. But since I possessed no information that could possibly help them, I fell back on bravado and shook my head defiantly.

At which point Kelly stunned me again my letting her head drop. "All right, I'll tell you what you want to know." She took her time, detailing how she'd been carrying the crystal for the first part of the voyage, our meeting at the crafts store, her clandestine visit to my cabin and later burglary of my hotel room. She didn't mention Beck or Dana and neither Sykes nor Davis asked any questions until she finished.

Davis cursed mildly and walked to the far corner of the room. Sykes sat back in his chair, stone faced. "Do you really expect us to believe that story?"

"Of course. You'll hear the same when your tame sorcerer arrives. That's what really happened. It won't do you any good so it doesn't hurt to tell you. Neither of us knows where the crystal is any longer. We're as much in the dark as you are and you've just wasted your time kidnapping us."

"Could Marks have reclaimed it?"

Kelly shrugged. "He may have, but if he did, he didn't tell me. And I have no idea where he is now or what he's planning to do next. I hope that he's already on his way to New Orleans and that it's too late for you to catch him. But if someone else took the crystal, then we're all out of luck."

"The Prussians perhaps?" Davis spoke without turning back to face us.

"Nonsense! Their agent on the *Warlock* was Beck, the false judge. She's too much of an amateur to have stolen a march on us." But Sykes didn't sound completely convinced.

"So either the young lady is lying to us and still knows where the crystal is, or she's telling the truth and it's most likely in the possession of her father."

Davis spun on his heel and walked back toward us. "Who could be well on his way by now."

"Possibly. If so, we're not likely to catch up to him easily. But what if it really is yet another party. The Iroquois perhaps, or even the Apache? The southwestern rebels would risk a lot to embarrass Ling and derail his efforts to suppress them. They've rarely intrigued outside their own territory in the past, but Laughing Cloud is a more intelligent and sophisticated leader than they've had in generations. He might have taken a seat at the table."

"I say it's Marks." Davis turned to Kelly. "Tell us how to identify him."

She smiled at him. "He's two meters tall, frightfully handsome, and has a dueling scar on his left cheek."

Davis pulled a notebook from his pocket but Sykes grabbed him by the arm. "Put it away. She's obviously lying. You can't expect the girl to betray her own father, at least not voluntarily. Wait till the gandalf gets here. He'll pull the truth out of her."

Her expression still so sweet that it might have drawn flies, Kelly turned to Sykes. "Possibly. But gandalfs aren't infallible, you know. I might very well send you off on a wild harpy chase."

Davis appeared to be growing more agitated by the moment. He extracted a short barreled pistol from somewhere inside his coat and pointed it, not at Kelly but at me. "I apologize for the melodramatics, but I won't waste any more time. Please reconsider my request, Miss Marks, for the sake of Mr. Parkhurst here. He's not privy to any information we're likely to find valuable, which makes him expendable."

There was an audible click as he cocked the pistol.

CHAPTER NINE

I have never thought of myself as a coward, but neither have I ever had any illusions that I was unusually courageous. As a young boy I had endured my share of encounters with local bullies, and sometimes I turned craven and did what was necessary to appease them, and sometimes I stood my ground and acquired some bruises, and sometimes I even managed to give as good or better than I received. My mandatory year of public service was spent in the Bureau of Trade rather than the military, a choice made following a family appraisal that I needed a wider knowledge of commerce if I was to enter the business, so I had no experience of more deadly conflicts. I knew there was a virtual state of war with the anarchists to the southeast, and there were occasional incidents along the border with Changsha, but these all seemed distant and irrelevant to my life. The closest that I'd been to actual physical danger prior to this trip was being caught by an unexpectedly fierce storm on Lake Supreme when I was twenty. Since I spent most of that experience huddled below deck, waiting to see if the crew and ship would hold up, there had been no real opportunity for me to discover how I would comport myself in a situation like this.

But at that moment, I felt a surge of unaccustomed bravado, probably because I couldn't abide the thought of losing face in front of Kelly. "Do as you wish, Moriarty. Just don't bore me with your endless chatter."

Sykes hesitated, his brows lifting inquisitively, his nose wrinkling as though he'd detected a foul odor. "Who's Moriarty?"

Davis burst out laughing and patted his associate on the shoulder. "He's quoting from one of those Sherlock Holmes things. 'The Case of the Confused Colonial', I think. You really should get out more, Sykes."

Sykes seemed neither pleased nor enlightened by the revelation. "I believe he's cast himself in a very short story then," he said at last, raising the muzzle to within a few inches of my face. I felt my pulse racing and sweat made my clothes stick to my body, but I forced myself to maintain a mildly aloof expression and not to flinch away. If I was going to die, it would be with dignity, even if no one I cared about ever learned about my final moments.

I think he really was going to fire, but that he was waiting for me to break down, and that hesitation saved my life. His hesitation, that is, plus the very unexpected and welcome events which came one upon another and so quickly that it was some time later, when Kelly and I were able to compare notes, that I could actually reconstruct the method of our deliverance.

As I said, Sykes was either preparing to kill me or had missed his calling as a dramatic actor. Davis and two other men were sitting at a table near the window, while a third thug leaned against the opposite wall, apparently bored with the proceedings, his eyes half closed. The zombie stood motionless in one corner. I was wondering how many seconds of life remained to me when there was the sharp crack of a weapon discharging and I thought the final one had come. Instead, Sykes' arm jerked to the side and the pistol flew out of his grip.

There were two more reports immediately following and I saw Commander Davis topple from his chair, the left side of his face a bloody ruin. One of his companions slumped in his seat as though he'd fallen asleep and the other recoiled, eyes wide, momentarily too shocked to take action.

Someone leaped in through the window, sending shattered glass flying in every direction. The figure carried two double barreled pistols and fired several more shots in rapid succession, so they must have had magical reloaders. I finally had the sense to duck down behind a chair so was unable to determine how effective this fusillade had been. Sykes rushed past me and out the front door while the two remaining men remained behind to meet the threat. Lacking orders, the zombie didn't react at all, even when one of the thugs groaned and toppled, caroming off its legs.

I recognized our rescuer when he paused for a moment to fire at the one remaining man, who had yet to decide whether or not to follow Sykes in ignominious retreat. It was Dana, the false steward, who had somehow picked up our trail and intervened at just the right strategic moment to save the day. Kelly had also dropped to the floor, and in the confusion neither of us saw all of what happened during the next few seconds, but shots were fired on both sides. Then there was a silence so loud that it hurt my eardrums and when I cautiously poked my head around the side of the chair, Dana was coming toward me.

"Get up. We have to get out of here quickly. Sykes has more men nearby, a party of Greenies camped by the stream. He was running in that direction when I lost track of him."

My legs were shaky and my ears were ringing, but I didn't need much urging to leave that place. Kelly was already on her feet, looking much calmer than she had any right to be. One of the downed men moaned slightly, but didn't appear capable of hindering us.

Kelly was regarding our rescuer pointedly. "Where did you come from?"

"What does it matter so long as he's here?" I had no time for subtleties, and now that there was a chance of surviving the night, I was suddenly much less courageous.

Dana didn't even appear to be breathing hard. "I watched you all leaving the hotel and hitched a ride on the back of the second car. Let's talk about it later, shall we?"

Dana led the way out the front door after cautiously poking his head through to see if we were about to be ambushed. There was no sign of life as we emerged, half running, but I could hear voices in the distance, raised voices. We ran to the first of the steamcars, which fortunately was free of anti-theft charms.

"You drive," Dana told me brusquely. "I'll disable the other one."

We were all huddled together at the rear of the lead vehicle. Dana took one step away from us and three shots rang out so close together that they could almost have been a single prolonged discharge. One round rushed past my cheek so closely that I felt the breeze, a second shattered the rear window of the Drake. The third, unfortunately, hit Dana high on the chest, lifted him from his feet and threw him back against the rear bumper.

He wasn't killed outright because I saw his arm move as he tried to bring up his pistol. More shots rang out – I don't know how many – and I heard one ricochet off metal. Dana's body jerked again and this time he dropped his weapon and slid down into a sitting position. I crouched beside him and spoke to him, encouraging him to get up and get into the steamcar. It was pointless. His eyes were wide open and unblinking.

Kelly stooped and retrieved the pistol he'd dropped. "Leave him," she hissed. "He's dead. We have to get out of here."

I was too stunned to think, let alone act. Dana's blood was smeared in a scarlet streak from my shoulder to my waist. Kelly rapped me painfully across one knee with the pistol as more shots rang out, passing over our heads, but fired from closer at hand. "Get in, damn it! I'll drive!"

Apparently our enemies had hit Dana more through luck than skill. We both squirmed around our respective sides of the Drake and got inside without being injured. I crouched on the passenger side, head lowered, my thoughts moving turgidly, probably as a result of mild shock. Kelly was less inhibited. After a cursory examination of the instrument panel, she began operating the controls just as another fusillade of shots pinged off the body and roof and shattered one of the side windows.

With a loud hiss, the steamcar shuddered, its turbine starting to build pressure. Kelly released the brake and we started forward, rolling at first thanks to a steep downgrade. I glanced back through the shattered window and saw a half dozen men running toward us, brandishing their weapons. We were slowly accelerating, but for those first few seconds I was absolutely certain that we would be overtaken, and I wondered if my reprieve had been just a temporary one. I crouched as low in the seat as possible, but Kelly remained upright, still manipulating the controls, trying to build pressure as quickly as possible without stalling.

"I hope they invested in sealing spells for the tires on this thing."

The tableau held for what seemed like hours but must have been a minute or less. Then the pressure of acceleration was strong enough that I knew we must be under full power, and almost immediately the shots and shouting died away behind us. Cautiously I poked my head up and looked around, but there was little to be seen. The night sky had continued to clear and with a nearly full moon, I could still make out the shape of the farmhouse receding behind us, until we rounded a curve and it was cut off by a line of trees.

We turned again, so violently that I was thrown against the door. Although we might be out of range for the moment, Kelly was taking no chances. The second Drake was still in operating order and if our pursuers were really Greenies, they undoubtedly had horses nearby. A straightaway opened up before us and she turned on the headlamps. Our route was flanked by fields of tobacco, apparently gone wild. We were halfway across them when the lights of the second steamcar appeared to our rear.

"They're coming," I said, marveling that my voice sounded almost natural.

"But they won't be any faster than we are. We should be safe for a while at least."

"Don't say that," I answered petulantly. "Every time I think I'm safe, someone else points a pistol at me."

She glanced toward me and smiled cheerily. It was actually quite an attractive smile, but under the circumstances I didn't feel any strong urge to respond in kind. "They'll have packed the car full. The extra weight will slow them down."

I wasn't reassured.

We reached a hard packed road a short while later and our speed reached a breathtaking sixty kilometers per hour. I'd only once traveled this rapidly before, on the trirail to Philadelphia, and I wondered if this particular steamcar was just better engineered than ordinary vehicles or if some very expensive spellcasting had enhanced its turbine. On pavement we could probably have managed to go even faster, but there are few paved roads outside of the major cities, and it would be dangerous to proceed at such a reckless pace on dirt tracks. There was not as yet enough motorized traffic to justify the expense of pavement in rural or suburban areas, although my father predicted that I would live to see the day when most main arteries were upgraded.

But that was the future. In the present, we enjoyed – if that's the right word – a rough, bruising drive at high speed over heavily rutted dirt roads and occasional patches where someone had spread gravel to ameliorate a tendency toward mud. I sat with my feet braced against the floor and both arms deployed to keep me from slamming into the front panel or the door handles, but there was little I could do when we hit the more exaggerated bumps or pits and my head was soon sore from its collisions with the ceiling.

Kelly, on the other hand, seemed to be taking every bump and jostle in stride. In fact, she looked as though she'd been born for just this role, caroming through the countryside ahead of a pack of ruthless killers. I was marveling at this when she turned her head slightly and gave me a dazzling smile.

"Two daredevil escapes in less than twenty four hours," she shouted merrily in order to be heard over the throbbing turbine. "You must lead a charmed life!"

"More likely I've been inflicted with a particularly sadistic curse!"

Whenever there was a long straightaway, our pursuers' lights were clearly visible behind us, and I didn't take much solace from the fact that they were smaller and more remote now than they had been at first. Kelly was a surprisingly skillful driver and she'd exploited every curve to increase our lead by small increments. Every so often the road would turn and run along a line of trees, a farmer's windbreak, and sometimes I'd lose sight of the other vehicle altogether, but it always reappeared eventually, doggedly following us. I worried about our fuel, about bad patches of road ahead, blown out tires, turbine trouble, and conjured other imagined delays that would land us in their hands once more.

The level ground gave way to an increasingly steep rise and we lost some of our speed, and some of our lead before the other steamcar was similarly inhibited. The road was dry and dusty here and I could mark their progress by a plume of dust spiraling up into the moonlight when I couldn't actually see their lights. Each time we crested a small hill we regained some of our speed, but never as much as we'd lost on the incline, and when I glanced over at the gauges I saw that we were perilously close to the danger zone on more than one dial. Hopefully Sykes and his companions were experiencing the same difficulties. We passed a small herd of unicorn, grazing on the dew, and they retreated from the edge of the road as we approached, watching balefully as we rumbled past. I glanced around hopefully for a shepherd, but even if one had been about, it would almost certainly be a child, since most adults no longer possess the quality required to tend these skittish beasts.

Anxiety, like any other emotion, cannot be maintained indefinitely without provocation, and against all good sense, I found myself relaxing slightly and actually enjoying the idea of being alone with an attractive young woman in the middle of the night, escaping a band of dangerous villains. It was a distorted fulfillment of one of my fondest dream fantasies; by right it should have been me driving and her huddled close at my side for protection and consolation. But I'll take my fantasies in diluted form if that's the best that's offered.

"Are you really Malachi Marks' daughter?"

She glanced in my direction and grinned impishly before turning her eyes back to the road. "I'm afraid so, although our family name really isn't Marks."

"Am I right in presuming that you've taken up the family business?"

"I dabble, help out when I think I can be useful. I spend most of my time writing. The Richard Grenadier books are my most successful efforts, but I do steamy romances as Paula Passion and children's books as Jane Coville."

"You created Eunice the Unicorn? My nieces are obsessed with the books, and can recite most of them word for word."

"I'll autograph copies for them if we get out of this."

I glanced ahead. "Do you have any idea where we're going?"

"Not really. In retrospect I should have taken the road in the opposite direction, since that's the way we came, although that would have meant running right at the gunmen. We're headed away from the river, and the city, roughly southeast."

"Greenie country?"

"Technically, not for a while yet, although they've sent raiding parties this far, obviously, and probably have lots of sympathizers in the area. But I'm not sure exactly where we are. I haven't seen any signs except the markers for a few farmhouses."

"Maybe we should head for one of them."

Kelly shook her head. "All that would accomplish would be to involve more innocent people in our problems. The bunch behind us wouldn't think twice about killing anybody who offered us shelter."

"So what's this all about? If I'm going to die, I'd at least like to know the reason."

"We're not going to die, at least not if I can help it. And I can't tell you any more than you know already. Sorry, but I don't even know the whole story myself."

"Is your father really involved in this as well?"

She hesitated. "Yes, he is. We like to make people believe that Malachi Marks always works alone, but it's not true, or at least not always. There are half a dozen agents who've helped him in the past, although some of them didn't know who they were partnering with. Involving myself gives me a taste of the action, the atmosphere. You write best when you write about the things you know."

Conversation flagged for a while after that. The sky was beginning to lighten in the distance and I realized that we must have been on this road for at least an hour. "We can't just keep driving forever," I said unnecessarily. "Can't we pull off the road and hide somewhere until they've gone past?"

She shook her head and tapped the control panel. "Too risky. They might see the steam rising from our turbine, or even hear it cooling down."

"Then we just keep driving until we reach a town?"

"Maybe. That kind of depends on which of us runs out of fuel first." She nodded toward the fuel gauge, which was now hovering below the one quarter mark. Suddenly anxious, I turned to look for our pursuers, but we'd just negotiated a curve and they were concealed by a row of poplars and the crest of the last hill we'd climbed.

"They haven't been able to gain on us but they're not losing ground any more. I have to keep our speed steady now to conserve fuel."

"So what are our chances?"

Kelly shrugged. "Probably slightly in our favor, unless they have more fuel left than we do. For the moment they can only react. Maybe something will come up that will improve the odds in our favor."

"Like what?"

"I have no idea."

I lapsed into a morose silence, feeling somewhat sorry for myself, and also a bit annoyed that I had been relegated to a supporting role in this mini-drama. Kelly's careful driving never faltered and I was actually nodding off to sleep when we hit a particularly deep pothole and I bit my tongue. "Sorry about that," she said without looking in my direction.

Half an hour later, the situation changed.

"Uh oh."

Alarmed, I straightened in my seat. "What does that mean?"

"Look what's coming up."

The road had leveled off as we raced down the longer axis of a narrow plateau, but in the distance I could just make out the curve of land angling upward again. The sky was noticeably brighter now, the stars and moon receding, the horizon glowing pink, and I could make out more details, although they were fuzzy. The road was about to become much steeper, and at the limit of my vision I saw where it doubled back at almost a one hundred eighty degree angle, twisting back and forth in a series of loops as it scaled the rugged hillside. At some point we would turn and start rushing back towards Sykes and company rather than away from them, although at a higher elevation. Not high enough to be safely out of range of their weapons, unfortunately.

"What do we do?"

"We don't have much choice, do we?" She produced the pistol she had recovered back at the farm and offered it to me. "Have you ever used one of these?"

I took the cold metal in my hands. It felt alien, even though I'd carried handguns in the past. It was an advanced Smith and Krupp pistol, with an eight position reloading chamber of which five were currently empty. Although I had heard this kind of weapon described, I had never seen one before.

"I've done some target shooting, but never with anything as lethal as this."

"Were you any good?"

"I can hit the side of the barn pretty consistently..."

"That's reassuring," she interrupted sarcastically.

"...so long as I'm standing in the barn at the time," I finished.

She turned to look at me and I grinned, and she smiled, acknowledging the joke. "That's okay. It's not a barn I want you to shoot at."

I let a second or two pass before giving her a serious answer. "I scored high enough to please my instructor, but I'm not a marksman."

"Could be worse. Why don't you refill the loading chambers?"

I was puzzled for a second, then remembered what I'd read. The bottom panel of the pistol butt slid free and six more rounds fell into my lap. I filled the empty slots and put the spare shell into my pocket.

"Loaded," I said quietly.

We reached the sharp turn moving a good deal faster than was probably wise. Kelly didn't want to sacrifice any more of our momentum than necessary. Fortunately it was a heavily built vehicle and although our rear end slewed alarmingly wide, all four tires remained on the ground. I was pressed hard against the door as she struggled to stay as close to the center of the road as possible. Runoff water from above had eroded deep ruts here and the road surface had obviously not been maintained for at least a couple of years.

"There they are."

The other set of lights, less distinct now that the sun was hovering just below the horizon, emerged from a stand of particularly tall scrub growth through which we'd passed perhaps five minutes earlier. They had yet to reach the steep incline so the gap was closing almost visibly. There was a sudden belch of steam from Sykes' vehicle, and for a moment I had hopes that something untoward had happened, and that we would make good our escape after all. Kelly immediately punctured my elation.

"That's what I was afraid of," she said quietly, more to herself than to me. I was about to ask what she meant when my eyes told me the answer.

The other steamcar had slowed significantly, and one of its passengers leaped out, briefly lost his footing, but recovered quickly. He crossed the road and immediately began to climb up the hillside toward the roadway ahead of us. Sykes and company were already accelerating again, although we'd gained some additional ground thanks to their diversion.

Kelly sighed significantly. "If you have any magical talents you haven't mentioned, now would be a good time."

I shook my head. "None whatsoever. I have an aunt who claims to be clairvoyant, but I think she's a fraud. How about you?"

"I levitated a hairpin once. It took half an hour and I was exhausted for the next two days."

The curve of the hillside concealed the climber from view so I wasn't able to measure his progress. It was possible that we might pass him before he reached the roadway, but it was just as possible that he'd be waiting for us with his weapon poised.

"You'd better get into the back seat."

"Why?"

"We don't know where he'll be when we reach him. Could be on either side of the road. If you're going to shoot him, I'd rather not be in the line of fire."

I'd never fired a weapon at a man in my life, but I thought that under the circumstances I'd have no qualms about thinking of him as a target. I clambered awkwardly into the rear. One of the side windows had been shot out already and I opened the other, letting it swing back on its tiny hinges.

"Fire a couple of shots as soon as we round this next curve," Kelly instructed. "I know you won't be able to see him yet, but if he's waiting for us, that might make him hesitate a second or two, or even duck for cover. The closer we get, the more likely it is that you'll be able to hit him."

The other Drake was directly below us now, but the landscape made it impossible for either of us to fire at the other. Time passed with glacial slowness. As much as I would have preferred to avoid this confrontation altogether, I also wanted it over with. Then, suddenly, we were sweeping around the corner and I extended my hand through the driver's side window and fired wildly.

Then I saw our adversary.

He hadn't quite reached the road, but he was close enough to be a menace, crouched against the side of a protruding rock ledge. The reloading charm chambered the next round and, more by instinct than plan, I fired a second round in his general direction. It ricocheted harmlessly off the rock a meter above his head, but it was close enough that he recoiled and ducked back out of sight.

"Good shot!"

I was absurdly pleased by the unwarranted compliment and put both hands on the pistol, trying to steady myself for the next shot. The steep incline had robbed us of so much momentum that it felt as though we were crawling toward him. Although the sun was up now, tendrils of mist rose on every side, and phantom movements kept distracting me.

When the gunman finally reappeared, he was not at all where I had expected him to be. He must have scurried up the rock out of our sight, then sprinted across the grassy verge. I could not shoot immediately because Kelly's head was almost directly in my line of fire, but she must have realized that because she made a quite unnecessary swerve toward the opposite side of the road. I fired but I don't know if I was even close, although the gunman ducked his head.

Kelly swerved back, fighting the wheel, and we hit another bad pothole just as I was shifting position. My wrist banged against the window frame and my fingers went numb, unclenched themselves against my will.

"Uh oh!" I exclaimed.

"What now?"

"I dropped the pistol!" I was suddenly sick with the realization that we were once again unarmed. There was little time to feel sorry for myself, however, because the gunman was standing on the road just ahead, raising his own weapon to point directly at our windshield.

"Keep your head down!" She swerved directly toward the man, doubly dangerous because he was standing at the very lip of the precipice. If we ran him down successfully, we would have to celebrate our victory very quickly if we were to fit it in before our crash.

Was Kelly crazy enough to kill both of us in order to take him with us? Apparently the gunman thought so, because he bolted without firing his weapon. At the last possible moment, she tugged hard on the wheel and we turned back toward the center of the road, but for a split second I think at least one of our wheels hovered over open space. Our ascent continued at a rate slightly faster than a man could run. I heard two futile shots from behind and then another curve shielded us.

"You can come back up front. We're safe for the time being."

I rejoined her, apologizing for losing our only weapon. "Don't worry about it. Couldn't be helped. Dad always tells me not to waste time on regrets."

The road rose steadily ahead of us as we maneuvered around another switchback and continued our ascent. I could almost have walked as fast as we were traveling now, and I wondered if Sykes was doing any better.

"We lost some ground to them, but they may give it back to us if they stop long enough to pick up their man."

"Now that it's light, we might be able to pick out some landmark that'll tell us where we are."

"I've got a pretty good idea, but it doesn't help us much. I think we're very close to the Mississippi wilderness. Greenie territory. Most of the farms in this area have been abandoned but there should be a few small towns."

"Don't the COPs ever patrol this area?"

"Out this far? You've got to be kidding. The Greenies have a lot of support from the locals. Most of them either lost their farms during the agricultural depression or ran businesses dependent upon the local economy. You won't find much respect for the federal authorities in this neck of the woods. If Congress would get off its collective butt and do something to improve the situation, they might be able to re-establish control in a few years, but the resentment will be with us for at least another generation."

We finally reached the crest and found ourselves heading down into a shallow, narrow valley dotted with clumps of tree and other growth that showed the pattern of old, abandoned farmland. There was a burnt out silo ahead of us and to our right, and beyond that a farmhouse and barn, both of which were clearly no longer in use. The roof of the barn had collapsed like a decayed tooth. We saw a sign indicating we were approaching Nixon's Corners, but it was an old sign. A few minutes later, we spotted a crossroad ahead, and at the intersection stood a gray shingled, single story building, devoid of windows or markings. A hunched object to one side looked very much like a doubleheaded pump. There was, as yet, no sign of Sykes behind us.

I glanced at the fuel gauge, which was nudging the empty mark. "That looks like a fuel stop." It was a tossup whether we'd run out of water or liquefied coal first, but both were imminent.

"Probably abandoned."

But as we drew closer, a figure emerged from the building and walked out past the pumps to stand in the road, presumably watching our approach.

"There's someone there."

"I see him," Kelly answered, but she didn't seem particularly pleased. As we drew closer, I realized that she was still building pressure.

"Aren't you going to stop? This may be our only chance to refuel!"

"Wouldn't surprise me at all." Her voice was tight with tension. "Keep your head down."

The bearded man moved to the side of the road as we approached, watched us with hands on his hips as we rumbled past. I noticed that he was armed, an old fashioned musket, but he didn't make any move toward his weapon, or any gesture at all for that matter, just turned his head slowly to watch us pass.

"Would you mind telling me why we didn't stop just then?" My voice was petulant and I knew it, but I was tired and I'd gotten over my guilt at dropping the pistol.

"Look, Jim, we have no way of knowing where that man's sympathies lie. He could be an honest businessman, but he might also be a Greenie or a bandit, or just a vagrant who slept in an abandoned building for the night. We don't know if those pumps were still working. There's so little traffic out this way that it seems unlikely. Even if he was selling fuel, we couldn't have taken on much before Sykes caught up to us. If you watch closely, you can see his dust plume. He's over the crest now. At best, all we would have accomplished is to lose our lead. At worse, we'd be overtaken and recaptured."

"But if they do sell fuel and Sykes stops, he'll outlast us. We can't have more than a half hour left in the tanks."

"If they stop, we'll gain some time to think of something else."

I understood her point, but I couldn't help looking at the fuel gauge. As things stood, we'd be on foot very soon, in the middle of nowhere with no idea in which direction help might lie.

A few minutes later, Kelly gave a grunt of satisfaction. "They've stopped. Their dust is gone. Best case is the pumps are empty and they've wasted the time. Worse case, they'll top up their tanks, which means we pick up ten or fifteen minutes. If we can reach a town of some sort, there's a good chance we can get out of this."

But naturally things weren't about to start breaking our way. It wasn't the fuel that stopped us though.

We had reached the head of the valley and entered a narrow pass that dropped very slowly ahead of us. The road curved slightly and was in worse repair than anything we'd encountered so far, and Kelly was hunched forward over the controls, trying not to sacrifice speed to safety. Suddenly there was a loud bang which startled me out of a light drowse, and I grabbed for handholds as we slewed violently to the left. Kelly fought the wheel as we hit the edge of the road, narrowly avoided colliding with a stately tree. There was a prolonged, grating sound and we were bumped and jostled before coming to a halt half on and half off the road.

"What happened?" I seemed to have developed a knack for asking unnecessary questions.

"Felt like we lost a wheel or broke an axle. Whatever it is, we're on foot now and we don't have much time."

We tumbled out of the car, stiff and sore both because of our bruises and the prolonged inactivity. As Kelly had predicted, we found the left rear wheel resting at an awkward angle. "Broken axle," she said curtly, already moving toward a line of trees to our left. "How are you at hiking and rock climbing?"

My stiff muscles soon had fresh cause for complaint. Although I enjoy good health and have avoided the tendency toward chunkiness that runs in my family, I live a predominantly sedentary life, punctuated by occasional games of tennis or hussade and even less frequent swims in the lake behind our house. But I was tired and sore already, and within a few minutes, the muscles in my calves were taut and aching, and shortly after that my feet and ankles began to hurt as well. Kelly seemed indefatigable, but I was resolved that she would be the one to call for our first rest. The trees provided a thick canopy here and we moved through a shadowy mock dusk. Once I thought I heard the thrum of a steam turbine to our rear, but if so it lasted only for a moment.

It would have been easier if we had followed the natural curve of the land down into the valley, but for reasons of her own, Kelly had decided to climb directly up the enclosing earth wall. The climb became progressively more difficult. The lower slopes had consisted of jumbled rocks heavily overgrown with vines, small bushes, and twisted trees. Although the footing was often treacherous, there were plenty of handholds and neither of us fell, although I nearly twisted my ankle on one occasion. The ground changed as we ascended, the trees shorter and less clustered, the ground sandy and uncertain under our feet. Sunlight spilled in ahead of us as the canopy was torn by gaps in the foliage, interspersed with gravelly slopes that forced us to make detours to more certain ground.

We passed the tree line about mid morning and paused for a few minutes to catch our breath. Although it had been quite cool, we were both soaked with perspiration and dust and I longed for a bath or a swim or even a nice strong downpour. When we felt somewhat restored, we moved parallel to the cliff face for a few minutes, emerging onto a ledge that provided a wonderful view of the roadway below. We could see the abandoned steamcar quite clearly, as well as the second Drake drawn up beside it. There was no sign of Sykes or his friends, who were presumably somewhere in the wooded hillside below us.

"I don't hear them," I whispered.

"Don't worry. They're coming. I think we've made them mad."

A cool, dry breeze sprang up, and I'd like to think that was why I shivered just then. Dana's blood had dried into a dark patch on the front of my shirt, and one of Kelly's sleeves was torn all the way up to the elbow thanks to a patch of bull briar we'd passed through a little before.

We reached the summit a few minutes later, taking advantage of a dry rill that was lined with conveniently exposed roots. I had hoped for good news but all that greeted us was more of the same, rolling hills, patches of dense forest, abandoned fields, and rocky upthrusts. At the very limit of our vision, there were a few parcels of land that seemed to be under active cultivation, but there was no other sign of human habitation except for a stretch of poorly maintained barbed wire fencing.

We wasted a few minutes searching the landscape with our hands shading our eyes, but it was profitless. "Let's follow along the ridge for a while."

I wasn't sure that was a good idea, since there was little cover at this elevation, but I was too tired to argue and followed Kelly's lead. She seemed to be favoring her right leg slightly. I couldn't remember seeing her injure it, but she might have pulled a muscle or banged a toe. Fifteen minutes later, the ridge made a slight jog to our right, providing a wider view of the depopulated landscape. But this time there was more definite evidence of human intervention – a narrow swathe of road ran from left to right.

Kelly gave me an inquisitive glance.

"It's better than nothing," I replied.

The descent was more dangerous than the climb had been. The ground underfoot was just as loose, crumbling and sliding away when we put our weight on it, and we were both very tired by now. We held onto small bushes to brace ourselves, but the soil was so uncertain that they often broke free when we put weight on them, and both of us fell a couple of times early on, which made us that much more hesitant to trust the footing. Once we finally reached firmer ground back under the tree line, our downward momentum made us move faster than was absolutely safe, and we were so tired that we weren't nearly as alert as we should have been.

We did finally hear a voice from somewhere behind us, almost certainly one of Sykes' party. It didn't sound nearly as far away as I'd hoped. We had made no serious effort to hide our trail. If Sykes had an experienced tracker with him, it would have done no good and would have cost precious time.

Both of us were staggering by the time we reached level ground. There was a field directly ahead of us through which we could have made excellent time, but Kelly insisted that we move through the scrub brush parallel to it, so that we were fairly well concealed from above. A stream, now almost completely dried up, had cut a narrow ravine that ran in the general direction we wanted, and the brush along its rim was more luxuriant than elsewhere.

We stopped for a rest just short of the road, which lacked cover. For a change I was the one to lead next. The water turned and ran parallel to the road to our left, so I started in that direction, since otherwise we would have been forced to leave what little cover remained to us. Kelly followed without comment and we plodded onward in silence. The road curved through a stand of trees and took its leave of the brook, but the curve would shield us after a quick sprint across an open stretch. I half expected to hear pistol fire or at least shouts of discovery, but the only sound was the breeze rushing through the branches over our heads and the persistent cackling of a crow somewhere in the distance.

There was an uncovered plank bridge ahead of us spanning our friendly brook's bigger brother. We paused there long enough to drink and wash our faces, and then found some dry stones beneath the bridge where we could sit and let our sore feet dangle in the cool water. After a few minutes of exhausted silence, my stomach rumbled and reminded me that we weren't out of the woods yet, literally or metaphorically.

"Now what?"

"Sorry, I'm fresh out of ideas, as well as breath." Kelly leaned back with her eyes shut and stretched and I was embarrassed as well as delighted to see how her sweat soaked clothing clung to her body. Her eyes opened, catching me in mid-leer, and I turned away hurriedly, then pulled my knees up to my chest and leaned forward, meaning to rest my eyes for a while.

I fell asleep, of course, although only for a moment or two. Then Kelly's hand was on my knee and when I raised my head she hissed at me. "Keep quiet. Someone's coming."

CHAPTER TEN

"Stay here." Kelly's voice crackled with command. Without waiting to see whether or not I obeyed, she crossed to the opposite side of the bridge and began climbing slowly up out of my line of sight. A few seconds passed while I waited breathlessly, expecting to hear shouts of discovery, or pistol fire, or some other indication that she'd been discovered. Then she was back, moving soundlessly down the slope and back under the bridge. Cautiously I moved to join her.

"It's a tinker's wagon. The Greenies tolerate them so long as they mind their own business. Wait here and keep out of sight until I call you."

She turned and was gone again before I could agree, or argue, or even react. This time she abandoned stealth and began openly climbing the slope, disturbing the soil as she did so. I moved as close to the edge of the bridge as I dared, trying to interpret what was happening above solely based on what I could hear.

A couple of minutes passed uneventfully during which I could clearly hear the sound of an approaching wagon, drawn by two horses. The rhythmic drumming came closer and closer and then slowed to a stop directly over my head. A man's voice grumbled "Whoa there!" and the plodding steps stopped, although I could still hear their harness jingling as the team moved their heads from side to side. I was surprised by Kelly's voice when she first spoke, because she was affecting a thick local accent.

"How d'ya do, sir? I wonder if I might beg a ride to the nearest town."

"Maybe. Maybe not. What's ya all doing out here by yerself?"

"My horse threw me last night, somewhere over that way. Hit my head real good and wandered around some in the dark. Started feelin' better this mornin', but damned if I know where exactly I am. My family just moved up here from down near Rawlins and I don't know my way around all that much."

There was a long pause and I imagined the tinker mulling the words over, looking for contradictions, or a trap, or possible trouble he might get into if he helped this stranger. Good Samaritans weren't that common in this part of the country. There were too many people ready to take advantage of a kind gesture.

"Nearest town's back the way I come a few miles. Crispinsville, it is."

"I wouldn't want to take you out of your way, but I have a few coins I could pay you for a ride back there. Of if there's someplace reasonably close ahead, that would be just as good. Near walked the bottoms off my feet already."

"I've got no more to do in Crispinsville. This here's a business and has to move forward. Next town's Lubbocks Mills."

"I know someone in Lubbocks Mills. That'd be fine with me."

"Get on up here then. I can't spend all day talkin' about it."

I almost stepped out from under cover at that point. Was Kelly going to abandon me here?

"I sure would appreciate a hand up, mister. I bruised my hip real good when I fell and I don't think I can climb up there without having it seize up on me."

There was an inarticulate grunt that might have been acquiescence. A few seconds of silence passed, then a thump, followed almost immediately by the sound of something heavy falling.

"Jim, get up here!"

I scrambled up the slope, not entirely sure what had happened, and when I reached the road level, I was more than slightly disconcerted. The tinker lay face down on the road, motionless, while his horses shifted their feet nervously and shook their heads back and forth. Kelly was leaning over the prostrate man, removing his tool belt. She stood up, fastening it around her own waist. The tinker's cap was lying in the dirt and she picked that up as well, adjusted it on her head and tucked her long hair up inside. She might pass for a boy if one didn't look too close, and stood a fair distance away, and suffered from poor vision. In the dark. "Luck's going our way for a change. This is just my size. How does it look?"

"Pretty awful. Did you kill him?" I was appalled at the idea, but I wouldn't have been surprised. Nothing was going to surprise me for some time, I suspected.

"No, he'll be fine when he wakes up. Sorry to have to hit him like that, but we need his rig a lot more than he does right now. We'll put him in the shade over there before we leave." She removed his identification card from a pouch on the belt, read it, and then replaced it. "If we get out of this all right, the government will compensate him for his losses."

"So what next?"

"There's no sign of our friends." She frowned. "If I were in their place, I'd have sent one man back to retrieve the steamcar while the others continued the search. They can't be far behind. Let's get this gentleman situated and head for that town he mentioned."

We carried the tinker to a grassy place under a large tree and made him as comfortable as possible. He moaned once but gave no indication of an imminent recovery. "Are you sure he'll be all right?"

"Trust me. I've done this before."

"Just what did you do?"

Kelly gave me an impish smile. "When he leaned down to offer me a hand up, I gave him a look inside my blouse. That distracted him long enough for me to pop him behind the ear with a stone. Let's get going."

The tinker's wagon was in good repair, with sideboards that opened up into a kind of canopy, displaying racks filled with tools, kitchenware, unidentifiable pieces of metal, a small steam lathe, rakes and hoes and other paraphernalia of his trade. There was also a considerable supply of medicines, some obviously homemade, which were presumably meant for sale. There was a small stock of foodstuffs, spare clothing, and other personal items clumped loosely in the center of the wagon along with a straw filled pad that probably served as his bed. Kelly spotted a threadbare flannel shirt and slipped it on to complete her disguise.

"You look disreputable enough already," she told me, and I glanced down at my clothing, realizing that my shirt and pants were stained and torn. "But you probably ought to stay out of sight for a while. They'll be looking for two people traveling together." So I hunkered down in the back while the tinker's stock and trade clinked and banged and jangled all around me.

The road forked around the next curve and there was no sign to help us. Kelly halted the horses and I poked my head up. "The right hand fork looks better maintained," I suggested.

"And is therefore more likely to lead to Lubbocks Mills. The right hand fork is is."

The next hour was tense but uneventful. I shifted position several times, trying to find the least uncomfortable way to lie concealed in a rough wooden wagon with worn springs and no padding. The road was anything but direct, winding back and forth so often that I suspected it was an old animal track.

"See if you can find anything we could use as a weapon back there. And you'd better find yourself a new shirt. You're covered with dried blood."

Dana's blood. I shuddered and did as I was told. Although I managed to find a woolen shirt that was almost new, it was a tight fit and I couldn't button the sleeves. The road surface was growing rapidly worse and the wagon lurched about uncertainly, forcing me to stay alert to avoid being struck by mallets and chisels and other items hanging from hooks above my head. I opened every container, burlaps sacks, wooden boxes, and a few skin pouches, but found nothing remotely weaponlike other than a hand axe with a cracked handle, a rusty sword blade lacking a hilt, and a dozen small knives, all meant for tanning or kitchen work, most of them badly in need of sharpening.

I reported my very limited success, crouched down behind the driver's bench, peering between the legs in an unsuccessful attempt to see ahead of us. My view, unfortunately, was blocked by the horses. "What do we do when we reach Lubbocks Mills?"

"Improvise. With luck we'll be able to find some alternate form of transportation. Sykes may have given up on us by now, but I wouldn't put money on it. He has a reputation for being very single minded. Make sure you stay out of sight if we run into anyone. I don't think they'll recognize me unless they're real close, but if they spot the two of us together, we won't be able to fool them for long."

"Where do you think they are anyway?" I felt my pulse accelerating again.

"I have no idea. They should have overtaken us by now if they're headed this way. Maybe they're out of fuel and coming on foot."

Despite my anxieties, I settled back down, cleared off one end of the tinker's pallet, and sat with my knees drawn up and my head down. The lurching and jostling seemed to recede, almost became soothing, and I dozed for awhile. I had missed an entire night's sleep and now that my adrenaline flow was back to normal, I was exhausted.

I must have slept for at least a couple of hours because the sun was high overhead when Kelly leaned back and hissed at me. "Stay sharp! We have company."

I peered out cautiously and saw that we were approaching the outskirts of a fairly good sized town, presumably Lubbocks Mills. The town was nestled against the side of a hill and our approach gave us a good view of the town center. I estimated there might be as many as two hundred buildings, mostly private houses, but also several storefronts, what looked to be a stable, a fuelstop, and one obvious tavern. There was an air of overall neglect and decay that became more apparent as we drew closer. Most of the buildings badly needed repainting, there were shingles missing from virtually every roof, some of the windows were broken, and scraps of paper and other trash littered the streets and adjoining yards. Some of the homes were obviously boarded up and abandoned, and when we reached the town proper, I saw only an occasional pedestrian, most of whom didn't even give us a curious look.

"What's next?" I whispered.

She shook her head just slightly. "This doesn't look promising. The town is half empty, more than half. The only ones left here are those too tired or too poor to move on."

We continued steadily forward and I shifted position, raising my head enough to get a better view. The road we were following merged with a rougher track on our left just as we reached the first of the outlying buildings.

I heard Kelly's sharp intake of breath and tensed, then saw what had alarmed her. Four men had emerged from one of the buildings ahead of us, and each of them wore a green sash. They glanced in our direction, but only for a moment. Although they were talking animatedly, one man gesturing dramatically back the way we'd just come, none of them gave us a second glance and the team plodded stolidly past them.

"We don't dare look for help here," Kelly said softly. "Those men may not have been looking for us, but if they can wear the green openly, there's no official presence here at all. I'm going to keep right on going and hope no one stops us because they need a knife sharpened or a kitchen wight repaired."

"Do you suppose those were Sykes' men?"

"Let's just say they'd be sympathetic to his cause even if they haven't heard from him yet."

The horses clipclopped along the hard packed dirt road, which fortunately was in somewhat better repair here. Otherwise, the town's decay was obvious and a bit sad. I saw more broken windows, and a couple of doors were missing. We passed the burnt out shells of two houses and a third had a collapsed roof. The economic downturn had hit this area hard, obviously, and Congress had consistently declined to address the problem. I felt a degree of sympathy for the Greenies, for their grievances rather than their methods. A handful of children passed us as we were leaving the town, playing some arcane game that involved running and shouting and getting very dirty. I saw a kite flying in the distance.

Fatigue overwhelmed my curiosity and I was settling back into my makeshift bed, feeling vaguely guilty because Kelly must also be exhausted by now, when I saw her back stiffen and she whispered, "Uh oh!"

I sat up cautiously. "Now what?"

She didn't turn her head, kept her voice low. "Steamcar just a little ways ahead of us, off the road on our left. It's a Drake and one of the men standing near it looks like Sykes."

"How could he be in front of us?" But I answered my own question. "They took the other road."

"Probably thought we'd avoid the main route to avoid being spotted. And they're considerably faster than we are."

"Have they seen us?"

"I don't think so, or they just aren't paying attention. Keep out of sight."

The horses plodded rhythmically onward and my head began to throb. Each second seemed infinitely prolonged, but they passed, one by one, and there was no outcry, no pistol shot, no indication that we'd been discovered.

"We're past them. It was Sykes, all right. He even glanced this way for a second."

I tried to relax, discovered that the muscles on the back of my neck seemed to have permanently knotted themselves into taut cords. I reached up with one hand and began massaging them with the tips of my fingers, and then froze in that position when Kelly hissed at me.

"Watch it! We've got trouble!"

A few seconds later, she jerked up on the reins and brought the wagon to a half.

"You just come in on the west road?"

It was a gravelly male voice with an odd accent, one I didn't recognize. Kelly answered in a throaty mumble that sounded vaguely male. "That's right. Who wants to know?"

"Green business so mind your manners. You see anybody out there, walking one way or the other?"

Kelly let a mildly insolent amount of time pass before answering. "Saw two kids out tending some 'corns about halfway between here and the bridge. Naught else. Who're you looking for?"

I don't know if Kelly misjudged the situation and made the man suspicious or if he had intended to search the wagon right from the outset, but his reply made my blood freeze. "All right, step down from there for me, real easy now."

"Mister, you got no call to point that pistol at me." This was undoubtedly for my benefit. I looked around again, even though I already knew there were no weapons available.

The man's voice had hardened. "Just do what I tell you and get down from that rig."

"Don't get all riled up. Just hold the reins for me, friend. Old Henry and his brother are a trifle skittish and I don't want them running off with me halfway down."

"Just get your ass down off that wagon!" But the man's voice was closer and I thought he'd taken the bait. I don't know if Kelly had some plan for dealing with him, but I was too tired and sore and frustrated to wait to be discovered. I took a quick peek under the seat to confirm where the man was standing, then reared up, swinging wildly with a cast iron frying pan.

He was slightly out of reach, but close enough to take alarm. He ducked instinctively and stepped sideways away from my blow, and Kelly lashed out with a booted foot, hitting him squarely on the side of the head. He staggered back as I climbed up onto the seat beside her, and this time I was able to land a solid blow to the crown of his head, driving him to his knees. Kelly dropped to the ground, spun on one foot and kicked out again, and I winced when I saw where her foot landed. He cried out hoarsely, doubled over in agony, temporarily uninterested in anything but his own private problems. Kelly snatched up his pistol and slammed it down on the back of his head, and this time he stopped moving.

She scrambled back up onto the wagon with her prize, tucked it into her belt, and picked up the reins, urging the horses forward. "No telling how long it'll be before he's missed or how fast he'll recover, but I think it's time we moved on."

We were out of town within minutes, the curve of a hill concealing the last of the buildings behind us, and there was still no sign of pursuit. Kelly kept the team moving smartly but not at a full run. "We'd wear them out and attract too much attention."

"I think it's a little late to keep a low profile."

After a few minutes I offered to relieve her so she could try to nap for a while, but she just shook her head. "I won't be able to sleep until we're out of this. But you can rest if you'd like."

I felt guilty about it, but once it was obvious that we weren't going to be immediately run down by our pursuers, my fatigue returned and I crawled into the back, dozing rather than sleeping. We stopped once to water the horses while I nervously watched the road back the way we'd come. I couldn't believe that the alarm had not been raised by now, but it appeared that for the moment at least we were still in the clear. A few minutes later we were underway again, and I was just about to nod off when Kelly called to me.

"We've got company!" The horses began to run and the wagon swayed back and forth alarmingly as I climbed awkwardly up beside her. We were near the top of a gentle incline with a slight curve, and I could just make out the shape of a steamcar coming into sight behind us. It was too far to be distinct, but it was painted black and I was certain it was a Drake.

Even if our horses had been thoroughbreds, which they weren't, they couldn't have outrun the steamcar for more than a few minutes. Our lead had slipped noticeably by the time we crested the hill.

The land dropped away before us very dramatically, the road a twisting ribbon that meandered through a patchwork of meadows and woodlots and a few long abandoned fields. Three parallel streams, or three branches of a single one, crisscrossed the landscape, their courses marked by a healthier growth of foliage. It must have rained somewhere in the hills recently, because the nearest was overflowing its banks. Some of the fields were fenced, but there were large gaps in places, and what remained standing was generally in poor repair.

I glanced back, even though there would be nothing to see until the steamcar crested the hill. "We can't outrun them."

"I know that." She sounded testy. Her head moved from side to side as she drove the rig onward, as though she was looking for something. We descended the hill at breakneck speed, and several pans and other small items bounced out of the wagon. "Throw out everything you can onto the roadway," she told me. "The load will be lighter and if we're really lucky, maybe we can blow out one of their tires."

"Not if they have sealing spells on them."

"Do it anyway. At worst it will surprise them. We're due for things to break our way for a change."

I felt a passing regret about the destruction of the tinker's stock, but if we got out of this alive, the government would probably pay him at least a portion of its value, and since our lives were at stake, I decided our rights overrode his. I began throwing out tools, rakes, hoes, cookware, hammers, bits of scrap metal, barrel hoops, pottery, a few machine parts, screws, nails, and everything else portable, even clothing and foodstuffs. The steamcar reappeared, frighteningly close and definitely a Drake, although the twisting road actually put them further away than it appeared. Freed of its stabilizing weight, the wagon moved faster but less predictably, swaying dramatically as Kelly negotiated one curve after another. When we finally reached the next straightaway, I thought we might even have gained some ground as the steamcar picked its way through the debris strewn road, but I had nothing left to throw out except the pallet, the sword blade, and the hand axe, and they'd be past the last of the obstacles soon.

I had also retained a heavy wrench with which I began loosening the tinker's wooden racks. Although I was being jostled too wildly to work efficiently, I finally freed one of them, and it fell free of its own volition, landing face down and blocking almost the entire road. They'd have to stop long enough to pull it out of the way, which would probably gain us a few minutes while they rebuilt steam pressure. My satisfaction was short lived however, because they were clearly visible when they reached it, and the steamcar simply slowed enough to leave the hard packed surface and bypass the obstruction by running briefly through the adjoining field before returning to the roadway. I had cost them, possibly, twenty seconds.

"Hold on!"

I twisted my upper body around to see what was happening and was almost thrown overboard despite her warning. Kelly deliberately turned the team off the road and I bit my lip as the wagon wheels slammed into a shallow ditch before being lifted and dragged further on. We were in an open field now, low scrub growth all around us, racing for a gap between two fences that seemed impossibly distant.

When I glanced back, the Drake had already turned from the roadway as well, angling to cut off our escape. For a change, Sykes seemed to have misjudged the situation, because the ground was soft and gave treacherously under his vehicle's considerable weight. He was losing speed quickly, and our chances of beating him to the fence rose from unlikely to just possible, and as the seconds raced by, steadily improved to probable.

I heard a distant popping and realized that someone was firing at us, but the range was too extreme for even a marksman, barring an incredibly lucky shot. The Drake slowed even further and when we reached the gap between the fences he was at least a hundred meters behind us. Sykes, or his driver, altered course again, ignoring the gap and striking the triple rail fence head on, bursting through a short distance to our left. Splintered wood flew through the air and the steamcar sprinted forward, the wheels having finally gotten purchase on firmer ground. I forced myself to look away from our pursuers and saw where Kelly had us headed. My stomach clenched when I realized what she intended.

"It's not wide enough!" I shouted.

"Just hold your breath when we reach it!" She flashed me a smile and I was amazed to see that she actually seemed to be enjoying this.

A major stream ran from right to left in front of us, an effective barrier to both our vehicles. But there was a small wooden plank bridge coming up, meant for pedestrian traffic and whatever animals may have grazed here once upon a time. You could have pushed a wheelbarrow over it, or even a small horse drawn cart. If it had been open and flat, we could have eased the horses slowly across with no difficulty; there was just room for the two of them abreast. But there were wooden railings on either side and at this breakneck pace, we'd more likely find ourselves in the water, if we survived the crash at all.

"We'll never make it across. Pull up in just shy of the bridge and we'll make a run for it!" The bridge would collapse under the weight of the steamcar, even if its wheel base was narrow enough to fit.

"No way! They'd catch us. We'll make it. Trust me."

The Drake was speeding up, angled to intercept us even before we reached the bridge. They were close enough to fire at us now with a remote chance of success; I heard the distinctive popping of their pistol fire and hunched my shoulders. Whoever the driver was, he was good at his job. They plowed through the grass like an ironclad through a gentle surf, and if the ground had been just a little bit more solid, provided slightly more traction, they might have caught us short of the bridge. As it was, I could see the driver's face quite clearly when we reached the bridge, still moving at full speed.

Kelly had us lined up perfectly. Both front wheels jumped the small step and banged onto the bridge floor. The guard rails exploded into fragments when the wagon body hit them, but they flew off to either side. One of the horses shied slightly and for a second I thought we were all going over the side, but Kelly worked the reins brilliantly and regained control. Then we had a split second to see the one thing Kelly hadn't anticipated.

The twin posts at the far end of the bridge weren't wooden. They were stone and concrete pillars.

The impact ripped both sideboards off the wagon. They tore away with a scream and were gone so quickly I didn't even have time to flinch. The two remaining racks mounted on the back fell to either side, metal screeching as the bolts were torn out of the floorboards. One fell away harmlessly to the left, the other toppled to the right, still partially bolted to the wagon, digging a shallow furrow in the soil that slowed our headlong race onward. The team perforce turned in that direction despite Kelly's attempts to hold them on a straight course. We were well off the bridge by then, but our speed was dropping quickly, and I stole a second to look back the way we had come.

The steamcar was drawn up at the edge of the water, its occupants watching us in what I hoped was helpless fury.

"Got you, you bastards!" I waved my fist wildly with elation, which lasted a distressingly short time.

"Jim, we've got another problem."

I twisted around to see what she was talking about. The dragging rack was threatening to tear the entire side off the wagon. "Find a place to stop and I'll undo the last of the bolts." It would only take me a moment or two to remove the last of the bolts and free us of our renegade rudder.

"That's the problem. I can't stop. I dropped the reins."

CHAPTER ELEVEN

"Why did you drop the reins!" It was a stupid question, but I couldn't help myself.

"I didn't do it on purpose!" The wagon lurched and I had to grab onto the seat to keep from being thrown off. Mercifully, the field had opened up in front of us and seemed to be relatively level, and despite our decided list to the right, we were still moving away from Sykes and company. Sooner or later the horses would grow tired and slow down, at which point we could either dismount or regain control. I had watched melodramas in which heroes jumped onto the horses and recovered the reins, but I knew it was beyond my capabilities and Kelly didn't seem inclined to try such a radical maneuver either.

I risked a quick glance backward and saw no sign of our pursuers. That wasn't good. Sykes would undoubtedly return to the road and try to intercept us somewhere further on.

It might have been possible to free the now thoroughly mangled rack without stopping, but I decided the drag was more likely to bring us to a halt. It was past midday and unusually warm. Earlier Kelly and I had filled our stomachs with some bread and cheese from the tinker's meager larder, but I was getting hungry again and I had tossed out the rest of the food during the chase. The team slowed and I began to relax a little. "We're out of Sykes' reach for the moment, and we have a pistol of our own now. All we have to do is keep our distance." And then I said something that I immediately knew was tempting fate. "Things could be worse."

No sooner were the words out of my mouth than things did in fact get worse. Much worse.

The right side horse stumbled, or put his foot in a hole. Everything happened too quickly after that for me to know exactly how it happened, and the results were the same in any case. The second horse shied away from the drag on its harness just as the forward edge of the wagon dropped. We swerved, the dangling rack slammed into the ground hard, and the harness twisted as we pivoted on the impact point. One of the horses screamed briefly and I felt myself thrown into the air. I hit the ground hard enough to take my breath away, and just managed to raise my arms over my face as splintered boards fell all around.

When the last of the debris had come to rest, I sat up and looked around, calling Kelly's name. She was lying not far away, cursing softly and kneading her left arm, which apparently had been twisted beneath her body when she landed. She picked herself up and we both brushed off our clothing, which looked more disreputable than ever. Kelly had a badly ripped pants leg to balance her tattered sleeve, and I had a cut over my eye that didn't hurt until she asked about it, but otherwise bruises and minor scratches were our worst injuries.

One of the horses was nowhere in sight. The other was casually cropping grass a short distance away.

"Lady, you sure know how to show a guy a good time." I was feeling light headed with relief at having survived yet another disaster. Kelly had lost her cap and her hair was matted with dirt and dried grass. She looked younger than ever and I felt the urge to say something protective, although so far I hadn't excelled at that role.

On the other hand, she seemed to have descended into a darker mood. "We can't stay here. They'll be looking for us." She eyed the horse speculatively. "Ever do any bareback riding?"

Our mount gave us a reproachful look when we both climbed aboard, but he didn't balk. Kelly sat in front of me, but she handed the reins back. "Your turn to drive. Stay away from the road and keep to cover as much as possible." She nodded toward a distant woodlot. "Wake me up if anything happens."

I don't know if I could have dropped off to sleep so readily on horseback, but Kelly managed just fine, and I have to admit it was pleasant having her slender body leaning back against me with my arms around her. I felt self conscious about it for the first few minutes, but that wore off quickly. We reached the wooded area and found a rough trail, and the horse followed it without requiring much guidance. Kelly roused occasionally and glanced around, but seemed satisfied with the course I had picked. The afternoon plodded by as slowly as our horse, and the sun began sinking down behind the distant hills. I noticed a stunted apple tree bearing insect laden fruit, but we were too hungry to be fastidious and gorged ourselves before remounting.

The sunlight was almost completely gone when we reached another stretch of open country, and clouds were crowding in to mask the moon and stars. I could see some lights far ahead of us, but whether they were farmhouses, headlamps, or torches I couldn't say. Kelly was awake by then, sounding much more alert, and she suggested that it might not be a good idea to make our presence known. As much as I longed to return to civilized parts and put this all behind me, I couldn't disagree with her assessment. Sykes was clearly in his element here, allied with the Greenies, and we had to assume everyone was our enemy.

"Would we have been better off doubling back? They have to know at least the general direction in which we were headed."

She shook her head. "Sykes is a seasoned operative. He would have anticipated that and left someone behind to watch for us. In all likelihood he's alerted the entire countryside and offered a reward. This is a hotbed of anti-government sentiment, and he'll play on that as well, even though he's no more concerned with their welfare than is Congress. We have to keep moving. I wouldn't be surprised if he could field a couple of hundred men to comb the area for us at first light. Our best chance is to put as much distance as possible between us and hope that he underestimates how far we can travel."

"But where do we go? It looks like we're heading even deeper into Greenie territory rather than out of it."

"If we're where I think we are, there's a large town northeast of us, Grand Junction. It's pretty well settled and there's a federal installation, Fort DiFilippo. They do some sort of arcane research there, pyrotics, I think, and they have a good sized garrison. The Greenies usually give it a wide berth. They'll have a telegraph and possibly even a mindlink. If we can get there safely, we'll probably be all right."

"Sykes presumably knows that too."

"I'm sure he does. He'll have people looking for us, but there's a lot of territory to cover and even with the Greenies helping him, he can't watch everything. But if you have a better suggestion, I'd be happy to hear it."

I didn't.

Our chances would probably have improved if we'd traveled through the night, but the woods were too thick to do so safely, our horse was tired, I was tired, and even Kelly was showing signs of exhaustion despite her napping. We found a small stand of trees atop a very small hill that gave us as good a field of view as we could hope to find, and enough cover to conceal us from casual observation. We tethered the horse where he could graze and I even found a pool of water nearby. It tasted brackish but the horse drank it readily and Kelly and I more tentatively. My stomach was grumbling unmercifully despite the apples we'd gorged ourselves upon earlier; we hadn't seen anything else edible since.

I made a tentative effort to gather some soft brush for bedding, but Kelly curled up against a tree trunk and was sleep immediately, and after a few minutes, I made myself as comfortable as possible, leaning against another tree, planning to stay awake and on watch for at least part of the night, but I doubt I lasted thirty minutes.

I was the first to waken, probably because I'd managed to give myself a stiff neck to add to my other aches and bruises. The sun had risen, but just barely, and a steamy mist was seeping through the brush, an eerie effect that only heightened my feeling that I was lost in an illusion play rather than reality. Birds and insects were already out and about, and their noise reassured me that no one was lurking just out of sight. I yawned and looked around without standing up, turning my head back and forth to try to relieve the strain in my neck and shoulders. A few meters away our horse was grazing contentedly on the grass and slapping at flies with his tail. Kelly was curled up just out of reach, her head tucked into the curve of one arm so that I couldn't see much of her face. I sat and watched her for quite some time before recollecting myself.

I was hungrier than ever. My woodcraft is pretty basic, but I thought I could recognize edible berries if I saw them, and even if the local farms were all abandoned, some of their crops should have survived. Moving quietly so that I wouldn't disturb Kelly, I stood up and stretched my arms and legs, then began exploring our surroundings.

To my surprise, I could see a small farm in the distance, and not an abandoned one either. There were two silos and a small barn, and a plume of smoke rose from the house where someone was presumably cooking breakfast. My mouth watered at the thought of bacon and eggs. I thought I saw a human figure moving near the building, but it was a fleeting glance and the distance was too great for me to be certain. A steamcar was parked adjacent to the house, but even from that far away I could tell it wasn't the one Sykes had been using. It was an older model, probably a Bentley or a Kaiser Kruzer, and it was light green rather than black.

There was a narrow road that ran in front of the farm, then turned and angled off toward another line of hills in the distance. At the extreme limit of my vision stood a second farm, or at least a silo poking its head up through the trees. While I watched, two figures began walking along the road, accompanied by a dog, coming from somewhere to my left. I shrank back into cover immediately, even though it was very unlikely that they could have seen me against the chaotic woodland background at this distance. I thought they were too small to be adults, but even a child could raise an alarm.

"See anything worth looking at?"

Kelly had joined me so silently that I jumped. "Judge for yourself. There's a road down there, and there are people as well, at least a couple of working farms."

"We could detour around them. Even if we were spotted, two people on horseback wouldn't look too suspicious unless they're watching for us. But it would be better if we stayed under cover for as long as possible. Isn't that an orchard?"

It took me a second to adjust to the abrupt change of topic, then look in the direction she was pointing. "Looks like apples." We could only see one corner of the orchard from our present position. "I don't think they're handing out free samples though. They probably shoot people for stealing around here. I doubt there's much official law enforcement."

"They only shoot the ones they can catch. If we circle around and slip across the road out of their line of sight, we can probably snag some breakfast and be on our way before anyone's the wiser."

We walked alongside the horse at first, bypassing the farm, taking advantage of whatever cover was available, but at Kelly's urging we didn't hurry unnecessarily. "Sooner or later, someone's going to notice us. If we're acting sneaky, they'll get suspicious. If we act as though we belong here, we'll be almost invisible." When we reached the unpaved road an hour later, there was no one around, and except for the top of one of the silos, we could no longer see either of the farms. I did hear a dog barking once, but it was too distant to be alarming.

"All right, let's do it." Kelly left me to lead the horse as she crossed into the orchard. After a momentary hesitation, I followed, the urgings of my stomach overcoming my anxieties. For the second time in twenty four hours I gorged myself on apples. We continued forward until we reached the far end of the orchard, which gave way to a thick woodlot, then mounted and turned to our left, Kelly holding the reins this time.

At the far end of the orchard, we found another road, a track really, too small for powered vehicles but just fine for horses. It turned in the direction we wanted, and although it looked as though it was rarely used, it presented no real difficulties and our horse had no trouble picking his way through the debris.

The forest began to open up very gradually, and by mid-morning we were passing meadows and pastureland, some of it in use, although we didn't see another human during that time. We stopped at a brook for a drink and a rest, and as we sat in the shade of an elm tree, a chickenhawk appeared overhead, circling slowly, then folded its wings and dropped to a branch on a tree not far from us. It stared at us curiously and I stared back, surprised that it would alight in such close proximity. A few seconds passed before I noticed that Kelly was suddenly tense, chewing her lower lip furiously.

"We're in trouble again."

I looked around frantically, expecting to see Sykes and his henchmen bearing down on us with drawn weapons. But our surroundings were unchanged. "What are you talking about?"

"I think they've got a remote viewer looking for us, and I think we've just been found. Let's get moving."

The hawk turned its head slowly as we mounted up and started off, then rose into the air with a flutter of wings and flew away to the north. Kelly gave me the reins, climbing up behind me and clasping her arms around my waist. "I have to think," she explained.

"Why didn't you shoot it?" I had no doubt that she was a good enough marksman to have managed it neatly.

"Unless they've got a top rated viewer, the best they'll get from the hawk is a fuzzy image. Their eyes work differently than ours. There's always a chance that we weren't identified. But if I'd shot the hawk..." She let the sentence die unfinished.

"Sykes doesn't strike me as the kind of man who'd employ an amateur."

"You're right. We have to get off this track. I don't know how far away they are, but you can bet that they'll at least send someone out to check on us before long."

I looked around, but our options were all of dubious value. To our left, a very wide stream ran parallel to the road, the water moving quite briskly and splashing over its banks, too deep, wide, and violent to chance a crossing. To our right was a not particularly tall set of hills, but their near face was sharply chiseled and virtually inaccessible.

"Unless you've acquired the power of levitation recently, we don't seem to have much choice right now."

"Pick up the pace. We need to have more choices."

I urged our mount to a canter, but it was absolute agony. Even with a saddle, I would have been sore by now. Bareback intensified the torture. "Do you think we might be better off abandoning the horse? We'd be slower, but quieter and harder to spot."

"Maybe. We need to gain some distance first."

The rock face to our right broke down and veered away, and we left the road a few minutes later, crossing an uncultivated meadow filled with wildflowers. A doe and her fawn bolted from our path and at least a dozen pheasants rose into the air, complaining shrilly about our interruption of their morning. Beyond the meadow was an impressive wall of trees, and we turned and ran alongside the border for a few minutes, then darted through a gap, following what was almost a tunnel until we emerged in another, smaller, and even more unruly meadow beyond.

Ten minutes later, we topped a small rise and I pulled up on the reins so sharply that Kelly almost lost her grip. A line of men were working their way through the brush below us, at least twenty of them walking steadily in our direction. They all seemed to be armed and at least some of them wore green sashes. Beyond them stood another road, where two men on horseback flanked a pair of horse drawn wagons.

We were spotted almost immediately. I couldn't make out the words, but they were shouting to one another and a few were pointing in our direction. We were well beyond pistol shot, so I wheeled away and urged the horse to what passed for a gallop, racing along the first rank of trees and parallel to their line of advance. I took Kelly's silence as tacit agreement with my choice of direction. There wasn't time to debate the pros and cons in any case.

The ground was rising slowly but steadily beneath us, and growing rockier by the minute. The soil was dry and broken, and our mount slowed down despite my urging. The summit was just ahead, but it took an agonizingly long time to reach it, and when we were finally at the top, I reined us in a second time. A second line of men was advancing up the hill toward us. The road we had seen curved around this hill and joined a larger one, and two steamcars and a horse and wagon were parked below us. One of them was a black Drake. My heart sank.

"If you have a suggestion, this would be a good time to mention it."

"Try that way!"

Kelly was pointing off to the right, which would force us to run right between the two converging picket lines. "They'll be expecting that."

"Then we don't want to disappoint them. Someone went to a lot of trouble to set up this trap, and it wouldn't be fair to just let them catch us right away and spoil their fun."

Fighting a renewed feeling that this was all an elaborate dream, I pulled the horse's head around and roused him into another headlong dash, although it didn't take an experienced horseman to know that he was flagging and couldn't keep up this pace much longer.

We might as well have saved the effort. We had barely begun the descent before a half dozen mounted men emerged from the trees ahead of us. Even if I had somehow managed to break through their line, our oversized draught horse would be no match for their mounts in a race. I tried to swerve away, but they were surrounding us on every side almost before we realized that we'd been captured.

I didn't recognize any of the men, but they all had firearms and when one of them gestured wordlessly for us to head toward the main road, I nodded resignedly and did as I was told.

When we reached the cluster of men who were waiting for us, one of them ordered us to dismount, sounding almost bored. As soon as we did so, our wrists were bound behind our backs with strips of rawhide. While we were being secured, Sykes emerged from the Drake, conversed briefly with two green sashed men in tones too low for me to overhear, then walked over to greet us.

"You two have caused me a great deal of time and money, almost certainly more than you're worth." He didn't sound amused although his expression was neutral. "Do you have any idea how many men I've had out looking for you? No, I didn't think so." Without warning, he made a fist and hit me on the left side, just above the belt. I'd been in fights before, as a boy, and I'd taken some pretty painful blows, but they'd always been delivered in the heat of anger and I'd always been somewhat prepared for them. This was cold blooded, precisely directed, completely unexpected, and painfully effective. I folded up and dropped to my knees, gasping for air.

"Your value in particular has never been very high, Mr. Parkhurst. You're nothing more than an annoying distraction." He turned toward Kelly and for a moment I thought he was going to hit her as well. Instead he just grabbed a handful of her blouse and yanked her forward. "I've hired nearly a hundred men for this little party, Miss Marks, and if I don't receive sufficient value to justify that expense, I may offer each of them a little non-monetary bonus." He raised his free hand and cupped one of her breasts just long enough to convey his message, then pushed her way. Kelly's expression had remained just as impassive as his.

He turned to a tall, bearded man, who had been watching the show with evident amusement. "Take them to Yeshuko's and wait for me there. The rest of the men can go. I'll stop at the tavern and arrange payment with Palestrina."

The tall man nodded and someone else jerked me to my feet. It hurt to draw breath and my knees were wobbling but I was able to keep my balance as Kelly and I were roughly pushed toward the second vehicle, a medium sized steamvan with doors mounted on the rear. I banged my knee climbing up into the rear compartment, but Kelly managed to jump up neatly. We were followed by two guards, one of whom was completely bald, had a blotchy complexion, a lazy eye, and several missing teeth. The second guard was smaller and older, his face almost completely obscured by a thick gray beard and a wide brimmed hat that he wore pulled down over his forehead. When the doors were closed, our only light came from small slit windows, and most of the noise was muted, but I could hear the other doors close as the driver and presumably a third guard took their places. There was a sliding panel between them and us, but it was currently closed.

The whine of a turbine started almost immediately.

We sat facing each other on the narrow benches, the guards next to us. No one said anything, although Kelly gave me a quick, not particularly reassuring smile. She looked tired and dispirited, but I suspected it was a mask concealing what was actually going on inside her head. I had no doubt she was already plotting an escape.

"We got us a long ride back." The bearded guard was talking to the bald one, not to us.

Baldy nodded, made an unpleasant snorting sound and wiped the back of his hand across his mouth. "Too long for what we're being paid. After Palestrina takes his cut and Wolf gets his, I could've made my share or more rustling unicorns in half the time."

"You with Wolf? I thought he was working up north somewheres. What's he doing down here?"

"Had to pull back. Too many federals around lately. They'll get tired of bruising their asses running around looking for us where we ain't no more and then they'll move on and we'll go back. Every time they come out hot and angry, Wolf takes us south for a while. Who're you with?"

"Galatin, from down south near Suffolk."

Baldy shook his head. "I thought Galatin got himself killed over a card game?"

"Naw. Punctured lung is all. He won't be able to ride a horse for another month or two, but the way I heard it, he doesn't mind spending so much time in bed. Gets a lot of company there."

Baldy laughed, or at least that was my interpretation of the ugly, irregular rasping sound that followed. "He still going either way?"

"Either or both. It don't make no big difference to him. Long as the body's warm and has holes in it."

This seemed to strike Baldy as incredibly funny, and his wheezing laugh grew even more raucous. When it finally ran down, the bearded man pointed at us, or more precisely, pointed at Kelly.

"What d'ya suppose Sykes got in mind for her?"

Baldy smirked. "He's royally pissed, he is. I don't think she's gonna have to worry about what's for breakfast tomorrow. Him neither." His thumb jerked in my direction.

"Damned shame. Wasting a fine looking woman like that, I mean."

Baldy shrugged. "There's more where she come from." But a new thought had apparently lodged in his piggish little mind because his head turned and he stared at Kelly a lot more intently than he had before. Kelly met his eyes squarely, and he was the one who broke the connection. "You got something in mind or you just jawing to pass the time?"

The other guard nodded. "Everybody else gets to go home. We get the extra duty so I figger we ought to give ourselves a little bonus, since no one else is going to remember us."

Baldy licked his lips. "Sykes won't like that none if he finds out."

"Sykes doesn't have to know. Who's he gonna believe, them or us? Hell, you heard him back there. He's probably gonna give her to us when he's done anyway. I don't know about you but I'd rather be at the front of the line then down near the end."

"That's a good point you got there, friend. You're talking straight, all right. We're pulling the extra duty here, so we oughta get something for it."

"Maybe we can get the guys up front to pull over and get their share too."

After a brief pause, Baldy shrugged. "Gussie's driving and he won't be much interested. Got his balls shot off in a skirmish a few years back. Calhoun though, he fancies himself a lady's man, might even romance her a little." His head moved from side to side as he examined the inside of the van. "Plenty of room in here." He turned back toward Kelly and I saw his eyes; they were smoldering, hungry, and cold. I shifted my position as unobtrusively as possible, knowing that I would have to try to intervene, knowing equally well that they'd brush me aside almost without noticing that I'd made the effort. If I was really lucky, I might be able to kick one of them in the groin and put him temporarily out of action, but even that was a long shot. I couldn't possibly stop both of them.

"Go ahead," urged the bearded one. "I don't mind sloppy seconds."

The steamvan was lurching from side to side as it moved over the uneven road surface, so Baldy raised both arms to brace himself as he stood up and moved to stand over Kelly. She glanced up at him with a look of utter contempt and absolute calm, and I sensed rather than saw the muscles in her legs and shoulders tensing, waiting for an opportunity to deal out some damage. The angle was bad for me, but I was more interested in the second man. If Kelly managed to keep the first occupied and I was incredibly lucky and temporarily disabled the second, we might actually have virtually no chance at all.

Baldy reached down toward Kelly's blouse and I caught my breath, and then things happened so quickly that I didn't actually understand what was happening until it was all over. The second guard came up off his feet with both arms out. One hand grabbed Baldy's hairless skull by an ear to steady it and the other dragged a small sheath knife across his scrawny throat, turning the body at the same time so that the spray of blood spattered against the wall and not all over Kelly. It is unlikely that Baldy even realized that he was dying before he collapsed to the floor of the van, twitched a couple of times, then subsided into a growing pool of blood.

The surviving guard doffed his hat and nodded to me and for the first time I got a good look at his face.

"Jeb Walker! What the hell are you doing here?"

CHAPTER TWELVE

"Explanations will have to wait a bit, son." Jeb dragged the body back to where Baldy had been sitting a moment earlier and propped him into place, leaning precariously against the wall of the van. "Move over a bit, girl." Kelly obligingly shifted to one side so that Jeb could open the sliding panel. "Hey there! Up front!"

"Yeah? What d'ya want back there?"

"Man I gotta piss like you wouldn't believe. Pull over for a minute, will ya?"

I could hear laughter from the driver's side. "Didn't your mommy teach you to always go potty before going for a ride?" More laughter.

Jeb's voice acquired a whine. "Aw, c'mon, have a heart. We got a long way to go yet. I'll just take a sec."

"You gotta piss, you can take a leak on those two you got back there with you. We don't get to go home 'til this delivery's over with, and I don't like being this close to the federals. I killed one of them once and they got paper out with my face on it."

Jeb made a small sound of exasperation which was certainly not audible to the men in the front of the van. "Look guys, I piss on them, I gotta smell it for the rest of the trip. Tell you what. Stop for just a minute and I'll buy you both a couple of drinks when we get paid off."

There was a brief silence and then a new voice spoke up. "All right. We're coming up on a covered bridge in a few minutes. We stop inside and you piss right there. Orders is not to stop at all, so I don't plan to do it anywhere we might be seen. You know how Palestrina keeps tabs on all of us."

"Much obliged, and I'll be as quick as I can." Jeb slid the panel shut. "Turn around folks so I can get you out of those ropes," he said softly.

He untied Kelly first, then me. My wrists were raw where I had been twisting them fruitlessly ever since we'd been loaded aboard, and the rush of returning circulation made me want to scream. From somewhere inside his jacket, Jeb pulled out two small pistols and handed one to each of us. "There's only four shots in those things, so make 'em count if you have to. Stay where you are for now, and keep your hands behind you when we stop, like you were still tied."

An endless few seconds passed and then the sound of our wheels changed. We had left the unpaved road surface in favor of a wooden bridge that creaked and groaned under our weight. Jeb produced a third pistol, larger than those he'd handed out, and held it just behind his hip as he stood and turned to face the rear doors.

The turbine's characteristic whine started down toward idle as we coasted to a stop, ending with a lurch as the driver applied the brakes. We heard a door slam up front, then a rattling as someone unlocked the rear door.

As it swung wide, Jeb broke into a wide smile. "Thank you kindly, young fellow. Mind giving an old man a hand down?"

But as the guard, whom I'd heard addressed as Calhoun earlier, reached up, Jeb raised his pistol and shot him precisely between the eyes.

Moving with surprising speed, Jeb was out of the van. The shot was loud enough to have alerted the driver, who unwisely chose to investigate. Jeb fired twice more and by the time Kelly and I had scrambled out the back, he was already dragging the driver's body over to the side of the bridge. There were slitted gaps in the wall every few meters, just wide enough to accommodate a human being. The driver hit the water with a splash, and a moment later I was helping carry the second man to the same fate.

Kelly and I climbed into the opposite side as Jeb scrambled into the driver's seat. It was a tight fit, but we managed, wriggling into the most comfortable position while Jeb examined the controls, then began tamping up the turbine. We rolled out of the bridge at a walking pace, and started to accelerate, but the van lacked the speed of regular passenger vehicles.

I was too stunned by the latest turn of events and too concerned about the possibility of discovery to say anything for the first several minutes. We reached a three way fork in the road and Jeb took the rightmost without hesitation, apparently having some destination in mind, although there were no signposts to tell us where we were. The condition of the road steadily worsened as we began to wind through overgrown, rocky country too harsh to farm and too ugly to enjoy. He surprised me again by making a sharp left just as we cleared a ragged looking promontory covered with pale lichen and moss, leaving the road entirely in favor of uneven ground covered with low brush. We slowed dramatically and aggravated our bruises by bouncing around a great deal, but the ground was marginally passable and, as it turned out, we didn't have far to go.

We reached a small glen hidden from the road by a stand of willow trees. A late model Cheviot steamcar was parked under a stand of evergreens, covered with cut branches so completely that I didn't notice it until we drew right up alongside. Just beyond was a wide expanse of water, a pond or perhaps even an arm of a nearby lake.

Jeb let the engine idle when we stopped and told us to get out. As soon as our feet touched the ground, the van began to move again, headed directly for the water. He must have done something to the controls because when he jumped out of the driver's side a moment later, it was still picking up speed and didn't stop until it toppled over the bank and into the water. It lurched forward a couple of meters and then there was an immense cloud of steam as cool water hit the hot turbine and it came to a halt, half submerged. There was a loud bang that might have been something metallic splitting under pressure and then just a hissing that gradually faded away.

"Let them scry that out," Jeb called to us. "She'll settle into the mud and be out of sight in an hour or so. They'll be able to see that she's in water, but there's a hundred or so little ponds like this scattered around, plus the river. It'd take them a couple of days just to check them even with Sykes' hired army. We need to get moving though. The faster we get out of here, the less chance there is that someone will suspect anything's wrong. We've got probably an hour before they start wondering why we haven't shown up."

This time I sat in the back while Kelly joined Jeb in the front of the Cheviot. We rolled back to the road, turned left, and started off in a generally southeasterly direction, which seemed to me just the opposite of what we wanted. I decided not to point that out. My adrenaline high was beginning to fade and when the turbine finally reached full speed and Jeb settled back to drive, my curiosity asserted itself.

"All right, just where in the hell did you come from, Jeb? The last I heard, you bought yourself passage to New Orleans on a barge. How did you find us? Just what's going on anyway?"

"Whoa, son. Slow down a mite. As a matter of fact, I did make plans to get out of Memphis, but things got rearranged a bit. Ran into a fellow who made me an offer I just couldn't refuse. Told me he wanted me to help look after his pretty little daughter." He nodded to his right and Kelly bobbed her head and turned away, but not before I saw her smile.

"But how did you find us? And what were you doing with the Greenies?"

Jeb gave me a quick glance and his eyes twinkled with amusement. "Told you I was a hunter, didn't I? Your trail wasn't all that hard to follow. This fellow who hired me, he told me about that farmhouse, said Sykes had used it as a waystation a time or two before this and that I should start looking there. I rented myself this here steamcar and had a look-see, and what I found was a couple of dead bodies, and one not quite so dead. I persuaded the latter to tell me what had happened, and with only one road leading out of there, it would've been pretty hard not to figure out you'd gone this way, since I'd come up from the other side." He hesitated, and when he resumed his voice was less playful. "This fellow I talked to was shot up pretty bad and he died before he could tell me the whole story. I don't suppose you'd mind explaining to me just who it was that showed up and helped you get loose?"

"It was Dana, the steward from the *Warlock*." Kelly answered for me.

"Dana wasn't really a steward. He was an agent working for Adjudicator Beck, except that she wasn't an adjudicator at all…" The words spilled out of me in a flood.

"She was an agent working for the Prussians," Jeb interrupted. "Everyone knows that."

"Everyone but me, apparently. Anyway, he rescued us but before we could get away Colonel Sykes showed up with a bunch of Greenies. Sykes was working with Commander Davis, incidentally, but Davis got killed in the fight. Anyway, one of Sykes' men shot Dana dead; his body was lying out front when we left."

"Maybe not so dead. He wasn't lying there when I passed through, but then I didn't take the time to stop and look around. Might be he crawled into the bushes. Anyways, I followed along that road for a while and when I stopped for fuel, I bought some information to go along with it. Seems the old thief who runs the fuel stop saw two vehicles come by earlier that day, the first without stopping at all, the second carrying four men with no sense of humor. A while later I found a wrecked Drake with some interesting tracks around it, six sets going up the hill, four coming back down to where a second vehicle had been parked."

"Sykes and his friends," Kelly broke in. "I thought maybe he wouldn't have the stomach for a foot chase across rough terrain like that. He followed longer than I expected before quitting."

"The stakes were pretty high. He's got half the countryside in an uproar trying to find you. Anyway, I figured it made more sense to follow the car than to drag these weary old bones up that hillside, so I kept going along until I came to this ugly little backwater town."

"Lubbocks Mills," I said. "We almost got caught there."

"You were the ones in the tinker's wagon then. I actually saw you from a distance but it never occurred to me that you'd been so resourceful." He gave Kelly a quick glance. "When the alarm got raised, I was too far away to reach you. By the time I got past the Greenies, you'd already taken to the hills and Sykes was back on the road, trying to figure out what to do next."

"Didn't seem to take him too long.

Jeb nodded. "The colonel is a resourceful man, and he's got a lot of influence locally. His dealings with the Greenies go way back. I'd guess he called in some old debts because he went straight to the Green Toad Tavern and a few minutes later riders were heading off in every direction. I went inside and bought myself a drink, trying to eavesdrop, but Sykes was using a private room. Took me a while to put together what was happening from bits and pieces dropped by the other customers, and by figuring out what I would have done in his place. I hid the Cheviot and commandeered a horse and sash from a passing Greenie, but by the time I made my way back to where the action was, you'd already been captured. Most of the men weren't too happy about being pressed into service like this – Greenies don't like authority even when it's their own authority – so it wasn't hard to volunteer as a guard for you folks. Everything after that, you saw for yourselves."

"So what do we do now? We seem to be headed deeper into Greenie country rather than away from it."

Jeb's shoulders rose and fell. "Which means they won't be looking as hard in this direction as they will in the other. There's a place along here a little ways called Nesbit. Small town, dying like most of the others, not many people, but they're not inclined to help the Greenies. Just outside town's a little hostelry; the people who run it aren't curious and don't ask questions so long as you pay in hard currency and on time. I've stayed there a time or two in the past. We can hold up there and wait for the hoo-rah to die down while we catch our breath."

Now that the immediate physical threat was over, I found myself trembling with reaction, mildly nauseated by the whipsaw of emotion I had recently experienced. "I really should be getting on to New Orleans. I don't suppose they have a steamcar rental service or anything like that?" It sounded inane even to me, but Jeb answered me seriously.

"Not likely, son. Small town, Nesbit is, like I said, and I don't suppose it's gotten any bigger since the last time I was here. More likely the opposite. It's kind of a pretty place though, and there's still a few businesses operating. But even if you got one of these," he tapped the driving wheel, "you'd have to drive through a whole lot of Greenie country to get to where you're planning to go, and they're still going to be out looking for you, and madder than hell about it."

I settled back into my seat and crossed my arms. "It doesn't look like I have much choice, does it? And I still don't know what any of this is about." Truthfully, given the choice I'd head back home. I'd had enough adventure to last me a lifetime, and not even the lure of a very profitable venture held much attraction for me at the moment. Then another thought occurred to me.

"This man who hired you. Did you catch his name?"

"Can't say that he threw it out. But if he's this young lady's father, then I reckon his name must be Masters, same as hers."

But Sykes had called her Miss Marks and she was supposedly Malachi's daughter. If Jeb didn't know that, I wasn't going to enlighten him just now. Everyone had secrets except me and I was feeling jealous. On the other hand, Kelly had told me Marks wasn't the real family name, so maybe it really was Masters. I was so confused at the moment, I wasn't entirely sure what my own name was.

"What did he look like? This Masters guy, I mean." I glanced toward Kelly, but she didn't voice any objection to my question. In fact, she didn't seem to be paying any attention, just stared out the window at the passing scenery.

"As to that, I couldn't rightly tell you. Never laid eyes on him. We conducted all our business by messenger."

"Oh." I turned to stare out the window, feeling half convinced that Jeb was lying to me, or perhaps just telling partial truths. He wasn't about to satisfy my curiosity and I wasn't about to let on that I suspected him. He'd saved my skin, after all, so let him keep his secrets if that's what he wanted.

An hour later we passed a hand painted sign that told us we entering the Republic of Mississippi and leaving the Kennessee Free State behind. The federal government didn't recognize either entity and claimed authority over both, but for all practical matters, they were ambiguously autonomous. Mississippi had been the last member of the Union to surrender its independent sovereignty during the consolidation a century earlier, following its disastrous attempt to conquer the adjoining Zulu colony. The already faltering local economy had bottomed out, and almost half of a generation of young men were either killed outright or maimed. King Chaka had counterattacked, chartering ships from the Carib states to carry his warriors to the coastland. They had never penetrated very far inland, but they'd held the coastal regions for almost four years before the collective leadership had made a deal with the federals, surrendering their status as an independent nation in exchange for an expeditionary force that finally drove out or killed the last of Chaka's invasion force.

There were lingering effects, however. The closer one came to the Gulf, the darker the average complexion, a legacy of occupation that was never talked about but which could not be escaped. The regional economy had been faltering even before the occupation, and the agricultural depression fell over the southeast a couple of years later, wiping out all the beneficial effects of their new status. Now an arguably large and inarguably noisy portion of the population had decided that the marriage was ending in divorce. Kennessee, on the other hand, had never been an independent entity, had been created out of whole cloth by the Greenie insurgents who still effectively governed it despite its annexation by Congress.

Jeb drove with a practiced hand and I nodded off during part of the drive, still exhausted physically as well as emotionally. We stopped briefly at a small, nameless crossroads village where Jeb bought us some sandwiches that weren't half bad, sliced ham and cheese, krakenfish salad, and some fried pastries filled with nuts and fruit. Kelly and I stayed out of sight; even if word of our flight hadn't reached this far, the state of our clothing would have made us too memorable for safety. The bloodstains on my clothing were long since dried, but I could still smell a faint hint of copper.

A short while after that we saw a sign warning us that we were approaching Nesbit, and Jeb turned right at the next crossroad, a meandering but well maintained little lane barely wide enough for our vehicle that led to a complex of five buildings set in a picturesque grove of trees adjacent to a small lake. We stayed out of sight as Jeb made arrangements in the office, then drove us to one of the smaller, outlying structures, choosing a parking space that concealed the Cheviot from casual passersby. He had rented the first of five adjoining cabins, registering us as his grown children. There was no one in sight, so we walked quickly to the first cabin and slipped inside.

There were three rooms, one for sitting and eating with a small coal stove and an icebox in the back, one room for sleeping, and a third that offered a shower and toilet but no bathtub. There was a tiny dressing table in one corner of the bathroom, currently buried under a stack of relatively clean towels. A large armoire in serious need of refinishing stood in the front room, but there were no other closets. The bed consisted of a double bunk and I was wondering about the sleeping arrangements until Kelly pulled a trundlebed out from behind the armoire.

Jeb carefully checked the latches on the windows and the lock on the door; a place this remote probably wouldn't hire anyone to install magical safeguards. Apparently satisfied, he cautioned us to remain out of sight, then left the cabin, walking around the grounds with an aimless air that almost fooled me even though I knew it was assumed. After a few minutes had passed he returned, stuck his head in the door long enough to tell us to lock up and stay put while he found us something to eat. I heard the steamcar's turbine fire up and then move away a few seconds later. Kelly was in the bathroom with the door closed, trying to wash the dirt and blood out of her clothing. I badly wanted to shower and do the same, but I was also suddenly very weary, or perhaps I just ran out of emotional strength, because I collapsed into a chair and dozed off.

I didn't open my eyes for some time and when I did, Kelly was sitting across the table from me, her clothing dark with damp but relatively clean, her head down on top of her folded forearms.

"Are you all right?" My voice sounded foreign to me, thin and strained.

She raised her head and nodded without smiling. "Just tired. Trying to get myself back together."

"Do you think we're safe here?" I glanced toward the door, wondering how long it would be before Jeb returned. His presence made me feel much more secure.

"For the time being. If Sykes locates the crystal or finds out who really has it, he might lose interest in us. If he doesn't, he'll move heaven and earth to find us."

I'd completely forgotten about the crystal. "Any idea who made off with it?"

Her chair creaked a protest as pushed herself away from the table and sat back. "Yes and no. There are so many parties with an interest in this, I could name a dozen agents who might have gotten lucky. And that doesn't even include freelancers hoping to sell it to the highest bidder."

"Could your father have taken it back without telling you? He might not have had time to contact you."

She surprised me by nodding. "That's a possibility. He knew I was going to move it and might have been forced to act quickly to trump someone else's play. It wouldn't be the first time he didn't tell me everything." She pursed her lips and looked just slightly miffed. "I'll have to ask him about it when I get the chance."

"Any idea what we should do next? Jeb said we can't hide out here for long. And if your father doesn't have the crystal, are you going to try to get it back or just give up and go home?" If the latter, I thought I might offer to escort her. I was pretty certain that I'd enjoy her company if I could experience it without risking my life in the process.

But she shook her head. "My assignment hasn't changed. I'm supposed to help deliver the crystal to New…to wherever it's supposed to go. If that means recovering it first, then that's what I'll have to do."

"How? For all we know, your father is downriver somewhere with the crystal in his pocket. If he doesn't have it, then as you just said, there could be a dozen or more different suspects, in a hundred or more locations. The only person we can be pretty certain doesn't have it is Sykes, or at least he didn't have it until recently. That may have changed in the past few hours."

She gave me a wry grin, a weary one, admittedly, but still distinctly wry. "I never said it was going to be easy. And you're forgetting Jeb. He's a link between me and my father, maybe a closer one than you think. I'm pretty sure Jeb can get hold of him if he wants to, and Dad has a knack for knowing where things are and what people are up to."

"Well, I suppose you know your own business better than I possibly could."

She gave me a thoughtful look. "There's another important question we haven't answered. What are you going to do?"

I raised my eyebrows. "What do you mean? I'm going to New Orleans if there's any chance I might still keep my appointment. Otherwise, it's back home and no more adventures for the rest of my life, thank you very much."

"And how are you going to accomplish either of those goals?"

I must have been really tired because I didn't have any idea what she was talking about, and my ignorance must have shown plainly on my face.

"You can't just show up at some port town and book passage, after all. Sykes will have people watching every embarkation point. He has lots of eyes and ears, and I'm sure he'll pay handsomely for information. Someone will see you and identify you, even if you managed to use a false name. And he'll be after you whether you run for home or try to make it to New Orleans."

"But I have to do something," I protested. "None of this matters to me. Well, it matters, but not personally, you understand."

"I understand what you're saying, but I don't think you understand the situation. If you go home before this is all resolved, all you'll do is put your entire family in jeopardy. Sykes is a ruthless man, and he's not even the worst of the parties interested in retrieving the crystal."

"Are you telling me that I have to see this through to the end?" I already knew the answer, but I was hoping that she would let me off the hook somehow.

"I'm afraid so. We might be able to arrange protective custody for a while, if you like, at least once we reach some place under federal control. There's no reason why you should have to tag along with us."

"No thank you. No protective custody. My experience with the COPs has done nothing to improve my opinion of their competence, and I trust the military even less. I'd feel a lot safer with you and Jeb. You both seem to know a lot more about what's going on than you're telling me and I have a feeling that might come in pretty handy before this is over with."

I thought she was going to put me off, tell me that they couldn't afford to drag around an amateur and worry about keeping me out of trouble while they were trying to do their job, but she surprised me. "Why thank you, Jim. I feel quite flattered."

We were quiet for a moment and I started thinking about a shower. I was also beginning to wonder where Jeb was. He seemed to have been gone for a very long time.

"Do you do this often? Go off on missions with your father, I mean?"

Kelly shrugged her shoulders. "It's not this glamorous, most of the time." I winced at her characterization of our recent adventures, but held my peace. "Most of the time I just run errands, lay false trails, help sift through stolen documents, carry messages, things like that. This isn't a typical assignment; the spy business is pretty dull most of the time. Don't judge it by my books either; a lot of what happens is based on real events, but I take a lot of liberties with the details and leave out all the dull stuff. Makes a better story that way."

"How did you, or your father for that matter, ever get into this business?"

For a brief moment, Kelly's expression turned melancholy, but it quickly returned to its former neutrality. "It kind of runs in the family," she answered at last. "But I'd rather not talk about that just now."

I took my shower and discovered more scratches, bruises, scrapes, and contusions than I had expected. The warm – not hot – water felt wonderful and washed away a lot of the accumulated stiffness and fatigue of the day, although I still felt as though I could sleep straight around the clock if given the opportunity. I had washed my shirt and pants in the sink and hung them up to dry, but they were still too wet to wear so I fastened one towel around my waist and wrapped a second around my neck and shoulders after rubbing my hair reasonably dry.

The shadows were growing longer outside and a cool breeze sneaked in around the window caulking. I tensed when I heard the distinctive sound of a steamcar and joined Kelly in the outer room, where she was already peering out the window.

"It's all right. Jeb's back, bearing provisions, it looks like."

Indeed he was, carrying two large parcels. The first contained a variety of foods including canned meat, two loaves of bread still warm from the oven, assorted fruit, a large bar of cheese, bottles of beer and fruit juice, and some odds and ends. Kelly and I broke off chunks of bread and cheese and washed them down with beer, which wasn't cold enough but tasted wonderful anyway. Jeb watched us with some amusement, gnawing on an apple of his own. I had never realized how wonderful food could taste and I had to force myself to stop even when my stomach felt normal again.

"What's in the other bag?" Kelly gestured with a hand still clutched around a spear of bread.

"I thought you two might want to change into something a little less bloody. I had to guess at your size, Jim, but I think I came pretty close."

Kelly sorted out the clothing, snatched up a pair of dark jeans and a cotton shirt, and disappeared into the bathroom to change. Still wrapped in towels, I sat by the window, staring out into the night. Jeb excused himself and went walking in the grounds, disappearing into the shadows almost immediately. I couldn't see any sign of him or any other living being except for a swarm of fireflies hovering over a patch of shrubbery that badly needed to be trimmed back.

Kelly emerged, looking considerably more composed and rather fetching as well. I was suddenly acutely conscious of the rather informal state of my clothing, so I took a pair of jeans and a flannel shirt from the table and imitated her. Jeb had chosen well; the pants were just a trifle too short, but the waist was fine. I examined my sash critically but it was clear that the stains were not going to come out, and I reluctantly did without it. I made a mostly successful attempt to clean off my shoes in the sink – they were so caked with dirt that I feared they were a complete lost – and when I emerged a moment later my spirits were greatly improved.

Jeb was back, sitting across from Kelly. They both turned toward me and I sensed that they'd been carrying on a hushed conversation in my absence. I started to discard my ruined clothing into the trash bin by the door but Jeb forestalled me. "Nope, put them in here." He held out one of the cloth bags. "We'll take them with us when we leave or bury them somewhere out in the woods. No point in leaving anything behind that might provide a clue to those who are looking for us."

We spent the night quietly, me in the upper bunk, Jeb in the lower, Kelly on the trundle. It was the first real bed I'd been in for a while and I was so tired that I suspect Sykes and his men could have dismantled the cabin around me without my knowing anything about it. Even the thought that Kelly was sleeping little more than a double arm's length away couldn't keep my daydreams from becoming real ones.

Jeb and Kelly were both up and dressed when I woke in the morning. A glance at the angle of light through the window told me the sun had just come up. I sat up and discovered that I'd acquired a prize headache during the night, and that various muscles were stiff and sore. As we breakfasted on fruit and what remained of the bread and cheese, Jeb told us that it would be best if we remained out of sight while he went into town to reconnoiter. I was restless and impatient to be gone, but recognized that he was right and held my peace.

I found my eyes drifting toward Kelly more and more frequently, and she caught me at it at least once or twice. When I made an effort to start a conversation while we waited for Jeb to return, she responded so casually and briefly that I took the hint and kept to myself. I paced for a while, which seemed to annoy her, so I climbed up onto the bunk to sulk and nurse my aches and pains.

We had one bad moment when someone knocked at the door. Kelly gestured for me to stay out of sight while she answered, but it was only an attendant from the main building telling us that he would bring a block of ice for the icebox later in the morning. Kelly thanked him and closed the door, and that brief moment of tension cleared the atmosphere somewhat and we got along much better after that. By mutual agreement, we avoided talking about our adventures during the past few days and traded stories of our childhood. Assuming that she was telling me the truth, Kelly had grown up in New England, a small town just outside Managansett. Her mother had died while she was still a child, a subject from which she immediately shied away, and she'd been raised by her father, when he was around, and an unmarried aunt who'd taught her to ride horses, shoot pistols, and all manner of unfeminine pursuits. "Aunt Agatha is really something. She raises horses for a living and goes mountain climbing, skiing, and deep sea diving for recreation even now, and she's almost sixty."

Jeb returned at mid-day, came in while we were splitting a can of spiced ham and drinking the last of the beer. His eyes were thoughtful, his expression otherwise unreadable.

"Everyone in town knows that something's up, but there's more different stories floating around than there are ears to hear them. The Greenies are on the move all over, apparently, upsetting the local folks something fierce. The most popular opinions are that they're planning a major raid against one of the federal held towns, or they're looking for one of their own people who turned out to be an informer, or there's been some kind of split in their leadership and they're getting ready to fight among themselves. A party of twenty or so hijacked a trawler just north of here and forced it to take them across to the west bank. That's probably true, since the details jibe pretty consistently; they even mentioned the captain by name, Sam Clemens. If that's the case, it's the first time I ever heard of them operating in that part of the country. That'll get the feds moving, I reckon, if only to keep them from provoking an incident along the border with Changsha."

Kelly frowned. "So where does that leave us?"

"We don't dare travel any further south overland. Sykes can't have hired all these Greenies; if he had that much cash, he'd have retired from this business altogether. He's a mercenary, not looking for honor or glory, and his only loyalty is to himself. On the other hand, he'll take advantage of the mobilization by posting a reward and passing the word along to everyone who'll listen. He might also have hinted that it would be to the Greenies' benefit to intercept the crystal, which is true up to a point. It wouldn't help them directly, but they could sell it or trade it for weapons and ammunition."

Kelly shifted in her seat impatiently. "Like I said, where does that leave us?"

Jeb gave an exaggerated sigh, like a parent dealing with a fractious child. "I found a man who'll sell us a boat and trailer tomorrow. It's not a big one, but it'll hold the three of us without capsizing. I told him I wanted to do some fishing on Percy's Lake back the way we came and I think he believed me, but we'll have to be careful when we pick it up tomorrow so he doesn't suspect anything. I picked up some fishing gear while I was out."

This time I was the one who twisted impatiently in my seat. "Then we have to spend another night here?"

"I'm afraid so. But I brought back fresh groceries with me."

It didn't occur to me until later that Jeb had mentioned the crystal. I couldn't recall Kelly saying anything about it earlier, but she might have done so when I was getting dressed, or he might have learned about it from her mysterious father. It did occur to me that Jeb might also be playing a double or even triple game, that he might be playing up to Kelly and I just so that he could find out where the crystal was and snatch it for himself. If so, he was going to be disappointed, since neither of us knew what had happened to it. And then I wondered if that was true either. Was it possible that Kelly really did know where it was, but didn't trust me enough to admit it?

But I didn't have time to consider that possibility in detail, because no sooner had Jeb spoken than someone knocked on the door. He tensed immediately and his hand moved toward the pistol in his pocket, but Kelly stood up, speaking softly. "It's probably just the man delivering ice. He said he'd be by about now."

But when she cautiously opened the door, it wasn't the iceman standing there. It was an old friend who smiled, bowed slightly at the waist, and glanced at each of us in turn.

"May I come in?"

It was Dana, the false steward, apparently returned from the dead.

CHAPTER THIRTEEN

"But you're dead!" I blurted it out without thinking, but only after Dana was inside and the door had been closed. "We saw you die back at the farm!"

"Appearances can sometimes be deceiving." Dana was quite cheerful and, I noticed, quite healthy as well. His clothing was neat and clean, although I don't think it was the same he'd been wearing when he'd rescued us. My eyes kept moving to a spot directly above his heart, where I'd seen what I thought must be a fatal wound. I subsided into uneasy quiet, not understanding this at all. He was too articulate to be a zombie, demonstrated none of the pallor or other attributes of a vampire, but he had obviously been reanimated in some fashion. Even if he had somehow survived his injuries, he could not have made so complete a recovery without magical assistance. It made my skin crawl and I began to understand why there had been such a violent reaction to unbridled sorcery back during the time of the great pogroms.

"Your blood was all over me," I said softly. "That was no illusion. Illusions don't travel well, and my clothes are still stained with it."

"Ah yes. The blood. You have it here somewhere, don't you?"

I was too shocked to answer and even Kelly's face had grown pale. Jeb was the only one who seemed unaffected. He had calmly moved to a position that gave him a clear shot at the mysteriously revivified steward, and his hand hovered near his jacket pocket. Dana seemed unconcerned, looking around curiously before finally spotting the bag of discarded clothing standing in one corner.

"Ah, there it is. May I?"

He looked at each of us in turn, took our silence as acquiescence, then crossed the room directly to the sack, which he opened and emptied onto the table where we'd been sitting, spreading out shirts and pants. The dark, crusty stains looked uglier than ever.

"You might want to avert your eyes for a moment. Most people find this rather unpleasant to watch." Without waiting for us to comply, Dana began unbuttoning the shirt he wore, revealing a pasty white, completely hairless chest. I couldn't tear my eyes away, kept looking for some evidence of the pistol round that I knew had pierced his heart. There wasn't even a blemish.

What happened next was not only beyond anything in my previous experience, it wasn't even something that I'd heard of theoretically, from illusions or books or hearsay or anything else. Dana stood motionless, leaning forward over the table, while tiny flecks of dried blood slowly detached themselves from the clothing, shivered slightly as though disturbed by a passing breeze, then rose into the air and drifted directly toward the exposed skin where they stuck, then slowly disappeared, absorbed into his flesh. The entire process could not have taken more than a couple of minutes and when it was done, the discarded clothing was still torn and filthy, but the discolorations were only dirt and sweat and probably a little bit of my own blood. The large, blotchy stains were completely gone.

"That feels better." He rebuttoned his shirt, then swept the clothing back into the bag and set it aside. "A rather distressing sensation, I must admit, and some is lost forever, of course, though not enough to matter. It takes a long time to replace it, but I'm a very patient person."

I think my mouth must have opened, but I couldn't come up with anything to say. It was Jeb who finally responded.

"You're a homunculus."

Dana's eyebrows lifted in surprise. "Why, yes, as a matter of fact. You're much better informed than I would have expected for a frontiersman like yourself. Our existence and nature is not widely known; the secret has been closely held for many generations. It's unlikely that there are more than a score of us in all, and we're pretty well scattered throughout the world. I haven't encountered another of my kind in more than a century. I'm impressed by the depth of your knowledge, sir, but then I'd expect no less."

"Homunculus?" I recognized the word from somewhere but couldn't put my mental finger on it. "Isn't that some kind of artificial person, a machine of some sort?"

"You're thinking of homodroids, mechanical men," Kelly corrected me. "Homodroids don't bleed, or impersonate human beings, and they can only function to fulfill a very limited purpose. Francis Bacon built one as a chess opponent, for example, and Queen Victoria had one to help her dress because she couldn't stand being seen so intimately by a mortal. You'd never mistake one of them for a real person. A homunculus is different, a kind of demon, I think."

Dana frowned. "A demon? Please, there's no reason to be insulting. Demons are from an entirely different world and they can only visit ours briefly and by a kind of proxy. They're powerful but generally not very bright. I, on the other hand, am a simple son of this Earth, although I confess the details of my origin differ rather dramatically from yours."

"Homunculi have been outlawed for more than a century." Jeb moved forward a step and I noticed that his hand was now inside his jacket pocket rather than just hovering near it. "Their creation is illegal in every nation in the world, even among the Zulu."

"Not precisely true. The creation of homunculi has been outlawed universally, it is true, as an offense against nature, although personally I think that jealousy played a part. We are, after all, theoretically immortal. Those of us who already existed found ourselves in a kind of legal limbo, since most countries did not apply the laws retroactively to prohibit our continued existence. We're not people in the sense that you three are, but we're not exactly things either. Since we tend to be reclusive, there was no real incentive to hunt us down."

"Are you saying you're more than a century old?" Kelly sounded skeptical, but after my experiences of the past couple of days, I was ready to believe just about anything. My entire image of the world had been shaken and it was not difficult to accept a few more tremors.

"Quite a bit over, as a matter of fact. I was created by Sir William Shakespeare, who planned an entire company of androgynous performers for his theater company, after having particular difficulty with his human players during the production of *Love's Labour Reclaimed*. Alas, he had completed only two of us when Parliament quietly outlawed the practice, and William himself died a short while later, although he did live long enough to see my performance in *Hamlet's Ghost*, which was quite outstanding if I do say so myself."

"Androgynous?" I'd never heard the word before.

"Yes, you know, both sexes at the same time, or neither actually. Wait, I'll show you."

Dana dropped his head and wrapped both arms around his face, covering it completely. There was a faint sound, like a distant wind blowing across a beach, and I recoiled when I saw that his hair was growing visibly longer with each passing second, the strands moving like slender worms. A full minute passed before he raised his head, revealing a familiar but subtly altered face. He had become a she, or perhaps I should say that it took on a feminine appearance. The lips were full, eyes heavily lidded, the structure of the face altered in very subtle ways. The hair had stopped growing when it reached the shoulders and his posture and musculature had changed, grown softer and less obvious. The new Dana even had a remarkably voluptuous figure, although his clothing was unaltered. The face was technically quite beautiful, but it was a characterless beauty like that of a sculpture rather than of a living being.

"I was ravishing as Desdemona. I received several marriage proposals following each performance, some of them quite tempting. I could have been Lady Daniela at least twice. I am fully functional sexually although barren, of course." Even the voice had changed, rising in pitch. "But I prefer the male form. No offense, Miss Masters, but it's much more practical. Men have greater freedom of movement, less chance of being remembered when it's desirable to leave no impressions behind."

"I've never felt at a disadvantage." Her voice was nakedly unfriendly and when I glanced in her direction, I noticed how stiffly she sat, how closely she was watching our unwelcome visitor.

Dana began to revert to his original form, without lowering his head this time. His features began to coarsen, his hair retreated into his scalp, and his body swelled and sank beneath his clothing. I found the sight so unsettling that I deliberately looked away until I was certain the transformation had ended.

Only Jeb seemed unaffected. "You've told us how you were born. Now tell us how you will die."

"I'm sorry. What was that question again?"

"You heard me the first time." Jeb's voice was suddenly deeper, commanding. "How will you die?"

Dana stared at him sullenly for a few seconds, his smile fading away, but it returned when he finally answered. "Very astute, Mr. Walker. You are indeed remarkably well informed. I will be fatally wounded by a hippogriff, and since the last few members of that species are all male and all captive, there's a very good chance that I will survive their extinction during this cycle of the universe and live until the species is reborn millennia from now." His smile became a smirk. "I will almost certainly outlive all of you."

Kelly looked just as confused as I felt, but Jeb took pity and enlightened us. "All homunculi know the specific manner of their death from the moment of their creation. They're bounded creatures with specific beginnings and endings. It is the one thing about which they cannot lie, the one answer they must always provide when asked, the only real control over their existence. It was a natural safeguard, a counterbalance against their immortality. They are also incapable of employing magic. Even charms prepared by others are usually ineffective if the homunculus itself employs them."

Dana nodded. "A shortcoming I find annoyingly inconvenient at times, although immortality is an adequate compensation."

"But you died at the farm," I protested. "You died in my arms."

"In a manner of speaking. We do become inactive when badly damaged, in order to hasten the repairs. I was trapped in a burning villa outside of Rome once and reduced to ashes. It took me almost a month to reconstitute enough of my body to leave the vicinity, and I wasn't fully restored until another year had passed. Fortunately, I don't experience pain in the same way as mortals; it's more like a sense of wrongness than an actual physical sensation. A pistol shot is easily cured, even through the heart. I lay there for almost an hour before the reconstruction was complete, and by then you were all long gone. I don't resent being abandoned, of course; I would have done the same thing in your place."

"You don't feel pain, but neither do you feel pity, or love, or anger, or any other emotion," Jeb added. "Not even hatred."

My head was spinning. I accepted the existence of supernatural entities, of course, although I had never seen one other than the time I had tickets to the Fairy Ballet. They weren't human but they were all mortal, even vampires, although they lived far longer than ordinary, unaltered humans. The notion that Dana could literally continue to survive until time caught up to its own tail was hard to accept. "You're saying that if we chopped you up into little pieces, you'd grow back?"

"Essentially, yes, that's the case. I'm a single, integral elemental, you know, forged from one drop of human blood, virgin blood as a matter of fact.. You might be surprised to discover how long it took Sir William to find a virgin willing to provide the raw material. The blood has to be collected from a particular part of the anatomy, you see."

"And that's how you found us. The blood called to you." Jeb's hand was visible again, but it still hovered near his pistol.

"Correct again. I can't really describe the sensation to you, I'm afraid, but I know in a general sense where the various parts of my body are at all times, even when we're quite far apart. There are traces of my blood running through the drains of this building and out into the brook. If I had time to wait, I could sit in this room and they would slowly reverse course and come back to me. As it is, I'm afraid I'll have to delay the reunion. The connection doesn't fade with the passage of time, and as I've already told you, I have all the time I could possibly want."

"All right," said Jeb. "We know how you found us. Now tell us why. What's your interest in our business?"

"I'm simply trying to perform the job for which I've been hired. Human or not, I do enjoy the creature comforts, good food, luxurious surroundings. I've developed quite sophisticated tastes and some of them are rather expensive indulgences. My immediate employer, alas, is no longer among the living and I'm afraid there's no possibility of reconstituting her. But I do try to honor my contracts, particularly when the rewards are so high."

"He was working for Beck," I interposed. "She told me she'd been hired to ensure that the crystal reached its intended destination."

"But Beck was working for the Prussians," Kelly objected.

"Which doesn't mean that we have to be at cross purposes." Dana made a soothing gesture. "Don't be concerned, Miss Masters. I'm not your enemy or even your rival. The Prussian government has decided that it is in their best interests in the long term if the crystal reaches its intended recipient. We're allies, at least in this matter. I'm here to help you."

"Who says we need your help?" Kelly stood up and began pacing slowly around the room, but her eyes never left Dana.

"You certainly needed it back at the farm." Dana crossed his arms smugly and sat back in his chair.

"Which doesn't mean we need you now." Jeb pulled out a chair and sat down, his voice hard but his body relaxed.

"Come now, sir. You three are hiding in a fleabag cabin in the middle of Greenie country with limited options, no allies, surrounded by your enemies. Even if you could get a message to a military post, the relief column would have to ride through territory swarming with aroused Greenies, and even if they reached you, there'd be no guarantee that you'd be safe. There are Greenie agents secreted among the federals, as I'm sure you know. Commander Davis was, after all, a highly respected officer. Even if we assume a successful rescue, word of your identities and whereabouts would almost certainly spread, making it virtually impossible for you to continue your mission."

Jeb nodded. "That's a fair assessment, although we have a few resources you've overlooked. Let's say that provisionally we agree to accept your help. I assume in return you'd like some form of acknowledgment of your assistance?"

"A quiet word to the Prussian embassy regarding my invaluable help would be deeply appreciated."

"I think that could be managed. We'll trust you, but only up to a point. No offense meant."

"None taken."

"I have a boat, or will have in the morning. It's not very big, but four will fit about as well as three. It'll be on a trailer and we're supposed to be taking it out to fish past Hiram's Hill, but we'll actually loop around and head for a sheltered spot down on the river coast. We won't be able to travel far on the river, because they'll be watching traffic there pretty closely, but we can cross to the opposite bank, hide the boat, and find land transport there."

"Didn't you tell us that the Greenies were operating on both sides of the river now?" I ventured.

"There's about twenty of them there and at least three or four hundred around here, with thousands more to the south of us. Which odds look more appealing to you?"

My three companions began discussing alternate routes on the west side of the Mississippi, and having nothing to contribute I quickly lost interest. Although Jeb seemed to have accepted Dana as one of us, it was clear that Kelly still felt uneasy. I wasn't sure how I felt. Objectively, everything he had done seemed to have benefited us, and his story was convincing, but I hadn't adjusted to the revelations about his true nature, which made me uneasy.

To my relief, Dana announced that he would not be spending the night with us. He left the cabin a few minutes later, promising to be back before sun up, barely missing the iceman who belatedly arrived with a block of ice wrapped in a heat retarding spell. It seemed to take him an inordinate amount of time to get it properly positioned in the icebox, but eventually he left.

When we were finally alone, Kelly rounded on Jeb, her eyes flashing. "I don't trust him, not for a moment."

Jeb raised one eyebrow. "The iceman? He seemed innocuous enough."

She stamped her foot. "You know who I mean! Dana. Isn't there something we can do to get rid of him?"

"Well, he did rescue the two of you from Sykes. And for the moment at least it appears that we have common interests. There aren't so many potential allies waiting in the wings that we can afford to turn up our noses when one walks in the door."

"I know that. But I still don't trust him."

"Nor do I, but he might be helpful, and I'd rather know where he is than where he isn't." Something struck me as odd, but it was a while before I realized that it was Jeb. His rustic accent had been slipping away steadily and he now sounded more forceful and sophisticated.

"He makes my skin crawl," Kelly continued. "There's something wrong about him. I can't explain it exactly but I know he's trouble."

"Then we'll deal with it, but not before we have to."

I didn't say anything but I felt sympathetic. I couldn't put my finger on it, but in addition to the fact that Dana just made me uneasy in general, I had the strangest feeling that I was forgetting something, or overlooking something very important connected to him. Something had happened while Dana was with us, either on the boat or at the farm, something that had left a mark deep in my memory, too deep to be easily recalled.

The balance of the day was a delicate, prolonged torture. The forced inactivity was getting on my nerves, and even the fact that

Kelly was sharing my informal imprisonment didn't compensate for the fact that I dared not go outside, risk being seen and recognized. Kelly was almost as jittery as I, but Jeb seemed completely at ease and even took a nap during the afternoon, then left for another trip into town, taking our discarded clothing with him to be buried somewhere along the way.

I tried to take a nap but I was too restless so I paced instead. That seemed to irritate Kelly, although she didn't say anything, and I stopped, but found myself up and walking again after a few minutes. Jeb came back well after darkness had fallen, carrying more food but no useful information other than that the search parties were still out, although the most popular rumor now was the federal agents had been identified within the ranks of the Greenies and that the traitors were in hiding.

I slept uneasily that night, tossing and turning, waking in a cold sweat from nightmares I couldn't remember.

Dana showed up just a few minutes after we got up the following morning and I had the strangest feeling that he hadn't really gone away at all, that he'd been lurking outside somewhere on business of his own, waiting for the appropriate time to reappear. Did homunculi even sleep? I had no idea. There were a number of questions I wanted to ask but I wasn't going to pose them to Dana. I made a mental note to ask Jeb some time when our new ally wasn't around.

His theoretical immortality didn't seem quite as daunting today. He might not die but he could certainly be incapacitated. He could be shot or burned or cut to pieces and would be out of action until he had time to reconstitute himself. He could be restrained or imprisoned, the way rogue vampires were incarcerated despite their superhuman strength. I suppose if he was convicted of a capital crime, a court could order that he be fed to a hippogriff.

We ate most of the remaining food and took the rest with us. Dana rode up front with Jeb while Kelly and I sat in the rear. Jeb had arranged to pick up the boat and trailer in a small hamlet just outside of Nesbit, a place called Stone's Banks, but he stopped short when we reached a woodlot so that Kelly and I could conceal ourselves while he and Dana made the pickup. We waited, swatting mosquitoes. Traffic was surprisingly heavy. A dozen horseback riders drifted past in twos and threes, a half dozen carriages, one of them drawn by centaurs, and even a couple of steamcars, though neither of them was the same model as Sykes was driving.

Kelly seemed preoccupied, almost brooding. I wasn't sure whether it was better to leave her alone or try talking, so I remained silent for a while. That felt even more awkward, so I searched for a way to open a conversation. "Are you worried about your father?"

She glanced at me with an odd expression, as though she hadn't understood the question. "What? Dad? No, not particularly. He's pretty good at taking care of himself. It's a family trait."

"You look concerned."

"I suppose I do. She sighed, gave me the briefest possible smile, then turned to look back at the currently empty road. "We've been in this kind of situation before, but the stakes have never been this high. It's more than just a dangerous game this time much more. If that crystal doesn't get into the right hands, thousands of people may die, tens of thousands."

That gave me pause. "What is this all about, Kelly? What was recorded on that crystal?"

Her smile lasted a tiny bit longer this time, but she shook her head. "You'll have to ask my father that. He might even tell you."

Jeb and Dana returned after slightly more than hour. A two wheeled trailer had been attached to the rear of the steamcar, and on it was mounted what appeared to me to be a perilously small boat in a questionable state of repair. There was a single slender mast and a furled sail, dismounted and lashed along one side at the moment, rudder and oars attached opposite. It was badly in need of fresh paint, but I couldn't see any obvious sprained boards or gaps in the seams.

We backtracked to the first main intersection, where Jeb surprised me by turning south rather than west toward the river. He'd had the fuel and water tanks topped up the previous evening and it was well that he did because we didn't pass a single fuel stop for the next two hours. The road began to turn southeast and improved in quality, and we also started seeing more signs for towns and hamlets. I began to breathe easier as we drew closer to the river because we were less likely to run into Greenies here, at least any obvious patrols. The COPs and the military contested this area with the anarchists and still controlled virtually all of the riverside communities.

We stopped for lunch at a roadside diner that obviously catered to travelers. Jeb bought the food and brought it out to the car, just to be on the safe side. Dana declined to eat anything and I wondered what powered his body if it wasn't food. Then we were on the road again, moving in traffic that grew so heavy we were forced to slow down to little more than a walking pace.

Jeb turned off the main road just outside a town named Friar's Point. We followed a winding dirt track that clearly wasn't meant for steam powered traffic, turning off onto an even narrower one toward Polson's Landing. It was obvious that the river was close; I could almost smell it even before it finally became visible through a gap in the trees. We were forced to slow to barely more than a walk but eventually we reached an open glade with a wide, gradual beach bracketed by a pair of wooden shacks. A pipestem thin man with a wispy beard walked out to meet the car.

"Wait," Jeb cautioned us as he killed the turbine and stepped outside to negotiate terms. They spoke with some animation, the thin man waving his arms and gesticulating, Jeb more restrained. They were obviously arguing.

"What's going on?" I whispered.

"They're trying to settle on a price for use of the slip and parking."

I laughed under my breath. "What, are we on a budget?"

She shook her head. "If we pay his asking price, he'll be talking about the bunch of suckers who showed up at his place to everyone he knows. Word might get back to the wrong people that a party of boaters was in too much of a hurry to complain about being gouged."

"Oh. Right."

The negotiations ended, money passed from one hand to another, and the thin man turned away, no longer interested. He made no move to assist us in positioning the trailer, lowering the boat, assembling the mast and rudder, or the actual launching, but we managed it all with minimal trouble and splashing around. The sun was warm and there was a cool breeze, so our water soaked clothing dried quickly once we were aboard and out from under the trees. It wasn't as tight a fit as I expected, fortunately, but the boat was lower in the water than I liked.

The breeze barely filled the sail and was coming from the wrong direction so Dana and I worked the oars while Jeb managed the rudder. Dana never seemed to grow tired, but my arms and shoulders were aching and I was feeling distinctly inferior, a situation aggravated when Kelly offered to take my place for a while. I declined but eventually flagged so badly that I had to give in when she asked a second time.

The current was against us so our progress was slow and incremental. I took over again after a while. The sun was dropping and we saw lights breaking up the dusk back the way we had come. They narrowed to pinpricks and then winked out and we still hadn't caught sight of the opposite shore.

"All right, ship your oars." It was almost the first time Jeb had spoken since we'd completed the launch. Dana complied immediately but I was so immersed in the routine that I made another couple of half strokes before I realized what he'd said. "We're in the main current," he explained. "Let's drift for a while. It should carry us pretty close to the far bank."

The sky had been clouding over when we'd left but it was clearing now, and a three quarter moon provided enough light for us to see one another. Kelly was sitting in the bow, staring forward into the darkness, with Jeb at the stern. Dana sat at ease, leaning against the oarlock, but I slid off the seat and stretched out my cramped limbs.

"How long?" I asked.

"Hard to say. A couple of hours probably. We'll drift a considerable way down river, but that's all to the good."

Jeb hadn't been particularly forthcoming about what we would do once we reached the west bank, but I didn't want to ask while Dana was around. I was also a bit concerned that he might admit that he was improvising as we went along, which would certainly have shaken my confidence. "Are we going to meet up with Malachi Marks?"

Dana laughed, a short, ugly sound. "That'd be a neat trick."

I already distrusted him, and his tone irritated me. "For your information," I said sarcastically and perhaps unwisely, "Kelly is Malachi Marks' daughter."

He shrugged. "So I've been told. I suppose it's true, though I don't see much family resemblance."

"You've met Marks then?" I sat up straighter.

"Of course I have. He's sitting right there next to you."

I hope that the darkness concealed the expression on my face. I felt as though I'd been struck from behind with a shovel. I slowly turned my head toward Jeb Walker. Or was he Jeb Walker?

"That's right," he admitted in slow, carefully pronounced syllables. "I have been known to use that name from time to time."

CHAPTER FOURTEEN

I'd had a few major surprises in my life, most of them in the span of a those last few days, but I think that was the first that actually hit me so hard that for a few seconds I couldn't formulate a meaningful thought. I glanced back and forth between Kelly and Jeb, waiting for a denial or an explanation, but they didn't even seem particularly surprised that Dana knew their secret.

"I think that I am very confused," I finally admitted.

"You probably would have figured it out on your own." Kelly was trying not to sound patronizing, but she was only partially successful. "We haven't had time to obscure the trail as well as in the past."

The paralysis slowly lifted from my mind. "I don't suppose you'd care to tell me how much of what you've told me is true? Have I understood anything of what has been going on these past few days?"

Father and daughter exchanged glances before she answered. "Everything else is pretty much what you've been told. The crystal really exists and until two nights ago I had no idea who had removed it from my room. There hasn't been an opportunity for us to compare notes for a while. Things have been happening too quickly."

I nodded and turned to Jeb. "You recovered the crystal, I take it. Do you have it with you now?"

Slowly he shook his head. "I don't have it, but I know where it is. It'll be safe there until we go and collect it."

I noticed that he made no effort to tell me the details, and I didn't bother to ask for information that wouldn't be forthcoming. "I don't suppose you could tell me what's so important about what it contains?" I was exasperated and a bit sulky and made no effort to hide my feelings. I had, after all, been threatened, kidnapped, diverted from my own business, lied to, inconvenienced, and placed in repeated and continuing danger of my life because of whatever information was contained in the elusive crystal, and I suddenly had the feeling that everyone in the world – or at least everyone else in the boat – knew much more about what was going on than I did.

To my surprise, it was Dana who answered. "It is the record of a meeting between Governor Ling of Changsha and a highly regarded emissary from the British Empire, and the subject was their scheme for partitioning the Federation."

I was still watching Jeb. His head moved, just perceptibly, and his eyes briefly betrayed surprise. "That's an interesting speculation," he said guardedly.

Dana smirked. "It's more than speculation, Mr. Marks. You're not the only competent agent on this mission. Beck was working for the Prussians, remember? Their intelligence service is second to none. They have a highly placed source within the most intimate circles of the British court, and no, I don't know who it is although I have it narrowed down to three people. I'm not sure how much her superiors knew, but they passed on enough that Beck was able to extrapolate, and she had some unofficial sources of her own. Changsha troop movements are hard to conceal and the rationale for some of their recent reorganization was pretty flimsy. We had a pretty good idea of the nature of the consultations even before you boarded the *Warlock*. Without proof, the Federation can't approach the Emperor and request that he reel in his subordinate, so the recording becomes the only real proof of Ling's treachery."

"I'm lost again," I admitted. "The British couldn't field a large enough army to seriously threaten the Federation, could they? Particularly with Toronto in open rebellion. I know the Emperor is still in a huff about that damned play, but it's an open secret that the frosty official relations are just to appease his overbearing wife. They don't reflect the true relationship between the Empire and the Federation, and he's too content with the status quo to start a war over trivia. For that matter, the border war with the Russians is still simmering, and they present a much more realistic threat."

"True all around," Jeb replied agreeably. "The Emperor is in fact completely unaware of the plot, officially at least. It's Governor Ling we have to worry about, an ambitious, ruthless, and quite unscrupulous man. He may be hoping to improve his standing with the Emperor at our expense or he may be planning to build a powerbase that will make him virtually independent."

"But the governor is only an arm of the empire. He has limited autonomy and certainly isn't empowered to conduct his own foreign policy."

"Traditionally that's been true, and the Empire is heavy on tradition. But it's not impossible that Emperor Deng and Ling cooked this up between themselves. If all goes well, then their partnership becomes public knowledge. If there's a disaster, Ling takes the fall for disobeying orders. On the other hand, Deng may really be ignorant of what's going on. Ling Hwa is a sophisticated man and a power unto himself, and he may have decided that with the Empire facing more pressing problems in Asia and Europe, he may be in a position to act on his own behalf."

"Ling sees himself as a future emperor," interposed Dana. "He'd prefer to succeed Deng but an expanded Changsha would be almost as good."

Jeb made a noncommittal sound. "Deng isn't entirely secure on the throne, for that matter. He survives only because he has great skill in manipulating the shifting alliances among his warlords and generals. If the Russian government collapses and that threat recedes, the Chinese would quite possibly turn their eyes inward. It would not surprise me in that event if Deng were to die accidentally or of some mysterious illness. Open rebellion or assassination would, of course, be unseemly."

"Which is why the Prussians have been unable to convince Deng to commit to a military alliance," added Kelly. "Their combined strength would certainly force the Russians to draw in their forces defensively. It is to Deng's advantage to maintain the status quo. It would be extremely risky for him to get entangled in any scheme of expansion on this side of the ocean unless it was a quick and obvious victory, so Ling has been given a relatively free hand. Deng can take credit for his successes and Ling takes the blame for his failures."

I shook my head, bewildered. "I thought the Changsha had all they could do just to hold the tribes in check."

Jeb snorted. "There hasn't been any real fighting down that way in more than a year, son. Ling negotiated with the Council of Chiefs a while back and promised them autonomy in return for their neutrality if hostilities started with the Federation. Except for a few hotheaded raiders, the border areas are peaceful. The Chiefs are being naïve, of course; if the Federation falls, Ling will turn on them at the first opportunity. You would have thought their experiences during the Federation's expansion would have taught them better than to believe in treaties."

"And don't underestimate the British," added Kelly. "Most of the navy stayed loyal to the throne. They could blockade the East Coast and tie up our own ships indefinitely. Toronto is a minor distraction they could deal with later, and the present troubles justify their positioning of a large ground force near the border. We think Toronto is a genuine rebel, but we've misjudged people in the past."

My mind was racing. It didn't seem possible. Half the population of the continent lived within the Federation, and one of the few things Congress agreed upon was maintaining the military as a deterrent to aggressors. "It still seems like an awfully big gamble."

"Not as big as you might think." Dana stirred from his seat. "The Federation isn't nearly as united as it was a century ago. Why do you think Sykes is getting so much help from the Greenies? Changsha and the British both have agents in Green territory, and I'd be very surprised if they hadn't been offered their own rump state in return for a coordinated uprising at the most opportune time. The Federals would have to move troops from the border to deal with the rebels, and if the timing was right, the Changsha could invade while everything was in flux. They'd hold the east bank of the Mississippi within days, if not hours."

I turned to Jeb, hoping he'd argue the point, but he was nodding. "The British have been very actively courting the Greens. Sykes was working with the late, unlamented Commander Davis, who served as the chief British negotiator. Davis promised them the city of New Orleans and formal recognition in return for their cooperation, but the treaty would be abrogated on some pretext or other once the shooting was over, probably by claiming Davis acted without official authority. And there are also some malcontents among the Federation military whose frustration with the vagaries of Congress might make them susceptible to temptation. Remember George Washington's perfidy during the Revolution. A mutiny behind the lines would throw any defensive effort into chaos."

"All right," I said at last. "Then why is this all being kept secret? Why not make the recordings public?"

"There's still time to move deliberately," Jeb reassured me, "and there's more to be gained by using the information we hold to entice traitors and spies into revealing themselves. A public scandal might well force the Emperor to back Ling and precipitate exactly what we're trying to avoid. No specific time frame was set at the meeting, but the parties will probably move in the spring. Ling needs more time to relocate his forces and ensure that they have the means to hold onto the territory they seize, and he can't be too abrupt without alerting the Federation that something is in the works. The British are already prepared on land with a massive troop buildup in the Toronto area, supposedly to contain the rebellion, but their naval forces are still dispersed around the world and will need to be realigned. We don't have much leverage with them directly and Congress is still dragging its feet about accepting Toronto as an ally. The key for us is the Emperor. We must convince him to move against Ling, either in assumed outrage or to prevent being exposed."

"And the crystal is key to all this?"

Jeb nodded. "He won't take our words for it without proof, even if he believes us. It would be too great a loss of face to admit he was convinced of the treachery of his most favored governor by an occidental. But if we can show him the recording, he will be forced to act regardless of whether or not he knows of the plot. And without Changsha, the British will not risk war."

It seemed quite reasonable, in an impossibly convoluted sort of way, and I sighed and shook my head, acknowledging the weight of their arguments as well as my own frustration. "So what do we do once we're ashore?"

"We recover the crystal and complete the mission, or at least Kelly and I do. We never intended to get you involved in this, but until it's over, Sykes is going to consider you an enemy." Jeb pointedly did not mention Dana, and I still wasn't certain of his status. Although he seemed to have been adopted into our company, I had a very strong feeling that Jeb didn't trust him. I was remembering my own suspicions when Dana spoke up.

"Under the circumstances, is it wise that only one of us knows the crystal's present whereabouts?"

On the surface, his question seemed completely reasonable, but I felt my hackles rise. There was something in his tone and manner that disturbed me, and I refused to believe that it was entirely subjective, or that Kelly and Jeb didn't share my misgivings. No matter how potentially usefully he might be as an ally, and despite the debt we owed him for our rescue back at the farm, I wished that we could part ways permanently with the homunculus.

"Never said I was the only one who knew where it was," Jeb replied casually. I assumed he meant Kelly. She had claimed ignorance, but even if she was telling the truth at the time, they might have had a chance to compare notes in private during the past day. Dana waited for him to elaborate, but Jeb turned his head away and squinted, staring into the night.

Conversation lapsed for a while as we slowly made our way across the river. In the darkness, far enough from both shores that no lights were visible, I had the strangest feeling that we were all alone in the universe, motionless on a limitless body of water, our progress merely an illusion. Kelly had turned away with her head bent forward, and I thought she might be dozing. Jeb relieved me on the oars and I moved to the stern of the boat, suddenly feeling a bit chilled by the damp night air. I wrapped my arms around myself and hunkered down, and if I didn't actually sleep, at least I slipped into some semi-conscious state where time passed at a different rate.

It was still pitch black when l was roused by the thump of something heavy striking the side of the boat.

"Give us a hand with this, Jim."

There were faint speckles of light in the distance, barely discernible, but probably located on the west bank. The clouds had begun to thin and a few stars were visible, but the moon was still swathed in a gray shroud. Kelly and Dana were leaning over the starboard side, struggling to disentangle us from what turned out to be the roots of an enormous tree which had broken loose from shore and gone adrift. Jeb worked the oars to provide some tension while the three of us poked and prodded and pushed. After several frustrating minutes we pulled free only to have a playful current immediately throw us back into the tree's dangerous embrace, but it was easier to disengage this time and we finally drew away, Jeb and Dana paddling furiously until we were far enough out of the way to avoid yet another collision.

Kelly promptly went back to sleep but I was restless again and replaced Jeb at the oars. Dana never slept, but he was clearly tiring and I had no trouble matching him stroke for stroke. He hadn't said anything for a while and I was getting bored so I asked Jeb how he'd managed to acquire the crystal in the first place, although I didn't really expect an answer. So naturally he surprised me by telling us the whole story.

"I'd like to say it was a well planned operation, but there was as much luck as skill involved. There had been rumors coming out of Daipeng for weeks that something big was happening, heavy security precautions, some of Ling's personal staff casting privacy spells and hiring local talent. I went down as part of a trade delegation – a legitimate one in fact – and did some poking around. The Isthmus might be physically separated from the rest of Changsha, but it's as secure as the regional capital. I hadn't been there more than a day or two before I knew something was up. There were too many troops, too many magic workers. The Mayan insurgents are troublesome but they haven't been capable of mounting a serious attack in more than a generation."

The moon had come out and I could see Jeb's face clearly. He looked older and more tired than I remembered and I turned my eyes away, uncomfortable.

"The first thing I figured was that Ling was going to move against the Canal. The Bolivarians are technically co-administrators, but if it ever came to a shooting war, they'd be sent packing pretty quick. Even the Carib States fought them to a draw a few years back. Anyway, it wouldn't do the Federation any good if Ling had exclusive control of the Canal. He could raise the tariffs or close off access to our shipping on some pretext and Congress wouldn't do more than posture about it. It wouldn't weaken us much militarily, since Ling's navy is no match for ours even if he somehow managed to get them all through the Canal, but the commercial damage would be substantial."

"The Chinese don't understand naval combat." Dana interrupted without turning his head in our direction. "The purpose of war is to seize territory and their greatest strength has always been in numbers. If the Federation had direct access to the Pacific, they could choke off the Empire's foreign trade within months."

Jeb acknowledged the point with a nod Dana could not possibly have seen. "Late one evening I went for a walk around the Orchid Palace, not really expecting to find anything. If Ling was plotting any kind of military adventure, he might have left some evidence hidden inside its formidable security system, and if there was a weak spot there I thought I might be able to find it. Hadn't half started the job when a large party arrived, large enough to set off a little alarm in my head, coming at that strange hour. I found a spot where I could watch them as they crossed the security perimeter and recognized Lord Chamberlain Jagger among the arrivals. Jagger was supposed to be recovering from an illness at his private estate in Labrador, so I knew right away that I'd stumbled into something important."

"Jagger was inside for less than an hour, and I had time to find myself a better vantage point before they came out. Jagger was brusque with his guard and they left quickly. I thought about following them, but I was more interested in finding out who else was in the Palace, so I waited around. We found out later that Jagger was staying with the head of the British Trade Mission, but his presence was very carefully concealed and even his staff thought that Jagger was an exiled mercantilist trying to negotiate concessions with Changsha. I was sitting in a tree, about ready to call it a night, when I saw a tiny puff of fire on one of the balconies, the one adjoining the royal suite. Only Ling would have the audacity to use the royal suite. He was smoking opium and, presumably, contemplating the empire he hopes to build."

I glanced toward shore. The lights were twinkling less and seemed more numerous, although they were still widely separated. Isolated homesteads then, rather than a city or even a town. I wondered if Jeb had any idea where we were, and how we would proceed once we were on land again, but I didn't ask. He was still talking.

He didn't provide the man's name, but there was a Federation spy among the Palace staff, a man recruited coercively because of a past indiscretion. Jeb applied pressure and received a half hearted promise. Fortunately, there was still time to make plans. If King Winston had come in person, negotiations might well have started in earnest on the following day, but Ling was a traditionalist. The disparity in rank between himself and Jagger was such that the Briton would be allowed to cool his heels for at least three days before anything substantive took place. The Orchid Palace included four identically laid out conference chambers, one each in silver, gold, pearl, and bamboo, but there was no way for Jeb to predict which one would be chosen. He already had a blank recording crystal, but only the one, and the local gandalfs were all likely in the pay of Changsha, or if not would still be unlikely to cross him.

There were at least five archmages in the Palace, which rivaled the magical power available to the Emperor or even King Chaka of the Zulus. Jeb's spy didn't know what safeguards they were planning, but his description of their preparations indicated they were going to erect a Sphere of Rejection, which would create a temporary impenetrable barrier around a limited area. No known weapon, listening device, or even magical spell could pass through its perimeter in either direction while it was in place. Jagger was also accompanied by a merlin, a formidable looking woman named Thatcher, but it seemed likely her job was to reassure Jagger that they were adequately protected rather than to add any wards of her own.

"I had to guess which chamber they would use and plant the crystal before the wards went up but after the merlins had made their sweep. So I asked our mole to find out which ceremonial robe had been prepared for Ling to wear that day. It was decorated with pearl, so I chose the corresponding chamber and my agent concealed the crystal, as planned, just as the Sphere was being conjured.

"Once they'd finished their business, neither Jagger nor Ling stayed around long, and the wards faded away a few hours later. The palace guard was relaxing after a long stint at full alert and it wasn't hard to get inside and recover the crystal. Unfortunately, my contact had a sudden attack of conscience and committed suicide, and his superiors were sufficiently suspicious to order a post mortem mind probe. The memories fade pretty quickly, but not fast enough. I knew they'd have peepers watching for me on all the escape routes back to the Federation, so I stole a boat and sailed up the coast until I reached New Peiping, then joined a wagon caravan headed east."

The lights on the distant shore were brighter now, but even more widely separated and I realized we must be drawing close. The indefatigable Dana and I were paired for the final leg. Jeb had lapsed into silence so I tried to prod him into continuing. "So how did they get on your trail again?"

"Thatcher's a powerful archmage, and we've met once or twice in the past. She's a sensitive and I'm lucky she didn't smell me out beforehand. Traveling over salt water usually breaks the trail, but she must have guessed where I was heading, more or less, and warned Sykes. And Sykes has a real personal reason for wanting to recover the crystal."

I waited, but Jeb didn't elaborate. After a few seconds, Dana snickered and shook his head. "Sykes was at the meeting, wasn't he? Beck thought he might have been, but she wasn't sure."

Jeb sighed. "Sykes is a bigger player than we thought, but his name is actually Grandison, and he's half Prussian. I'm still not sure what his game is, but I don't think I like the rules he plays by."

CHAPTER FIFTEEN

We finally reached shore only a few minutes before dawn, not far from a little town Jeb identified as Elaine. I couldn't imagine how he could possibly have known where we were, or how he had navigated us accurately considering the circumstances of our passage, but I had learned by now to trust his judgment. Not that I had any real choice in the matter. At his insistence, we dragged the boat up onto shore and over to a shallow pond where we weighted it down with stones until it sank out of sight beneath the reeds and rushes.

The farms were much more prosperous on this side of the river. We walked roughly southwestward past neatly tilled fields of corn, tobacco, barley, and other crops, mostly grains. The roads were in various states of repair, varying from tracks accessible only to foot traffic to hard packed dirt roads whose surface was as solid as pavement. Jeb seemed to know exactly where he was going, occasionally leaving the road to cut across a fallow field or woodlot, and neither Kelly nor Dana seemed inclined to question him, so neither did I. No further mention had been made of my leaving the party, although I imagine I could have done so at any time. Somehow it didn't seem proper to abandon them at this point, even if I was actually more burden than help. For the most part, we didn't speak, and the pace was fast enough that I was just as happy to save my breath.

As the morning progressed, we saw an increasing amount of traffic, most of it on foot. Farmers worked their crops, and travelers passed us in the opposite direction, sometimes with a friendly nod or greeting, sometimes with suspicious glances that we all ignored. Two hours after touching land, Jeb hailed a commercial steambus and we boarded, Jeb paying for the lot of us, and found seats together near the back. According to the sign on the front of the bus, we were headed for Snow Lake, a name I actually recognized although I had never been there. It was a sprawling town on the verge of incorporating as a city, a natural transit point for traders heading west into Changsha, a way station for river travelers, and home to a small but thriving manufacturing complex.

A block from the terminal, we had a hearty breakfast at the Purple Harpy Tavern. I noticed with interest that Dana acted as though he was famished, ate half again as much as any of the rest of us, so I concluded that homunculi were not completely exempt from the laws of conservation of mass, energy, and magic. The tavern was crowded, the tables close upon each other, so our conversation was limited to general observations of the city around us, the weather, the quality of the food, and other inconsequentials. Jeb appeared to be in no great hurry; in fact, it struck me that he had the air of someone early for an appointment.

This impression was reinforced by the circuitous course upon which he led us when we were finished eating. I held my tongue, but Dana irritably complained that we were wasting time.

"Just being cautious, my friend. I don't think we've been spotted but there's no reason to take any unnecessary chances."

Our course did become more direct from that point, however, and we left the retail district behind and entered a warren of small manufacturing concerns and warehouses, silversmiths, alchemists, woodworking shops, amulet makers, tinworkers and toolmakers and a large and noisy steamcar assembly plant. There were a few shops scattered about as well, a bakery, a fortuneteller, a disreputable looking storefront advertising magical potions. One garishly painted shop with a broken window caught my attention, advertising "Martha the Medium, Your Loved Ones Last Words Don't Have To Be Their Last"..

Jeb took a sudden right turn into a narrow alley between two unidentified warehouses, differentiated only by coded numbers stenciled on their walls in letters nearly as tall as I. WR54 was to our right, WR55 to our left. Halfway down the block, opposing stairways led to unmarked doors, and Jeb climbed those leading to WR55 and removed something from his pocket. It was a piece of chalk. We stood silently and watched as he drew a series of runes across both the door and the adjacent wall. They seemed very elaborate and I was beginning to grow impatient again when he leaned back, nodded to himself, and made the chalk disappear back into his pocket. In its place he now held a long, slender bar of metal which he touched to the solid locking plate mounted on the door. There was an audible metallic sound and the door shuddered slightly, then swung open a few inches. Jeb gestured to us to follow and led us inside.

The interior of the warehouse was partitioned into a series of storage compartments. There were skylights far above us, but the light was so dim that I had to stop and wait for my eyes to adjust before proceeding. From where I stood, it appeared that the warehouse was near capacity, with crates piled up in every compartment, sometimes protruding into the already narrow aisles. They varied a great deal in size and some of them were open frameworks through which I could see unidentifiable machinery and other merchandise. Lengths of teakwood, metal ingots, and various bulky objects were strapped to wooden pallets in other compartments, and there was an entire row of the latter bearing coconuts, held in place by tightly wrapped hemp webbing, presumably also protected by preservation spells.

"What are we doing here?" I asked, whispering.

We had reached the first intersecting aisle and Jeb halted. He made no effort to pitch his voice lower when he turned back toward us. "I had made arrangements to leave Memphis on *The Golden Arch*, a cargo carrier that spends most of its time running cattle down to New Orleans and imported delicacies back north. Since the Ranchers' Union went on strike last month, they've been picking up whatever freight they can find, and they were more than happy to let me book some deck space. While I was checking the accommodations, I managed to conceal the crystal in one of their consignments, carefully noting the warehouse to which it was being delivered."

"Wasn't that taking rather a chance?" asked Dana. "What if someone has already picked it up?"

Jeb shook his head. "Not likely. The bill of lading was stamped with a government lien for non-payment of import duties. This is a bonded warehouse that specializes in disputed merchandise and government seizures. Even if the owners pay all of the fines and duties owed, they'll still have to deal with the local federal bureaucracy to have the seals lifted. They're not going to have clear title for at least another month even if they grease a few palms along the way. It has the added advantage of a scrying barrier, which meant that no one could use a locating spell to find the crystal."

Dana shrugged as though none of this really interested him. "All right, where is it?"

Jeb sighed. "Well, that's the hard part. Unless we can find some sort of directory, we're going to have to check every stall until we find the right one. The bill of lading number was stenciled on all of the crates so we shouldn't have any trouble identifying it. But we have to find it first. A homing wand would help if you have one. Now that we're inside the warehouse, the barrier isn't a factor."

Dana sniffed impatiently. "You know I don't carry anything like that. Magical artifacts don't work for me."

I glanced down the seemingly endless rows. "This is a big place."

"Let's look for some kind of inventory records first." Jeb chose the fork that led toward the front of the building, Dana only a step behind. Kelly started to follow, but I hadn't moved and she hesitated.

"Is something wrong?"

I wasn't sure and I said so. Although I'd been suspicious of Dana from the outset, I hadn't felt any real sense of alarm. Until now. There was something wrong about him, and I didn't think I was just reacting to his unnatural creation. Even more unnerving was the sense that the reason was right within my grasp, slightly out of focus, or hovering at the periphery of my inner vision. "I don't know. Something's not right."

She tensed and looked slowly around. "I don't see anything."

"Neither do I, but we're in some sort of danger."

I was pleased to notice that she was taking me seriously. "I thought you didn't have any magical talents."

"I don't. It might just be my imagination." I started to shake my head disparagingly and dismiss the feeling as a long delayed reaction to our earlier adventures, but instead I froze. "Kelly," I whispered. "Dana has been lying to us."

Her expression didn't change; she didn't seem to be particularly surprised. "About anything in particular?"

Jeb and Dana were well out of earshot by now. "Look, he told us he'd been working for Beck aboard the *River Warlock*, right? That she hired him before they even came aboard?"

She nodded without answering.

"Well, Beck told me that the person working with her was an aura reader and a precog. That was how she knew I was going to get entangled in this mess."

Kelly's eyes narrowed but she still hadn't made the connection.

"Dana just now mentioned that he can't work magic. He said it earlier, back at the cabin, but I'd forgotten about it until now."

Her expression changed. "Very good, Jim. I told Dad you were smart."

She didn't seem to be particularly alarmed by my revelation, and I began to have doubts. "Am I missing something here?"

"No, of course not." She glanced over her shoulder. Jeb and Dana were out of sight. "Just play along with us for a while, okay? We have things under control."

I felt suddenly deflated. "You already knew, didn't you?"

She nodded, a bit shamefaced. "We knew who Beck's partner was while we were still on board. It was Captain Martin. They've worked together several times in the past, and Dad hired him once or twice as well, though never directly. He's a distant relation of the Duke of Toronto, believe it or not. And his family on the other side is named Kaiser; one of the royal families of early imperial Prussia. His talent is unreliable, but when it's working, he's quite valuable."

"Then who is Dana actually working for?"

"Dad thinks he's freelancing and wants the crystal so that he can auction it off to the highest bidder. Given his nature, it seems unlikely that he's motivated by patriotism or personal loyalty." She made an unpleasant face. "I really don't care so long as he's neutralized. He makes my skin crawl, and not because he's inhuman. One of my cousins was converted to vampirism and we're still just as friendly as before, at least during the daylight. With Dana it's personal. I just don't like him."

I glanced nervously toward the front of the building. "Neutralized? Do you mean killed?"

"If necessary," and her tone was so firm and businesslike that I caught a glimpse of an alternate Kelly I hadn't seen before. "Though that might be difficult since we don't have a hippogriff handy. I'll be satisfied if we just manage to remove him from the equation, which might be sooner than you'd expect. Come on, let's find the others."

We walked briskly down the poorly lighted aisle and turned to our right, passing through an arched entranceway that led to yet another row of packed storage compartments. Jeb and Dana were standing at a desk, examining the papers strewn across its surface, when four figures emerged from the shadows, closing in on them from all sides. I froze in mid-step, my heart racing, but Kelly touched my arm.

"It's all right. They're with us."

And so it was. Two of the newcomers caught Dana by the arms before he had time to more than half turn in their direction. As far as I could see, he made no effort to resist. One of the other two held a pistol in one hand, rather pointless given the homunculus' immunity to gunfire, although I suppose a serious wound would have inconvenienced him at the very least. The last man shook hands vigorously with Jeb, and I finally began to relax. "What's going on?" I asked.

"Dad set this up by mindlink while we were holed up in the cabin. These are people we know we can trust. There are fewer of them lately, but still enough to deal with annoying problems like Dana."

Dana had made no effort to resist, not even a protest, and he seemed relaxed and even in good spirits when we reached them.

"How have you been, Axel?" Kelly greeted the man who had shaken hands with her father, a middle-aged fellow with a bushy beard and moustache, unruly hair, and arms as thick as my thighs.

"Pining away in your absence, Miss Kelly. You really should visit with us more often."

They hugged each other familiarly and Jeb introduced us all around, but first names only. "Axel's an old friend of the family. If things had worked out a bit differently, Kelly's mother might have married him instead of me." The other three were Mike, who held the pistol, and Yevgeny and Hamelin, who held Dana. Despite his name, Yevgeny was at least half Zulu, and his forehead and cheeks were marked with clan signs.

"Now what shall we do with this gentleman?" Jeb had turned to Dana, who met his eyes without flinching.

"I don't suppose we could come to some mutually acceptable business arrangement." Dana hesitated only a second before continuing. "No, I suppose not. I never will understand this human facility for holding loyalties to particular social systems or isolated geographical regions. Enlightened self interest is so much more practical. I suppose you need to acquire the experience of a century or two before you can appreciate the transitory nature of human artifacts, however elaborate."

"If you're not troubled by such matters, then you won't have any qualms about telling us who you're really working for."

Dana smiled. "I could argue that my personal reputation requires that I conceal my employer's identity, but I don't suppose my future job potential is of much concern to you."

Axel made an impatient gesture. "If I were you, I'd be more interested in my present personal liberty than anything else. We might not be able to kill you, at least not without resorting to considerable inconvenience, but we could arrange to have you forgotten in federal custody for a century or so."

Dana's smile went away but he still didn't look to be particularly alarmed. "It would be rather boring, I confess, although I've been confined before and something always comes up to cut my sentence short. Your government might find itself in need of my services, for example, and offer me a pardon in exchange for my assistance. But I admit I would rather avoid the uncertainty. Suppose I agreed to answer all of your questions. What would you offer me in return?"

Axel and Jeb exchanged glances, and it was Jeb who answered. "Axel here is curator of the Snow Lake Zoo. Cooperate with us and you'll be held incommunicado there until the current situation is resolved, then set free. We would prefer that you left the Federation, but won't insist upon it."

"I have your word that you'll release me?"

"We have no serious quarrel with you. Once our interests no longer conflict, we can go our separate ways. Until the next time our paths cross, of course. I can't speak to that."

Dana nodded slowly. "All right, I can't see that it will do any harm. I was hired by High Chief Three Oaks of the Iroquois Free State. The High Council has, or at least had, only the vaguest idea of what might be happening, but given the turmoil in Toronto and the Crown's well known expansionist inclination, they're interested in acquiring bargaining chips to buttress their position."

I wasn't entirely convinced that he was telling the truth even now. The IFS was so militantly isolationist that they didn't even have full embassies in neighboring countries, and diplomatic matters were routinely handled by their trade missions. There had never even been rumors that they employed spies, although I realized now that I was probably being very naïve to believe that they didn't take an interest in international affairs, at least those affairs which could impact their own security. This trip was proving to be very educational.

If Jeb was surprised, there was no evidence of it on his face or in his voice. "And when did you decide to doublecross them?"

Dana smiled but his eyes hardened. "As soon as I realized how important the crystal could be. And how valuable to whoever possessed it. Ling or King Winston's government would happily pay ten times what the Iroquois offered. It would be catastrophic for them if the crystal ever reached the Emperor in such a way that he could no longer pretend he didn't know of the plot's existence. I would have allowed the Federation to bid as well, of course, but by the time your bureaucrats finished arguing about how to finance the deal, events would long since have played themselves out. Democracy is a hideously inefficient form of government, you know. I much prefer dealing with a well defined hierarchy."

"How did you know I was in Beck's room?" I hadn't meant to speak, but the question had been bothering me and it burst out before I realized what I was doing.

Dana turned and regarded me with cold, unblinking eyes. "I didn't, as a matter of fact. I went there to discover what she'd learned from Captain Martin. I'm afraid he died rather than tell me himself. A weak heart, apparently, and the pain was too much for him. I knew he was working for Beck so I hired a minor gandalf to neutralize the locking charms on her room. We were hiding in a closet to await her return, although I never expected her to appear with you in tow. My gandalf attempted to neutralize you both with a sleep spell, and you dropped off obediently enough. Unfortunately, she wore a warding charm and drew her weapon. I assure you that her death was completely accidental; she took me by surprise and I over reacted. That left you, Mr. Parkhurst, as the only possible lead."

"And that's when you decided to pose as her agent?"

"I'd listened in to your conversation and knew she hadn't identified Martin by name. Considering how short a time I had in which to improvise, I thought I'd done rather well. If Miss Marks hadn't struck me at the first opportunity, and quite unprovoked I might add, chances are I could have fooled her as well. That would have saved us all considerable trouble."

"I'm less gullible than you might think," said Kelly dryly, and then realized what this implied about my own perceptiveness. "Experience has taught me not to accept anything at face value." She gave me an apologetic look that did no good at all.

Jeb had apparently heard enough. He turned to Axel, dismissing Dana. "We've wasted enough time here. Have you made arrangements for our transportation?"

Axel nodded. "Yev and Mike will drive you to Vicksburg. You'll be met there by our mutual friends. They'll be fully equipped."

"All right. I'm sure you'll have no trouble dealing with our friend here."

Dana suddenly shifted his weight and spoke up. "If you don't mind my asking, would you satisfy my curiosity about one matter? Would you tell me how you got the crystal out of Memphis? I assume the story about stashing it in a cargo container was just a fiction to get me here."

"Not entirely." Jeb measured his words carefully. "But this isn't the right warehouse."

What happened next was so fast and so unexpected that it was all over before I realized what was taking place. Dana hardly seemed to move but Yev and Hamelin were suddenly off balance and slamming into each other. Yev was stunned and fell heavily to the floor, but Hamelin somehow became airborne, and he crashed into Mike before the latter could fire his weapon. The two men slammed into a section of wire fencing and the pistol went skittering across the floor.

Jeb and Axel were drawing their own weapons, but Dana spun on his heel and raced toward me. I barely had time to raise my arms defensively before we collided, and even as I flew backward, I found a split second to wonder at the immense strength in his wiry frame. Then I hit something with my back so hard that I think I cried out and I know I lay stunned and gasping like a grounded fish for at least several seconds, although at the time it seemed hours. I heard raised voices but couldn't make out the words and I thought I was going to lose consciousness. I didn't quite, but what roused me was Dana's voice, sounding entirely too cheerful for my liking.

"Are you still with us, Mr. Parkhurst?"

I blinked and raised myself up on one elbow. My surroundings were blurry at first and it still hurt slightly to breathe, but I was beginning to recover what remained of my wits. Dana was standing directly in my line of sight, holding the small pistol that Jeb had given Kelly. She was sitting on the floor beside him, looking dazed, and beyond I could see Jeb and Axel standing with their arms raised, and no sign of their weapons. Yev and Hamelin were both motionless, but Mike was moaning softly where he lay.

"On your feet, if you please, Mr. Parkhurst. I require your assistance."

I rose shakily and reluctantly, acutely aware of the fact that my own pistol remained in my thigh pocket. It would be a heroic gesture to attempt to reverse the situation by drawing my weapon, but it would also likely be suicidal. I decided to bide my time.

"Very good, Mr. Parkhurst. Now if you wouldn't mind, I would like you to walk very slowly over to your friends there and kick their weapons toward me. Please don't be so rash as to attempt to pick them up or interfere in any way. I assure you that if they don't fancy the odds for themselves, they would be even longer in your case. My reflexes are quite superior to that of any human being, and I could break Miss Marks' neck and possibly put a round into everyone in this room before you could aim and fire."

There were actually only four rounds in the weapon he held, but that would be more than enough to deal with those of us still conscious, and his superhuman strength and speed, which apparently not even Jeb had anticipated, would probably be enough even without the weapon. Moving very slowly, I followed Dana's instructions. Both weapons were lying on the floor out of my direct line of sight, but I found them and kicked them close to where he stood, though deliberately not so close as to put them easily within his reach.

"You're doing quite well, Mr. Parkhurst. Now if all three of you would very slowly sit down on the floor, with your hands beneath you. That's right."

With Axel in the middle, the three of us sat on our hands. Jeb's face was expressionless but Axel's jaw muscles twitched in quite obvious fury. Dana, on the other hand, was uncharacteristically cheery.

"Let me tell you all what's going to happen next. You, Mr. Marks, are going to identify the proper warehouse and provide the bill of lading number, as well as an explanation of how I might find the crystal. Mr. Parkhurst will then help me to lock you all in one of the storage chambers while he, Miss Marks, and I go to collect it. If all goes well, I will release my companions as soon as I'm confident that I'm beyond your immediate reach. You will attempt to follow me, of course, but I doubt very much if you will be able to pick up the trail quickly enough. If, on the other hand, the information you provide proves false, things will not go well for the young lady." He glanced down at her; Kelly still hadn't raised her head. "Nothing personal, Miss Marks. I assure you that I bear you no personal animosity despite your obvious hostility. I consider myself a professional, just like you, and I do whatever is necessary to complete the job."

Jeb's face was calm but alert, and I saw him exchange looks with Axel, who nodded almost imperceptibly. But if I noticed it, so did Dana. "It would be best for all of us if no one attempted any heroics. I assure you I'm quite willing to kill any or all of you as necessary, but I would prefer not to be forced into anything quite that drastic. As you noted earlier, Mr. Marks, I do not feel remorse, although I find that under certain circumstances I do experience something akin to human anger."

Axel had closed his eyes but he seemed tense, shaking just perceptibly. I thought I heard something from somewhere out of my line of sight, a hint of movement, and wondered if there were other members of his group, a reserve force waiting in concealment. Suddenly shadows shifted on the warehouse walls, very large shadows.

Something emerged from the darkness at the far end of the aisle, something far too big to be a human being. I recognized a wing, saw a clawed foot, and then it stepped out into the open. It was a full grown hippogriff. I had been a child when I last saw one at a zoo, but its shape was unmistakable, the powerful catlike body, furled wings, and sharply curving beak. It was a magnificent beast, the claws on its oversized feet clacking against the concrete floor as it approached. There were very few of the creatures left in the world;

they had been hunted to extinction in the wild and only lingered on in a score of zoos scattered about the world. Attempts to breed them had been largely ineffective and their numbers were dwindling. Jeb had indicated that Axel managed the local zoo, but I would never have imagined that such a small community could have obtained such a rare exhibit.

Dana recoiled as though he'd seen death personified, as indeed might well be the case. I was wondering if I dared draw my pistol when Kelly reacted more quickly than I. She lunged toward one of the discarded weapons, her arms outstretched. Dana recovered quickly from his initial shock, leaped into the air, twisting and kicking out. One foot caught Kelly behind her left ear, and she crashed to the floor, half rolled up onto her side, then fell back, unconscious.

"Very resourceful of you, Mr. Marks." There was tension in the homunculus' voice, but no indication of fear.

The hippogriff had come to a halt about twenty meters away, its head slowly moving from side to side as though it was seeking prey. Jeb's eyes were on Kelly and I thought I sensed a difference in his posture, a tension I hadn't noticed before. Axel remained motionless, eyes still closed, a distant expression on his face. His reaction struck me as curious, but Dana interpreted it almost immediately.

"And clever as well. Tell me, is your associate here really associated with the zoo or was that just a device to prepare me for this little game?"

Jeb hesitated, then nodded. "He's the director, as a matter of fact. That's why his reconstructions are so realistic." He nudged Axel with an elbow. "Game's up, Axel. He didn't buy it." The larger man shivered slightly, shook his head, and the hippogriff blinked out of existence.

"And a very powerful projective illusionist as a sideline. I'm impressed. Sound as well as vision. That's a very rare talent. Unfortunately, I have a very sensitive nose and hippogriffs have a distinctive scent, something to do with the mix of fur and feathers I suspect. If there had actually been one of the beasts anywhere in the vicinity, I would have known it instantly. But you did fool me for a moment, I confess, and that hasn't happened in a long time."

Axel shrugged and dropped his eyes. I glanced toward Kelly, but she hadn't moved since she'd fallen.

The revolver felt very heavy in my pocket.

CHAPTER SIXTEEN

A small internal voice cautioned me to wait for a better opportunity, or preferably for someone else to take the initiative, but I knew that no better circumstances were likely, particularly once the party separated. I slid my hand into my thigh pocket, trying to be casual about it, probably telegraphing my intentions if anyone had bothered to take notice of what I was doing. I knew that pistol fire would not kill the homunculus, but I also knew from our experience back at the farm that it would at least incapacitate him for a while, and I'm sure Jeb and his friends could arrange something more durable while he was recovering.

Frankly, I didn't expect to get away with it, and I actually froze in surprise when I realized the pistol was in my hand and that Dana hadn't noticed. Jeb must have seen what I was doing, but his face remained impassive and his eyes never so much as flickered. The honorable thing to do would have been to call on Dana to throw down his weapon and submit, but I couldn't take that chance. Lives were at stake here, including my own. I fired all four rounds in rapid succession. I've never been more than a fair shot with a pistol and the angle was awkward, but I'm still a bit ashamed at my dismal aim.

The first two shots missed to his right, although one came close enough to rip the sleeve of his jacket, and the third went over his head because he ducked as he spun around, bringing his own weapon to bear. More through luck than skill, my final round hit him squarely in the forehead, and he flew backward as though hit by a cannonball, slamming into a wire mesh partition and then crumpling to the floor. I was so elated that it was a few seconds before I realized that my left shoulder was on fire and I raised a hand to the pain and felt something hot and sticky. Dana had managed to fire back at least once.

I don't remember sitting down, or falling down, and I think I was semi-conscious for some time because I had a hazy sense of time passing and then Kelly and Jeb were squatting beside me and my shirt was half open. Kelly was sprinkling some kind of antiseptic powder over my wound and it must have been treated with a painkiller charm because the burning pain stopped almost immediately. I tried to thank her but my stomach was churning and I half turned away, expecting to vomit, and instead fainted.

When I recovered for the second time, I was lying on a tattered couch in a small office. I raised my head cautiously, but felt so much better that I carefully sat up and swung my feet down to the floor. Kelly was sitting in a padded chair in one corner of the room, with what appeared to be an icepack pressed against the back of her head.

"How are you feeling?"

There was a slight ache in my shoulder and I was still a bit light headed, but under the circumstances I felt pretty good and said so. "How about you?"

She wiggled the ice pack to draw attention to it. "A kingsized headache and some bruises, but I'll survive."

"Where are the others? What's happening?"

"Axel and his friends just took Dana away. The next time he opens his eyes, he's going to find himself in a cage in the zoo's infirmary. If it's up to me, that's where he'll stay," she said ruefully.

"How are the others?"

"Hamelin's got a concussion and Mike has a broken elbow. Dad and Yev went to get the crystal. They'll be back soon."

"And then what?"

"We'll get you to a local healer. A discrete one. I'm sorry that we dragged you into all this, Jim. I suppose it's my fault. I shouldn't have planted the crystal in your luggage. It was just too much of a temptation; I never stopped to think about the consequences."

She sounded genuinely contrite and I was tempted to try to take advantage of her feelings, but I'm happy to say that honor overcame baseness. "Don't worry about it. I can't say that this has been the most pleasant experience of my life, but now that no one's actually threatening to kill us and we're in friendly hands, I have to admit that it's been rather exciting, something I can tell my children about. When I have children. Or maybe I'll read about it in one of your books." I started to stand up but my head spun so crazily that I thought better of it and sat back down.

"You shouldn't do that yet," Kelly warned unnecessarily and belatedly.

"So I noticed." Someone had bandaged my injured shoulder while I was unconscious. I could move my arm, so long as I did so slowly and within very narrow limits; it ached a little and the muscles felt as though they'd been drawn tight, but there was very little pain. "It doesn't feel too bad."

"It's lucky you're as tall as you are. The bullet came up at an angle and just cut a furrow through your muscle. The blessing powder should take care of any infection and I didn't have any trouble stitching you up." Uncertainty must have shown on my face because she laughed. "Don't worry. I've done it before. I've probably sewn more flesh than cloth in my time. It's a nice, neat job, and if there's any chance of scarring, you can get the healer to take care of it. We'll have you there in a couple of hours at the outside."

"Can we afford the time?"

Her eyes skipped away and I knew she was going to be evasive even before she spoke. "We know someone who has dealt with this kind of situation before. She'll keep you out of sight until it's safe for you to take up your old life."

"If I'm going to be in danger anyway, I'd rather stay with you and Jeb. I have the feeling that if Sykes, or Grandison, or whoever he is, really wants to find me, he will, regardless of whatever precautions we might take."

"He won't be interested in you if he knows you're not with us any longer. Sykes is smart enough to realize you were an innocent bystander and that you can't help him now. He's a professional, and professionals don't waste time on revenge."

I made another effort to stand up, and this time succeeded, although my knees felt rubbery and it took a few seconds before the room was stationary. "I'm not betting my life on his forbearance, and frankly, I'm mad enough now that I want to see this through. Patriotism aside, I've been hounded, threatened, shot at, and wounded, and I want the chance to even the score a little."

"You already did that with Dana. We'd all be in very serious bind if you hadn't acted when you did."

"Dana isn't Sykes. I can understand Dana in a way; he's not human and has no reason to be loyal to the Federation. But Sykes is a citizen and a traitor. I want to help."

She seemed prepared to argue further, but instead smiled slightly and shook her head. "It's not up to me. Talk to Dad when he gets back. He's the one you have to convince."

I tried flexing my injured arm. If I concentrated, I could feel the pain, but it was distant and muffled. I was more concerned that my shoulder would stiffen up and hamper my movements than that it would actually start to hurt.

"Why don't you lie down and try to rest? We won't be leaving before dark regardless of what we decide to do."

"All right. But I'll never be able to get to sleep." I laid back and, of course, fell asleep almost immediately. My dreams were a succession of dark sequences in which shadowy figures lurked just outside my field of perception.

I was wakened by the touch of a hand on my good shoulder.

"Wake up, Jim. It's time to go." It was Kelly, who had somehow managed to obtain a fresh set of clothing while I was asleep. Baggy cotton trousers and a durable dragonsilk blouse, practical rather than decorative. "Here, try putting this on."

She handed me a button front shirt, not really in style at the moment but not so odd that it would attract attention. A pair of denim jeans had been draped over a nearby chair, and a plain, neutral colored sash. My shoulder was still stiff, but not so much as before, and I was able to strip off the bloodstained clothing I was wearing and get into my new garb without too much difficulty. I felt dizzy for a few seconds when I stood up, but it passed quickly.

"How's the shoulder?"

I raised my arm tentatively. "Still a little stiff, but better than it was before. Where are we off to?"

"You'll have to ask Dad about that."

Jeb and several others were waiting at the warehouse entrance. He offered me a rare smile and shook my hand warmly. "When this is all over, Jim, I'll thank you more properly. Kelly tells me you want to tag along with us."

I had been quietly marshalling my arguments, which seemed woefully inadequate, but Jeb derailed me instantly. "I wouldn't ask it of you, but if you really want to come along, you're welcome to do so. You've brought us good luck so far and we could use a lot more of it."

I stammered some sort of thank you but Jeb was already leading the way outside into the darkness. A late model Norton steamcar was parked near the entrance, dark blue or black and almost invisible despite the security lights. Yev was behind the wheel and Jeb slid in beside him. Kelly indicated that I should precede her into the back seat and one of the men whose name I didn't know climbed into the boot compartment. The newcomer, whose name I later learned was Ted, carried a long barreled weapon that I thought might be some variation of the Gatling streamshooter. It was so large that it was awkward to hold, but it fitted into a locking mechanism mounted at the rear of the steamcar, and swiveled back and forth so that its operator could sweep a trail of rounds across a considerable perimeter, firing as fast as the reloading charm could move rounds into the firing chamber. Gatling's were rare outside of the military, but I had ceased being surprised by Jeb's resourcefulness.

Once we were moving, no one seemed inclined to talk, and in fact Jeb slouched down in his seat and went to sleep. Kelly seemed to be dozing as well, leaning against the window opposite me at first, then shifting so that she was leaning toward me. I edged tentatively in her direction and she put her head against my shoulder, fortunately the uninjured one. I found the sensation quite pleasant and slowly raised my arm, moved it along the back of the seat, and then I was holding her, lightly but securely, trying not to disturb her sleep. She moved quite deliberately then, slipping one arm around my waist, and I realized to my delight that she wasn't asleep at all. I felt absurdly like a teenager making out in the back of a hay wagon.

I could see very little despite the city's lights, which were smaller and at greater intervals than those I was used to. Within an hour, we were out of their range anyway, and I could see nothing at all. Yev drove efficiently, making good time without attracting attention. Although I hadn't been able to note our route, we crossed a small bridge from which I could see the illuminated upper deck of a riverboat. It was to our left, which meant we were headed south, not much of a surprise. We were close enough to the river that I could faintly hear the sound of the liner's orchestra, entertaining the first class tourists, and it occurred to me that just a few days ago I had been similarly blissful.

We were headed toward New Orleans again, presumably, and unless I had miscounted days, it was still theoretically possible for me to arrive in time for my conference. Somehow the consequences of that meeting, to which I had devoted a good portion of a year's efforts, no longer seemed quite as significant as they had when I had set out. To pass the time, I began to develop alternate strategies, possible new markets, promotions, anything that would enable us to move some of the merchandise out of our presently bulging warehouses. If my plans collapsed entirely, it would cost us a considerable portion of our assets, but not a ruinous amount, and we'd done quite well when the Northern Provinces dumped large quantities of gold and jewelry into our markets in anticipation of King Winston's new confiscatory tax policies.

After a while, I drifted off to sleep myself, although every so often I'd waken, look around tentatively, discover that nothing appeared to have changed, and close my eyes again.

Eventually the sun came up. Kelly and I disentangled ourselves and stared around, blinking and stretching stiff muscles. I was relieved to find that my shoulder was no worse; if anything it felt slightly more limber. We were crossing open country, cleared but largely untilled land interspersed with stretches of heavy forest. Much of it seemed to be pasturage and I counted almost a score of centaurs, mostly mares and their young, but at least one magnificent stallion that stood at the fence and glared at us as we drove past. Scientists and sorcerers alike have been telling us for years that centaurs aren't truly sentient, that they simply imitate human behaviors in the same fashion as a parrot, but they still disconcert me with their human features and facial expressions. I keep expecting them to speak in intelligible English, although their vocal chords aren't up to the task.

Ted turned in his seat and I got a good look at him for the first time. He had a rather impressive scar running up one cheek, and it must have been inflicted with a magical weapon since he hadn't had it removed. Unless he liked having it there. You never know. He nodded at us and shouted so he could be heard above the laboring turbine. "Yev, it's not much further ahead."

Our driver acknowledged with a wave but didn't turn his head. "Algernon Point. I remember."

Kelly was looking out her side window curiously. "Whereabouts are we?"

Jeb swiveled around to look at us. "We're in northern Georgiana." Georgiana was the only member of the Federation never to have had an independent government prior to its incorporation into the union. Congress had negotiated the purchase of what was then a largely undeveloped tract of land from King George IX when he desperately needed funds to finance his war against the Scandinavian Hegemony. The sales treaty had stipulated that New Orleans was to remain an international port open to British merchants, but with the passage of time, that provision had been slowly eroded and was now little more than an historical curiosity.

"We'll be changing vehicles in a few minutes. Just as a precaution, in case someone spotted us leaving the city and sent word ahead. There should be food waiting as well."

Fifteen minutes later, the turbine changed tone as Yev slowed, then turned abruptly into a narrow road marked by a sign that read "Algernon Point. No Trespassing." We made our way up a gentle incline that ended at a large circular drive that ran along the crest of the rise, then down through the trees almost to the shore of a small lake or large pond. I saw three or four log cabins scattered about, but there were no people in sight, no boats on the water. An older steamcar, a bright red Drake, was parked alongside the boathouse, whose roof was in serious need of repair.

"Stop here," Jeb ordered while we were still some distance away.

Yev complied, cut the fuel to the turbine, which slowly began to wind down. Ted dismounted the Gatling gun and climbed out of the back while Jeb and Yev opened their doors. Kelly and I were both preparing to follow them when Ted drew his pistol and fired a shot into the sky.

Jeb and Yev spun around as several men emerged from hiding, all carrying leveled weapons. We were completely surrounded, having driven into a well laid trap. Ted rapped the barrel of his pistol against my window. "Come out of there this way, both of you. Nice and slow." My hand had automatically gone to my thigh pocket, but the pistol was gone. I didn't know whether or not Kelly was armed, but the question seemed moot at this point. We were outnumbered and outgunned. Ted stepped back so that he could cover us as we emerged.

Our two companions had already dropped their weapons, Jeb's face impassive but his eyes alert. More figures emerged from the distance and I recognized one of them right off.

"Fate, it seems, has once more brought us together, my friends." It was Colonel Sykes, as I still thought of him, looking extraordinarily pleased with himself. "You've given us quite a run. I'd admire you for it if I had the time."

Yev was clearly at a loss. "How could you do this, Ted? We've been friends for six years."

Ted had the grace to look uncomfortable, but his weapon never wavered. "You're all on the wrong side this time. The Federation is coming apart at the seams. Congress and the state legislatures will never iron out their differences and form a coherent union. We should never have broken away from the Empire in the first place and we've been drifting toward disaster ever since. The Throne will provide the structure we need to pull together as a people, and the discipline to put down the Greenies and restore order within our borders. It was a childish dream to think we could survive independently."

"And Changsha," Jeb said quietly. "What will they be contributing to this Utopian dream of yours? You don't think they'll be content with just half the continent, do you?"

Ted's eyes betrayed uncertainty but his voice remained firm. "We'll lose some of the western territories, at least for the time being. It's a necessary sacrifice. We're spread too thin. Better to draw back to a defensible border than risk everything to hold untenable ground. You told me that, Jeb. Remember? They're a corrupt and inferior people. In the long run, we'll push them back to the Pacific."

"As a much as I enjoy listening to all this," Sykes interrupted sarcastically, "I'm afraid you'll have to argue politics on your own time. You should be grateful to your old friend, Marks. If I had my way you'd all be dead now. But I'm a man of my word and Ted insisted that we spare you in exchange for his cooperation."

Jeb gave Ted a last look that was so contemptuously dismissive that I half expected the man to wither away on the spot. "So where are we off to this time?"

"You're not going anywhere, none of you, at least for a few days. We, on the other hand, will be relieving you of the responsibility of the crystal, which I will soon exchange for a king's ransom, or at least a duke's. The four of you will be detained in one of these cabins," he gestured over his shoulder, "with ample supplies and an armed guard to make certain you don't wander off and injure yourselves. Ted will be looking after you for the duration, at the end of which time he and the other guard will leave. We're sufficiently secluded here that it should take a day or so after that before you can raise the alarm, and by then matters will have resolved themselves to my satisfaction. I'll be retiring after this, so I don't suppose there will be any reason for us to speak again."

"I wouldn't bet the farm on that."

Sykes pursed his lips. "I'd be a bit more politic if I were you, Marks. You're surviving this on my sufferance, after all. Don't press the issue. And I'll take the crystal now, if you please."

Jeb hesitated and I caught my breath, half expecting him to refuse. It would have been a meaningless gesture, however, and after an uncomfortable few seconds, he reached into his pocket, withdrew a small, carved ivory box, and tossed it to the ground at Sykes' feet.

The Colonel frowned but bent to retrieve the box. I was close enough to see that the cover was decorated with a carved, semi-circular pattern. Sykes withdrew the crystal, which was so small that it was lost in his palm, and handed it to one of his companions, a nervous looking woman who cupped it briefly and closed her eyes, then handed it back.

"It's the one you're after," she said quietly. "I can feel the images within it."

"At last!" Sykes replaced the crystal in its box and made the box disappear into his sash. "Now if you will excuse my hasty departure, I have a schedule to maintain. This business has been, if not pleasant, at least interesting." He spun on his heel, followed closely by the woman and three of the armed men.

None of the rest of us moved or spoke a word until the bright red Drake had disappeared back in the direction of the main road. Ted, who wasn't looking nearly as happy as a triumphant villain should, pointed toward one of the cabins with the barrel of his pistol. "All right, let's get this over with. There's food and bedding inside. The shower works but the water's cold, I'm afraid. We'll be camped outside until sometime tomorrow night, so you'll just have to make yourselves as comfortable as possible until then. After that, you're welcome to break down the door, or the whole damned cabin if you want. The nearest town is six hours away by foot if you cut cross country and go directly southeast. By road it's more like eight, but you might catch a ride. You can try to track me down if you want to, but I have no idea where Sykes is going so you'll just be wasting your time. I'm out of it now anyway."

Ted and one other man had remained behind. They flanked us as we walked single file, Jeb in the lead, followed by Yev, myself, and Kelly in the rear. Ted walked to Kelly's right, a step behind her, and the nameless man to Jeb's left.

Just as Jeb reached the cabin door he stumbled and fell to one knee, or at least that was what I thought had happened. Yev had been watching the guard and bumped into Jeb, lost his own balance and fell forward. It was artfully done. Yev's body masked Jeb's movements for a split second, during which he drew a knife from somewhere inside his clothing and tossed it underhanded but with enough force that it embedded itself in the guard's throat. His eyes opened wide and he half reached for the hilt of the knife, but fell over onto his back, motionless, without ever having touched it.

If I'd had time to think about it, I might have been terrified by the prospect of being shot in the back by Ted, but Kelly had already spun around on one foot and kicked with the other. Ted instinctively drew back but the side of her foot knocked the pistol from his hand. He hesitated, torn between attempting to retrieve the pistol and racing back to the Gatling, and that was his undoing. Kelly shifted her weight and kicked out again, but this time Ted skipped back a couple of steps, made up his mind, and bolted toward the Gatling.

He almost made it. There were two shots and he went down in mid-stride, slid across the ground, and came to rest against the rear wheel of the steamcar. Jeb had recovered the other guard's weapon and fired with deadly accuracy. Kelly and I stood motionless, but Yev knelt beside the fallen man.

"He's dead." His voice sounded hollow.

Jeb nodded, more to himself than to anyone else, I imagine. "Better that way. Let's get moving. We don't have time to waste here."

We climbed into the steamcar, in the same places as before, but the boot compartment was empty now, the Gatling dismounted and unmanned. The turbine was barely turning when we started moving, negotiating a tight circle and heading back toward the main road.

"Do you think we can catch him?" I asked.

"There's a chance." Jeb didn't sound worried at all. "But if he's headed where I think he's going, we might not get there in time."

We retraced our way along the poorly maintained road at such a hectic pace that I wondered if we'd hold together long enough to reach the exit. Kelly and I braced ourselves with arms and legs as we were bumped and tossed mercilessly, and my sore shoulder complained about this fresh mistreatment. Then Jeb said something I didn't hear and Yev turned onto an even rougher track, one I hadn't noticed on the way up. The slope became much steeper and trees closed in tightly on both sides, their branches slashing at our windows. A few more endless minutes of torture passed and we were in the open, with shoulder high grass and reeds on either side, headed toward a small jetty and what must have been the Little Mo River. Beyond the jetty, so close to shore that we could still make out individual figures moving on the deck, a ferry boat was slowly pulling its way across to the opposite bank. A steam funnel belched pearly white spumes into the air and the rear mounted paddle threshed steadily through the water.

A bright red Drake steamcar was visible on the afterdeck.

CHAPTER SEVENTEEN

The road surface was much better here, but Yev had already begun to slow the turbine. It was obvious that we were too late to catch Sykes. Kelly leaned forward over the seat. "Where do you think he's headed?"

"Texicana, most likely. He can choose a dozen different routes to the west, and if they're willing to switch to horseback somewhere along the way, they could cross the border at any number of places. Neither side spends much time patrolling the desert, and there aren't any significant military posts near enough to help. Not in the time we have left."

"We can take the ferry once it comes back, can't we?" I was suddenly infuriated at the prospect of being bested by Sykes. "They won't have more than an hour or two's lead."

"I doubt very much the ferry will be back today." Kelly sounded very tired and discouraged for the first time since I'd met her. "They'll almost certainly disable it when they reach the other side. Engine trouble, quietly contrived by his gandalf, most likely. He won't want to raise any unnecessary alarm. Even if Sykes is confident that we're out of the picture, he's thorough enough to take precautions. It gets to be second nature to cover your tracks when you can."

We reached the jetty and stopped but none of us left our seats. Jeb was obviously preoccupied and we remained quiet for several minutes, while the turbine hissed and burbled. After what seemed an endless wait, he turned to Yev. "Isn't there a trirail junction in Wainwright?"

"Sure is. That's back north a ways, though, maybe an hour's drive."

"It can't be helped. Sykes won't rest until he's considerably west of here, far enough to have put at least a couple of route changes between us. He'll relax some after that, figuring there hasn't been enough time for anyone to check out all the possibilities fast enough to catch him."

"What good will the trirail do us?" asked Kelly. "We can probably get ahead of him, but the farther we go, the more choices he'll have. It would take a small army to cut off all of his escape routes."

"Maybe, maybe not," Jeb answered cryptically, then settled back into his seat as we turned in a tight circle and started back the way we'd come. "Wake me when we get to Wainwright. I've got some sleeping to catch up on."

Which put an end to that conversation.

The trip to Wainwright was rough on my nerves. Kelly was lost in thoughts of her own, stared blankly out at the passing countryside, and frankly I wasn't in the mood for conversation myself. Despite Jeb's optimism, I was convinced that we were on a futile quest. Wagon trains had been lost in the area where Sykes had gone, entire towns existed unknown to the territorial government. The Apache raided there occasionally, although they were usually preoccupied with harassing the Changsha border settlements, the dregs of the Federation drifted to the region because they were effectively beyond the reach of the law, and the land itself was barren and sometimes actively hostile. Jeb stirred himself while we were still on the outskirts of the small trade town, and he surprised me by telling Yev to pull over when we saw a small farmers' market ahead. He bought fresh fruit, dried beef, bottled beer, and a few other supplies and we ate quietly and without much appetite for most of the remainder of the trip.

Wainwright was small but obviously prosperous, the buildings mostly new and universally well maintained. It was rapidly becoming one of the more important rail junctions and would probably swell to city size within a generation. We found the booking office with no difficulty and parked between two steam lorries laden with bundled grain and crated machine parts. The terminal was very crowded and my temper was wearing thin by the time we had our turn, and the booking agent disappointed us all by advising us that there were no trains heading west until the following morning.

"We had a washout a few miles east and the crews won't have the rails back in place until this evening."

Jeb paid for our tickets and asked directions to the nearest hostelry. The Bread Basket was not up to my usual standards, but it was clean and convenient and they had rooms available. Yev and I shared one, Jeb and Kelly each had their own. My roommate immediately took to his bed, and I realized he had slept less than any of the rest of us during the past day so I left him in peace and wandered down to the lobby. Kelly appeared a couple of minutes later, obviously restless and depressed.

"Let's take a walk. I need to stretch my legs."

She didn't have to ask me twice. The world might be about to collapse into war and anarchy all around us, but that wouldn't take the luster off spending time with an attractive and assertive young woman. I knew such an animal existed, of course, but rarely in the circles where I normally traveled. The mercantile class is still largely male dominated, just as the medical profession consists mostly of females, but merchants of either sex tended to be cool, calculating, and unimaginative. Myself included, I suppose. It just hadn't occurred to me how colorless my life had been until I had a few bright sparks with which to compare it.

We walked the entire length of the town, rarely speaking except to point out one or another interesting feature. An extensive addition to the switching yards was half completed, only one of the many signs of growth that we noticed. Several buildings were under construction or renovation, land was being cleared for a district courthouse, and we saw at least a dozen steamcars with carts in tow, carts filled with furniture, clothing, and other indications that immigration was rapid and steady. We started back by a slightly different route, angling toward the downtown, and bought pastry stuffed with spiced meat paste from a roadside vendor.

Time passed surprisingly quickly, but our feet got tired and I started looking for someplace where we could sit down for a while. My spirits were considerably improved but Kelly was still preoccupied and glum and when I spotted an Illusion Chamber, I decided that a diversion might help. Kelly was less than enthusiastic but let herself be persuaded, probably just to make me shut up. The exterior was unprepossessing, but the interior was very well fitted and a sign boasted that they had the most modern equipment west of the Mississippi.

Illusion Chambers are still banned in a few locations, those where the Calvinist holdouts against Benedict Arnold's Reformation are still a significant political force. The general and first President of the Federation Congress had alienated his original constituency by endorsing the liberalization of his church, and many conservative holdouts had retreated to remote enclaves where they became even more zealous than they had been in the past. In general, however, the popularity of this new form of entertainment has increased so dramatically that they're among the few commercial establishments allowed to build in residential zones in many of our larger cities. Each illusion is created by a team of technicians and magic wielders who carefully interweave spells and technology to create a nearly perfect counterfeit of reality. While experiencing a first rate illusion, the customer perceives the entire story from the point of view of an omniscient observer or, for a substantially higher fee, can even occupy the "body" of one of the characters in the story, although only as a passenger unable to change the dialogue or action in even the slightest fashion.

We spent the late afternoon watching a musical comedy about Lafayette written by someone name Ronald Hubbard. I found the lyrics inane and derivative myself, and the music was unmemorable, but it seemed to lift Kelly's spirits a bit and we returned to the hotel at dusk in a much more optimistic mood. The knowledge that Kelly and I were from two different worlds gnawed at the edge of my consciousness, but I ignored the warnings. Jeb was sitting in the lobby, reading the local paper, and he never said a word about our long mutual absence, which I chose to interpret as a favorable sign.

I found it difficult to sleep that night even though I knew I needed to rest. Yev was in and out; he'd slept through most of the day and was refreshed, but he'd become much more withdrawn, brooding over Ted's defection, I think. My shoulder was still sore, but I managed to find a relatively comfortable position and dropped off eventually, but only after concocting a half dozen totally impractical schemes. The most elaborate involved dispersing a team of prescients along the border, but the strongest documented prescient vision had only reached a little more than two hours into the future, and that wouldn't give us time to react to Sykes' movements even if we could distribute a picket line of psychics across his path. Countermeasures against prescients were easy, in any case. Most sporting events employed a blanket shield for each contest to keep the outcome secret until the game had actually been played. And that was my best idea. I'd be hopelessly embarrassed if I ever committed some of my wilder schemes to paper.

Yev roused me before the sun was up the following morning. We breakfasted in the hostelry, which had excellent food, and eventually boarded a passenger car bound for Dallas, capital of Texicana. The cabin steward welcomed us aboard and launched into his canned speech expounding upon the virtues of trirail travel, a list of the amenities available to us during our trip, assurances that the rail grippers were all manufactured from the finest elvish iron imported from the Balkan mines before the outbreak of the war with Russia. I'd experienced a minor derailment in the Michigan-Doddsylvania disputed zone once and had no desire to repeat the experience. The border dispute between the two states made it very difficult to upgrade the rail lines and would likely continue until Congress finally compelled the two parties to reconcile.

Jeb had booked a private compartment with anti-eavesdropping spells and after we'd explored the train a bit, we all ended up there. I still had no idea what he was planning or how we could possibly hope to anticipate Sykes' next move, but Jeb had surprised me often enough already that I was still hopeful.

Yev slumped in his seat, staring into his lap. Kelly stood at the window with her hands clasped behind her back. Jeb and I sat facing each other and I waited for as long as I could stand it before asking.

"How are we going to find Sykes now? He's had more than a full day's head start and there are plenty of different routes he could have taken. He might be hundreds of miles from Dallas when he crosses the border." The trirail would reach Dallas in a matter of only a few hours so we would leapfrog him if he was headed that way, but he might have turned sharply southward, or even cut back to the north. "He could have doubled back across the Little Mo and gone up into the Kansas territory."

Jeb reached into his pocket and withdrew an object which I recognized as a duplicate of the small, ornate box which had held the crystal and which was now in Sykes' possession. He tossed it across to me and I caught it, popped it open, half expecting to find the real crystal inside, although that was clearly impossible. The gandalf had verified that he had the real thing. The one in my hand was empty.

"Keep the cover open and hold it as level as possible, then run your finger around the interior rim. Slowly."

Mystified, I did as I was told. One edge seemed slightly warmer, presumably where it had been pressed against Jeb's body, but otherwise I could detect nothing out of the ordinary. "I don't get it."

"Don't you feel the heat, lad?"

"Well, one side is just a bit warmer than the other." I thought about that. "Some kind of directional device?"

"Right you are, Jimmy. I don't suppose you've ever heard of kinship boxes before now?" I shook my head and handed the box back to him. "They're not common; the preparation takes a long time, and just one deviant cut of the knife and they're too different for the charm to work. Both of these were carved from the very same troll horn long before any of us were born, and they've been in my family for eight generations. They have to be mirrors of each other, stroke for stroke, and if they do, they grow warm on the sides that face at a range of as much as a thousand miles, though it would be so faint at that distance that we'd need precision instruments to detect the temperature differential. We won't let Sykes get anywhere near that far away from us."

"But what if he discards the box? I mean, it's the crystal he's interested in, after all."

Jeb seemed unperturbed by that thought. "Then we'll have to think of something else. But he hasn't yet. I've been checking regularly and the other box has been moving steadily since before dawn. He's headed generally west, dipping southwards from time to time. I can't say that he's going to Dallas, but he's going in that general direction."

For the first time since we'd watched the ferry moving away from us, I felt as though we might have a chance after all.

"Then all we have to do is lay a trap for him."

Jeb scratched his head. "Well, it's not going to be quite that simple. He could turn away from us at any time and pick a route further to the south, although he's already missed some of his best chances to do that. It would certainly help if he planned to go through Dallas, but I suspect he'll stay clear of any city that size. Too many chances that someone will be watching for him. We'll just have to hope for the best and improvise as we go along. Texicana might be culturally homogeneous with the Federation, but Dallas has its own distinct personality, and cooperation with the federal authorities isn't considered a virtue thereabouts. There are still powerful interests who'd like to see the monarchy restored. Sykes' still has the best cards showing, but I'd say there's a good chance we'll get to renew our acquaintance within the next couple of days."

We reached Dallas early in the afternoon. Jeb sent Yev to buy or rent a steamcar, drawing once more against on what appeared to be an endless supply of hard credit, while Kelly and I shopped for provisions. Jeb disappeared on a mission of his own, to "gather intelligence". Two hours later when we rendezvoused not far from the station, he was weighed down with packages which we stored in the back of a used, older model Cheviot purchased from a local dealership. Yev, who appeared to be in better spirits now that we were actually doing something, told us that it had formerly been a COP vehicle, that it had a supercharged turbine and a reinforced frame.

We made one additional stop on our way out of the city, a pawn shop that looked like every other pawn shop in the world, located in an industrial district. Kelly and I waited while Jeb and Yev went inside, and she told me that the proprietor did a lively trade in black market weapons and ammunition. Our companions returned after a very short interval carrying two large packages which they stored in the rear compartment with our food. One of them looked to be the right size to hold a Gatling gun.

Jeb consulted the kinship box regularly after that, studying a detailed map he'd obtained in Dallas. Once we were beyond the city limits and moving through unsettled, flat country, he announced that Sykes had made better progress than expected. "We're not ahead of him, exactly, but we're in a good position to intercept him if he continues along his present course. He's almost directly south of us and traveling due east, but he's on one of the hunting tracks and won't be able to move as fast as we can on this nice modern highway." The last was meant sarcastically. The road was rutted and filled with potholes, covered with drifting sagebrush and other debris. We were probably going faster than Sykes, but not by a significant margin.

Jeb used a pencil to mark various locations on his map, interception points based on different choices Sykes might make as he passed a handful of intersecting routes. "None of them are any better than the track he's on, and my guess is he'll stick to it for a while. He has no reason to believe we know where he is, or that we're this close."

"Where are we likely to catch him?" I was growing more anxious with the passage of time, and had begun wondering what exactly my role would be in the confrontation to come. Spectator or participant?

"It all depends on Sykes. We can cut his trail no matter which way he goes, but we have no way of anticipating his choices in advance. My best guess is somewhere between Brownwood and Junction City. If he runs into bad road, we might make it into Brownwood before him."

"How soon?"

Jeb hesitated. "Sometime around midnight, if everything goes in our favor. Mid-morning at the outside unless one of us runs into serious delays. That's assuming he doesn't turn directly south for some reason, which would force us to chase him rather than cut him off. I don't think that's likely, but Sykes has surprised me more than once in the past."

The sun had already reached its highest point in the sky and we had fed ourselves from our supplies without stopping. We had lots of water in addition to the beer, but Jeb cautioned us not to over indulge.

"What if he stops some place for the night?" I asked.

"He won't. They'll sleep in the car and drive in shifts. Sykes isn't about to give us any unnecessary advantages."

"But he doesn't even know we're chasing him."

"In our profession, it's safest to assume that we're always being chased. One of the chores I took care of back in Dallas was to set someone watching our trail, in case some of Sykes' friends decide to find out what happened to Ted and his buddy."

We drove steadily throughout the afternoon and evening. Jeb spelled Yev for a while but the younger man obviously chafed at the inactivity and took over again after a very short interval. Our only breaks came at fuel stops and they were as quick as we could manage. Every time we reached a small town we were forced to slow down, but they were few and far between and didn't seriously impede our progress. We encountered other traffic rarely outside the towns proper, a handful of steamcars passing the other way or quickly overtaken, an occasional horse drawn wagon or individual rider. On two occasions we saw unicorns carrying passengers as well, invariably young children. Our only significant delay was at a toll bridge; it was an unofficial one not sanctioned by the Texican government, but Jeb paid without comment rather than argue the point, observing that illegal enterprises like this had sprung up throughout Texicana in recent years.

Occasionally Kelly or I would make some desultory effort to start a conversation, but Jeb was preoccupied and Yev had retreated into himself again, so our efforts all died stillborn. Jeb used a pocket charm to light his map now and then, and checked the kinship box more frequently. He was slowly eliminating possibilities from the map, narrowing the area with which we needed to concern ourselves. We changed course once, diverting onto a narrower roadway with no pavement and a cloud of dust rose behind us, but it was full dark by then so we weren't likely to give away our presence even if someone was looking for us.

Our surroundings hadn't been particularly interesting during the daylight and were even less so in the darkness. The long wait jangled my nerves and I tried to doze. Even if my nerves had been willing to cooperate, the rough road surface would not, and the jostling steadily worsened until we were holding onto the door handles with white knuckles. Our lights picked out the hunched shapes of cactus and little else, and we'd only encountered two other vehicles since leaving the paved road, both of them long haul steamvans. We swerved once when an unidentified animal ran out in front of us and Yev said something crude under his breath.

The sun was threatening to peek over the horizon when we reached the small town of Zephyr, and it came up a few minutes later as we approached the Colorado River crossing. Daylight restored my spirits slightly, although I hadn't managed to get much rest during the night. Fatigue had further dulled my anxiety and I just wanted to get things over with.

"They're close now, very close." Jeb folded the map into a more compact surface. "He either crossed further down and is following the highway on the other side of the river or he's on one of these two tributary roads, both of which merge with this one up ahead a few kilometers."

I reassured myself that my brand new pistol was in my pocket, and looked out the window with renewed interest. The road was winding its way back and forth up the face of the first in a series of steep though not particularly tall hills, barren plateaus actually with flat tops and little vegetation. It was hotter and drier than the previous morning, and our plume of dust was thick and dark.

"Would one of you youngsters mind unwrapping that large package when you have a moment?" Jeb gave us a broad wink. He had deflected our questions about the second parcel, the one I suspected held a Gatling gun. "I brought along a little surprise for our friend the colonel. With luck we won't need to use it, but luck hasn't chosen sides yet."

Kelly and I both attacked the wrapping, because she was as much in the dark as I. It was stiff butcher's paper, several layers thick, secured by heavy twine with knots that had been crimped with tin seals. It wasn't a Gatling after all, but some other weapon, one with which I was unfamiliar. It looked like a large version of the flare launcher that Jeb had used aboard the *River Warlock*. Three smaller boxes were arranged around it, each the length of my forearm. We opened one of these as well and saw two slender metallic cylinders with tapered heads. There were three narrow fins at the blunt end. I'd never seen anything like them before and said so.

"Explosive rockets," Jeb explained. "Restricted to military personnel, at least in theory, and too expensive to be common. I was quite surprised to find one in Quintaro's stockroom, but he always has been a resourceful fellow."

We began encountering heavier traffic after we passed through the first line of hills, most of it bound for the crossing, some of it coming toward us from the opposite side. Yev was forced to slow down and wait for opportunities to pass the slower vehicles, and the turbine labored heavily to speed up when we started into the second tier of rises. On the opposite side of that obstruction, we merged onto a paved and well maintained highway.

Jeb consulted his map and frowned. "I think they're ahead of us on this road now. We'll have to catch up to them."

"I'm not going to be able to coax much more out of the turbine," complained Yev. "And we're going to need to refuel pretty soon."

"Well, we'll just have to hope that Sykes runs into lengthier delays than we do. He has to be feeling more secure with each mile he covers, so there's a chance he'll stop for a break before crossing."

We saw a fuel stop a few minutes later and, although Jeb visibly chafed at the delay, it was best to take advantage of the opportunity now rather than risk having to hunt for one later. Kelly and I ran inside to use the facilities but the other two stayed in their seats. We had barely returned when we were on the move again, not even waiting for our change.

Signs warned us that we were approaching a toll bridge. I thought at first it was the Colorado Crossing, but it was a smaller tributary instead. Jeb told us that the kinship box was warm enough that he knew we were quite close. "They're either at the bridge or just beyond it." We did not, however, catch them before reaching the bridge, a narrow but serviceable span built by a private company some twenty years previously. Toll stations had been provided on either side, manned rather laconically judging by the significant backlog of traffic. We were stop and go for the last half mile, most of it along a road laid in a deep gully with little room to either side. Yev suggested abandoning the steamcar and going ahead on foot.

"No, we'll wait for a bit." Jeb settled back in his seat although he must have been as impatient as the rest of us. "Odds are they're on the bridge already. We'd never reach them in time." A few minutes later we could see directly onto the bridge, and although it was impossible to identify the vehicle from that distance, a red steamcar disappeared over the crest as we watched.

We had just emerged from the gully into relatively flat land. Jeb took a quick look out the side window and barked an order. "All right, take us around!"

Yev heaved on the wheel and pulled out of line. There was a lurch as we left the roadway and I slid partway off the seat, wrenching my good shoulder this time and banging my knee as well. I pushed myself back up and saw that we were rushing alongside the line of traffic now, while drivers and passengers stared at us with expressions of astonishment or anger.

We maneuvered deftly around cactus, mesquite, stunted trees, and other obstacles, banged our way across a shallow depression, then turned directly toward the bridge gates. The tollbooth was slightly to our right and an overweight man stood beside it, collecting payment from each car and painstakingly writing receipts when requested. The delay was such that no more than two vehicles were actually on the bridge at any given moment and the road beyond was clear except for one vehicle laboring up the slope. He must have heard the roar of our charge or perhaps the horns of those outraged by our unauthorized shortcut, because he raised his head, shading his eyes with one hand.

When it became obvious that we had no intention of stopping, he pulled a pistol from his belt holster and started to point it in our direction, but thought better of it as we bore down on him. He leaped aside just as we rushed pass, rebounding as we glanced off the front end of a steamvan waiting for the gates to lift. The barrier disintegrated into shards of splintered wood, one of which slammed into the windshield and sent jagged fault lines starring through the glass. Then we were past it and on the bridge, the turbine laboring to deal with the sudden incline.

There was only a single travel lane for each direction, so when we caught up to the steamcar in front of us, Yev swerved into the oncoming lane. We seemed to crawl past the other vehicle, whose driver shook her fist at us, and then we were over the crest and pulling back into the proper lane just before slamming into a horsedrawn wagon approaching from the opposite side. There was no barrier ahead of us at this end, but the tollkeeper frowned and waved angrily because of our reckless speed, shouting something we couldn't hear. There was a jolting thump as we reached solid ground and then we were laying another dust trail as we moved forward.

The road split into four diverging routes here, the largest of which led to the Crossing. One of the others ran roughly back eastwards and two turned west. Jeb consulted the map and swore softly. "They're not going for the river after all. Turn right, here. They're somewhere ahead of us. Keep your speed down for the time being. I want to know where he's heading. If you see them, don't close up yet."

But we didn't see them. Half an hour later we reached another intersection. Most of the traffic turned left here, but Jeb indicated we should continue straight through. A few minutes later I noticed a red car ahead of us, with two other vehicles in between. I leaned forward and, unaccountably, whispered. "Is that Sykes?"

"I think so, but he might be a bit further on. There aren't that many red Drakes around though." Yev made no effort to close the gap.

"How are we going to stop them?" My mouth was dry and my pulse was racing.

"We're not. They'll oblige us themselves sooner or later. Food or fuel or both."

A few minutes later the Kaiser Kruzer directly ahead of us turned into a private road. Only one vehicle separated us now, but Jeb cautioned Yev against getting too close. "We don't want Sykes to spot us. Surprise works to our advantage this time."

We continued onward, separated from our prey by a late model Roosevelt Roadster. Sykes' party must have accelerated because the space between them and the Roadster grew longer and longer until we could barely see them. Yev looked a question at Jeb who nodded, and at the next opportunity, he pulled out and began to pass.

The Roadster was driven by a rather attractive young woman who glanced in our direction, smiled and waved as we went by. Feeling foolish, I waved back. Then we were past her and accelerating.

"Don't get too close," warned Jeb. "I don't want to make them suspicious."

But that's when the situation took another drunken turn away from its original course. There was a loud roar and a violent concussion jolted us. Kelly slid across the seat and hit me in the side and I bumped my head against the windowframe.

"What the hell?" I gasped as the steamcar swerved despite Yev's efforts to hold it on the road.

And then we were hit a second time.

CHAPTER EIGHTEEN

We swerved again but Yev was better prepared this time and he managed to stay on the road. I twisted around to look behind us and saw that the Roadster was only a few meters behind. The young woman was closing on us again, and behind her a dark haired man was leaning out of the rear window, aiming at us with a pistol. We were close enough that the driver's eyes met mine and she smiled and even waved an insolent greeting as she tried to ram us for a third time.

Yev was waiting for the right moment to act. He yanked on the wheel suddenly and there was a high pitched metallic squeal as our bumpers scraped, but it was a glancing blow rather than a collision. The woman lost some ground but began to accelerate again as we wove back and forth, and it was obvious that her lighter vehicle was faster than we were. A horse drawn carriage coming from the opposite direction abruptly abandoned the road just as we roared past, careening from one lane to the other.

"They must be working for Sykes!" I shouted unnecessarily. My pistol was in my hand, although I don't remember actually drawing it. The words were hardly out of my mouth when the rear window disintegrated in a shower of broken glass.

"Remarkably fine shot that was," Jeb said dryly. "These people aren't amateurs."

"You don't have any idea how happy it makes me to hear you say that." I tried to brace myself and aim the pistol back through the broken window, but we were bumping up and down and weaving from side to side so rapidly that I couldn't get a proper aim. I fired one round in the general direction of our attackers, but it was more to assure myself I was doing something than from any hope of actually hitting anything. The Roadster was keeping pace with us now, no longer attempting to ram, more likely trying to get into position for another pistol shot. The shooter was patient and when he fired, the round whistled through our vehicle, exiting through the window on Kelly's side.

Yev twisted the wheel and there was a loud thump as we left the road. I glanced forward and thought we were going to hit a stunted tree head on but he somehow avoided it and climbed a slightly elevated ridge that ran parallel to the pavement. The Roadster didn't act quickly enough and couldn't follow because of a low rocky shelf that separated us, so instead they ran parallel, quickly closing the gap so that we were almost side by side. The marksman slid across the seat and I saw the pistol appear at the near side window.

"Any suggestions?" Yev sounded surprisingly calm given the circumstances, even more remarkable when I noticed that our improvised roadway ended not far ahead, ended in a pile of tumbled boulders in fact.

"You dealt the cards," said Jeb. "You play the hand." I think Yev actually laughed, but then he surprised me again by accelerating and swerving suddenly to the left, toward the road.

I thought we were going to flip over or break an axle. There were still rocks between us and the road, though not as large as at first, and I heard metal tearing as we scraped across them. We did manage to make it back to the pavement, but we lost most of our forward momentum, as well as paint and metal scrapings, and actually ended up behind the Roadster. Its driver must have been caught by surprise because she slowed suddenly, not realizing her danger. Our turbine complained shrilly at how it was being mistreated, but we began to speed up, closing the gap quickly, and if the woman had a split second in which to realize her mistake, it was not enough time for her to do anything about it.

We hit them hard, and our greater weight worked to our advantage now. The Roadster's rear end whipsawed back and forth as the driver fought for control, coming perilously close to the left side of the road, which was bordered by a drop long enough to have put them out of action permanently if they'd gone over. She was skillful enough to avoid that fate, but only by braking hard, and we leaped past them and took the lead again, a lead that increased dramatically in the first few seconds. The Roadster was motionless, its engine stalled. Kelly and I cheered and congratulated Yev, but our elation was short lived. By the time we crested the next gentle rise, we could see them behind us once again, and the gap was already closing.

They continued to gain on us but very slowly. Either the driver had grown more cautious or the Roadster had sustained some damage that was impeding its progress. They followed us for the better part of an hour, up and down gentle rises, across stretches of barren land that were indistinguishable from each other. The Roadster eventually closed to within a hundred meters and the marksman occasionally stuck his head out the window, as though measuring his chances, but the distance was too great and he fired no shots. For the same reason we made no effort to shoot at them. Our one consolation was that the ground was dry in this area and they must be breathing our dust, another good reason for keeping their distance.

Almost another hour passed before we spotted the red Drake, presumably carrying Sykes, slightly more than a kilometer ahead of us. That heartened us considerably even though we were now caught between two parties of the enemy. Sykes almost certainly knew of our presence now, although he might not know our identities.

"He may have noticed the warm spots on the kinship box and realized what it was," Jeb speculated. "Fortunately, he couldn't have known until we were close. If he'd guessed earlier, he'd have sent the box off with someone else to lead us astray." I couldn't help wondering if that had not in fact happened. We had no proof that Sykes was actually riding up ahead of us. But I kept my mouth shut. We'd had enough bad news already.

Jeb was studying his map again. "There's a road coming up on your right. Take it."

Yev turned and blinked, but didn't argue. Kelly and I exchanged glances and she shrugged. I certainly wasn't going to ask. Within a minute or two the road curved sharply to avoid some jagged rocks and I saw a narrow dirt road ahead that led off toward a humpbacked ridge. We slowed dramatically and made the turn, tires protesting as we spewed dust and gravel to the side. Behind us, the Roadster came to a stop at the turn, as though its driver couldn't decide whether to follow us or to continue as before and rejoin the rest of their party. They were still in sight when they backed up and turned away, and then we were passing through more rocky outcroppings and could no longer see them.

"We'll never catch up to them now!" I protested impatiently.

Kelly's voice was calmer. "What are we up to, Dad?"

"There's another bridge up ahead, a small one across the Runnins River. It's the only way across unless they backtrack and make their way along to one of the other minor crossings to the north. Which means they'd have to go back to one of the crossroads we passed an hour or so back."

"Well unless the bridge is out, I don't see how that's going to help us." I knew I sounded irritated but I didn't care. I didn't want Sykes to get away just when we had him in sight again.

"Then we'll just have to arrange for the bridge to be out when he gets there."

We came out of the rocks and turned right to parallel a narrow, fast moving body of water that was probably a tributary of the Runnins. I glanced over Jeb's shoulder to look at the map and saw that we were headed straight out onto a wedge shaped peninsula that pointed directly at the bridge, but which had no access to it except back the way we'd come. I had completely forgotten about the oversized weapon in the rear compartment, so I had no idea what Jeb could possibly have in mind, and he didn't enlighten me until we had rolled to a stop and climbed out of the battered Cheviot.

The bridge was so close that we could see a horse drawn carriage half way across. There was no other traffic at the moment and we couldn't see any sign of Sykes or the Roadster, which would have had to circumnavigate a wide expanse of rocky ground to reach the approach. Yev and Jeb carried the rocket launcher and tripod around to the front of the car and began assembling it.

"Are you really going to blow up the bridge?" I was watching the horse and carriage with one hand shading my eyes. They had almost finished the crossing, but a steamvan had just started from the opposite side.

"If I have to, that's what I'll do. This is too important to be fastidious, Jimmy. But I'm hoping we can get away with something a little less drastic."

The bridge was built almost entirely of wood, probably treated with stress spells and other bindings to reinforce its structure. There was a very slight rise in the middle but it was mostly level. The suspension cables looked like spider webs from this distance where they were draped over two pair of central towers. Yev cautioned us to stay away from the launcher and joined us at the side of the steamcar. "They say these things never blow up beforehand, but I still don't trust them."

Jeb was taking his time with the sights and I kept looking at the approach road, expecting to see the red Drake or the Roadster at any moment. In fact I was looking that way when there was a whoosh and bang like a firecracker and a projectile shot away from us trailing smoke and sparks.

It looked to me like Jeb had overshot his mark by a considerable distance. The missile passed through the web of cables near the top of the rightmost pair of towers and disappeared beyond. There was a dull thud and an enormous spray of water rose into the air. The steamvan slowed halfway across and then came to a stop.

"Damned fool!" complained Jeb. "He's just where I don't want him to be."

The seconds ticked past and a movement at the periphery of my vision caught my eye. "Here he comes!" I shouted. "It's Sykes!"

Sure enough, Sykes' distinctive vehicle had nosed up to the bridge ramp.

"Can't be helped then," muttered Jeb and bent over the launcher. Almost immediately there was another hiss and bang and a second missile shot away from us, this one with a slightly lower trajectory. I thought he had overshot a second time, but I had misjudged his target. Jeb wasn't aiming for the roadbed. The missile struck the nearside support tower squarely and the entire top third exploded into a cloud of torn wood and shredded cables. The debris fell partially over one side into the water, but most of it crashed down onto the roadway, some of it narrowly missing the van, which suddenly lurched forward, pulling away from the wreckage. Jeb was already loading another round, which seemed unnecessary to me. It was obvious that the center of the span was now impassable and would be until the wreckage was cleared away.

The red Drake had stopped and was now slowly backing off the bridge. Jeb was turning the tripod in that direction. He fired just as they reached solid ground, but his aim wasn't quite as good this time, or more likely he wasn't intending to actually hit them. That might have destroyed the crystal. The missile left its usual sooty wake, but its flight seemed erratic and it veered off to the right, impacting harmlessly against a rocky bluff. Jeb had started to load another round but whoever was driving had reversed course quickly and had already started toward the cover provided by the bluff. Jeb shook his head resignedly. "All right, let's get moving."

I helped them bundle the launcher back into storage. The muzzle was so hot that I burned the palm of my hand maneuvering it into place, just one more in a long string of minor injuries I'd sustained during the past few days. Yev was already winding the turbine and we were barely inside before we were backing around to face the way we'd come.

If anything we traveled even faster on the return trip, bouncing on our seats and bracing ourselves to avoid further damage to our bruised and aching bodies. Jeb made us stop just shy of the intersection and park between two large boulders so that we couldn't be seen from the main road. We set up the rocket launcher on a mostly level piece of ground slightly higher, with one round chambered and the two remaining near at hand. From where we sat, we commanded the intersection through which Sykes would have to pass to escape, and there was no way for attackers to approach us on foot without being spotted.

"What if they abandon the steamcars and try to walk out of here? They must know we're responsible for the damage to the bridge. Will Sykes risk letting us have another shot at him?"

"Sykes knows I don't dare fire directly at him. If the crystal is destroyed, the game is lost. He'll be trying to outmaneuver us, find an escape route we don't have covered. The nearest settlement is ten miles, but I don't underestimate the man. He's got nerve and he's fast on his feet. He has managed to outthink us a few times already, and I don't expect that he'll just throw up his hands and accept defeat. And he won't abandon his transport unless he has no other choice."

So we settled down to wait. And waited. And waited some more. It was Kelly who finally articulated what we all were feeling. "Something's gone wrong."

As though wakening from a slumber, Jed stirred from his resting place. "You're right. He's had more than enough time to meet up with the Roadster, compare notes, make plans, and get back here." He pulled the map from his pocket and began scrutinizing it again. "Damned if I can see any other practical way out of there, but maps have been wrong before. Let's go, but carefully. He may be counting on us poking our noses into a trap."

We packed up and headed out, cautiously, in the direction of the bridge. We were extraordinarily careful because there were any number of places from which we could have been ambushed, but the minutes passed uneventfully and I began to chafe at the inactivity. Imperturbable, Jeb ordered a pause every so often to investigate an area where they might have left the road and concealed their tracks, but each time without profit.

We weren't quite far enough along to see the ruined bridge when we found the rough track leading off to our right. As Jeb had feared, it wasn't on his map, not surprising since it wasn't a proper road at all. The ground formed a natural ramp for the first few meters, but quickly deteriorated as it passed through two crumbling spires and twisted off out of sight behind a jagged knoll.

We stopped again and Jeb got out, walked ahead of us and studied the ground for endless seconds. He picked up a handful of soil, rubbed it between his fingers, stared off into the distance for a few seconds and then let it trickle back down to the ground before returning to us.

"Two cars went off this way and not long ago," he said curtly. "Stay alert. They may be waiting for us to follow them."

The whine of our turbine was loud and unmistakable. If there was someone lying in wait for us ahead, they'd hear us coming well in advance. We couldn't possibly sneak up on them except on foot, and that was impossible until we knew where they were. I had developed a blinding headache that was as much tension as the heat, which had turned the land around us into a gigantic baking pan. The romantic appeal of being involved in such a dramatic situation had worn thin a long time ago, and it was only my sense of dignity that prevented me from getting out and leaving them to go on without me.

And Kelly's presence no doubt had something to do with it. I would not have wanted her to think badly of me.

We passed between the spires without incident, made the turn and found ourselves looking out over a gentle slope dotted with widely interspersed boulders, a few narrow defiles, and patches of sparse desert growth. The curve of the Runnins was a darker line in the distance. On the far side of the water, a paved road ran along the shoreline, but without a bridge or ferry, it was as remote as the moon. The ground was passable, though rather bumpy, and Yev picked his way carefully, watching for signs of our quarry. We passed the entrance to a small mine, boarded shut and undisturbed for years, and the rough path we'd been following became even less hospitable from that point onward. At the top of the next rise, we could see a small wooden shack in the distance, leaning drunkenly to one side and with its roof collapsed.

There were two steamcars parked behind the shack, one of them bright red, the other a late model Roosevelt Roadster.

We came to a stop, the turbine idling. "They'll be set up and waiting for us, probably scattered through the rocks in a crescent. I'd guess there's six of them, counting Sykes, but there could be one or two more, so don't take anything for granted."

Kelly and I unloaded the launcher and carried it to a sheltered spot where the ground was level enough to support the tripod. Yev disappeared into the rocks with drawn pistol, to make sure we hadn't already been flanked. Jeb seemed unperturbed as he stared toward the shack, but I noticed that he stayed behind cover and that he held a pistol in his hand. After a few minutes that stretched on forever, he came over to where Kelly and I crouched in hiding.

"They must know that we're here," I ventured. "Why haven't they started shooting?"

"They're biding their time. Right now we can only guess where they're hiding themselves. That all changes once the shooting starts."

As if on cue, three shots rang out in rapid succession. We all, Jeb included, ducked behind cover, but the firing stopped immediately.

"Where are they?" I whispered this time.

Jeb made an unhappy sound. "One of them's down near the vehicles. That's the one with the nervous trigger finger. No sign of the others yet."

There was another report, this time from somewhere off to our left, and a spit of dust flew up near the shack. "That's Yev," explained Jeb. "Politely answering the greeting. He'll be moving now so they won't know where he is."

A few minutes passed and a single shot ran out from somewhere distant. It wasn't even close. The silence stretched onward.

"All right," said Jeb. "Let's step on the nest and see what we can stir up." He checked the box to make sure he wasn't aiming at the crystal, then began sighting the rocket launcher and Kelly and I moved to one side. When he was satisfied, he fired and this time his aim was right on target.. The rocket hit the scarlet Drake directly on the side of the turbine chamber, which exploded with a loud hiss of escaping steam, then immediately burst into flames. Within seconds the fire reached the fuel compartment, which caused a second explosion, a double thump. Flaming fuel sprayed in every direction and thick clouds of ropy, black smoke coiled up into the sky. Some of the fuel landed on the hood of the Roadster, which was quickly engulfed, and more liquid fire spread across the ground. The ruined shack was dry and rotten and it went up like tinder, the flames spreading so eagerly that we heard the pops of the wood as it burst apart.

From somewhere behind the cabin, a hunting rifle came flying through the air and a male voice shouted, "I'm coming out! Don't shoot! I'm not armed!"

"All right!" Jeb called back. "Show yourself, and particularly your hands!"

A man I'd never seen before stepped out into the open, tentatively at first, but more hastily as the shack began to burn even more intensely, showering him with sparks. He approached us steadily but once he was beyond the immediate reach of the fire, Jeb called out to him again.

'Lie down on your stomach and spread your arms and legs!"

The man hesitated only a second before complying, then waited patiently without speaking. Jeb made no move and neither did we, until Yev emerged from the rocks, surprisingly close to the conflagration and waved to us. He crossed to the prone man and patted him down, then beckoned for us to come out.

Jeb and Kelly stepped out of cover immediately and I followed suit after a short delay, although I felt as though a target had been drawn on my chest. "Aren't we taking a chance doing this?" I whispered.

Kelly shrugged. "Doesn't matter. The rest of them are gone."

"Gone? Gone where?" I scanned the countryside and saw nothing but more of the same.

"Across the river," Jeb tossed back over his shoulder. "I don't imagine they tried swimming, although it's manageable enough. My guess is they had an inflatable in one of the cars."

CHAPTER NINETEEN

We left Sykes' crony, minus his weapon, since there was no point in holding him captive. It took almost two hours to drive to the next intact bridge, including a fuel stop, and something less than half that to retrace our way along the coast highway. After a very brief search, we found an inflatable boat crumpled and concealed in a rocky cleft. There was very little conversation among us, and for the first time even Jeb seemed less than optimistic. Sykes had remained one step ahead of us, and the race was getting near the finish line.

I had taken some comfort from the fact that the other party was on foot now and would not be able to move as quickly as before, but that faint hope was dashed when Yev spotted a flash of color from the tall grass that grew along the shore. It was the body of a middle-aged man, lying on his back, one arm across his eyes, the other flung to the side. He was wearing overalls and a plaid shirt, his face sported an uneven beard, and he'd been shot through the heart, a dark, formless blotch of darkness on his chest. The expression on his face was more surprise than pain.

"Where did he come from?" I asked hoarsely. "Are they fighting among themselves now?"

"Hardly. Sykes needed transportation and this poor soul was the first to come by." Jeb leaned forward, close to the body, breathing deeply. "He smells of horse, so it must have been a carriage of some sort." He straightened up, looked back along the roadway which turned west and cut between two spurs of rubble. "He'll be looking for something faster, so let's close the gap while we still have the advantage."

We left the body where it lay despite my personal misgivings, but there really wasn't anything we could do about it. Yev coaxed as much speed as possible out of the turbine, but there was a faint irregularity in its throbbing that all of us heard but none of us mentioned. A breakdown couldn't come at a worse possible time and we all held our metaphorical breath. There was very little traffic coming from the opposite direction, and all of it horse drawn. We overtook four carriages ourselves, slowing each time and watching closely to make sure we weren't bypassing our quarry. There were no other steam driven vehicles, which was heartening.

And if Sykes had commandeered one already, we should have seen the abandoned wagon, because the country had opened up again and there was no place to conceal one even if the horses were driven off. This was one of the least settled parts of Texicana, with no cities nearby, and there was a good chance that Sykes would find it impossible to upgrade his transportation in the short term.

Jeb consulted the map and the kinship box and he didn't frown, but he didn't smile either.

"What if he discards the other box?" I ventured.

Jeb shrugged. "More likely he'll keep it so he knows where we arc."

We reached a town of sorts eventually, Ulager's Folly. There were fewer than a score of buildings and some of them were no longer in use. It was a crossroads community, but that was its only reason for existence, and not a particularly good one. We refueled even though we really didn't need to and we stretched our legs while Jeb talked to the attendant, telling him we were looking for a party of our friends who had come this way earlier in the day. She was amiable and a bit of a talker but couldn't help. Wagons passed all the time, and she didn't pay attention to any of them unless they stopped to buy feed or water or any of the trinkets and conveniences she sold inside. Jeb asked about business in general and was pleased to hear that we were the first powered vehicle to come by in at least two days except that "one of them big steamvans came through last night at some ungodly hour and woke everyone up for miles around".

Three of the buildings in Ulager's Folly were taverns and one claimed to be a hotel but was probably actually a bordello. There was a hardware store, another, dingier hotel that might actually rent rooms, and a feed and grain store that looked as though it hadn't been open in a while. I found it all rather depressing and was greatly relieved when we were on the move again, ignoring the crossroad after Jeb consulted the kinship box. The road curved to the northwest and another small river appeared on our right. The map showed that our present route would take us parallel to this tributary, the Black Snake River, for almost a hundred miles, then jog left through slightly more hospitable country until it reached Clyde, one of the larger towns in this part of the world. I had visited Clyde once, as a boy traveling with my father, who was negotiating to buy mutton and centaur futures, but my memories of it were vague and incomplete and no doubt hopelessly out of date by now. I did remember an elaborately decorated confectionary stand and wondered if it would still be there.

As it happened, we never got that far and I still don't know.

Jeb had been holding the kinship box in his hand, trying to estimate the distance separating us by the relative warmth of the facing edge. He made a sudden, unintelligible sound of surprise. "Slow down. There's nothing on the map, but the road is more or less straight ahead and they've gone right, not too far ahead of us either."

Kelly and I leaned forward over the seats and watched as we negotiated a gentle left turn to bypass a grassy knoll that hugged the side of the river. The road turned back almost immediately, but still diverged from the river by quite a wide margin, far enough that we occasionally lost sight of it depending upon the rise and fall of the intervening prairie. We reached a straightaway and our speed edged up slightly, but dropped again as Jeb pointed to a rough track that cut away to our right. A small, hand painted, very faded sign said "Private" and there were two posts for a gate, but no other barrier. The ground had been rising slightly for the last few kilometers, and it did so now even more steeply as we left the main road and followed the track. Then it dipped suddenly into a natural crevice that was barely wide enough to accommodate us.

"Stay alert. They're very close now." I hadn't needed Jeb's warning; my pistol was already in my hand, although once again I didn't remember drawing it.

Two sharp, twisting curves later, the road dropped away, ending at an elliptical parking area adjacent to a good sized, grayish brown building that had been built half on shore, half protruding out over the Black Snake. As we advanced, I recognized the housing was designed for a hydroelectric paddlewheel, from which the paddle itself was missing. The building, although superficially intact, showed clear signs of abandonment. And not recently either. Brush had blown up against the walls, the windows were boarded over, and the roof, though largely intact, was sagging.

Off to our left, two harnessed horses were cropping unenthusiastically at some brush. They were still attached to an open topped wagon, which looked to be empty. There were no signs of life, but I very much doubted that we were alone, or unobserved. The sound of our turbine must have been audible from the moment we left the road.

We stopped at a respectable distance and Yev killed the engine.

"What is this place?" asked Kelly, craning her head around.

"An abandoned mill of some sort," I ventured. "There's good farmland not far to the north. I'd guess they used to bring the grain downriver on barges and mill it right here. Generated their own power, looks like. The whole thing probably failed when the trirail went through Clyde and offered a quicker, cheaper, and more reliable way to move crops to the major markets. I've seen dozens of places like this, backwaters that couldn't compete with the cities and modern mass transportation."

With our weapons in hand, we stepped out of the car, separating and approaching circumspectly, taking advantage of what cover was available, which wasn't much. Other than the horses, there was no sign of anything alive. If Sykes had checked his kinship box, he must have realized we were close on his heels again, and since he couldn't outrun us, his only alternative would be to lay a trap.

There were three visible entrances to the mill. The first was a double door which had been boarded shut, although the left side jamb had become separated from the wall and sagged inward, providing enough access that a child or small adult could have slipped through. A smaller door to one side was closed and apparently undamaged. On the side opposite the river, a loading dock sagged precariously, its interior so cloaked in shadows that I couldn't make out the details, but there would certainly be an entrance there as well. The building itself was barrel shaped until it reached the water, and buttressed on the opposite end by two small silos and the housing for a grain elevator. Three smaller buildings, probably for tool storage or something similar, stood separate from the mill itself. One of them had lost its roof and a second was leaning at a precarious angle.

"Any suggestions?" Jeb asked wryly. "Other than waiting for them to get hungry or thirsty?"

"How about the fire escape?" We were crouched behind a sandy rise halfway between the steamcar and the mill. Yev was referring to a wooden ladder that had been nailed to the side of the main building. The bottom rung was a good two meters off the ground and the top parallel to a partially boarded window near the top of the mill. It was right at the corner closest to the river, where tall grass and scrub growth were crowding up against the wall. It would provide some cover, but not much.

"Think you can get to it all right?" Jeb sounded dubious.

"I'll manage." He moved away from us, retreating backwards and then disappearing into the hillocks to our left.

Jeb waited till he was gone before turning to us. "Anyone else got any good ideas?"

Kelly spoke up immediately. "I'll take the front. I'm the only one who'll fit."

Her father accepted her offer without argument, and I felt compelled to volunteer for something. "I can try the other door. If it's locked, maybe I can work my way around to the loading dock and find a way inside from there."

"Try the back first. There might be some kind of rear entrance. The loading area's probably where they got in, and they'll have it covered." He laughed humorlessly. "They'll have them all covered, actually, but I figure there's only five of them so their resources are almost as limited as ours. But don't take chances. Remember that gentleman we found back by the river. Sykes may play the gentleman, but he's ruthless. He'll kill us all and it won't disturb his appetite any."

I hoped my nervousness wasn't painted all over my face as I nodded. My heart was pounding and my mouth was dry, and it wasn't until sometime later that I realized Jeb had never said anything about what he intended to do. Kelly was already slithering over the rise and I followed suit, at a slightly different angle. I snagged a sleeve on a twisted root and banged my knee against a half buried rock but when I finally ran out of cover and sprinted the rest of the way to the side of the mill, there had been no gunfire, no shouts of alarm, nothing to indicate I'd been seen. I stood there for a few seconds, catching my breath, and spotted Jeb for just a split second as he moved from cover to cover, and it was only then that I realized he was headed toward the loading area. I cursed him for a fool, but under my breath.

Kelly broke cover a second later and made it to the sagging door, slipped through so quickly that it was as if she'd fallen into a hole. There was no sign of Yev, but from where I stood, I couldn't see the area from which he'd be approaching. As quickly as that, I was alone.

I was struck by how quiet it was. The river ran smooth and untroubled, there was only the hint of a breeze, and I had yet to hear either a bird or an insect. Our cooling turbine let out a pop every once in a while, and one of the horses whinnied nervously for a few seconds, but nothing else disturbed the silence. It occurred to me that I was horribly miscast for my part in this little melodrama. Even as a child I hadn't been fond of violent games like Rebels and Redcoats or Find the Greenies. I was a merchant by nature as well as profession, and here I was, pistol in hand, preparing to break into an abandoned building filled with killer spies. My knees suddenly felt rubbery and my eyes went out of focus. What in the world was I doing here?

I told myself to breathe deeply and evenly, reminded myself how important it was to prevent Sykes from getting away, remembered the various indignities he'd inflicted upon me and remembered as well the way Kelly had looked at me with admittedly surprised respect after I'd dealt with Dana at the warehouse. Slowly self control returned, and I turned to the task at hand.

I edged carefully to the door and tried the handle, but one look told me that I wasn't going to enter this way. The lock may or may not have been engaged, but it didn't matter; the beam above the doorway had dropped, smashing the mantle and pressing down onto the door itself. It was wedged immovably in place.

My next best chance was to follow Kelly through the rent in the wall, but it proved to be too narrow. I scraped some skin off my shoulder and hip discovering that fact. Beyond was the corner of the building and the fire ladder, and I tried there next, with equal lack of success. Yev might be capable of the prodigious leap necessary to reach the lowest rung, which was in fact better than two meters from ground level, but the task was beyond me.

So I started cautiously toward the hydroelectric annex. From a distance, it looked more hopeful. A large section of the abutting structure had collapsed into the river and portions of the flooring were completely gone. There were gaping holes in the walls as well, and it wouldn't be long before this entire wing was reduced to a skeleton. Much of the roof had survived, however, and the interior was filled with shadows. I climbed in through one of several gaps, brushing away generations of spiderwebs.

The passageway from the annex to the mill was open, a narrow but clear corridor, at least as far as the light penetrated. I crouched at the entrance for several seconds, letting my eyes adjust to the darkness, but the shadows were so thick that I used my hands to ward off invisible cables that hung from the ceiling, and splinters of wood that jutted out from the walls. There was some minor debris on the floor, and I stumbled once, the noise alarming me more than the possibility of falling, and I picked my way much more carefully from that point onward.

The interior damage was extensive. Water dripped somewhere in the distance, a rhythmic drumming sound, as though it were falling on a piece of sheet metal. The corridor ended in a large open space, and I could see the housings for machinery which had apparently been removed when the mill failed. Some of the interior walls, which probably had enclosed offices and storage compartments, had collapsed partially or completely. There were, or had been, two levels above me, connected by staircases, catwalks, and ramps. Some of these remained in place, but others had collapsed into twisted piles of rotting timber or rusting metal.

I advanced slowly and carefully, my pistol raised, my free hand warding off the ever present spider webs and other, more substantial, obstacles. The silence was uncanny. Neither Sykes' party nor my companions made any sound.

Moving to the left, around the periphery of the main milling floor, I discovered two more corridors. The first led to a collection of large wooden vats, arranged in a double row, with some enigmatic mechanical devices hovering overhead. The other was in better condition than most of the rest of the building, and several doors, all closed, concealed what lay in those rooms. There was a bright gleam from my right, the entrance through which Kelly had entered, but I could see no sign of her or anyone else. I was beginning to wonder if this was going to turn out to be more show than substance, like our confrontation at the ruined shack.

I reached a wooden staircase that led to the second level and tested it by climbing up onto the first two steps. It was firm underfoot and accepted my weight without making a protesting sound. Moving very cautiously, I had advanced three more steps when something disturbed the shadows above and ahead of me.

I raised my weapon and started to retreat down the stairs and almost lost my footing in the process. There was an echoing crash and a burst of light and something flashed past my face. Later it would occur to me that the stumble had probably saved my life. Two more shots rang out as I crouched, my back pressed against the handrail, and I was about to fire back when the rail gave way with a scream of tearing wood. There may have been an additional shot or two, but for the next few seconds all I could do was throw my arms around my face and hope that I would not be impaled on something sharp when I hit the floor.

I slammed into something hard enough to stun me and a heavy object fell across my thighs. Cautiously I dropped my arms, overjoyed to find myself still alive and – insofar as I could tell – relatively unharmed. Debris was still falling, small pieces of torn wood, a seemingly endless quantity of dust, some of which got into my eyes which immediately began tearing. Blinking furiously, I rolled over into a prone position and pulled my legs up close to my body. I was considering trying to stand up when someone whispered from close at hand.

"Are you all right, Jim?"

I couldn't see her in the darkness, but the voice was Kelly's. "What happened?" I whispered back.

"One down the rest to go." A shape moved in the shadows as she emerged from her hiding place behind a pile of crumbling wooden crates. I stood up and brushed off my clothing, then stopped when I saw the body sprawled on the floor only a meter away. The light was poor and it wasn't Sykes or the woman. I thought it might be the marksman from the Roadster, but couldn't be sure. Kelly had shot him in the face.

We moved away from the staircase. There was a quick, soft creaking sound from overhead, but I couldn't tell whether it was an unwary tread or just the settling sounds common to decaying buildings. I made a tentative move back toward the staircase but Kelly caught hold of my arm, then nodded toward a row of chin high wooden stalls along the far wall.

"Let's check those out first. We don't want to have someone waiting to cut off our retreat."

I nodded and we moved in that direction, with more confidence in my case. We'd accounted for one of the enemy, or Kelly had, and I'd survived the encounter with nothing more than fresh bruises. If our count was right, it was now four to four, and I figured Jeb was worth any two of them. I should have remembered that pride goes before a fall. I was completely unprepared for the attack when it came.

A large section of the ceiling had come loose and was hanging precariously, and through the gap I could see all the way to the roof, which had also partially collapsed. Bright light streamed in through a few small openings, just enough to be dazzling without actually illuminating much of anything. Kelly and I were about three meters apart as we reached the row of stalls, which were clearly meant for storage. A torn bag of grain slumped in the corner of the leftmost, although most of its contents had long since disappeared. Kelly checked two stalls and I tried the next, found it empty except for cobwebs and a rusted shovel. There were only two left, and Kelly was a step ahead of me, clearing hers and turning away just as I reached for the door to the last.

The moment my fingers touched the cool metal of the handle, the door burst open, sending me staggering away, windmilling my arms to keep from falling.

The shaft of light from the collapsed doorway danced with dust particles for a split second, then vanished as a massive figure came toward me. Despite my surprise, I fired two rounds into its chest, and it staggered to a stop but didn't go down. It was bright enough for me to see that there was a bloodless bullet wound in my attacker's forehead as well; it was the zombie that we'd first seen back at the farm.

Shaken by the two slugs, it hesitated but then it was coming toward me again and only its innate clumsiness allowed me to avoid the clenched fist it swung toward my face. Unfortunately there was a supporting column directly behind me and I backed into it, stalling my retreat. The other arm came at me and struck me a glancing blow, glancing but still powerful enough to knock me off my feet and into a nearby work table, which obligingly collapsed under my weight, depositing me ungently on the floor. I hit my left elbow so hard that my entire arm went numb.

I heard more firing, but didn't count the shots this time. During the fall I had lost sight of my attacker and was in such a near panic that I rolled away recklessly, tucking my pistol against my side so that I wouldn't drop it. When I reached clear floor, I sprang to my feet, but managed only two steps before I lost my footing again and fell against a waist high partition of mesh wire in a wooden frame. It held together but I caught my sleeve on the wire and it wouldn't pull free. Terrified, I turned back the way I'd come and raised the pistol.

Zombies aren't very bright, can follow only the simplest of instructions, and are incapable of making independent decisions. This one was no exception. It stood motionless, its head swiveling back and forth between me and Kelly, who stood with her back braced against the wall, both hands holding her pistol level. Some small differential must have pushed it down one horn of the dilemma because it lurched toward Kelly and raised both arms above its shoulders.

I tugged furiously at my snagged sleeve, finally tore enough of the fabric that I was able to pull free. Another shot rang out as I started forward, but from an entirely different quarter this time. The zombie's head jerked wildly and it stopped moving, but only for a second. Jeb stepped out into the open and advanced, shouting something I couldn't make out. The zombie hesitated again, then turned toward him and Kelly bolted in my direction. Her father remained where he was until the creature was dangerously close, then ducked under an outflung arm and slipped away, running easily toward the base of the staircase.

The zombie lumbered after him and Kelly spun and fired two shots directly into its back. I added two of my own, but there was no noticeable change in its movements. Although they can be destroyed by conventional means that only occurs when enough of the internal organs are destroyed that the animating magic can no longer maintain its integrity. Unfortunately, I had no idea how much damage was required, and so far this one seemed barely inconvenienced. Nor had I forgotten the others. Sykes and the young woman were still unaccounted for, and there was probably at least one person we hadn't seen yet.

Jeb climbed the first three stairs, spun around, and fired again. I saw the creature's head jerk and it even missed a step, but then it was moving again. Kelly crouched and shouted something at me, but she had to repeat herself before I realized what she was saying. "The knees! Shoot it in the knees!"

Like I said, I'm not the world's greatest shot, but we were so close that I could hardly miss. Both of us fired, at the same knee as it happened, and the zombie staggered and started to fall as the shattered leg gave way. It was still half erect, leaning against one of the staircase supports, and either through blind rage, bad luck, or from some residual intelligence, it fought back in the only way remaining. Both arms went around the support and it heaved, pulled the upright out of place. Boards snapped and nails tore free. The entire staircase slewed abruptly to one side, swayed, and then began to collapse. With an agility I could only envy, Jeb leaped into the air, passed directly over the laboring monster, and landed deftly on his feet.

I thought that would be the end of it, but the zombie somehow pulled itself upright, hopping on its good leg and dragging the other behind. Jeb joined Kelly and I and we all turned to fire, but Kelly and I had emptied our pistols, and Jeb had only a single remaining round. We were about to run for it when something dropped from the gaping hole in the ceiling, striking the zombie squarely in the back with both feet. It fell forward and the newcomer wrapped one arm under its chin and pulled the head back. There was a sharp CRACK! and the creature stopped moving.

"A timely entrance, Yev." Jeb started to reload his weapon and Kelly and I belatedly imitated him.

Yev stepped away from the zombie and started toward us, and that moment of inattention almost cost him his life. Even though its neck was twisted at an impossible angle, the zombie rose onto one forearm and reached out with the other hand to grab a length of splintered wood, formerly part of the guard rail. Yev sensed the motion but not quite quickly enough. He was hit directly on one shoulder, lifted into the air, and crashed to the floor a meter away.

There was pistol fire from my left and from my right as Jeb fired his last round into the zombie's head. Kelly had picked up Yev's weapon and emptied it as quickly as she could work the trigger. It wasn't until the din and its echoes had died down and the monstrous form was finally motionless, all spark of its unnatural life extinguished, that I drew my next real breath.

Yev was conscious but in severe pain when we reached him. His left arm was broken in two places and one cheek was scraped raw. Kelly immediately set about making a splint; fortunately, we had enough wood scattered about to have ministered to a small army of casualties. When she was done, he insisted upon standing up and did so, although he seemed a bit unsteady.

Throughout all of this, Jeb had stood guard with his reloaded weapon ready, his eyes watching the superstructure above us.

"There's no one up there." Yev sounded apologetic. "I searched what's left of the building, but most of it is ready to collapse. There's no sign of them."

Jeb looked skeptical, but he reached into his pocket and took out the kinship box. He held it, concentrating as he slowly turned in a semicircle, then sighed and put it away. A moment later he was extracting an identical carving from the pocket of what remained of the zombie.

It was empty, of course. Sykes had taken the crystal out before planting it as part of this ambush. He was out there somewhere with the crystal, at least two companions, and we hadn't the slightest idea where he was or in which direction he was moving.

Even Jeb looked discouraged.

CHAPTER TWENTY

We walked, or in the cases of Yev and I, limped back to the steamcar. Yev slid into the back seat; he was clearly in no condition to drive. I was going to volunteer, but Kelly was behind the wheel and charging the turbine before I had a chance to open my mouth. Jeb got in beside her and I took the last seat in the back.

"Where to?" She sounded less than enthusiastic.

"Back to Ulager's Folly." Jeb's voice was barely audible. "That's the most likely place for them to have split up."

Jeb carried an analgesic potion which seemed to lessen Yev's pain and he drifted off into an uneasy sleep. I declined the offer of some for my own comparatively minor hurts, which I was beginning to consider badges of honor.

"Could they have been hiding in Ulager's Folly when we passed through?" Kelly spoke without taking her eyes from the road.

"Either that or they'd already left somehow. The diversion would gain them some time at worst. At best, their playmates might have killed one or more of us."

I searched my memory. "I don't remember seeing any powered vehicles in town. There was an old bus parked behind one of the buildings, but all of its tires were missing. They must have gotten riding stock or another wagon and team."

Jeb nodded noncommittally. "Maybe, but Sykes wouldn't be happy unless he had a chance of outrunning us. He wouldn't settle for anything that slow unless he had no alternative. My guess is he'd stay put until something faster came by and then commandeer it like he did the wagon."

"He might have a long wait," I observed. "We haven't seen anything powered going in either direction."

"There's one logical place for them to have staked out. The fuel stop right on the edge of town."

Everything looked normal until we were close enough to see the vultures circling. Jeb cursed and I heard Kelly draw a sharp breath. A few seconds later we found the bodies of an elderly couple lying behind a berm not far from the pump, along with the attendant. All three had been shot through the heart.

"Why'd he have to kill them?" I turned away, sickened as much by the callous way the bodies had been discarded as by the deadly act itself. "They weren't any threat to him. He stole their vehicle; what could they possibly have done about it?"

"They would have notified the COPs," Jeb said quietly. "But more to the point, they might have told us what happened and which way they went."

"So which way did they go?" Kelly turned her head, spanning the roads south, west, and north. "Not the way we just came, but did they backtrack or take the side road?"

"The western road winds around and peters out in the middle of nowhere. My guess is he went back south. There's another place he could turn west there, not a great piece of road but it connects to a better one after a few miles. That one runs almost due west to the border."

We dragged the bodies inside to protect them from the birds, then set out again, making the best speed we could manage. The turbine was audibly laboring now, but Kelly nursed it along and we made good progress. We reached the side road shortly after noon and I suppose I must have been hungry, but the muscles around my stomach were so taut with tension and anger that I declined the offer of food when Yev roused and pulled out some of our provisions from the rear compartment. I also felt a tinge of despair, because I was beginning to accept the possibility that we were going to lose this race, and that would have been a personal as well as a national tragedy.

As it happened, we caught up to Sykes so quickly that even Jeb was momentarily startled.

There were only two people in the car, Sykes and the young woman from the Roadster. We could tell that right away because they were in a two-seater Stanley Steamer, almost an antique. If there'd been a third in their party, he'd been left behind somewhere along the line. With its oversized and inefficient turbine chugging away at full power, the Stanley couldn't have managed more than half of our own somewhat reduced speed, and only the fact that they enjoyed a substantial head start had allowed them to stay ahead of us for as long as they had.

They must have recognized us immediately when we appeared to their rear, and as soon as we were in range, the woman turned around and leveled a pistol toward us, although she didn't fire it until we were much closer. Even from that range she was wildly off target. The Stanleys were famous for their bad suspension system and she bobbed up and down like a kite on a windy day.

"Let's see how they like it for a change!" Kelly gripped the wheel tightly and coaxed the last bit of power from the turbine.

We hit them squarely and the jolt made Sykes momentarily lose control, although he recovered just before they ran completely off the road, swerving back onto the relatively smooth track. The Steamer was cumbersome and unresponsive, which helped us, but it was much heavier than we were, which helped them. Our front lights shattered and the hood buckled and Kelly seemed to be having trouble holding a straight course, probably because the alignment had been knocked out of true.

"I don't think I can force them off the road this way. Any ideas, anyone?"

"Can you get past them and cut them off?" asked Jeb. It looked unlikely to me. The road was so narrow that if we'd encountered someone coming from the other direction, one party would have been forced off to allow the other to pass. Kelly edged as far to her left as possible, but it was obvious that there was insufficient clearance to pass.

We continued like that for five minutes, then ten. We were too low on ammunition to waste any of it in low percentage shooting, and apparently the same held true for our adversaries. The road eventually veered sharply to the left to avoid a steep defile. It was a bit wider here and Kelly tried once more to pass, but Sykes kept weaving back and forth, obviously anticipating what she was trying to accomplish.

We traveled some considerable distance in this fashion. On two occasions, the woman fired at us, but she was clearly not as good as the marksman who'd been her passenger earlier and neither shot came even close, although the second caromed off the roof with a metallic ping. I considered leaning out the window and returning her fire, but the ride was so rough that I had trouble holding onto the pistol let alone aiming it from such an awkward position.

"Any towns out this way?" I asked.

Jeb shook his head. "Almost a hundred miles to the next marked settlement. We'll need fuel by then; I don't know about our friends there. The Steamer isn't as efficient but they've got a much bigger tank, and I'm sure Sykes would have topped it off."

The road we were on eventually crossed one marked much bolder on the map, presumably paved, but it was quite a way off and the surrounding landscape was getting rougher than ever. Fields of sharply carved rock grew up out of treacherous plains pockmarked with pits and ravines. Even cactus seemed reluctant to grow here. Just looking around made me thirsty.

The road seemed to be an endless succession of short, sharp turns to left and right, and I finally settled back in my seat, resigned to a long chase, determined to save my energy for what would happen next. I even closed my eyes, intending to nap for a bit, and of course that's when everything changed again.

We had just started a tight leftward spiral in the general direction of a pair of conical hills. Kelly had dropped back a dozen meters or so to discourage gunfire, since it was obvious that Sykes could counter every attempt to pass. They couldn't outrun us, but they might have enough fuel to outlast us.

Three prairie goats had wandered out onto the roadway. Under ordinary circumstances, there would have been plenty of time to pass them, buy Sykes was still hugging the center line to prevent us from pulling alongside, and possibly something distracted him at the crucial moment. He jerked the wheel hard to the right, just managing to avoid running into the closest of the animals, but he overcompensated or underestimated his momentum. The right front wheel caught in a deep rut and the Stanley was pulled even further in that direction. Whatever he may have tried in the next few seconds was ill advised or ineffective. The Stanley left the road entirely, then veered sharply away, rolling and bumping down a gravelly decline.

Kelly was almost as startled as Sykes. She turned in the opposite direction, missing the goats by a fair margin, but there wasn't quite enough room to get between them and a wall of tumbled rock and sand. We struck it glancingly and the front quarter panel buckled and then flew up over our heads. All of us were thrown hard against the roof and Yev let out a short, involuntary cry of pain as his injured arm slammed against the side of the car. The turbine coughed and began to wind down, hissing furiously, as we rolled forward another few meters and came to a stop.

From where we sat, Sykes' vehicle was as invisible as if it had fallen over the edge of the world.

"Is everybody all right?" Kelly sounded breathless, but she was already opening her door. Yev gave me a high sign but made no effort to move and I could see that his smile was really a grimace. Jeb was on the move as well so I nodded reassuringly, and opened my door.

We crossed the road cautiously, weapons drawn, and peered over the edge. Either through skill or luck, or more likely both, Sykes had managed to retain some control of the Stanley as it plunged down the shallow hillside. We could see the skid marks, two lines furrowing down to the base of the hill. He must have still been under power because the Stanley had moved forward from that point, perpendicular to the road, and into the desert beyond, but only a few dozen meters. It was motionless now, faced with impassable terrain, half concealed by a needlelike promontory, although I could hear the turbine, still winding happily. Just beyond was a chaotic collection of boulders and low brush, providing enough cover for a hundred snipers, let alone two desperate fugitives.

"There they are!" Jeb pointed toward a spot in the distance, and after a second or two I saw what he meant. Something was moving on the opposite side of the arroyo, moving furtively although the cover there was sparse and low enough that it couldn't quite conceal them from us. Our quarry had fled with surprising alacrity and already had a considerable lead.

"One or both?" asked Kelly, shading her eyes.

I was pretty sure I had seen Sykes, but he might well have been alone. Jeb's eyes must have been better than mine because he said he'd seen two figures.

Sykes must have been desperate because he was taking his life in his hands by chancing the desert. Even if they managed to elude us, there was a good chance that they'd perish out there. On the other hand, we were going after them, so maybe we were just as foolhardy.

We made sure Yev was as comfortable as possible and took as much water as we could carry, then started down the treacherous slope. It was even more difficult than I expected because the gravel tended to shift under our feet. We would have been easy targets for a sharpshooter, but Sykes and his companion were well out of range as well as out of sight by now. The Stanley had finally fallen silent, probably out of fuel, which meant we would have overtaken them shortly, another missed opportunity. When we reached the bottom, Jeb made a cursory search of the vehicle, but without finding anything of interest.

Climbing down had been dangerous enough, climbing up the opposite slope was both dangerous and exhausting. There was always the chance that one or both of our opponents was lying in wait ahead to pop up and shoot at us when we were at our most vulnerable. The footing became a bit more secure once we were halfway up, but the heat from the sun was like a firm hand, constantly trying to push us back. There was no sign of Sykes or the woman, nor sound either.

As we approached the top of the ridge, we became more cautious and sought common shelter beneath an overhang which protected us from ambush from above. Jeb kept his voice low. "There's a good chance they're waiting somewhere nearby, hoping we'll stick our heads up and provide them with targets."

I glanced to either side. "We could try to circle around them."

He considered that, then shook his head. "If they're lying in wait, they'll have anticipated that. If they're still running, we'll just give them that much more time to put distance between us."

"What can they hope for out here?" asked Kelly, sounding tired and dispirited. "We're in the middle of nowhere. There isn't a road in this direction for almost fifty miles."

"No, but there might be something along the rim of the desert. There aren't any big ranches out here, but there's good range not far to the south, and they'll have wayposts out this way. Sykes won't find any transport if they stumble onto one of them, but there might well be stockpiles of food and water, and maybe ammunition. And we've already found more than one route not on the map. I don't think Sykes knows this territory any better than we do but he might, and he's been lucky more than once in the past."

He cautioned us to keep our heads down as much as possible until we cleared the top of the ridge and found shelter on the other side, and we started to separate and finish the climb. Jeb and I were barely two meters apart when he stumbled and then fell headlong.

Kelly and I were both at his side within seconds, relieved when he rolled over, cursing, and extended an arm for me to help him up. He rose easily, but when he tried to put weight on his right ankle, his leg buckled and I had to grab him to keep him from falling again.

"Damn!" He sat down on a spur of rock and began massaging his ankle. "It's swelling already. Twisted and sprained but not broken." He craned his head to look back at the crest of the ridge. "I'll never be able to keep up. The two of you will have to go on by yourselves." His face was deadly serious. "We can't let them get away, Jim. I know you didn't exactly sign on for this, but we can't just hope that Sykes dies in the desert. We need that crystal to prove what's being cooked up and get the Emperor to reign in Ling."

I didn't trust myself to speak but I nodded.

"Will you be all right?" asked Kelly.

Jeb snorted with some of his old vigor. "I'll be able to hobble back and keep Yev company till you folks are done. Be careful, both of you. Sykes is likely to be even more dangerous when he's cornered."

And so it was that Kelly and I slid across the top of the ridge, relieved to discover no one was lying in wait for us, dismayed when there was no sign of Sykes visible anywhere on the opposite side.

The terrain was flatter but no less inviting ahead of us. At the foot of the ridge lay a relatively clear band of uninterrupted sand, but it was narrow, giving way to a deeply cut ravine that must once have channeled water many generations back. Beyond that was another ridge like the one we'd just climbed, but it was taller and hid the horizon. There was some cactus scattered about and sagebrush with no breeze to disturb it. The ridge facing us was covered with broken rock and small crevices just large enough to conceal a sniper. The woman had been wearing a bright green blouse, which would stand out against the dull red and tan background, but Sykes had been wearing khaki and could blend right in.

Further delay would accomplish nothing so we started our descent, using cover whenever possible, moving quickly when it was not. My shoulders were hunched in anticipation of gunfire, but the near silence remained unbroken and I became more and more convinced that they had continued onward rather than risk setting a trap. So when the attack finally came, it caught me completely by surprise.

The gunshot was from behind and above us, and so totally unexpected that I froze in astonishment rather than duck for cover. Recovering myself, I slipped into the shadow of a cracked boulder just as a second shot struck quite close to where I had been standing a second before. I moved carefully to the opposite side of the boulder, trying to spot Kelly, and saw her lying face down and motionless, sprawled across a swathe of gravel. A third shot rang out and I glanced upward in time to see a flash of bright green before it disappeared back behind a granite spire.

My first instinct was to go to Kelly, but she lay in such an exposed area that I would be taking too great a risk. Despair and fury warred within me, but happily common sense prevailed. If I was going to help Kelly, I would first have to deal with the more immediate ongoing threat from above.

In order to go up, I first had to go down. At least if I didn't want to be killed in the attempt. I retreated until there was sufficient cover that I could make my way horizontally along the length of the ravine without being observed from above. I had a pretty good idea where the shooter was, unless she too was on the move, but I suspected that she wouldn't abandon her vantage point too quickly. Sykes might be up there as well, but only the woman had fired at us, and I was pretty sure she had been left behind just like the others, to give him time to get away.

When I felt confident that my location was sufficiently uncertain to give me a chance, I started climbing, moving slowly so that I wouldn't disturb any loose rock and give away my presence, keeping to cover as much as possible. It seemed to take forever but it was less than a half hour before I was approaching the spire from an oblique angle. I was rewarded with a flash of green, just barely visible through a narrow cleft, and I became even more circumspect as I slowly closed the gap. I had to be close enough to get her with my first shot, because I didn't think she'd allow me a second chance.

I was just beginning to feel optimistic again when a voice shattered my illusions.

"Hold it right where you are."

It was a woman's voice, from somewhere close behind me, and I had no doubt at all that I'd been outfoxed.

"Set your weapon down on the rock ahead of you and stand up. Do it slowly, and don't turn around until I tell you to."

CHAPTER TWENTY ONE

I hesitated, knowing that if I failed now, there was no chance of stopping Sykes from escaping with the crystal and collecting his bounty for returning it to Ling. To say nothing of the fact that Kelly was lying wounded or dead not far away.

"Don't be a fool," the woman called to me. "You've made a good effort, did your heroic best, but it's all over now. Sykes is long gone. I'm not after your blood, although you've caused me considerable trouble and discomfort over the past day. I don't want to kill you; I'd far rather trade you back to your friends for free conduct to the nearest town."

I suppose that if I had been the protagonist in a Malachi Marks novel, I would have spun around unexpectedly and shot her dead before she could react. There was no way I could do it. I'm a mediocre shot, I was standing in an awkward position, and I didn't even have a very good idea of where exactly she was. Regretfully I decided to wait for a better opportunity, so I slowly laid my weapon down on a flat rock.

"Very sensible of you." She seemed relieved, even happy. "Now raise your hands above your head and turn around, and do it slowly."

I did as I was told, and there she was, only about three meters away. She would have been remarkably attractive if she hadn't been holding a gun pointed at me. She had shed her green blouse and I hoped that she'd get at least a very painful sunburn in exchange, likely since her complexion was very fair. Her hair was shoulder length, and tied back, but it was dark with perspiration. The left knee of her jeans was badly torn and darkened further by dried blood. I silently hoped it was hurting her a lot.

She'd been standing behind a chest high boulder, but having satisfied herself that I was no immediate threat, she stepped out into the open. I was willing her to come closer, hoping that some misstep would give me a chance to wrestle the weapon away, but she took only a single step in my direction before stopping.

"Can we go check on my friend?" I asked with false calm. "The one you didn't mind shooting a few minutes back."

"She's not going anywhere. I'm a pretty good shot."

Actually, she wasn't, which was why I was still alive. I was searching my mind for a suitable rejoinder when there was a faint pop, her eyes widened, and she gave a little jerk. Something dark appeared on her pale skin, just above the top of her brassiere, and I thought an insect might have lighted upon her. But it grew in size and she staggered forward, her gun hand wavering, then collapsed without ever making another sound.

"But I'm a better one."

I turned at the sound, glanced upslope and saw Kelly leaning heavily against a long dead tree. Both of her hands were wrapped around her pistol, which she still held at arm's length. Pausing only to assure myself that the woman was indeed dead and to collect both her weapon and my own, I scrambled up the loose shale.

Kelly was still bleeding but she'd managed to staunch the worst of it by tearing a section out of her skimpy sash. The round had hit her high in the shoulder and was apparently lodged somewhere near the collarbone. I helped to rewrap the makeshift bandage, pulled it tight and tied it in place, and added an inadequate sling made out of my own sash. Her face was pale and she was trembling, but she only flinched a little bit in the process and declared herself capable of walking on her own, but not very quickly.

"You still have to go after Sykes," she insisted. "We can't let him get away now, not after everything we've been through."

I wanted to protest that it was more important that I help her back to the others so that all three of them could get the medical attention they needed. I wanted to decline on the grounds that I was not suited, temperamentally or by my skills, for a desperate chase across the desert in pursuit of a master spy. But I didn't. I knew there was no alternative, and if I'd been trapped in a role beyond my capacity, then there it was. I'd have to play the cards I'd drawn to the best of my ability.

"Will you be all right?"

She nodded. "I'm a little light headed, but I'm not feverish and the pain isn't so bad. I've had worse, actually. You'd better get going. He's got quite a lead on you now."

"Right." I reloaded both pistols and took all of Kelly's spare ammunition.

When I was ready to go, Kelly pushed herself to her feet and surprised me by grabbing hold of me. It wasn't a sisterly kiss and for a few seconds I couldn't have cared less where Sykes was or what he was doing. Then she broke it off, leaving me breathless.

"Come back to us, James Parkhurst. I have plans for you."

I climbed and descended two more ridges before the landscape flattened out, and from the top of the last I spotted a single human figure, far ahead of me, moving slowly away. Impatient to have this over with, even if it was going to end in my defeat or death, I quickened my pace when I reached the sand. But I could only maintain that pace for a short period. The blistering sun, the cracked dry surface underfoot, and the odds against my succeeding all added invisible weights to my limbs. When I finished the first of my two canteens, I discarded it to lighten my load and plodded onward.

Although I really had no way to measure time, I imagine more than another hour passed before I realized that the stick figure I occasionally managed to glimpse ahead of me had taken on more solid form and was discernibly human. That puzzled me at first, but then my slowly cooking brain suggested that, just possibly, I was gaining on Sykes. Hardened military man he might be, but he was also at least twenty years my senior. From somewhere I found the energy to move slightly faster, though at times I staggered rather than walked.

I'm not sure when they first became visible, but some time later I raised my eyes to make sure I was still moving directly toward Sykes and noticed some irregularities on the horizon. At first I thought they were more rocks; I was having some trouble focusing and the heat shimmers made details uncertain under the best of conditions. But after another few score paces, I knew for certain that they were buildings, a ranch perhaps, or some other settlement, although I couldn't imagine any reason to build one in such a remote location.

The prospect of civilization was both encouraging and alarming. I couldn't go on indefinitely. If Sykes could find some form of transportation here, all of my efforts to close the gap between us might well be in vain. Although the muscles in my legs protested and my head ached intolerably, I forced myself to alternate walking twenty paces with jogging another twenty.

If I had started a little earlier, I might have caught him before he reached the buildings. As it was, I couldn't have been more than a couple of minutes behind when he reached the nearest and disappeared around its corner. By then I already suspected the truth, that this was neither a working ranch nor a settled outpost but actually the remains of some small endeavor long since abandoned. There were a great many of them in this area, I knew, Fundamentalist Calvinists and a few other extremist philosophies who worshipped a harsh god and wanted to live beyond the reach of the authorities and at the mercy of their deity. He hadn't shown much mercy, and almost every one of these newborn communities had died away in less than a generation. Dust storms, unrelenting heat, tornadoes, unresponsive soil, and occasional raids by the savages to the west claimed one after another.

As I closed the distance, I saw a church to my right, and the steeple was built in the style of the Church of the Living Martyr, a now largely extinct set that claimed that Christ had risen following the Crucifixion but had not ascended to Heaven. Instead, he still walked the Earth, checking on the behavior of the faithful, rewarding the virtuous and punishing the sinful. Next to it was a squat, square building whose front was so covered with sagebrush and drifted sand that I could not discern its purpose, although I guessed it to be a general store or possibly a meeting hall.

I was carrying one of my pistols and moving more deliberately, and not just because I was physically exhausted. There had been neither sight nor sound of Sykes since he'd first disappeared, but I was less worried now about his escaping. It was obvious that he would find no transportation here, not even a horse let alone a steamcar. Although there must have been a road from here to one of the connecting roads at some point, drifting sand had long since covered it up and I had no idea where it lay.

I passed through the first line of buildings and realized that the town had been built in the form of a cross with a large open space in the center and the church at the end of the shortest leg. The open space was broken only by a well housing, the sight of which made me so thirsty that I sipped some of my remaining water.

Still no sign of Sykes. I rested for a minute or two, sitting on the crumbling porch of someone's abandoned home. My legs began to cramp, and when I finally stood up again, I hobbled a bit until my muscles relented and consented to work properly. I stuck my head around the corner, scanning the surrounding ruins.

"Sykes!" I shouted. "You might as well give up! There's no way out of here!"

I thought I might have heard distant laughter in response to my show of bravado, but it could just as easily have been my imagination. I was also acutely aware that everything depended on me, more than just my life, possibly the lives of everyone I knew and loved. Although I was not a seasoned killer like Sykes, I was pretty sure I could prevent him from leaving the settlement, at least by daylight. But what would I do when night fell? He could slip away and I would never know that he'd gone.

So I decided to bluff. "Sykes! The game is over, do you understand? The others will be here as soon as they find a way around the rocks, and there's a patrol from Fort Glover on its way as well. You're surrounded and outnumbered."

If that really had been Sykes I'd heard before, he wasn't laughing this time. He might not actually believe me, but he couldn't entirely disregard what I'd said either. I didn't expect an answer; I just hoped to add another drop of uncertainty to what I hoped was a growing pool.

So he surprised me by answering.

"Parkhurst? Is that you? I admit I'm impressed by your tenacity, if not your good sense. I never thought you'd be the type to stick it out this far. Pampered upbringing, always had the best of everything, doting parents. A perfect citizen. Marks must have you really brainwashed, or maybe it's that slut daughter of his."

I wouldn't have considered his faint praise a compliment even if he hadn't added the last. Although I'd expected him to be somewhere to my left, his voice sounded as though it came from the church, or close by. I must have walked within a few meters of him. It worked both ways, of course. He surely had a pretty good idea of where I was as well. I eased back around the corner of the porch and ducked my head, suddenly feeling very exposed.

"Parkhurst? What about coming over to my side? I could use someone with your resourcefulness, and you're bright enough to know that the Federation is doomed. They can't even control their own population, let alone a foreign army. This is my last job, you know. I'm going to retire somewhere up north and live to a ripe old age. The fee is more than enough for me; I'll cut you in on part of it and give you a recommendation to my employers. Who knows? We might end up neighbors someday."

I didn't say anything. Even if it was meant as a genuine offer, which I doubted, I was not tempted in the slightest, and in truth I thought it simply a ruse to convince me to expose myself. Sykes had left enough corpses behind during this little adventure; one more certainly wouldn't give him pause.

The ground immediately separating me from the church was relatively clear of debris and afforded no cover, but there was an abandoned wagon, a tumbledown storage shack, and what appeared to be the skeleton of a threshing machine arrayed in a line that extended roughly from the opposite side of the porch to the side yard of the church. I was reluctant to expose myself by crossing the porch so I retreated along the side of the house, and then picked my way around its rear, carefully because the back wall had collapsed outward. From the opposite side, I studied the church more closely. There were two windows flanking the central double doors, and the side I could see was an unbroken expanse of stucco, in much better condition than most of the other structures.

The wind had carved a low ridge and I crawled on hands and knees until I reached the thresher. Although I was confident now that Sykes was inside the church, there was enough debris out front that I couldn't entirely discount the possibility that he was lurking there, waiting to pick me off if I gave him the opportunity. Crouching, I ran to the shack, paused to catch my breath, then sprinted to the wagon, which lay up on one side, although several planks were missing from the bed.

There really wasn't any choice unless I was willing to give it up and retreat. I took a deep breath, drank some more of my water, then bolted toward the church.

My audacity may have surprised Sykes, because when he finally fired, he was just the slightest bit too late. His first shot was well behind me and the second kicked up dirt next to my right foot. The angle was bad for him and I reached the church wall safely, though out of breath. He'd been firing from above, far above. He had taken refuge in the steeple.

I edged around to the front of the building, protected from above by the slight overhang of the roof, and reached the first window. The glass was long since gone, of course, but it was too small for me to climb through. The wall was clear here, but on the other side of the door sagebrush and other dead plants had been blown up against the stucco and had become an almost impenetrable, tangled mass. I skipped past the door and plunged into it, forcing my way until I could reach the second window, which also gaped open.

Heedless of the abrasions to my hands, I began breaking off branches and pulling free entire plants, pitching each bit of dried vegetation through the window. Sykes didn't call to me, and I suspected he might be quietly creeping back down from his lofty perch, but I didn't pause to think about that. I kept ripping and tearing and throwing until I felt confident I'd piled a substantial amount of debris inside. Then I pulled loose one more chunk of dried vegetation, lit it with my fancy lighter, and tossed it inside.

The fire caught with a gratifying crackle and rush and in less than a minute flames were licking out through the window, followed by black, viscous smoke. I retreated back the way I had come and then started along the side of the church. There would almost certainly be a rear entrance, and that was where I expected to have my final meeting with Sykes. A section of the sloped roof exploded in a shower of sparks and I realized the conflagration was spreading even faster than I had expected. The building had been dried to tinder.

The rear of the church was relatively free of debris and had a small door that appeared intact. There was virtually no cover, so I stayed at the corner, a pistol in each hand, and waited for Sykes to emerge.

So naturally he fooled me by braving the flames long enough to use the front entrance.

I was saved by purest chance. A portion of the roof blew out and rained flaming shards down into the yard just as he was preparing to shoot me in the back. His bullet missed, ricocheted off the wall above my head, and I twisted and dropped simultaneously, firing blindly with both pistols, not stopping until both of them were empty. I thought I was probably dead then, but Sykes stood without returning fire, looking surprised and a bit disappointed. He turned and staggered out of sight, and I was elated to realize that I must have hit him at least once. I carefully reloaded both of my weapons before following.

When I poked my head around the corner of the church, it seemed at first that Sykes had vanished into thin air. A pistol lay on the ground but flames erupted from the windows and I retreated quickly, one arm shielding my face. It was then that I saw Sykes, halfway between the church and the communal well, weaving back and forth as though he'd just finished a monumental drinking spree without benefit of a sobriety potion.

I set out after him.

He fell to his knees just short of the well and slowly began to turn back in my direction. The front of his shirt and his sash were both dark with blood. He didn't appear to be armed, but I was too cautious to take that for granted and I approached slowly and deliberately and remained well beyond his reach.

"Wait!" His voice was unsteady but still reflected the phenomenal strength of the man. "You've been lucky, Parkhurst, but not lucky enough."

I hesitated, wondering what new devilment he planned, and that's when I noticed that he was holding something in the palm of one hand. The thought that it might be some magical charm or mundane weapon, perhaps an explosive device, caused me to retreat a few steps, but I was reluctant to shoot the man down in cold blood, even though I could have done so easily from this range. He chuckled, half turned his body, and lobbed whatever he'd been holding into the ruined well. It vanished without a sound.

I knew then what it must have been and rushed forward heedlessly and unwisely, but it didn't matter. Sykes died with that last gesture, fell to the sand and never moved again.

I won't bore you with my exploits in the well. Sykes' last desperate act of defiance was an empty one. Years of disuse had filled the well with sand and trash. A nest of scorpions gave me some bad moments while I was searching, but I used a piece of rotten wood to bat them away. I managed to break a finger while climbing up the crumbling wall and wrenched my wounded shoulder again, but I just added these to my tally of injuries.

Now that I finally had the crystal in my possession, or knowingly at least, it seemed like a very trivial thing to have cost so much effort and so many lives, even if I did know that it was not the crystal itself but the knowledge it contained that was important. Sykes was wearing a canteen, but it was empty, and I wasn't looking forward to a dry return trip, but as it turned out, that proved unnecessary. I was only a couple of hundred meters away from the ruins when I saw a plume of steam on my left, and a few minutes later spotted a Cheviot racing across the sand in my direction. I had a bad moment during which I feared that Sykes had more confederates and that they were about to undo my efforts, but then I recognized who it was, and even found the energy to run a few paces in their direction.

My three companions – no, my three friends – had found a way around the line of ridges and had come rushing to the rescue.

The days that followed were anticlimactic, to say the least. It was pretty disappointing to realize that if we achieved our purpose, only a very few people would ever know what had happened during the past few days.

We headed south until we reached a safe house Jeb trusted, got medical attention, good food, and fresh clothing, then took a ferry back across the Mississippi. We were in New Orleans the following day, just in time for me to make my conference, which seemed extraordinarily tame and tedious but resulted in a very favorable agreement which made my father a very happy and considerably richer man.

One other bit of information needs to be recorded here, although I'm afraid no one will be able to read any of this until the political climate has changed, perhaps not even in my lifetime. Kelly is transforming it unrecognizably as the plot for her latest Malachi Marks novel.

It's Malachi Marks that I want to tell you about. During our last day together, I took Jeb and Kelly aside and asked them point blank if their name really was Marks. Kelly laughed softly and glanced at her father, who was thoughtful for a moment, then smiled. "There is no Malachi Marks, Jim. There never has been one, at least in the conventional sense."

I frowned. "I don't think I understand."

"The original Malachi Marks was Kelly's mother, although that wasn't her real name either. She recruited me and eventually talked me into marrying her. Marks was a fiction she had created to mask her activities when she was in England. The Ministry of Security expended considerable effort to track down the spy, Marks, and never suspected for a moment that he was actually a woman."

"Then I still haven't met the real Malachi Marks?"

"Yes and no. Julia died five years ago, Jim, and before you ask, it was natural causes. She died at home, in Wisconsin, and we were both there with her at the end. But Malachi Marks had already become a family business by then, and his reputation was so intimidating that we couldn't let him just pass away. Kelly and I and another man, Axel's brother in fact, all started using the name, circumspectly, planting a rumor here, making a furtive appearance there. Kelly hit on the idea of writing up his adventures, and that just made him seem more elusive and forbidding. No one of us is Malachi Marks, but we all are, even you. News is already spreading that Marks killed Sykes in a duel out in the desert."

I felt pretty good, all of a sudden. I was Malachi Marks, after a fashion. I looked at Kelly. "Okay, so that means your real name isn't Kelly Marks either, I assume."

"Nope. Afraid not."

"Care to tell me what it really is?"

She tossed her head. "To be honest, I've used so many different names over the last three years, I've almost forgotten which is the right one. Maybe they all are. I suppose I'll have to choose one and stick to it, just so I don't forget whom I really am. Actually, I've sort of picked one out already."

I sighed. "And that would be?"

"I think I'd like to try being Kelly Parkhurst," she said. "That is, if you don't mind."

And eventually she got her wish, but that's another story entirely.

www.ingramcontent.com/pod-product-compliance
Lightning Source LLC
Chambersburg PA
CBHW072213170626
46813CB00003B/920